CRAZY IN LOVE
LOVE & WAR

EMILIA FINN

beelieve
PUBLISHING, Pty Ltd.

Copyright © 2025 Emilia Finn

All rights reserved. No part of this publication may be reproduced, distributed, or transmitted in any form or by any means, including photocopying, recording, or other electronic or mechanical methods, without the prior written permission of the publisher, except in the case of brief quotations embodied in critical reviews and certain other noncommercial uses permitted by copyright law. For permission requests, write to the publisher, addressed "Attention: Permissions Coordinator," at the address below:

info@beelievepublishing.com

ISBN: (paperback) 978 1 922623 99 7

ISBN: (hard cover) 978 1 923515 00 0

Any references to historical events, real people, or real places are used fictitiously. Names, characters, and places are products of the author's imagination.

Cover Design:-

eBook and Paperback: Amy Queue @ Q Design

Hardcover: Emilia Finn

Cover Photography: Katie Cadwallader

Cover Model: Jordyn

Editing: Brit @ Bookish B Editing

Proofreading: Lindsi Labar

First printing edition 2025.

Beelieve Publishing, Pty Ltd

PO Box 407,

Woy Woy, NSW, 2256

Australia

www.emiliafinn.com

EMILIA FINN, the ROLLERS logo, the CHECKMATE SECURITY logo, STACKED DECK logo, and INAMORATA are all trade marks of Beelieve Publishing, Pty Ltd

FOREWORD

Crazy In Love contains *lots* of sex.
Butt sex. Mouth sex. Hand sex. All the sex.
My editor suggested I warn you ahead of time.

Also, this book contains discussion of maternal/infant mortality rates, and dark humor. Please take care of your mental health when reading.

AUTHOR'S NOTE

No hamsters were harmed in the making of this story.
She was joking. I swear!

CRAZY IN LOVE
LOVE AND WAR BOOK 2

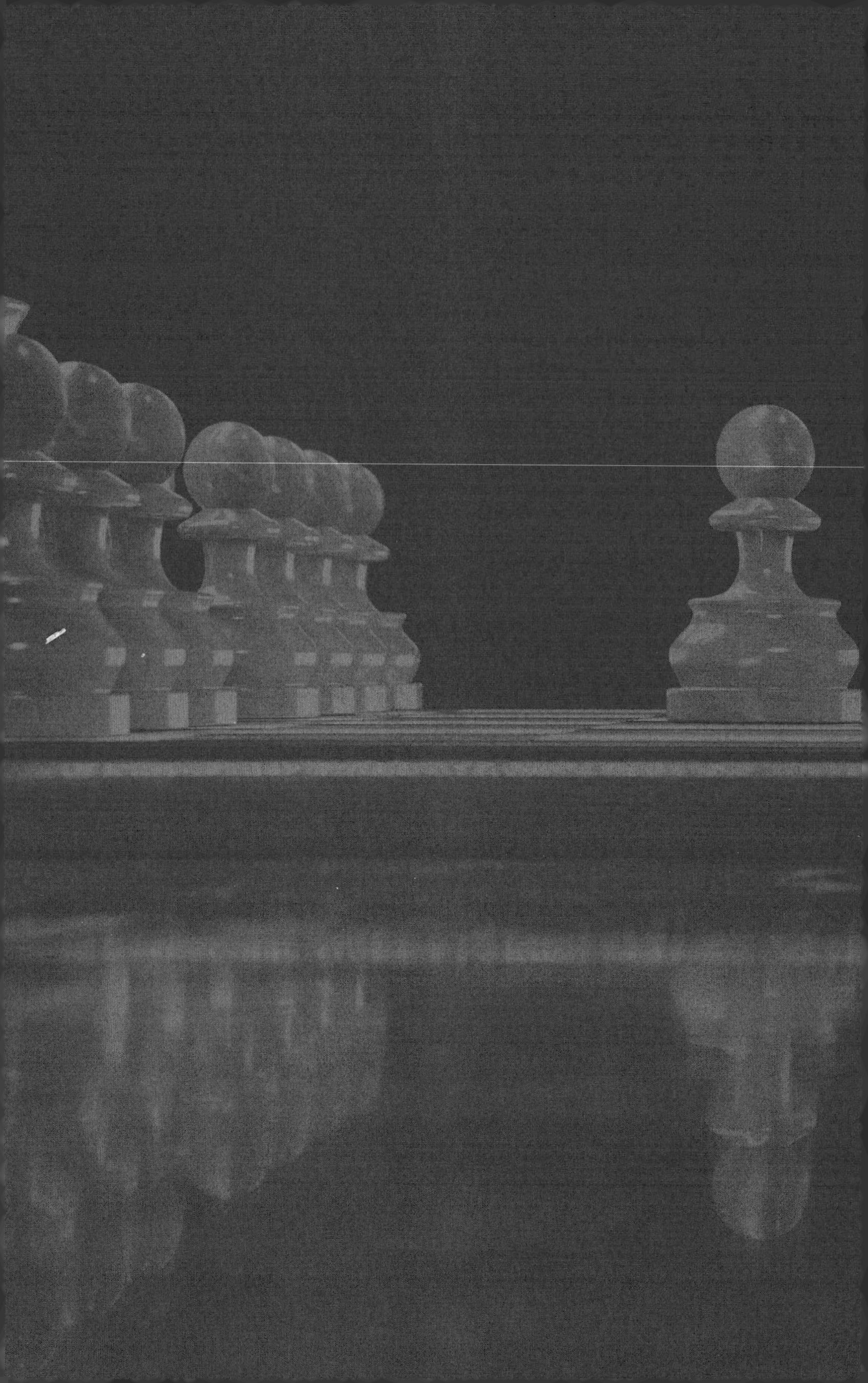

ROUND ONE
FOX

"See you when you get back, Fox!"
"Be safe out there, Fox."
"Come back to us, Fox."
Sure, one could assume by my honor-guard-esque sendoff that I'm leaving for an around-the-world expedition.
Or war.
Or missionary work somewhere far worse off than those of us in New York City.
"Be safe, Fox!"
"We're gonna miss you, Fox."
Have I donated my organs?
No.
Cured world hunger?
Not even close.
Invented insulin and sold the patent for a mere dollar?
Nope.
Although most of my coworkers press their backs to the walls of my Manhattan office and wave their goodbyes, Brenna breaks formation, stumbling forward and wrapping me in a hug that smells of peaches and coffee.
She's twice my age and barely more than half my height. She's also the first face anyone sees on their way into Gable, Gains, and Hemingway—a Fortune 50 Marketing Firm set prestigiously amongst some of the tallest

buildings in New York—so I suppose it's a good thing her face is particularly kind.

Pulling back with glittering eyes, she holds on and rubs my arms with her buttery-smooth palms. "It's just six weeks, right? You're *only* going for six weeks?"

"Six weeks." I tug her in and squeeze until her warm breath bursts against my neck, then backing away, I show her my smile and take comfort in the fact I'm adequately fucked up—*child of trauma and all that*—which means my eyes remain blissfully dry. "I promise. And I'll be available by email the whole time I'm gone."

"Bye, Fox!"

"I'm gonna miss you, Fox."

"Come back soon, Fox."

I quicken my steps, my four-inch heels *click-click-clicking* against the ornate tile flooring on the fifty-first floor of a business that turns over two hundred million dollars a year. Easily. Clearing the crowd and bursting through my office door, I swing back and close it again, only to hear the throaty, happy chuckle of a man I would recognize anywhere. Anytime. Any world.

Booker Hemingway is my boss's boss's boss—*or something like that*—but his office is a mere few feet from mine, and our friendship is something every worker bee aspires for.

"Is there a reason you're trespassing in my office, Booker?" Turning with a sigh, I lean against the door and study the man perched on the edge of my desk. He wears an expensive suit, not the kind one can buy off the rack, and a watch I wouldn't wear alone at night in a not-so-good neighborhood.

He's barely a few years older than my twenty-eight, which makes his rise to one-third owner of a highly regarded marketing firm a hell of a lot more impressive than Gable and Gains—*who are closing in on sixty and seventy, respectively.*

Booker's piercing brown eyes flicker with humor, and his short brown hair creates nothing more than a shadow against his scalp. The dude is handsome. There's no denying it. But he transforms to obnoxious easily, snatching up my desk football—I keep it for stress relief—and tosses it from one hand to the other.

In Booker's case, obnoxious rarely translates to annoying.

"You'd be hard-pressed to find a judge who agrees this is trespassing, considering my name on the side of the building. But yeah. There's a reason." He tosses the ball, catching it on its downward arc. "I needed to say goodbye before you left, but I'm not the type who'll line up in the hall like the rest of them."

"Because you consider yourself above them?" I push away from the door and catch my ball while it's in the air, squishing the soft foam in my palm and striding around my desk to set it in my top drawer.

That ball was a gift from my best-little-buddy, Franklin Page. And Booker Hemingway has already been warned not to touch what's not his.

Warned by Franky, that is. Not me.

"Six weeks is a long time." Unruffled, he flops into my visitor chair, lazy and languid, which is everything he's *not* allowed to be if anyone on the other side of my office door just happened to look in.

At thirty-one, he must prove himself in ways Gable and Gains never have to. Worse, because he's neither middle-aged, nor white, he has to work harder than his business partners *and* always appear thrilled while doing it.

"Remind me again where you're going?" He drops his legs open and rolls his head back. *Not so thrilled.* "For six *whole* weeks."

"Plainview." *Ugh.* Just saying the name out loud makes me pout. "Population: thirty-two... or so. They have one street running through town, one grocery store, four churches, and an uncountable number of old folks just begging for a scrap of gossip."

"And the chicken poo," he teases. *I may have mentioned the plethora of poo in the past.* "You're scheduled for six weeks off, but I bet you'll be back in one."

"Can't." I grab my purse and set it on my desk, then I open the thick leather and toss my things in. Phone. Laptop. Keys. My lucky pen with chew marks on the lid, though, truly, it's no different from the thirty other pens from the multi-box I took it from. "My best friend is having her baby, and her son needs me. This is a massive change, and change, for him, is upsetting."

"He's nine years old! Surely, he's old enough to understand that things are gonna be different now. He'll be fine."

"He's ten, actually. He's more intelligent than anyone I've ever met and a genuinely sweet boy who would never begrudge his mom's happiness or the little sister on the way. But he's also autistic, thrives on routine and familiarity, and though Alana will do her best to cater to both of her children, having a baby is a major medical episode." I open my top drawer and grab my notebook—*just in case*—and a packet of gum. "I've been in Franky's life since the day he was born, and their move to Plainview is still kinda fresh. Alana just bought a bookstore, and Tommy—her baby daddy—is busy with his own business. Everyone is already juggling, so I see no reason not to help my friends." I drop everything into my purse and bring my eyes back to Booker's. "That's what kind people do."

He snorts, perfect white teeth flashing behind a smile most others would gleefully pay for. "You're trying to hurt my feelings, huh? Because you're excited to see your friend, but you're also gonna miss us."

"I'll miss Brenna." Lie. I'll miss them all. But saying so to confident men is how larger egos are created. "I'll be back in six weeks, plus you're heading to Rome while I'm gone, so you'll hardly even notice my absence. Once I'm back, life will go on as it always has, and this will be just a memory. I'll be available via email." I repeat the words I've spoken a thousand times already today, flattening my voice into an unfeeling monotone. "You can call if you need something, and I'll send updates anyway. Other than that," I close my drawer with a satisfying snick, "I'm entitled to my time off, and complaining about it achieves nothing except to prove you're a big baby."

"Big baby." Grunting like a jolly old man, he leans forward and sets his elbows on his knees, dangling his hands between his legs. "You speak to your superiors with such disrespect, Ms. Tatum. It's hardly acceptable in the workplace."

"Yeah, but we were friends before you got stupid-rich, so it hardly counts." I quickly scan my computer screen and the emails that sit unread; countless, and all with similar subject lines: *goodbye*. I dismiss them and jump across to the dozen web tabs I've left open; newspaper articles about a certain fight sensation, coaching success, and prodigy maker—since it's smart business to research your rival—then I switch the screen off and straighten my back. And finally, I release a deep breath and empty my lungs. "I'm leaving now. Don't try to stop me."

"You think awfully highly of yourself." He pushes off my chair and tidies his suit jacket. Because once we leave this office, he must be *Mr. Hemingway* again. The heat of his following eyes lingers on my back as I stroll to the closet built into my office wall and tug the door open. While he straightens his tie and clears his throat, I drag a ridiculously heavy suitcase out and miss running over my toes by a hair, then I grab my carry-on case and a pair of Nike high-tops to change into once I get to the airport.

"Would you like me to call up a car? Since you seem to think you're king shit around here."

"I don't *think* I'm king shit." I set my purse on top of my suitcase, draping the straps over the handle to keep it from tumbling right off. "I'm told how amazing I am every single day. It's hardly conjecture at this point. Also," I peek over my shoulder, "no need to call a car."

"You'd rather catch a cab?"

"No. No need to call. Michael's already downstairs waiting for me."

He laughs. "Of course he is."

"Walk me down?" My heart thuds with emotion, taking what is supposed to be an exciting adventure and adding a sheen of dread because of the work-family I know I'll miss while I'm gone. Plainview is not just *not-Manhattan*, which is a massive *con* in the pros and cons list anyway, but it's a small town in the middle of Hell, with nothing to do and nowhere to go, not a single restaurant operational past ten at night—*for those late-night adventures I enjoy going on when the apartment is too lonely*—and no one within its town limits for me to spend my time with—*besides Alana and Franky.*

Well, them and the Watkins twins.

Tommy will be Alana's husband soon, and Chris is… strange, in the '*don't look at me*' and '*don't sit in my seat*' kind of way.

In the silence, Booker takes my large suitcase and rolls it across my office, spires of glittering light flaring from the sparkling exterior as he passes in front of my window. He opens the door, only to reveal more faces. More goodbyes. More teary smiles and emotional eyes.

"They're attached to you," he murmurs, waiting as I grab my smaller case and follow him out. He leads me over expensive tile and into his office, then into a private elevator gleaming with shiny steel and a boldly painted artwork on the back wall. Selecting the ground floor and folding his arms, he studies my coworkers who mingle and wave, his eyes warm on the side of my face as I step in beside him and bring my carry-on case closer.

"Six weeks can feel like a lifetime for those who rely on your presence."

"Which is how I feel about Alana and Franky." Mirroring his pose, I lean against the side wall and draw my bottom lip between my teeth. "I saw them every single day for ten years. Now they're gone. Six weeks away from here will feel like a long time, but three-quarters of a year away from them feels like death by a thousand paper cuts. It feels like I can't breathe half the time."

"I know." His dark eyes slide over my features, a million thoughts going unspoken. A decade of friendship sits over our heads. And because I *know* he wants to say something, but doesn't, my heart thrums just a little faster.

"What?"

Thoughtful, but silent, he grabs my suitcase handle, so when the elevator doors open on the ground level, he strides out and leaves me behind.

"Booker!"

"Michael." He wheels my suitcase to the rear of the waiting car, palming a wad of cash toward the driver faster than my eyes can keep up. Then, he hands my purse back to me and takes my carry-on, placing it in the trunk.

Finally, he spins and looks down into my eyes, forcing me to fold at the neck because of how impressively tall he is, even compared to my respectable five-nine.

"You're thinking things that are probably going to annoy me."

He chuckles. "Actually, I was thinking about how sad you've been since Alana left. I know it, even if you think you're good at hiding it."

"Booker—"

"*They* probably don't notice." He glances briefly toward our building. "Because you're damn good at your job. But I knew you before. I've known you since you stumbled into the wrong lecture hall and stayed for an advanced marketing lecture you had no business being in."

I breathe out a soft, almost silent snicker. "That was a fun day."

"It matters that you're happy, Fox. Business aside, I care that you're okay. So go for your six-week sabbatical in the swamplands of nowhere, and try not to catch a nasty case of listeria or whatever it is those tiny towns carry."

"You're being mean. Truthful," I amend. "But mean."

"Stay in contact. And when you're back, bring your A-game because I have big plans for us and a hell of a lot of shaking up to do here at Gable and Gains."

"Gable, Gains, and Hemingway," I counter. My heart swells with pride for the man too humble to be loud. "You forgot your name is on the building, too."

He smirks. "I didn't forget. We have things to discuss when you're back, okay? So keep your schedule open for a dinner meeting. Non-negotiable."

"A dinner meeting?"

"I have a proposal I'd like you to mull over."

"When I get back?"

"There's no point discussing it now, since I still need to iron out a few of the details. Besides, you're going on vacation. Don't overthink this, and don't stress. Just know that once you return, I hope to have some pretty exciting news for you."

"Oh sure, because that wasn't vague and intriguing as hell! Why don't you whack me with that carrot-dangling stick now and get it over with?"

"Because you need to focus on that sweet baby arriving any day now." He opens the car door and steps back to pull it wide. "Plus, Sherry wants to be there for our chat, too. Give Alana my best, and tell Franklin I'm ready for a chess re-match. I've been studying."

Because losing to a ten-year-old is embarrassing.

"Send pictures of the baby once she's here." He places his hand under my elbow and guides me toward the back seat. "And don't pick fights with the folk down there. They have a lot of cousins to fight for them, seeing as how they're all related."

"You're being a jerk." But I laugh and slide into the car, twisting when he closes the door and leaning on the window frame to keep him in view. "You're generalizing an entire community. That's harmful and unkind."

"Eh." He smirks. "Oh, and since you're not as good at hiding shit as you think you are, I feel it's my duty to warn you *not* to pick at Christian Watkins anymore."

Stunned, I pull away from the window and narrow my eyes. "What?"

"I know you, Fox, and I'm friends with Alana, too. Maybe not talk-every-day friends, like you are, but we say *hey*. She told me how you and Chris bickered every damn minute the last time you were in the same room."

"We didn't bicker!"

We totally, absolutely did.

"She told me he's his brother's opposite. Tommy's loud and outgoing. But Chris depends on routine. Quiet. Rules." He pins me with a look. "You, my dear Fox, are the anti-routine rule-breaking nutcracker. You know exactly how to screw with him, and I know you well enough to be certain you've already decided on your mission."

"You make me sound like an asshole. I'm not mean. I'm just... me. And that sometimes bothers him."

"You're protective and possessive of the people you love, and one of those people now defers to Chris for comfort—*instead of you*. You've become obsessed about this." He takes a step back and taps the roof of the car. "Consider sharing that little boy instead of tearing him in two. And be nice. I don't want you to get stabbed by the hillbillies."

"You're being an asshole, you know that?"

"Come back in six weeks, and we'll talk about it." His phone trills, so while he backs up, he drops his hand into his pocket and fishes the device out, grinning from ear to ear as he reads the name on the screen. "Sherry. Hey. I was just putting her in the car."

"JFK, Ms. Tatum?" Michael's eyes wait for mine in the rearview mirror, so when I nod and settle back into my seat, he pulls away from our building and into New York traffic.

JFK. And then... Bumfuck Nowhere.

Yee haw.

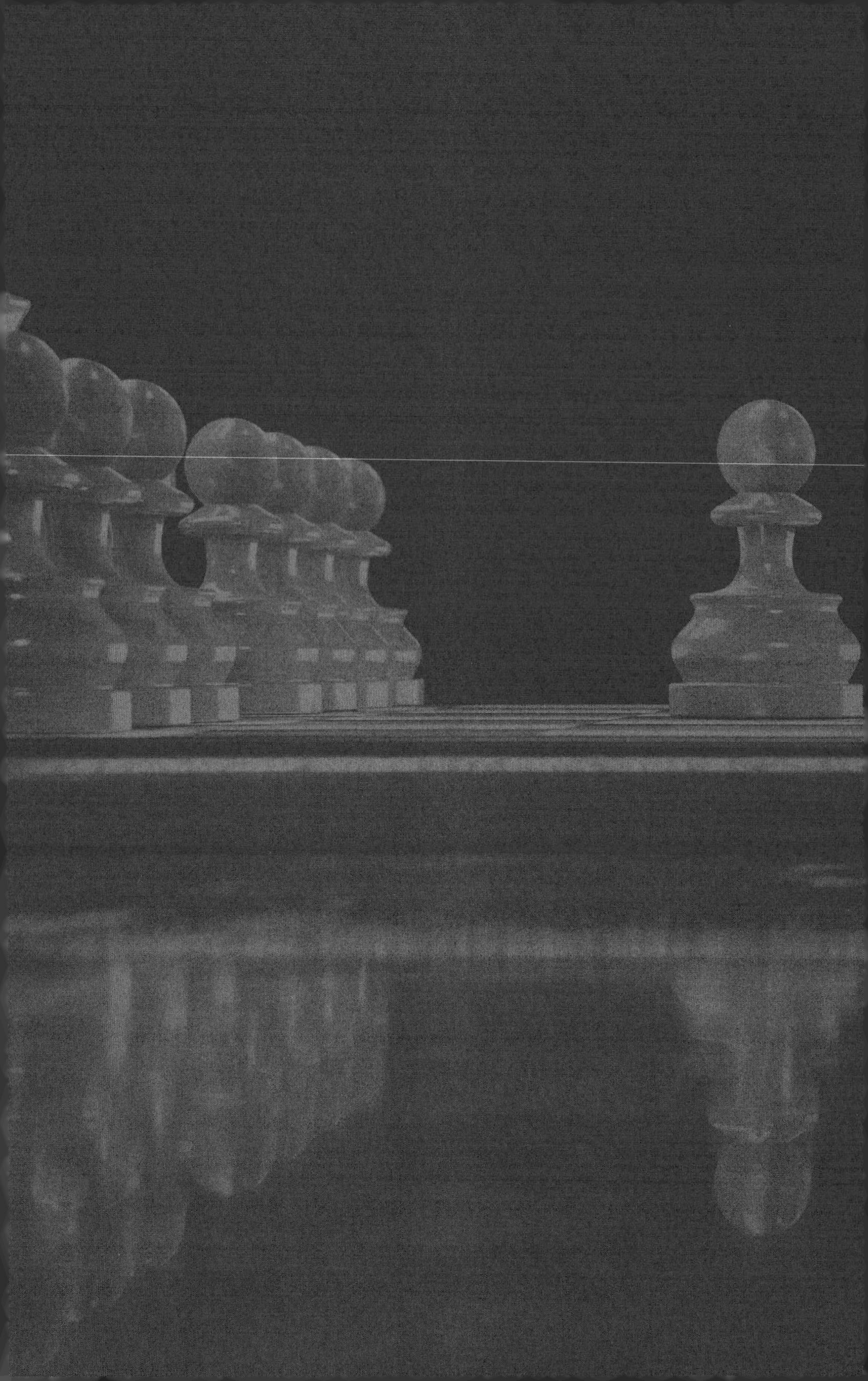

ROUND TWO
CHRIS

"You're embarrassing me, dude." I stand over my fighters—Cliff and Tommy—and shake my head with frustration. Tommy is my best friend. He's my twin brother. Honestly, he's my whole fucking world, but right now, he's the enemy, and though everyone expects him to be the better fighter—the title belt hung on his office wall kinda says so—the years I've spent working with Cliff on his ground game are starting to feel like an exercise in insanity.

He's not ready to defeat the champ. Not even close.

"Bridge your hips." I lower into a crouch and stare into Cliff's widening eyes. His dark red face. His white neck, wrapped in Tommy's furious lock. "You gave him your back, then your front. Now you're all tangled up and about to go to sleep."

"He can't escape this one," Tommy grunts past his mouthguard. "Ready to reset?"

"Nope." To reset would be to give my fighter a *pass*. Which is how we repeat our mistakes. So I deny him the out and tap his left ankle. "You gotta get this leg around. Snake it under and use your knee to force that space."

"He's not breathing. Reset?"

"Bring your leg under!" I reach between the two of them and grab Cliff's ankle, dragging it around while I ignore his reddening face. "You fucked up when you put your neck on the chopping block, so now you fight for your life, or you accept your fate and close your eyes."

"Chris—"

"You wanna win at the next Stacked Deck tournament? Means you've gotta focus on your ground and pound. The Rollers dominate on the mats, and they sure as fuck aren't screwing around when they're supposed to be training. Right now? You're embarrassing *our* gym."

"Yeah. But I'm making friends." Cliff wiggles and steals an inch of space, drawing a deep breath into his lungs and snaking his leg around Tommy's to lock in his hooks. "They like me there. So that's nice."

"So retire and become the next Mrs. Kincaid." Tommy slams his elbow into the side of Cliff's neck, breaking their grips and rolling away until he flops to his back. Panting, his sweaty chest lifts and falls in search of air. "You're more focused on flirting with those girl fighters than you are about bringing one of those belts back to our gym."

"I mean…" Cliff starfishes the canvas, arms and legs spread wide, and a goofy ass grin plastered across his face. "I'm not flirting with them or anythin', since most of 'em are married already. But I enjoy the tournaments and training with the champs every year."

"You're training with the champ right now," Tommy snarls. "Fuck you very much."

He laughs. "*Different* champs, Boss. Geez. Don't get your feelings hurt. If you'd make the drive with me in December, you could fight Conner and put that beef to bed. But you won't, so you—"

"Can't," I insert. "Contracts were already signed, and some of us like money." I drop to my ass and rest my elbows on my knees, dangling my head until the stretch in the back of my neck feels good. "He chose right, and Conner chose right. Their paths were heading in different directions. But you," I meet his smug gaze, "you're just a shitty fighter, no matter where you're competing."

"That was unkind." He runs a gloved hand through his hair, cut short when it's typically on the shaggier side. "Why do you insist on being mean to me, Coach?"

"Because you won't fight the way I want you to."

"With the mongrel in my blood," he snickers. "You want me to be a killer, when mostly, I just enjoy the sport and meeting new people."

Literally the opposite of everything I stand for.

"You asked for our blessing to fight at Stacked Deck." Tommy rolls to his hands and knees and crawls to his water bottle. "You're never going pro the traditional way, and the Rollers are happy to take your five hundred bucks. We were cool with it. But Jesus."

"You're not cool with it anymore?"

"You keep losing!" I lift my head and tilt it backward, extending my throat instead. "You mosey on over to that other gym every December and twirl around like you have no worries in the world. But everyone else is there to win. It's war for them, but it's just a fun adventure for you."

"They fight for the money and belt. I fight for the chance to see those girls in their booty shorts." His lips curl into a long, arrogant grin. "Maybe they're married up and happy, but their booties are booties worth looking at, ya know? The Rollers have got way more girl fighters than we do. You could do with a little diversity, Coach. The War Room's looking a little '*Ol Boys Club*' right now."

"We have Eliza." Tommy gestures toward the boxing bag currently being decimated by Eliza Darling—*not a darling in any sense of the word*. She may be small, but she's strong as an ox, and her roundhouse kick will knock even the fiercest competitor down a notch.

"Sure. We have Eliza." Cliff twitches at every blow Eliza slams against the bag, a sprinkle of sand hitting the mats after every strike until it becomes the playlist to today's sweat session. "But we don't watch *her* booty if we wanna keep our insides *inside*. Feel like we learned that lesson a long time ago."

"And here I thought you were a decent, respectful ally to womankind. Turns out you're a secret perv looking to scam on girls."

"Nah." Re-energized, he pops to his feet and wanders to the cage. "I'm allowed to appreciate so long as I'm not a dick about it. But not Eliza. I've known her since she was a kid, so it feels weird checking out her bum."

"Check out my bum, and I'll gut you." Eliza rotates into a ferocious spinning kick, stabbing the bag with her heel and knocking a heap more sand to the floor. She lowers her hands and folds at the hips, panting past her mouthguard. But she hits us with a heated glare. *A warning most others know to heed.* "Stop talking about me while I'm training. It's rude."

"Was just trying to make a point, Ms. Darling." Blowing an obnoxious kiss, Cliff turns his back to the best chick fighter in this town and the next, too oblivious to be afraid. Then he leans against the cage and stares at me square on. "I live in Plainview. I train in Plainview. My allegiances belong to this gym, this family, and this shitty town that doesn't even have a decent strip club to relax in after a long day of work. But a little skippity-hop a couple states over once a year makes for a nice vacation. I'm not there for the belt, Coach. And if that bothers you, then I guess that's gonna be a you-problem."

His *non*-desire for a win irks me on a soul-deep level, since we train for a purpose, and entering a tournament *should* come with the intention of winning. But I clamp my lips shut and save myself from their mocking barbs.

Something about routine and being highly strung.

"Somebody help me."

Ready for war, Tommy's eyes swing toward the door, his shoulders coming up defensively. Then Alana waddles through with her nine-month-pregnant belly and a groan. Her face is red with exertion, and her bow lips move into a pout. "I'm begging you. Get a steak knife and put me out of my misery."

"Not really something you should say in public." Tommy pops to his feet and tosses his water bottle, then he bursts through the cage door in three long strides, wrapping himself around her exhausted body and placing his hand under her belly. "You're almost done, baby." He presses a kiss on her cheek. Then the other. Her lips. Her forehead. "We already hit forty weeks. We're just waiting for her to decide she's ready to come out."

"I don't want to do this anymore." She drapes her arms over his shoulders, giving him her weight to hold. "I can't sleep. I can't hardly eat." She pulls back and growls. "I can't breathe! She's crushing my lungs *and* bladder at the same damn time."

Franky meanders through the door with his nose hidden behind a book and his blue-framed glasses slipping along his nose. He doesn't watch where he's walking, which, for a clumsy kid, makes for a treacherous trek, but muscle memory allows him to walk past his mother, scowl as he passes Tommy—*that bastard stole his mom*—and come all the way to the cage door without stumbling.

Finally, he brings his eyes up and blinks until they focus on me.

"Hey, little dude." Playful, Cliff strolls across the canvas and peels his fingerless gloves off his hands. "How was school? Make new friends? Beat anyone up?"

Franky merely stares. He's got this savage ability to look straight through a man and keep his mouth shut, and though society says he *should* speak, and most others will toss out a '*hey*' just to appease the masses, Franky merely shrugs and brings his eyes back to mine.

He's *my* buddy. Not Cliff's.

"How was school? Molly still causing a ruckus in class?"

He closes his book and sets it on the step, then he toes his shoes off and carefully sets his glasses inside one for safekeeping. "Molly makes a ruckus every single day. But I kinda like it because then everyone pays attention to her and leaves me alone."

"Wow." Cliff rolls his eyes—and his head for extra emphasis—before stepping through the cage door. "I'll get you someday, little dude. I'll secure that *hello* and finally become one of the cool crowd."

Franky watches him in silence, eyes narrowed and breaths measured. And only when Cliff passes into the hall does he bring his gaze back to me. "He's loud, too. He doesn't care about my day. He just wants me to talk to him."

I lower to my knees, a muscle memory I'm not sure I remember creating, and offer my fist for him to tap. Then I grin and slowly circle. *Fight.* "Cliff is a pretty nice guy, so if he's asking about your day, I reckon he cares. But he's also a showoff and loud as hell, so I believe him when he says he's aiming for that *hello*. Doesn't mean he's an ass for it. He's just a friendly type."

"Christian Watkins!" Alana snaps. "Don't say ass while talking with my son."

"Yeah. Don't say ass to me." Taking his chance, Franky superman jumps and snakes around my arm, throwing his weight backward in what I know he means to be an arm-bar. I outweigh him by a long shot, so he couldn't *actually* pull me down, but he's learning, so I fall to the ground and give him a chance to inch closer to my shoulder.

"I'm getting better at this, don't you think?"

Better? *Sure.*

Good? *Not really.*

"You sure are. Move closer on this side." I grab his leg to show him. "You wanna have your butt touching me," then I tap his ankle, "and lock these in. You gotta cross your feet."

He unhooks his ankles, then re-links them again and scoots toward my shoulder. In a competition, he would've already lost his position. But this is practice, so I become one with the floor.

I'll be his training dummy.

"Fun fact." Grunting, he folds my arm back against his chest and digs his heels into my ribs. "Forty-three percent of airbus pilots admit to falling asleep while flying long haul."

"Really? That's kinda terrifying." I turn my hand to remind him which way my thumb should point: *upwards.* "Probably why I never wanna fly anywhere."

"Also, you know how airplane food sometimes tastes bland?" He yanks on my arm with the viciousness of a dozen angry kittens. "Well, cabin humidity and high-altitude pressure hamper our sensitivity to flavors by up to thirty percent. So maybe the food isn't actually gross. Maybe your tastebuds are just not doing their job."

"And now I know." I wait… wait… wait… for him to drag my arm over his shoulder and complete the bar, and when I figure it's as close as it's gonna get, I pat his thigh, proud as he rolls out of his lock.

Victorious.

"I'm getting better, Mom!" He spins toward her and Tommy, wrapped in each other's arms while they whisper things *we* don't need to hear. "I got him in an arm bar. Did you see?"

She turns and leans against Tommy's side, forcing him to hold her weight. "Great job, honey. That basically makes you the world champ, huh? Chris trained Tommy. So that's pretty much the same thing."

He spins back to face me. "I'm not even close to being the world champ. She's just saying that because she's my mom."

"Moms sometimes do that." *Not my mom.* Mine preferred to beat the shit out of me and Tommy for fun, and only when we weren't busy getting the shit beat out of us by our dad. "She likes to build you up because that's what people do for those they love."

He resets his stance, widening his legs and bending at the knees. Then he extends his hand, ready for me to bump it. "I know. Did you know my Aunty Fox is flying in tonight?"

"Hmm?"

He throws himself at me—*same move, same battle cry, same arm*—and falls backward, tugging me to the floor and locking me exactly how he did the first time.

"That's why I was saying about the plane food and stuff. She already texted my mom and said she was at the airport and getting ready to board."

"Yeah?"

"Mmhm." He wriggles closer and twists my wrist into place. "She'll land after dinnertime. Tommy said he'll drive to the airport and get her so Mom can stay home and rest."

"You excited to see her?"

"Uh-huh." He squeezes my hand and tries to hyperextend my elbow. But his grip isn't right, and his hips are too far from my body, which makes his lock as weak as my brother's '*oops, I forgot to mention my plans*' attempt at shielding me from something *uncomfortable*. "I miss her," he explains. "Haven't seen her since Vegas. And that was a fast visit, 'cos we had to rush back here for Mom's baby appointments. But she's staying for six weeks this time."

I tap and let him win, but when he bounds to his feet, ready for a third round, I stay on the canvas and stare up at the cobwebbed ceiling instead. "She staying at the house with you guys?"

Game over. He drops to the floor beside me, arms and legs splayed wide, while his chest lifts and falls in search of air. "For tonight. But she's staying at the apartment above the bookstore most of the time 'cos she's gonna run the shop while Mom's at home with the baby. She promised to stay at the house on the days we need her."

"Like the day your sister's born?"

"Right." He peeks across with glittering, fearful eyes. "Having a baby is dangerous, ya know? There are a lot of things that can go wrong."

"True. But science and medicine are pretty good nowadays. And Ollie will be there, since he's the doctor. Tommy won't leave her side because besides you, who on the planet is the most protective of your mom?"

Apprehensive, his brows pinch closer, and his teeth come forward to nibble on his bottom lip. "He's protective of her. And you."

"And me," I accept with a smile. "But since I'm not the one having a baby this month, why don't you let Tommy take care of the Alana stuff, and I'll take care of the Franky stuff? Fox could probably even stay at the bookstore and not worry, since I'll hang with you. We don't need her."

"But she's coming to visit for exactly this." Like me, Franklin Page relies on rules and expectations. On fulfilling the roles we're supposed to fulfill and abiding by the rules set down around us. "She flew all the way from New York *because* Mom asked her to help."

"Sure. And she can help with the shop." I tilt my head to the side and glimpse Tommy and Alana whispering again. Smirking. Flirting. His hands on her body, and her belly pressed snugly against his. He's shirtless and sweaty, and she's as professional as a woman can be while elastic bands keep her pants up. "The shop will need someone to run it, and the apartment above sounds like the perfect place for her to stay. It's convenient. And since you and your mom moved out to Tommy's place a few months back, and I live right next door, that means I can hang out with you while she and your sister are in the hospital. Convenient again."

He shakes his head. Though *shaking* is actually *rolling*. "Aunty Fox wants to hang out with me, too. She already said so." He brings his eyes back around. "Did you know she has a magic ability to make people happy?"

"You think?" Sweat creates a vacuum seal between my back and the canvas, so each time I move, the slurping release is audible. "I wouldn't know about that, kid. She's yet to use that magic in front of me."

"It's her actual job. And she's really good at it, except when she wants me to dance."

"Dance?"

"Mmm." He purses his lips. "I don't even mean, like, dancing at a party or whatever. I mean, when I would get mad and wanted to be left alone, she'd grab my hands and tell me to *dance it out*." He sighs up at the ceiling. "I don't even wanna dance when I'm happy. I *especially* don't want to dance when I'm mad."

"That would make me *extra* mad. If I'm already pissed about something, dancing ain't gonna simmer shit down."

"Christian Watkins!" Alana growls. "Stop swearing in front of him! He's ten. He is *not* your twenty-five-year-old best friend."

"You don't get to dictate how I interact with my own brother." I wink for the boy and push up to sit, the slurping release of my back traveling all the way across the gym—and probably into the next building, too. "I know it's all a bit confusing, considering blood relations and all that mess, but you never hissed at me for swearing in front of Tommy when he was ten."

"Because you were ten, too!"

"A mess is a mess is a mess." I climb to my feet and meet Tommy's watchful gaze. Our silent observer. Our loud protector. "Franky said you're gonna drive over and get that chick from the airport in a couple of hours. You should stay with Alana. I'll go get her."

"That chick?" Alana cuts in. "*That chick* is my best friend. She has a name."

"Yeah, but it's kinda weird. *Fox*. Fox." Done for today, I bend and scoop up a towel to mop the sweat from my face. "It's not even short for anything. It's just... Fox. I don't get it."

"You don't have to get it. You only have to respect it."

"*Fox*." I roll her name over my tongue, testing each sound while I wipe the sweat from my chest. "I'll drive over and get *Fox*, since you need to keep your backside at home. Forty weeks is not the time to screw around with travel."

"I wasn't going. Tommy was."

"Forty weeks isn't the right time for *him* to be traveling, either. You know McMaster's Bridge is finicky as hell, and we had all that rain last week. We've got more forecast for tonight, so sending him to the other side while the river level is already high is not smart. You three stay here. I'll go get her."

"You only wanna do it so you can lecture her on the way back and set down your rules." Tommy, that traitorous bastard, laughs. "She can't come over to the house too often. Can't be loud. Can't demand too much of anyone's attention. Can't come into the gym." He slides his tongue acrosss the front of his teeth. "Did I miss any?"

"I've never said any of that!"

Out loud.

"You don't have to say it for us to know." Alana snickers. "You feel a certain way about me and Franky—me, because of our history, and Franky, because of blood—but Fox matters, too. She's been with us since the day he came home from the hospital. Since before then, really. It bothers you that she's our family, even if we don't share blood."

"She's not your family! She's a friend. And she lives on the other side of the country. Honestly? You should let her go. She's not a part of your life anymore."

With a shake of his head, Tommy moves to stand in front of her. Because she's the type to try out the superman dive her son is so fond of. "Ignore him. Relax your face. The baby feels your stress." He cups her cheeks and draws her to her toes. "Caaaaaaaalm. Happpppppy. Kumbaya and all that shit."

"You're lucky she's weighed down by that bowling ball." Franky's cheeks burn red over the laughter he swallows down. "You don't get to say bad things about Fox and live to talk about it."

I toss my towel and snatch up my water bottle. I have new plans for today that include a shower, a drive, and an airport. And if I'm lucky, I might convince our guest to turn her ass around and fly east, all before bedtime. "I didn't say bad things about her. I just said she was unneeded."

"Unneeded is mean."

"It's not mean! It's facts. Tommy's gonna help Alana with whatever she needs. I'll help you. And Caroline has offered a million times to run the shop while your mom is off. Fox being in a town she doesn't wanna be in, to run a shop she doesn't wanna run, is dumb."

"You wanna hear a new fun fact?" He crawls to his feet and stares up at me through eyes that match mine damn near exactly. "Did you know a hundred and fifty thousand people die every single day all over the world?" His lips curl into a devious grin. "If you keep this up, you might be one of them."

"Yeah? Well, fun fact, kiddo. Shut the hell up."

"Christian!"

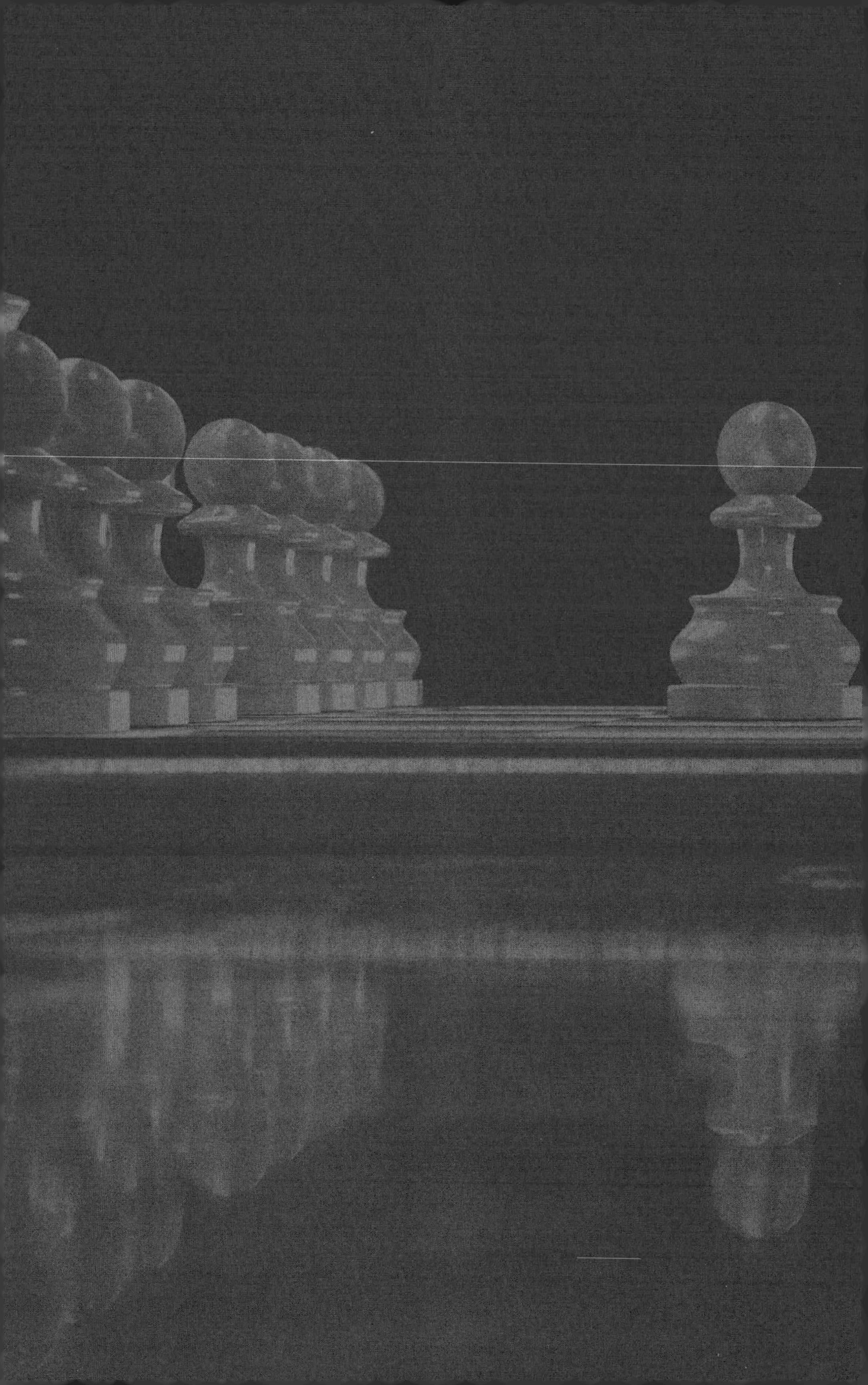

ROUND THREE
FOX

Anyone would think I'd get used to a tiny ass airport by the second or third time I flew into it. The single runway, the Lego-sized building. Lord, the luggage buggy—not a carousel, like we have literally everywhere else—but a golf-buggy-looking thing that zooms around like ice-cream trucks in suburban neighborhoods.

Instead of slinging dessert, it slings suitcases.

May means the winter harshness is long gone, and with that change comes the absence of three-foot-deep snow and ugly, naked trees. Instead, this small town named Barlespy—a town *barely* larger than Plainview—blooms with seasonal color and swells happily in that sweet spot between winter and summer. It's neither hot nor cold. The sun remains in the sky just a little longer each night than it did a month ago, and the summer bugs are not yet at make-you-want-to-kill-yourself level.

Oh, but they're coming.

Still, the suitcase-man sets my nerves on edge, zooming around the airport while he drags our luggage behind his little cart. I trudge off the plane—no tunnel or ramps here—and traverse the rickety steel stairs until I'm standing ten-toes down on the runway. The actual runway.

Folks would be arrested for this in New York!

The warm spring breeze whips my hair back while the sun flirts with the horizon. Not quite dark, but not really light, either. Best of all, Tommy Watkins waits by the airport terminal's back door—no JFK security out here—and dips his chin when our eyes meet.

Just like that, a welcoming face releases my lungs and allows my pent-up breath to escape.

I set my carry-on case on its wheels and make quick work of tugging the handle up, but when I try to place my purse on top, my nerves make my movements jerky, and my rushed actions end with it spilling onto the ground. "Shit." Crouching, I toss my pen back into the leather bag, then my keys and lip balm.

"You need help, ma'am?" A broad, tanned hand stops in my peripherals, and when I follow it along a muscular arm, which leads to a wide chest and then, further up, a sweet smile and kind eyes, I gulp and stare.

So he places his hand under my elbow and draws me to my feet.

"Uh... thank you." He smells nice, and when he reaches across and takes the handle of my carry-on, the delicious scents of cologne and coffee fill my lungs, replacing stale plane air. I study his handsome face and expensively bought smile, and moving the straps of my purse to the crook of my arm, I hardly clock Tommy's approaching form on my right. "Kinda wish they'd give us the inflatable slide to get out of those planes. Way better than the stairs."

He draws me around and leads me toward the terminal... *Lego building*. "You dread leaving New York and visiting places like this as much as I do?"

"Eh. I'm not visiting the place. I'm visiting the people. You here for a funeral or someone's fiftieth wedding anniversary?"

He snorts. "Basically the only valid reasons to come here. My mom and dad's anniversary, actually." He brings me toward the left, out of the other passengers' way, since it's clear *they* have somewhere to rush to. "Name's Wade Perkins." He offers his hand and a charming grin. "Bugging out of my skin already and can't wait to fly east again."

"Fox Tatum." I take his hand and shake. "Excited aunt counting down the minutes until her brand-new niece's birth."

"Fox." Tommy comes to a stop on my right, his hands in his pockets and a baseball cap pulled low over his eyes. He wears jeans not a great deal different from Wade's and a plain black t-shirt that hugs his chest... also similar to Wade's.

I guess they make them big out here.

"Hey." I drag my favorite fighter into a hug—*he's the only fighter I know, but still.* I squeeze extra tight and revel in the goodness of *almost-Alana* for a single beat of time. Then I step back and exhale a relieved breath as he takes my carry-on from Wade, then the handbag that weighs a ton.

Awkwardly, Wade drops his hands into his pockets and clears his throat.

"Oh! I'm sorry. Uh... Tommy Watkins, Wade Perkins." I point between the pair. "Wade, Tommy."

"We have to go." Tommy pinches the hem of my jacket and tugs me away. "Alana's waiting for you."

"Is she okay?" *Wade who?* I move fast, hurrying over the blacktop in his wake, two hurried steps to every one of his long strides. "Hey? Is there a problem? Why are we rushing?"

"Not rushing, and nothing's wrong. We've got a drive ahead of us, and I wanna get home."

"But she's okay, right?" I *step-step-jog* to keep up. "Healthy? Baby's okay?"

"Baby's fine." He drags me to a stop by the other passengers, catching my elbow when my feet tangle and the ground promises to hurt. Then he lifts a brow, glaring toward the suitcase buggy.

One might assume he's waiting for instructions, unsure which case to select. But then the ice-cream man presents a glittering spectacle completely unlike the blacks and beiges and browns surrounding it. With a heaving grunt and strained face, he tosses it unceremoniously onto the concrete, its bulk landing with a splat that leaves me worried about the zippers. But Tommy lowers his questioning brow and steps forward to collect my things. Then we're off again, moving toward the exit. "Alana's tired of being pregnant. She's swollen and exhausted and said she's not sleeping very well."

"I mean... She's full-term with a giant Watkins baby. I'd expect nothing less."

"Right."

"And Franky?"

He tugs me out the doors and through the parking lot, straight toward a truck of rusted silver and scratched fenders that would never clue the world into the fortune he has socked away after back-to-back title wins. Lifting my suitcase, his back and shoulders flaring under the weight, he tosses it into the bed of his truck, then he turns and grabs my carry-on, lobbing it in, too. "Franky's working on his armbar and getting kinda decent at it."

"No, I meant..." I stroll to the passenger door, narrowing my eyes. Intuition niggles at the back of my brain. "How's he doing *emotionally*? His mom's going through some stuff, and his baby sister is about to turn his life upside down. I imagine he's stressed but determined not to let Alana know."

"Oh, yeah. He's doing that." He follows me to the door and jerks it open, gesturing none-too-friendly into the cab. "Let's go."

"A-are you alright?" I inch past him and carefully climb in. "You seem kinda tense. You insisted on picking me up tonight, but if I'd known it would make you cranky—"

"I'm not cranky." He slams the door and strides around the hood, digging a hand into his pocket and freeing his keys. In seconds, he slides in on his side, his aftershave smacking me with a wafting cloud, his flexing jaw like a neon sign in the dark, illuminated under the harsh overhead light that extinguishes the moment he tugs his door closed. Finally, he releases all but one key, so the rest dangle on the hoop, and a fancy, monogrammed keyring catches my attention.

CW.

C friggin W!

"Christian?" I recoil and slam my elbow on the window, hissing from the pain as his menacing eyes look me up and down. "What the hell? You're not Tommy!"

"Didn't say I was." He stabs the key into the ignition and turns over the engine, pressing his foot to the clutch and rolling the truck forward, all in the time it takes my heart to beat. "You assumed."

"You *let* me assume! I said, '*Hey, Tommy!*' And *you* leaned in for a hug."

"You grabbed me for a hug. I neither consented nor did I make it into a big deal or act like an asshole in front of your friend. I didn't want to embarrass you."

"Bullshit! You *know* I was only being polite because I thought you were someone else."

"You don't think I deserve your general politeness?"

"After you emailed me twenty-three times in the last six days?" I slump back and fix my seatbelt, folding my arms and making myself as small as possible, if only so I don't have to be near him. "Twenty-three times! All to say the same thing. That's grounds for a harassment order in *any* state."

He firms his jaw in the waning light. "I was letting you know that we had this under control. So if you wanted to stay in New York, you could."

"And I hit reply to the first three emails, informing you that I heard you, and that I intended to visit anyway. The twenty after that were unnecessary."

"It was five emails." He pulls out of the airport parking lot and onto a single-lane road. *Because that's all they need out here. One lane.* "Exaggerating is the same as lying. Don't be that person."

"I told you your opinion was noted and disregarded. Yet, you continued to fill my inbox." I purse my lips and stare daggers at the side of his face. "Don't be that guy. It's not cute. Neither is being a dick."

"I wasn't trying to be a dick." He lounges back, one hand on the steering wheel and the other spinning the window crank until a warm breeze sprints through the cab. "I was trying to ensure everyone was clear on the details. I was formal, friendly, and not at all harassing. Your presence is *not* necessary. That's factual. You're taking it personally."

Of course, I'm taking it personally, you jackass! "It seems *your* presence is equally unnecessary. Alana asked *me* to be there for her. Did she ask you?"

Target decimated. The stony grip he has on his jaw breaks, and his hardened eyes slide across to mine. "I live here. She knows she can count on me, so it was hardly worth vocalizing."

"Mmhm." I open my purse and dig through its contents, snagging my phone just as soon as I catch sight of the illuminated screen. Then, setting my bag on the floor between my feet, I unlock the device with a fast swipe of my thumb, switch off plane mode, and jump to my text inbox until, of course, a half dozen texts ding and vibrate to announce their arrival.

> Chris is coming to get you. He insisted.

> Be nice to him! He appears grouchy and tough, but his feelings are easily hurt if you find the right words.

> You should be landing soon. I hope your flight was good.

> My flight tracker app says you're taxiing. Welcome! Hurry to me. I miss the hell out of you.

> Don't forget the thing I said about Chris. He's a sweetheart, and I'm kinda protective. So don't pick at him.

> Franky says hey and to hurry! Also, Tommy says hey and to not be mean to his brother. We know you, Fox! I know you. So don't be a jerk.

"Coulda sent those texts *before* I went into airplane mode." Grumbling under my breath, I tap out a fast reply.

> I'm here, I'm in the truck, and Tommy owes me a giant apology for sending his identical proxy without adequate warning. I would've preferred hitching a ride with the suitcase flingerer. Seems safer.

"Unfortunately, Alana wants us to get along." Sending the message, I lower my phone and peer over at the guy who won't say a word unless it's pried out of his mouth with a crowbar... or spite. "She said we have to."

"We are getting along." He drops his legs open and turns the radio up just enough to catch the tune, but not the words. "I don't know about you, but I don't make a habit of arguing with perfect strangers."

"But you'd send me twenty-three—"

"Five."

"Five emails in seven days—"

"Sixteen days."

Argh! "Fine! Five emails in sixteen days *gently* suggesting I stay the hell out of your state and leave your family alone. That's not nice, Christian. It doesn't take an emotionally healthy adult to recognize that you're highly strung and a little controlling."

"I'm not controlling—"

"Maybe you feel a certain possessiveness, since you knew Alana when you were younger. But she's *my* friend, too. She's practically my sister. We went through hell and back together, raising a little boy and winging every damn aspect of it because we were clueless and doing our best. And all along, you and your brother actively *hated* her. So while you're out here in Bumfuck Idaho, thinking you get to round them up and keep them all to yourself, I'm here to tell you that's not gonna happen. I'm *not* going away. You *won't* keep me out of their lives, and you *can't* stop me from coming when they need me, no matter how many emails you send."

"I didn't say any of that."

He's entirely too relaxed, tapping the steering wheel with the tips of his fingers and rocking, barely perceptibly, to the music on the radio. Which is all good and dandy for him. Meanwhile, there's a part of me that wants to deck the smug prick, and *most of me* that wants to curl up in the corner and cry a little bit.

Fuck him, and fuck his emails, too.

"I said Caroline offered to help at the shop," he continues, "Tommy would be with Alana, and I could be with Franky. My emails were a professional courtesy, informing you that flying all this way was not necessary."

"Yeah? Well, your professional courtesy was received. And dismissed. I replied to your first email with the same polite detachment and informative tone yours had, which should have been the end of this discussion. Yet, here we are. Still bickering about a topic I consider moot."

"We're not bickering." *So fucking calm.* He sets his elbow on the door frame and chills. "You're here now. Not only that, but I was courteous enough to pick you up and bring you to the woman you're nagging me about. Which implies the subject is closed." But then he glances over, quietly optimistic. "Unless you'd like me to turn around? If you catch the next flight out, you could be back in your apartment by midnight."

Snarling, I ball my fist and consider striking out at the two-hundred-something-pound wall of muscle.

Hating a guy doesn't exclude me from noticing the body he created inside a fight gym. The proud lines of his jaw and the broad swelling of his chest. His literal job is to work out seven days a week, which means he wears his muscles the way I wear a skirt suit. But before I can smack the jerk, my phone vibrates with an incoming text and the rage bubbling in my blood turns to something else entirely.

Because Alana's name pops onto my screen.

Saved by the bell... ish.

> I'm counting down the minutes till you arrive. The baby's kicking up a storm, so I think she knows something's happening. Tommy said he'll make Chris wear a name tag if it helps… but I think he was joking. So probably don't expect that to happen.

> You have a 45 minute drive, and I'm not entirely sure I know which of you will fare better. So just… ya know. Think of me, and be nice. Chris is apt to pull over and put you on the highway if you annoy him too much. He can only handle so much noise before he's done. So don't push him too hard.

> 44 minutes. I'm honestly freaking the hell out and dying to see you. Please hurry.

I draw a long sigh, filling my chest and washing away the anger that brews in my veins. Then I exhale again and study my driver.

A faceless, nameless, personality-less service provider. That's all he is.

"What?" He peeks my way. "Why are you staring at me?"

"Because she's *begging* me to hurry." I turn my phone and show him the screen, though I doubt he can read fast enough to capture more than a word or two. "She's freaking out and *needs* me there." I quickly type, '*love you, see you soon*' and hit send, then I lock the screen and accept my new reality.

Be quiet. Don't fight. Forty-three more minutes.

"She *wants* me in Plainview. So it would be best for all involved if you stopped asking me to leave."

Okay, so one more barb. That's it. No more.

"Does she send you texts like that?"

Oy. The next six weeks are gonna be rough.

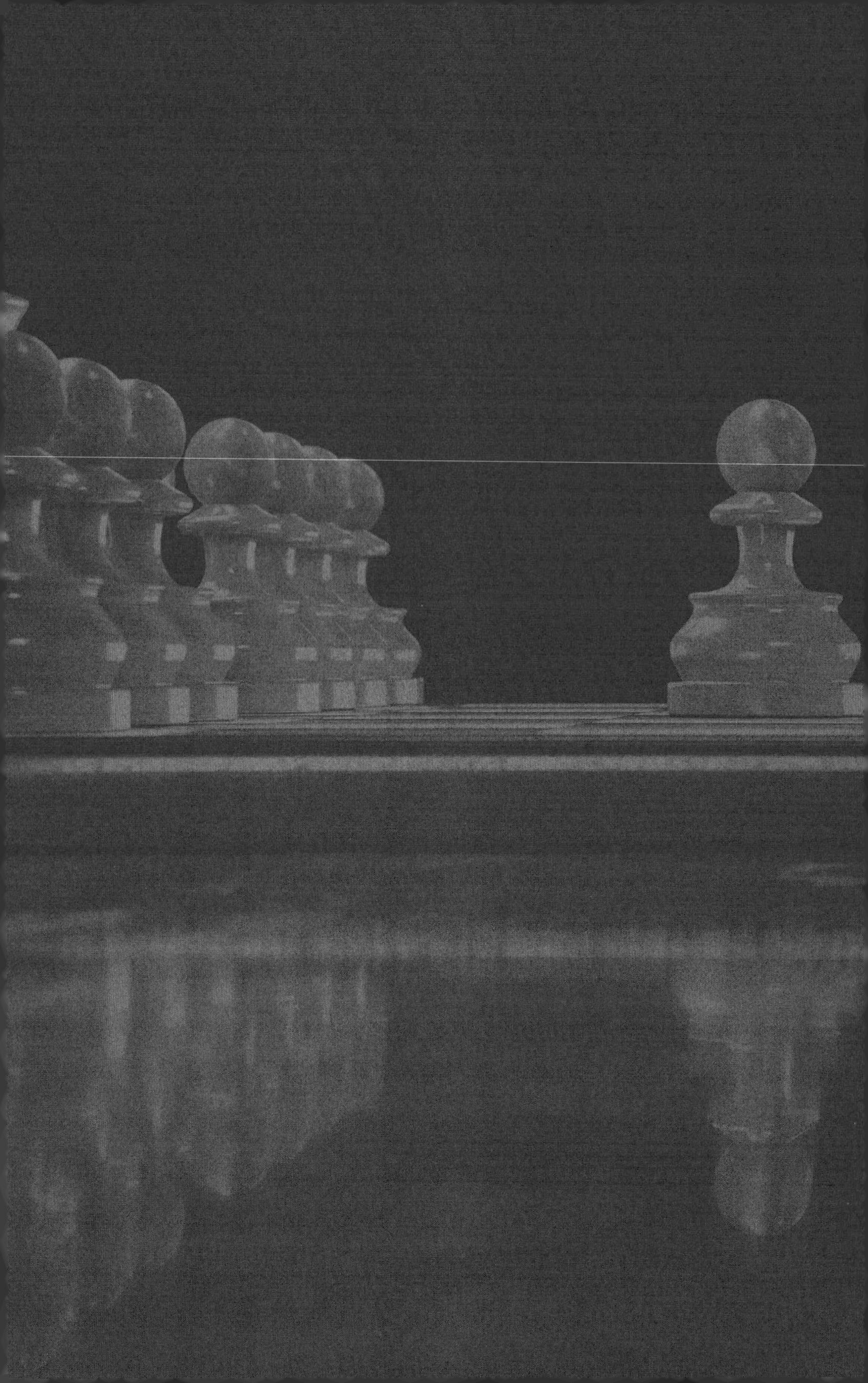

ROUND FOUR
CHRIS

"Oh my God. Oh my God. Oh my God." The very moment I bring the truck to a stop in Tommy's driveway and kill the engine, Fox whips her seatbelt off and shoves her door open. "Oh my God! Ahhh!" She leaves her purse behind. Her suitcases. Her bad attitude, too, and bounds out of the truck, dashing toward Alana's top-heavy form waiting on the porch. "Lana!"

She sprints up the steps and crashes into her best friend with a violence Tommy and I would *never*. They squeeze and hug, squeal, and hell, there's a little jumping, too.

I had no clue Alana could do that anymore.

"I missed you so much!" Alana blubbers, pregnancy tears sliding onto her cheeks and a sob making her chest bounce.

I roll my eyes and climb out of the truck, moving to the back so I can get Fox's shit and toss it on the lawn.

Tommy, being the smart man he is, circles the women and heads this way, too.

It's dark out now, and the cicadas are already screaming. But his eyes are on me, his hands in his pockets while his walk is part escape, part swagger.

"They didn't do that last time they were together." He comes to the back of the truck and drops the tailgate open, reaching in to grab the larger of the two suitcases. *Geez, it's almost like he knows I intend to disrespect the glittering purple eyesore.* "Was she squeaking and whatnot while you were driving?"

"Nope." I snatch the carry-on case and set it in the dirt—*oops*—before stepping back and digging my hands into my pockets. "She was snippy and rude and annoying, actually." I tip my chin toward the cab. "Her purse is in there, on the floor. She kicked it over when she bolted, so you're gonna need to get it."

He follows my gaze and chuckles. But at least he starts toward the passenger door. "You have a real problem with this, huh?" He grabs her things, tossing random women-shit into the depths of her purse. "I'm not sure I've ever seen you so *pre*-annoyed before."

"I'm not pre-annoyed. I'm adequately post-annoyed because she's... she's..."

"She's what?" He leans into the truck to make sure he's got everything. "From a time in Alana's life that we're not a part of? Confident and louder than you'd like? Someone who has a whole decade of Alana's history tucked away in her heart? If anyone gets to be toxically defensive about all this, it's me. But I'm not, because I'm pretty fuckin' glad Lana had someone to count on while she was dealing with things we had no clue about."

"Tommy—"

"Never, when I think of that woman, can I muster even an ounce of irritation. She was there for them when I wasn't. I won't shit on that." He closes the truck door and glances at the lady-duo on the porch, and then at Franky—*my buddy, my pal*—who looks up at the pair with an expression verging on intolerance.

My boy.

"Alana smiles because Fox is in her life." He comes around the truck and grabs the larger suitcase. "That's all I need to know. If my girl wants her friend, then I'm gonna make damn sure she sees her friend. I don't give a fuck about anything else."

"What if she tries to take over?" I grab the carry-on case, since I'm not a complete douchebag—*sometimes*—and follow him toward the house. "What if the baby arrives, and when it's your turn to hold her, Fox inserts herself instead?"

"She won't. She's here to help, and that baby is mine, too. *I* get to say who holds her. Not Fox."

"What if she convinces Alana to move back to New York at the end of the six weeks? Maybe it'll be like, '*You've needed me this whole time, since babies are hard work. Come back with me.*' Then maybe she'll look at you like, '*Just for a little while, Tommy. You gotta focus on your fights. Alana can return to Plainview when the baby is twenty-one.*'"

"Jesus." He shakes his head and drags the suitcase in his wake. "Sounds like you have some insecurities to work through. Alana's life is here now, and Fox already let her go once."

"What kinda name is that, anyway?" I quicken my stride, because I'll be damned if we leave those two alone for too long and risk Fox buying return tickets for *my* family. "Fox isn't even a name. It's not even a nickname. It's not even a shortened version of a real name. It's just..."

"None of our business?" He taunts me with dancing eyes and lugs the overweight suitcase up the stairs. And because our approach is noisy, drawing his guest's curious eyes, he sets the case by the door and circles back for a hug. "Glad you arrived safe. Flight was okay?"

She squeezes him long enough to almost make it weird, holding on when he would have stepped back. But then she releases him and scoops Alana closer until they're hip to hip. "Flight was uneventful. Food was bland. But," she adds when Franky's eyes alight with his fun fact, "I heard that cabin pressure can affect our tastebuds. So maybe the food wasn't bland at all."

"Maybe." Tommy grins, reaching over and swiping a wet tear track from Alana's cheek. "We're happy to have you. I'm especially happy that Alana's happy."

"Will you change your mind and stay here at the house?" Alana pleads. "You could take any of the spare rooms and not be in the way."

"There's plenty of room for you," Tommy agrees. "We'd love to have you."

"I'll stay here tonight, since it's already dark, and I missed the hell out of you. But tomorrow, I'm hiring a car and moving into the apartment above the bookstore. I want to give you your space."

"But—"

"I'll want my space, too," she cuts in with a playful smile. "You know me, Lana. I spread out and occupy every inch of my living quarters. So unless you want my heels in your kitchen and my hair straightener between the couch cushions, this is best. Six weeks is both a long time and a blink of an eye. I don't want to waste a single second of it worrying about getting under each other's feet."

"I'm gonna help you at the shop," Franky declares, pushing his glasses up his nose. "*I* set up the spreadsheets and stocking system, so *I'll* have to explain it so you don't mess it up."

"See." Fox gestures toward him. "The shop will need my full concentration. I would hate to mess up a flawless system."

"What about when the baby comes?" Alana's eyes dance with unshed tears. "I'll want Franky to be with me, but I'll need him to be with you, too. I don't want him staying at the bookshop—"

"I'll be around." *It's time to remind these people that I exist, dammit.* I carry the smaller suitcase up the stairs and draw four sets of eyes, though only one set narrows and frames with fiery ire. "I'm just next door, remember? I'll sleep on the couch for a few nights after the baby arrives, so I can help with Franky, but he'll still be in his own home."

"I'll stay at the house," Fox inserts, oh-so-fucking-sweetly. "You've set up a room for me already, so I'll sleep in there tonight and whatever other nights you need me. When you want me around and need Franky close, that's where I'll be. And when you need me less, I'll be at the shop." She purses her lips and stares defiantly into my eyes. "No need for you to sleep on the couch, Christian. Not for as long as I'm in Plainview."

"Listen—"

Tommy steps between us, his back to me, and forces out a fake chuckle. And because he's still holding it, he offers her purse, hanging it from two fingers. "We have cheesecake inside and movie snacks. Why don't you girls head in? Alana's been waiting for tonight with a fierce desperation."

"Oh, fun!" Fox takes her purse and tilts to the left, just far enough to meet my eyes. "Could you bring my bag in? That would be *so* helpful." Then she turns on her heels and drags Alana into the house.

"It's like she's not even being careful!" Frustrated, I release her carry-on and watch it tumble back down the stairs—*bang, bang, thud, bang*—until it hits the dirt with a splat. "We're out here treating Alana like glass, but that chick is manhandling her without a single care in the world."

Shaking his head, Tommy trudges down the stairs and collects the case, pulling the handle out so he can use it and patting dust off the shell exterior. "You need to chill the hell out."

"I'm just saying that Alana's in pain, she's tired, she's already friggin' crowning. She can't just be running around and forgetting to be careful. But Fox comes in and body slams her? How is that okay?"

"Fox has already been with Alana during pregnancy and birth." He sets the suitcase on the porch and gestures toward Franky, who merely watches us through smudged glasses. "He turned out fine, right? In reality, those two women have more experience on this front than you or I *ever* will. So let them do whatever the hell they wanna do."

"Tommy—"

"I just care that my daughter arrives safely, and that Alana gets through in one piece. Fox can say and do whatever the fuck she wants because she has a track record of not screwing this up. We don't mess with a winning formula, Christian."

"How come you don't like Aunt Fox?" Franky grabs the smaller suitcase handle and wipes dust from the top. "What'd she do to you?"

"She—"

"She did nothing," Tommy cuts in. "Chris struggles with inclusion sometimes. It's not that he wants to be mean. He just doesn't know how to accommodate Aunt Fox while she's in Plainview to help with the baby. It makes him feel a little—"

"Wary?" I suggest. "Appropriately concerned."

"Redundant." He flashes a taunting smile and places one hand on Franky's shoulder, then he turns them both and starts toward the door. "Chris' feelings are hurt because way, way, way back before you existed, there was just me, your mom, and Chris. We were a team, and we had a lot of fun together. Now there's you, your mom, me, Chris, and Fox. And unfortunately for Fox, she's outspoken enough to grate on his nerves and unlucky enough that Chris acts like she's stepping on toes when she's not."

"Stop talking about me like I'm not here." Anger bristles in my veins, throbbing to the beat of my heart. But do I turn around and leave? Fuck no. I blow out a huff of exasperation and follow them into the house, slamming the wire door in my wake and locking the wooden door to keep intruders away.

Then, I follow the sound of girly giggles and a cheesy rom-com playing on the television.

"Oh my gosh!" Fox's face glows, her hands pressed to Alana's belly. "She's jumping like crazy!"

"That's what I told you!" Alana's long blonde hair sits high on her head in a messy ponytail, which is a stark contrast to Fox's sleek mahogany locks, delicately draped over an off-white blouse suited to the office.

"Tommy thinks she's gonna be a fighter," Alana giggles. "She's got strong legs already."

"We'll see how it shakes out," Tommy counters, stalking past me to the kitchen, then back again with bowls already filled with dessert. "I like the idea of teaching my baby girl how to whoop some ass. But sending her into the cage is a whole other thing. If some other brat hits her, I'm gonna hunt her daddy down and take care of business. Here." He leans over the back of the couch and places the first bowl in Alana's line of sight. He drops a kiss to her forehead and another on the tip of her nose, then he moves on to Fox... though he skips the kissing part. "Franky and Alana made cheesecake this morning."

"Mmm." Fox digs in and makes sounds in the back of her throat that belong in the bedroom. It's inappropriate. It's rude! *There's a kid listening!* "I would have known even if you didn't tell me." She scoops dessert onto her tongue and whimpers happily. "Alana has *alllllways* been the queen of baking. In fact, before she moved here, I offered her *free* accommodation for the rest of her life at my apartment in the village in exchange for monthly brownies." She closes her eyes and savors her snack. "Lord, I've missed this."

"You're making it into a whole thing." Blushing, Alana eats, too. Though she manages to do it with less oohing and noisy aahing. "I'm not working very much right now, but sitting down all day hurts my hips. So I've revisited my love of baking."

"Which is funny, since you started at the end of your first pregnancy." Smug, Fox peeks over and pins me with a look that screams *fuck you*! "It sucks you guys never experienced that baking. It changed my life."

"I'll show you around the bookstore tomorrow if you want, Aunt Fox." Franky strolls around the couch and climbs up to sit on the arm, tucking his feet under Alana's thigh. "I can teach you the computer system and the storage room and stuff. We need to make a new book order, but Mom said we could save it for when you get here so you could see."

"That sounds fantastic." She lounges back, burying herself in the couch cushions, and hugs her bowl to her chest. "I'll be up, bright and early, so whenever you're ready to rock and roll, I'm ready to learn." She meets his eyes and grins. "I'm quick on the job and *always* have glowing references. Would you like to see them?"

He giggles. "I believe you. And I already talked to Booker to make sure."

"You talked to Booker?" she laughs. "Checking up on me?"

"What is your job, anyway?"

Dammit, Chris! Shut the fuck up.

Four sets of eyes swing across, like tractor beams burning my skin and clawing at my face. They watch me, stare at me. Silence hangs but for the movie playing on the screen. Then Fox smirks, grabs a little more cheesecake, and slides it onto her tongue. "What do *I* do?"

I could have gone straight home. I could be sitting on my couch right now, all alone, exactly how I like to be. I could be comfortable in a pair of sweatpants instead of jeans and barefoot, which is way better than the boots that itch the soles of my feet.

But no. I insisted on driving to the fucking airport and collecting a socialite whose mere existence bothers me in ways I can't explain.

"Yes." I push the single syllable past gritted teeth. "You."

"I'm the CHO at Gable, Gains, and Hemingway."

"That's a marketing firm!" Franky *fun facts* me. "Their building is in Manhattan, and it's huge. It's not the tallest, but it's one of them. You can see it from miles and miles outside the city."

I draw my eyes back to Fox, my nose twitching with displeasure when I find her brown gaze waiting for mine. "So you're in marketing? You write ads and stuff?"

"No. My boss writes ads and stuff." She allows a lazy, languid smile to spread across her lips. "I'm the CHO. My job is much more important."

I dig my hands deeper into my pockets. "Chief... *something* officer. Sounds prestigious. You must've worked hard to get there at..." I look her up and down. "Thirty-five?"

I'm a bastard, I know.

"Twenty-eight," she bites out. "In fact, I had a birthday just a few days ago."

Alana gasps, grabbing her friend. "I'm sorry I couldn't fly out for the party! You know I would've if I could, right? There's no chance I would've skipped it if I had literally any other choice."

"You're seventy-five months pregnant. You're not *allowed* to fly, and sitting in the car for two days would send anyone crazy." She places her hands on Alana's baby bump. "I forgive you."

"We'll make it up to you while you're here. I promise. I'm gonna do something special for you just as soon as this giant baby is out of me."

"I already told you what I wanted for my birthday, anyway. But since that bambina is still locked inside the vault of Alana, I guess I'll trade birthday buddy for a birthday *month* buddy." Smirking, Fox glances over her shoulder and catches me staring. "I'm Chief Happiness Officer, by the way."

Her words don't make sense. The phraseology doesn't compute. I blink, and then I blink again. I open my mouth to speak, and then I snap it closed again. Then I reach up and scratch the back of my neck. "What?"

"Chief Happiness Officer. That's what I do."

"Your... Your job is *happiness*?"

"I work within a stressful industry where burnout is real and too common, and business executives perform exponentially better when that stress is mitigated. My job, specifically, is to make them happy."

"You're a—" *Hooker? Paid companion? Massage therapist with the happy ending services?* "You're a high-end escort?"

Alana gasps. "Christian!"

Tommy throws his head back, barking out a laugh that leaves his chest bouncing.

Franky, thankfully, is oblivious.

"No." Unphased, Fox scoops more cheesecake onto her tongue. "I already told you what I am. The fact you took to it with a scarlet-colored crayon is something you should discuss with your therapist." She brings her eyes back to Alana. "Do they have those out here in the hills?"

"But what the hell is a chief happiness officer?" Why are they laughing at me? There's no such thing. "I don't get it."

"You're gonna get yourself shot," Tommy giggles. *He giggles*!

"She plans team bonding experiences," Alana explains. "She decorates the office to prioritize peaceful flow and good energy."

"You're shitting me?"

"Her job is to reduce stress within the workplace. Ergonomic furniture, clearer computer monitors, blue lens glasses. Office flow, maximizing break times, catering with healthy, clean food, since junk food is often the first a stressed person will go for, which actually makes stress worse."

"My job is to assess my company and find ways to make it better. Relaxed staff members perform more efficiently. It's statistically proven."

"That's just... that's..." I look at Tommy and search for sense. For confirmation that this is all a joke. "That's not even a real job!"

Alana scowls. "Chris!"

"My paycheck says otherwise," Fox counters. "And the plaque on my office door."

"And your ergonomic chair," Franky helpfully adds. "And your coworkers are always smiling. I saw it every time I visited."

Fox hooks a thumb over her shoulder. "See? It's real."

I turn on my heels and stride away *because the irony isn't lost on me that when I'm around her, my stress levels rise*. I have nothing to say that won't get me in trouble with Alana and no fucking way to end this conversation with anything remotely kind. So I stalk across the kitchen, echoing laughter hitting my back like an obnoxious slap from a drunken friend.

Flipping the locks, I yank the door open and move onto the porch. I can't deal with her. I can't deal with fake ass people or ulterior motives. I can't deal with the woman who so clearly wants Alana to choose her over Plainview and the one who will, no doubt, lay claim over the sweet little baby I get to call my niece.

"She's not even related to them!" I slam the door and stomp down the stairs. "And that's *not* a real job."

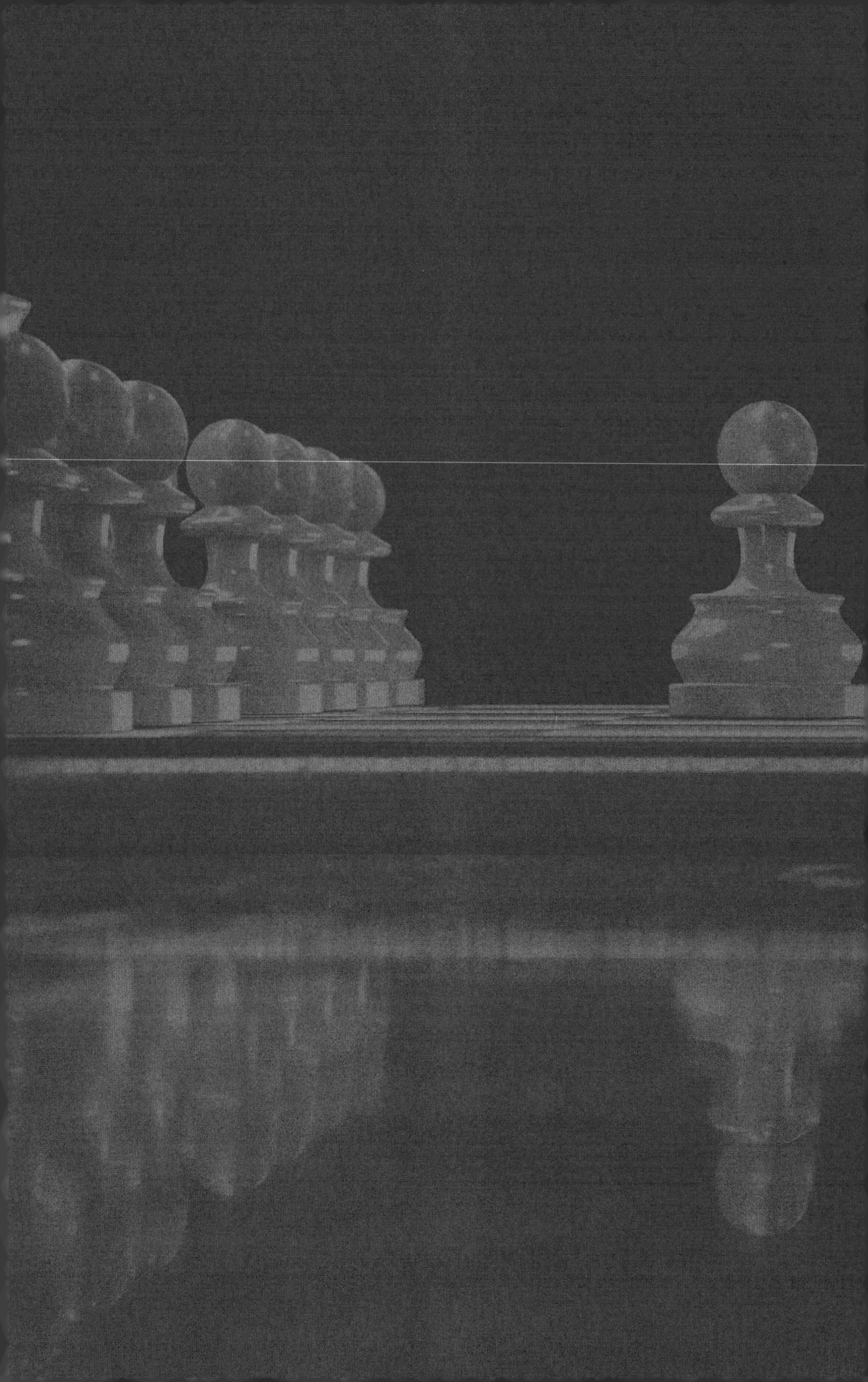

ROUND FIVE
FOX

I wake the next morning before anyone else, with the sun slowly creeping toward the horizon and the chirp of birds outside invading my dreams.

It's not that I mind a noisy world—New York City traffic is a constant hum I'm not sure I'll ever stop hearing—but a robin's call is pretty enough, and loud enough, to drag me toward consciousness and remind me where I am.

In Satan's asshole.

Though, the room Tommy and Alana have set me up in is luxurious enough to make the rest tolerable.

Crawling off my bed and into a pair of buttery soft yoga pants, I tiptoe acrosss my room with eager anticipation bubbling in my veins. The memory of the lake from last night playing in my mind, and the reality that I'll get to enjoy it all alone for a few moments, means I move quickly. Too quickly. Because in my rush, I slam my toe against the corner of a heavy set of drawers. Pain radiates up through my leg and into my belly, forcing me to grit my teeth and swallow my hiss before I wake the rest of the household. Instead, I pause right where I am, squeezing my fists and slowly opening my lips to allow fresh air into my lungs.

When the sharpest blades of pain subside, I limp toward the door, carefully pulling it open to reveal a still-dark house and out the windows on both sides, trees and water as far as the eye can see. Most magical of all is the dock that stretches halfway across the water, disappearing into the fog of an early morning.

From the moment we drove in last night, and Chris' headlights played off the water, I knew what I wanted to explore. More than that, I knew I wanted to do it all alone, before the rest of the world woke. And since New York is a couple of hours ahead of Plainview, that means I get a head start on everyone else.

Eagerness is like electricity in my blood, pulsing in my veins as I head downstairs in silence. The rich scent of freshly brewed coffee leads me to the kitchen and, mercifully, to a coffee pot that clearly works on a timer. I snag a mug and fill it to the brim with steaming black liquid, then whipping my hair into a ponytail to keep it off my face, I skip creamer altogether and move toward the door.

Already, the pain of a stubbed toe is a long-gone memory.

Carefully, as quietly as I can, I flip the locks and peek back to ensure no one stirs upstairs, and when the coast is clear, I step outside into the glorious morning chill.

Fresh air never tasted so good. The smell of moss in my nostrils and the soft movement of the lake, just fifty feet from Tommy's back door, is better than whatever Heaven is likely to offer.

Being born and raised in New York City means the stench of traffic and subway grates is in my blood. It's not even a smell I dislike. The glitz and glamor of Broadway makes my heart swell, and the constant lights in Times Square leaves me with a happy sense of belonging.

Harmony.

We're all in this together-ness.

None of which Plainview could ever hope to have. But this lake... this view...

I traverse the porch steps and tiptoe from dirt to grass, soft dew-coated blades tickling the soles of my bare feet. Goosebumps track along my exposed arms, just cold enough to remind me that it's early, but not so bad that I'm tempted to trade this for the comfort of inside.

Instead, I stop in the middle of the yard and tilt my head back, closing my eyes and hugging my coffee between both hands. And I take this moment to simply... *be*. To breathe. To remember and bathe in the knowledge that I'm with my family again for the first time in way too long, so close I could sprint inside and jump in their bed and steal a hug that won't ever be denied.

When Alana and Franky left New York, they took my heart and a chunk of my soul with them.

I would never tell them their absence haunts me or that the loneliness I feel now is akin to abandonment. They're entitled to their happiness just as much as anyone else. More, really. But that doesn't mean I'm spared from the consequences of their move. It doesn't mean that pain isn't a beating drum, day after day, while the cruel, dark side of my subconscious reminds me that I wasn't good enough for them to stay.

There's what I know to be true, and of course, their move wasn't about *leaving* me, so much as it was about *moving toward* something else. But then there's that childhood trauma I keep tucked away, rearing its ugly head and stomping on me during my darker, achier days.

But those are problems for New York Fox Tatum. For this moment, I choose appreciation and *being*. I choose the outdoors, solitude, and silence. And when I can't stand the darkness any longer, I open my eyes and take in the beauty of this paradise my best friend has stumbled upon.

It's all so pretty.

So clean.

So tranquil, as frogs croak and crickets chirp. Strolling toward the dock, I take in the lake that may actually be a river... a stream of some sort, considering the slow-moving water. Grass grows all the way to the edge, and flowers spring up in every available patch of dirt, so what isn't green, is yellow and pink and blue and white.

The morning fog rolls ominously across the water's surface, thinning with every inch of sunlight that spills over the mountains surrounding this town.

This house is nice, certainly. The land is lovely and sprawling.

But the water is otherworldly, so mesmerizing, I wonder how many mornings Alana and Tommy have snuck out to snuggle in each other's arms and revisit the love they had pre-Franky's conception. The relationship they have now is beautiful, but the love between teenagers, before they knew true heartache... that's something else entirely.

I slowly wander the grass, in no rush to arrive anywhere, and scrunch my toes in the thicker patches of the lawn until dew sneaks between each one. Moisture soaks into the bottoms of my pants, darkening against the gray fabric until I'm tempted to fold the hems up.

But I don't.

I don't truly mind.

I sip my coffee instead and move from grass to dirt, then dirt to rocks, and when I'm close enough, I skip from rocks to the dock, all so I can stroll amongst the fog.

This is where magic happens. It's where the world holds no pain, hearts never break, and the vulnerable are simply... okay.

It's where everything is perfect.

I walk on my toes and look everywhere at once, fearful that I might miss something beautiful. I hold my coffee in one hand and raise the other above my head, stretching my arm, my shoulder, my back. My shirt rides up, revealing my stomach. But that, too, is okay. Because I'm the only person who exists right now, and modesty is hardly a necessity when I'm the only person alive.

I tuck loose tendrils of hair behind my ear, only for the soft breeze to knock them loose again, and when I try a second time—and lose—I leave the locks on my face and meander to the very end of the dock until I'm gifted with a view more perfect than any painting could try to imitate.

Not even the most talented artist could capture this with tools as ordinary as a canvas and paints.

I draw a deep breath, sucking air into my lungs until I taste the dew in my throat and feel the cold inside my belly, and exhaling again, I turn and lean against the railing someone—perhaps Tommy, or maybe whoever owned this land before him—built to make the dock safer. I tilt my head back and smile, though I have no clue why, *exactly*, I do, and I search my five senses, since the literature says to do that.

I *smell* the water, and I *feel* the rough wood under my feet.

I *hear* the birds, and I *taste* my coffee.

Then I *see*... I see Chris Watkins sprint across his front yard.

Dammit.

Just like that, my delicate glass pane of peace shatters, replaced immediately with worry. Because he runs toward Tommy's house. Toward Alana. *Is she okay? Is there an emergency?* Straight away, I push off the railing and prepare to run, too, but before he crosses yard boundaries, he skids to a stop, touches the ground, and turns again. He pumps his arms, head down, powerful legs carrying him faster than five o'clock in the morning should allow. Until he reaches another invisible boundary, touches the grass, and spins back again.

Exercise. Shuttle runs.

Not an emergency.

Exhaling, I rest against the railing and explore my senses again. I still feel the wood and smell the water. I hear the birds and taste my coffee, but my eyes take in more than all the others combined. Chris' black shorts, sitting low on his hips and the ends touching his knees.

No shoes.

I have no shoes on either, but his lack of footwear becomes a detail that sticks in my side. His chest glistens with sweat despite the chill in the air, and his back burns a light shade of red... beneath the ink, that is. So much of it littered from shoulder to shoulder.

It's too bad he's an insufferable control freak. Because even a blind woman would acknowledge he's a treat to look at.

I hide amongst the morning fog and sample my coffee in the quiet, and when Chris switches from running like a lunatic to lifting weights that may or may not consist of a tractor engine, I merely shake my head and know *this* is the purest version of that man I'll ever know.

When he thinks he's alone, not competing for Tommy's attention, or Alana's, or even Franky's. When he has no clue I'm near, and because he doesn't, lacks the massive chip on his shoulder and his unfair claim to the only family I've ever truly known. When it's just him, and he's not imagining false things to be defensive about, he creates an image of serenity.

Just a man working his body to the point of failure. Building muscle and forcing his heart to a thunderous pace.

I settle in and watch him lift things and throw things. Squat and roll. He sweats and grunts, and when I think he's ready to take a break, he wipes his face and starts all over again.

Five in the morning is for lazy sleep-ins or quiet moments by the water. A romantic book and a cup of coffee. Or a hug, the kind that never ends. But Chris's preference for a punishing '*I must be stronger than Rambo*' routine leaves me with a deep sadness in the base of my belly.

Because only the most guarded, wounded man would work himself the way he does while no one else is watching.

"Fox?"

Startled, I tear my gaze across to Alana's door, and in front of it, the woman herself, in tiny sleep shorts and a shirt that can't possibly hide all of her belly. She squints, searching for me in the yard and tracking all the way to the dock, until finally, our eyes meet, and the worry in hers extinguishes, replaced by sweet happiness.

She places her hand on the railing and sumo-walks her way down the stairs, so while she's busy with that, I cast my eyes back to *the Chris show*. But of course, his workout is over, and his eyes burn against mine.

It should be impossible that a human being's *light* could change so visibly from one moment to the next. But the darkness that surrounds him now is entirely different from the darkness of an early morning. His unfounded anger, as obvious as if he were facing me, with two middle fingers pointed to the sky.

His chest lifts and falls, oxygen flooding his veins and filling his lungs, and by his sides, his hands flex and ball. His arms swell with adrenaline and the added blood flow from his workout. But if he receives a serotonin boost from exercise, he shows none of it to me.

He merely frowns, and when Alana emerges from the front of her yard and starts onto the dock, his eyes flicker her way.

And damn him, they soften.

"What are you doing out here so early?" Oblivious to our audience, Alana pads across the rough wood, massaging the side of her stomach with a kneading roll of her hand. "I know you're a morning person, but this is kinda ridiculous. It's barely six o'clock."

"It's six already?" I don't have a watch, and I didn't bring my phone outside. But I cast a look to the sun, crawling just a little higher. "I didn't even realize. Why are you awake so early?"

"I smelled the coffee Tommy banned me from having." She walks straight toward me, her belly hitting mine and her hands wrapping around my mug before I can stop her. Then she brings it up and sticks her nose as close to the liquid as she can, drawing the smell all the way to the base of her lungs. "That's the good stuff. Jesus." She takes another whiff and comes up again with a goofy grin. "This baby is coming today."

Just like that, my heart splats, and my eyes drop to her stomach. "I'm sorry... what? Are you having contractions?"

"Everything feels a little tighter, that's all. It hasn't begun, but I have a sneaking suspicion she was waiting for you." She hands my coffee back and comes around to lean against the railing. "What were you looking at?"

My eyes swing back to Chris'... or, well, the place Chris stood a mere moment ago. But his yard is empty now.

"Fox?"

"Nothing. Just enjoying the quiet. Do you normally come out here at this hour?"

"I think about it a lot. But most of the time, I stay in."

"Lazy bones."

She snickers. "I can't leave until Tommy's ready to let go."

"Because he won't let you?"

"Nah... Because *I* won't let me." Smiling, she brings her eyes around to mine. "Sometimes Franky climbs into bed with us, so when that happens, and we have nowhere else to be, we usually switch the TV on and, before we know it, it's nearly the middle of the day, and we didn't even notice we were hungry."

I *tut-tut-tut.* "That Watkins boy not feeding you?"

"Seems he's obsessed with taking care of me. Food. Water. Comfort. He's bought two dozen different shapes and sizes of pillow in the last six months, all for me to try because he's worried my stomach hurts when I lie on my side."

"Does it?"

"No." She takes another long, silly sniff of my coffee. "He worries, though. Like, a *lot*. So I rarely complain, and the times I do, it's usually about how hard he's working. That's when I tell him he needs to come home."

"Devious." I scan Chris' yard without being entirely obvious about it. "He won't hear '*you're working too hard*.' Instead, he'll hear that you want him at home. At which point, he'll fall into bed with you anyway."

"It's a system. He felt like his Vegas fight was only okay."

"But he won."

She snorts. "I know. Still, he thinks he could've done better, and *not* fighting Conner makes him feel like he's not the true champion. It's like he's worried we'll go hungry if he only wins a fight by a *little bit*."

"As opposed to a clean knockout?"

"Right. Never mind the fact he owns the house outright, the gym has no debts, and his clientele is loyal. He could lose every fight, and everything would still be okay. But he's Tommy Watkins." Sad, she drops her gaze and sighs. "He always fed me, even when he was starving. Me leaving for ten years caused a lot of damage."

"You can't seriously think you were in the wrong for—"

"No. I don't." She nibbles on her bottom lip, rolling it between her teeth. "But that doesn't erase the things he thought and the ways he felt for all those years. He and Chris are caretakers, and even though Tommy was thrilled about this baby, it doesn't stop him from freaking the hell out."

"Which is why you asked me to come to Plainview." I take back my coffee and knock her shoulder with mine. "Sure, you want me to help. Especially when the explosive poo arrives."

She giggles.

"But mostly, you want that extra set of eyes and hands, so if Tommy's losing his mind and the baby is crying and Franky is ridiculously dysregulated, you could call on me to pick up a couple of the pieces while you save Tommy from a menty-b."

"A menty-b," she snickers. "You always did have a skill for taking something serious and destroying its power. Mental breakdown is scary. Menty-b is…" She shrugs. "Meh."

"Have you considered that Tommy isn't the one you should worry about?" I don't bother hiding my intentions this time. I cast my gaze toward Chris' deserted yard and search for him in the shadows. "That dude is Franky on steroids, Alana. But he's a grown man with no clue how to emotionally regulate or calm the hell down. He's all knotted up, scared to death of this unknown world you're walking toward. And instead of being a healed, normal person who admits, *'hey, I'm kinda out of my depth here, so can someone help?'* he loses his mind trying to fit a square peg into a round hole."

"Fox—"

"You and Tommy and Chris are the *old* round hole. He was even able to jam Franky in there. But now, this baby... and me..." I exhale a soft laugh. "Jesus. He'd rather smack me with a rubber mallet than let me suggest a different, larger, potentially newer hole."

"I told you how things were when we were younger, right? How we created this odd codependence and obsession with keeping each other safe?"

"Yeah. Child of trauma, abusive situation." I tilt my head to the side and stretch my neck. "I know."

"He's terrified of being left behind. He's grown now, and outside of all this, he's brave and strong and entirely capable of living his life. But the baby scares him. The possibility that something will go wrong terrifies him. And the nagging fear that I'll leave Plainview and go back to New York makes him sweat."

"Because he's in love with you?"

"Me?" She chokes out a quiet laugh. "Love, yes. *In love*, no. If I leave, then Tommy will follow. And obviously, Franky will come, too. I think this scenario scares him most of all, even though, really, if we ever moved, we'd take him with us anyway. Christian's fear of rejection is *almost* as toxic as yours." Taunting, she peeks across and smirks. "You would curl into a ball and die. He would curl his fists and kill. It's different."

I tamp down on the bubbling anxiety that swells within my stomach. "Is he aware of how utterly mentally fucked up he is? There are therapists that can help with that sort of stuff."

"He's aware. But there's no therapist on the planet who can help him." She leans into me, setting her cheek on my shoulder. "He needs to be reminded that he's loved, that's all. He needs that unwavering reinforcement, since he was told every single day of his youth how *unwanted* and *unloved* he was."

"Sounds needy."

She clicks her tongue, which, in Alana code, means I'm about to cop an elbow to my ribs. "And then there's you, dying for acceptance and silently begging for the same things he is. But not only don't you stroll into town and make friends with the man not entirely different from you, but you're out here actively throwing his insecurities in his face. You told him he was unneeded, Fox."

"He told you I said that? What a snitch!"

"He didn't tell me. But I suspected, and you just confirmed." She turns her head and searches my eyes. "Don't do that, okay?"

Busted. I grit my teeth.

"For me? Don't say things like that to him. He's not just any guy you get to play with, and poking at him is not the same as poking at Booker or Colin or anyone else we know. Christian isn't needy in the way you think he is. But he's fragile." She lays her cheek on my shoulder once more. "He needs to be handled with care."

I'm fragile.
I need to be handled with care.
And he told me in five different emails how unwanted I was.

But no one wants to hear about that.

"Please?" She takes my hand and tangles our fingers together. "It would reduce my stress by a whole lot if I knew he was okay when we're not in the same room. This matters to me."

"Fine," I grumble, petulant and proud of it. "For you. Because I love you."

"I love you, too."

"I won't tell him he's unwanted," I clarify, since I'm all about the details. "I promise nothing about irritating him in general."

She snickers and tightens her fingers around mine. "I figured as much."

"I'll just be me. And I won't intentionally hurt his feelings. But if my existence is a bother, then that's something he's gonna have to handle all on his own."

"This is going to be a bumpy six weeks," she sighs. But then she hisses and grabs her stomach. "She's talking business now. Ouch. She's gonna come out swinging."

"Little fighter baby." I set my coffee on the railing and press my palms to her stomach. "Sheesh. You weren't kidding. Your stomach is tight as hell."

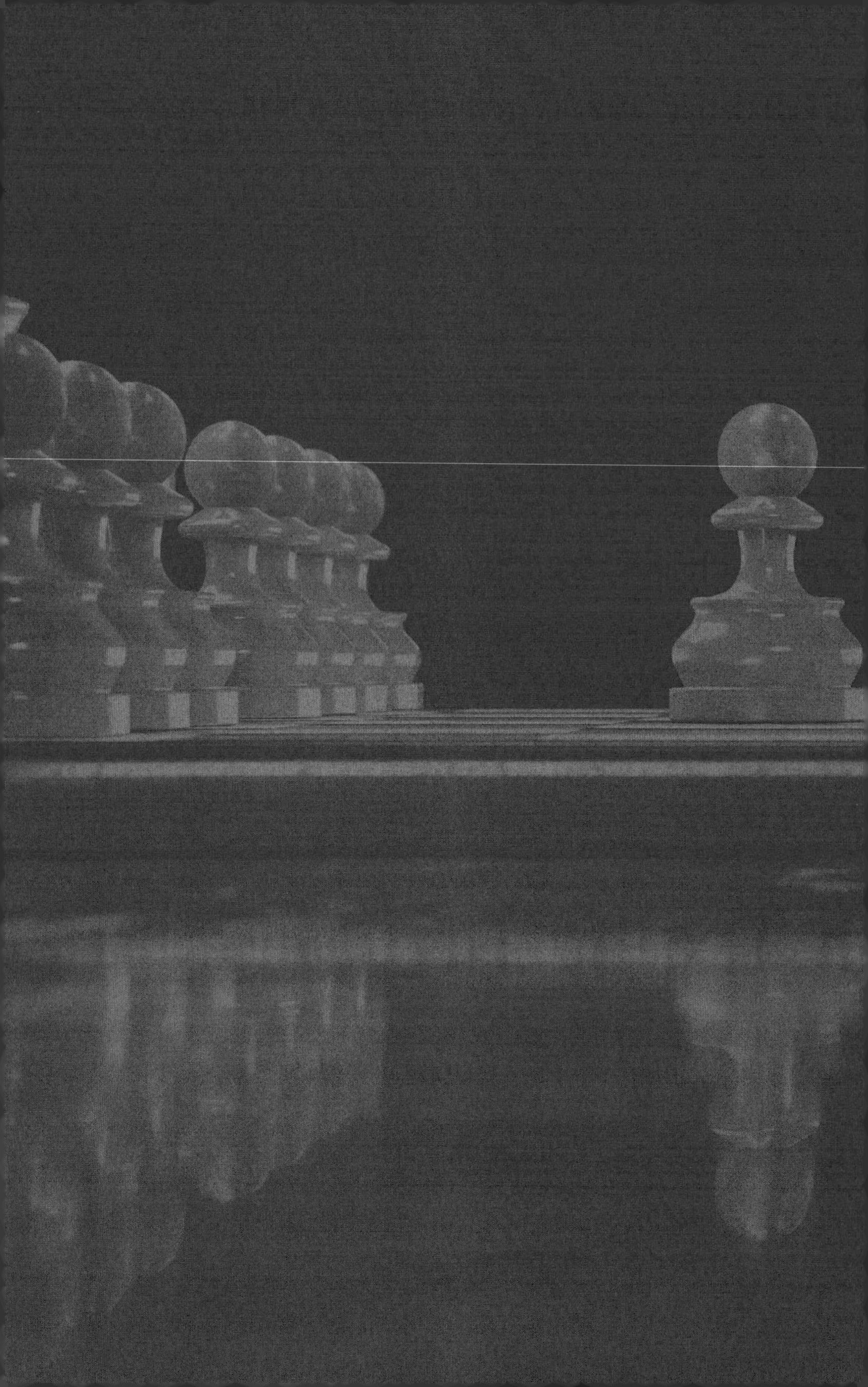

ROUND SIX
CHRIS

The bell above the bookstore front door jingles downstairs, alerting me to visitors. Though I know they're not customers.

They're Franky and Fox, here to settle in and discuss business.

I carefully set my wrench in my toolbox and take a step back from the spout that, an hour ago, leaked a constant *drip-drip-drip* into a shower that hasn't been used in months. Perhaps even years. And though turning the mains off to conserve water briefly passed through my mind, it took only a moment more to realize those same pipes feed the shop downstairs, too. If I cut one half of the building off, the other half goes without. Which means no toilets. No sink. No way to refill the coffee machine to appease the steady stream of customers Alana has cultivated over the past few months.

No coffee means the old ladies of Plainview might revolt. And shit, but they were young in the sixties. Every smart man knows not to fuck with folks from that era.

"I'll show you upstairs soon, Aunt Fox." Franky closes the front door, his voice echoing throughout the long shop and up the stairs into the apartment Fox will move into soon. He clomps across the store and flicks the lights on, and after that, the computer.

I know his routine almost as well as he knows it himself.

He moves to the cash register and powers it on so the Wi-Fi has time to catch up, then he switches the coffee machine on so customers have something delicious to drink while they peruse books.

"My mom sometimes bakes things herself for the fridges. And other times, the bakery up the street supplies us."

"Does your mom call them the day before to let them know?"

"Yep." He drags a stool over the old flooring, a tooth-aching screech announcing exactly where he is. *At the computer.* "She usually writes a list each day of all the things we need for the next day, and then she decides which ones she'll bake herself. Whatever is left over, she tells that to the baker, and the baker takes care of it."

"Sounds like a good system." There's no click-click-click of heels on the floor. So… sneakers? Flip flops? "Do you usually sell a lot of baked items?"

"We sell them all. Every single day."

Fuck, I don't have to see him to know his face glows with pride.

"We sell them *faster* when Mom bakes them," he adds smugly. "And usually, whoever the first customer is, asks, then they tell everyone else, 'cos this town is run on a grapevine."

"A grapevine?"

"Yeah, like, *gossip*. We don't even need TVs around here. Everyone knows everything about everyone else anyway."

He shudders.

I mean, I don't see it.

But he shudders. I'm sure of it.

"I miss that about New York," he murmurs. "Where people leave me alone, and no one talks about anyone else."

"It sure is nice," she agrees. And because I can't see her, and I don't know her well enough to know where she intends to take this conversation, I stalk out of the bathroom and into the studio apartment that hasn't been lived in since… the civil war, maybe. If Fox Tatum thinks she can manipulate an impressionable Franky into wanting to return to New York, then I consider it my right, my damn duty, to stand guard.

I have no desire to hide my presence, so I stomp across the apartment and close the door with a noisy slam—her one and only warning I'm on my way—then I jog down the interior staircase, the squeaky steps providing music for my approach. If Fox is my opponent, then the stairs are my fight song.

I move quickly, skipping off the final two steps, and come to a stop at the very opposite end of the bookstore where Franky and Fox wait.

One of them smiles when our eyes meet.

The other sets her hands on her hips and scowls.

"Why were you up there?" Agitated, Fox strides away from the front counter and stops an easy twenty feet from where I stand. Her brows pinch tight, and her eyes burn me in my skin. It's almost like she thinks her bad mood and five feet, nine inches are scary. "I thought the shop was locked and empty."

"It was." But I dig a hand into my pocket and pull out my keys, showing her that CW charm Franky gifted me for my birthday. "Fortunately, I have access and permission to enter anytime I like." *And I've been fixing your living quarters, you ungrateful shit.* Dismissing her, I tilt to the left and meet Franky's glasses-covered eyes. "Your mom and Tommy resting at home?"

"No. But Whacky's at home and being a total jerk. He chased me all the way to Aunt Fox's car."

"The rooster?"

"Do you know anyone else named Whacky?" He pushes his glasses up his nose and softens his expression. "And Mom and Tommy are at the hospital."

Fear spears through my blood, like the sting of a thousand furious hornets. "Why are they at the hospital? Is Alana okay?"

"She's fine." Where I expect derision, Fox offers kindness. When I expect snark, she presents a friendly grin and a slow walk forward. "Alana's having contractions, but they're slow and mild." She pauses in front of me, tilting her head back and meeting my eyes. "The baby will be here soon."

"Like, in twenty minutes soon? Or three hours soon?"

"Three days soon?" She comes around and stops beside me, so we're facing Franky's curious observation and presenting a united front. "Could be today, could be tomorrow. But we're calm and relaxed." She digs her hands into the pockets of her daisy dukes and leans, ever so gently to the side, until her shoulder touches my arm. "There's no emergency, and we're not panicking like there is one. We're just gonna get the shop ready for business and wait by the phone for Tommy's progress texts."

"I just..." *Relaxed? Who the fuck is relaxed?* "She's in labor now?"

"She's having contractions now. Which is not labor. It's *pre*-labor."

"Contractions means baby! That's labor."

"Good lord. This is gonna be more difficult than I thought." She gestures toward Franky. "Your mom is fine, right? She's safe, and everything is okay."

"Everything's fine," he answers in monotone. "Fun fact: there are three stages to having a baby. And my mom is only in the first stage. We have loads of time."

I read the book. *I read the book, dammit*! "Stage one leads to stage two. Why is no one concerned about the impending arrival of stage two?"

"Because we're calm." Fox turns to me and presents her hands, a silent question flashing through her eyes. Then she places two fingers on my chest, right between my breastbones.

"What are you—"

"I know Alana was your zen master all the way through childhood, and I know she has this special ability to simmer you the hell down. I won't even pretend to be as cool as she is. But," she glances up, grinning, "did you know you have a pressure point right here at your sternum? When you press on it and take a long, deep breath, your nervous system catches on that everything is okay, which then makes it possible to calm down."

"I'm not *not* calm!" *Stop touching me.* I like it. "I'm asking questions about a time-sensitive matter. If Alana is in labor, then a baby is coming. If the baby is coming, then I think I'd like to be there for the actual, literal birth of my niece."

She increases the compression of her fingers, massaging my breastbone and filling her lungs with a deep breath. And fuck, I don't mean to do the same, but I inhale anyway, expanding my chest and stretching my lungs. *Damn her and her witchcraft.*

"The baby is coming... at some point this week," she murmurs. "And you'll be there for the big reveal, I promise. Though, no matter how fond Alana is of you, I know for a damn fact you're not invited into the birthing suite. So why don't you trust me to handle the logistics, deal with the timing, and eventually, get you and Franky where you need to be when you need to be there?"

"*Trust* you? Woman, you already don't like me! You'd be happy if I missed out on this."

Her eyes shutter, from faux comfort to the real, angry person she is beneath. "I do not intend to miss it, Christian. Not the end, when Tommy comes out and tells us everything is okay. Which means for as long as I'm right here in front of you, you haven't missed anything. Now breathe." She inhales again and nods when my lungs do the same.

Traitorous fuckers.

"Feels better already, doesn't it?"

"I don't..." Shit. She's not wrong. "You—"

"You're lucky she didn't tell you to dance," Franky drawls. "She's real annoying when she thinks dancing will fix a bad mood."

Pleased, she drops her hands and strides away, the absence of her touch as startling as if she'd smacked me on the side of the head with a two-by-four. Instead, she claps her hands and beams for Franky. "Do we have to go to the bakery to get the stuff, or does the bakery deliver to us?"

"They come to us." He studies his computer screen, the reflection of spreadsheets bouncing off the lenses of his glasses. Hell, it's almost like his world wasn't just fucking turned on its head, right here in the middle of Alana's bookstore. "They usually come at nine, right after Mom takes me to school and opens up. But since it's Saturday, they'll come at about ten-thirty."

"Makes sense. Not many folks are heading to the bookstore as soon as they wake on the weekend."

She has a way of dancing while she walks. It's not an overt sashay and sway, but a more discreet roll of her hips. Which, unfortunately for me, is a million times more pronounced now that she's wearing denim shorts and those high-top sneakers she seems to favor.

"Can you teach me how to work the coffee machine?" She wanders around Franky's desk and kisses the back of his head. "Aunty Fox needs a hit of caffeine before she turns herself inside out. You know how dangerous no-coffee can be, right?"

He scoffs in agreement.

"So if you could peel yourself away from all those numbers, I'd be hella grateful."

"Hella is not a real word." But he slides off the stool and walks her to the machine, tapping buttons and catering to her the way he does his mother. He likes caring for them, and I think both women know it. So they give him tasks and save him from his racing brain.

It's me. My brain is racing.

"I'll go get the pastries." I stalk toward the front door, hunching my shoulders and digging my hands into my pockets. And though I draw both sets of eyes, curious stares following my progress across the store, I stride through the doorway and onto the sidewalk outside without a single added word.

Fresh air hits me like a wall, pushing my hair back and attacking my lungs. And though it *should* erase that suffocating squeeze crushing me from the inside out, I can't quite find a way to get my brain to talk to my lungs. So I press my fingers to the blazing point in the center of my chest instead, right where Fox touched only a moment ago.

But I don't have that same magic touch she has.

It doesn't work when I do it.

I can't find the calm.

"Shoulda told her not to fuckin' touch me." Frustrated, I lower my hand and stomp toward the bakery. "Should've smacked her away and told her to get jacked."

Yeah, right, dickhead. You wouldn't dare.

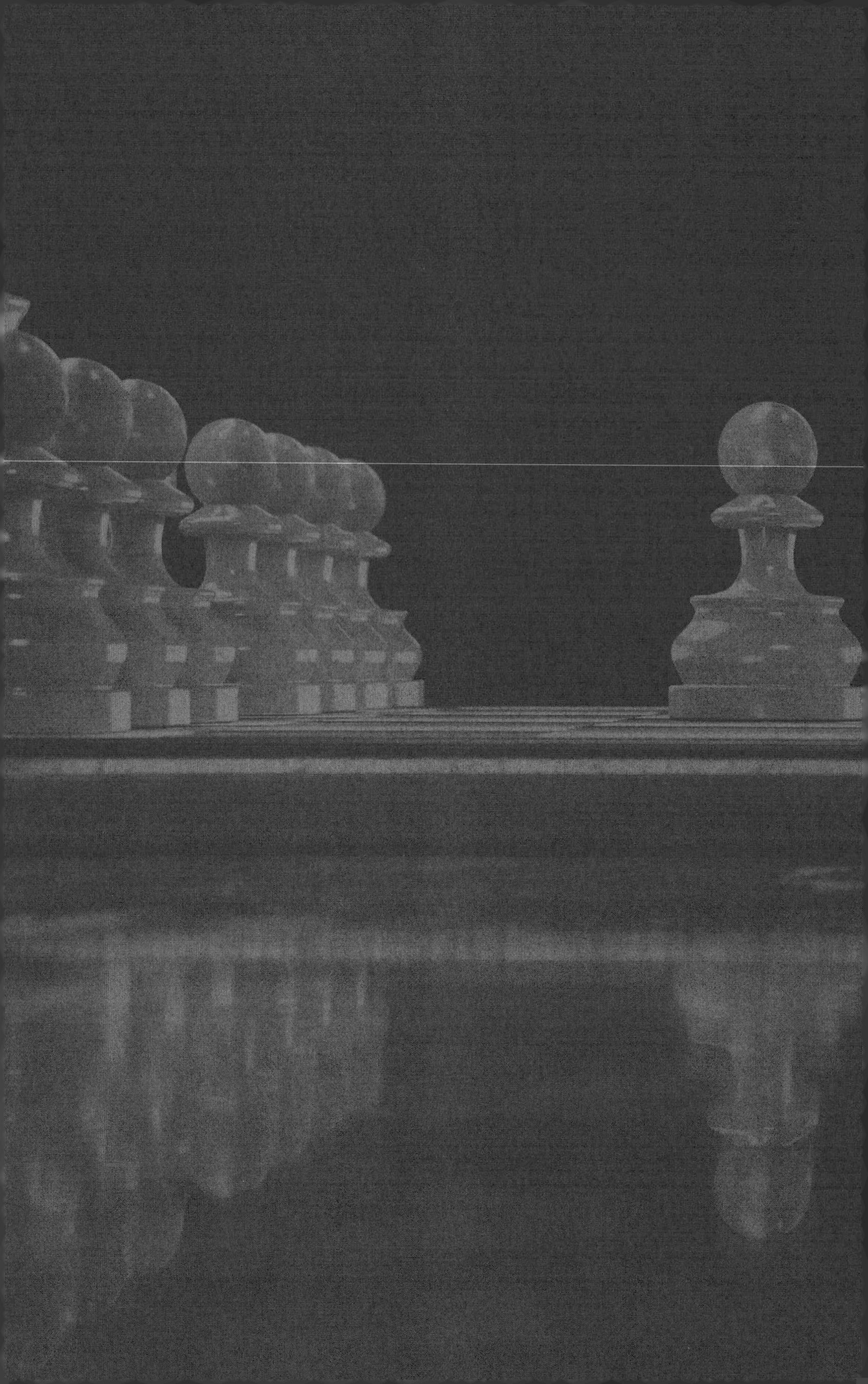

ROUND SEVEN
FOX

"How is she doing?" Barbara—that's her name, according to the discreet note Franky slides under my nose—hands me just enough money to pay for her pastry. No tip. No payment for the book she's been reading between the stacks. Not even a kind smile. Just a sneer and enough derision in her stare to make my hands twitch. "I heard Alana and Tommy are at the hospital."

"She's doing as well as we can expect." *Be nice, Fox. Be polite.* I ring up her purchase and make a note for Alana to deal with when she gets back.

Barbara's a cheap ass wench who steals entertainment, but thinks it's not stealing, because she hasn't left the store yet.

"Tommy sent a text a little while ago saying everything is fine."

"And how about you, Franklin?" The old bitty shuffles along, dragging her purse across the desk and hunching until they're on the same level. "How are you feeling about all this? A new sister will take all of your mom's attention, don't you think?"

Unimpressed, he stares right into her eyes, flat lips, expressionless face, and like the pro he is, unflinchingly cold until she gives up, snatches up her purse, and turns away.

The moment she's gone, his lips curl into a cute little smirk.

"Sometimes you do that because *you're* uncomfortable," I mumble under my breath. "Other times, you do it to make *them* uncomfortable."

"She doesn't need to know about my feelings." He makes a note on his computer about the sale, since, clearly he's into data and loves to track pastry trends amongst small-town folk. Then he taps enter and meets my eyes. "She could have said something positive, like how the baby will be an exciting addition to the family. Or how nice it'll be when I become a big brother. Or she could have even said how the baby will be fat and cute. Instead, she chose negativity." He shrugs. "She doesn't care about my feelings. She only wanted to make me sad."

"Which is as good a reason as any to ignore her." I bring my eyes back around and find our next customer stepping forward. One book, a cup of coffee—though those are free—and a bear claw stocked by none other than a pouting Christian Watkins. "Find everything you need?"

"Yep. You got one of those New York accents, huh?" A little old lady—miraculously, littler, older, and meaner than Barbara—digs through her tiny coin purse and lays silver on the desk between us. "You staying for long, Ms. Tatum?"

"Only six weeks," Franky answers, misinterpreting her question for kindness, when I hear, clear as day, the *we don't like you* dripping from her tongue. "She lives really far away, but she came to Plainview to help me and Tommy and my mom with the baby."

"Will you move out here?" Another silver coin. Then another. "Real estate may be cheaper in Plainview, but I don't imagine it's the kind that appeals to someone from New York."

No shit! I'd pay ten times the asking price and still consider New York superior to this place. However, I'm under strict instructions to be nice to the customers, so I paste on a saccharine smile and *fake, fake, fake* it. "I'm enjoying my visit for as long as I'm here. And I'm very lucky to have a wonderful job to return to when it's time, an amazing boss, and an apartment that overlooks Washington Square. I love living there and getting to visit here."

"New York is nothing but overpriced real estate," she *tuts*. "Have no clue how you afford it."

Be nice, be nice, be nice! "I'm paid well."

"She's the chief happiness officer," Franky declares. "Did you know that's even a thing?"

"A…" The old lady stops counting coins and drags her wrinkle-rounded eyes up. "Happiness officer?"

"Yes, ma'am. And I get to dip my toes into the marketing world, too, which is what I went to college for. I enjoy the best of both worlds, guided by a wildly successful man who loves to teach. I'm very fortunate."

"I-I'm not sure what a happiness officer does," Betty—that's probably her name—stammers. "Oddly, all I can conjure is an image of a children's entertainer. You know, like, balloon animals and whatnot."

Across the shop and stacking books, Chris snorts.

"It's okay if you don't understand it. It's obvious Plainview isn't looking for someone with my particular resume, so I figure I needn't bore you with the details. Can I help you count that?" I don't wait for her permission. I grab her coins and slide them into groupings as quickly as my fingers can move. Two dollars. Three. Four. I drop the coins into the register. "Do you need a receipt?"

"No, thank you." Snippy and sour-faced, she grabs her things and shakes her head. Then, just like Barbara, she spins away.

"I'm not very good at making friends in Plainview, Franklin." I close the till drawer and side-eye the little boy who has *never* made me feel less-than because of my job or living status. But then again, he wasn't raised in this godforsaken hellhole, nor was he raised by an asshole.

So there's that.

"It's hard being new in a town like this," he agrees. "My mom's only friends were Tommy and Chris, and even they were mean when we first got here."

"Newcomers are like a virus they insist on studying and poking at. Alana's the nicest human being I know, and she's a helluva lot nicer than me. I think that means I'm shit out of luck."

"You're not supposed to say shit in front of me." Smirking, he closes his spreadsheet and brings his eyes up. But not to me. He looks at Chris instead and watches the older Watkins slowly swagger this way. He's in no rush. No fuss. He sets his hands on his hips and likes to pretend his focus doesn't stray to my phone for the thousandth time in the span of a single second.

"Tommy call?"

"Not since the last one." *Be kind, Fox. You're not allowed to hurt his feelings.* Jesus, it takes every ounce of willpower I possess not to scream in his face that the world *isn't* kind. It's not gentle for those who need it. It sure as shit isn't about fluffing pillows and patting heads to save an aching soul from pain. *I know that better than anyone.* "She's still cruising at two centimeters," I explain past tight teeth. "She and Tommy are walking laps of the hospital. Like I said, I'll let you know if I hear something. Besides, you have your own phone. You might get the news before I do, seeing as how you're—" *delicate* "—his twin."

He harrumphs, exhaling a bull-ish breath, and tilts his head toward Franky. "Did you need something?"

"Fox's suitcases are in the car outside." He hooks a thumb over his shoulder. "Could you bring them up to the apartment for her?"

My stomach jumps. The thought of asking that guy for *anything* feels as foolish as stepping in front of a speeding car. "That's okay, Franky. I can take care of my own things."

"It's fine." Chris stalks toward the desk and snatches up my keys. "I'll do it."

"Wait—" I dive forward to grab them back, but Chris is faster, turning on his heels and striding toward the door. Frustrated, I swing my gaze around to Franky. "Dude! I didn't ask for help."

"No. *I* asked for it." He pushes his glasses up his nose. "Chris'll do it because he likes to be busy when he's worried. Besides, your suitcase weighs a ton, and there are stairs. Sounds logical to me."

"It's *not* logical because I didn't ask for help! Now he's gonna act like I owe him a million *thank yous* and my first-born son. Jesus." I cast a fast glance around the shop to make sure no one needs me, then I grab my cell and stride around the desk. "Stay here and watch the place for me, okay?"

"You're going to argue with him?"

"I'm going to take care of my own luggage. Stay here."

He pulls out a book and flips it open to a page marked by a pen, and resting on his elbows, he goes to work solving a crime.

Good.

I turn on my heels and charge through the shop door, and since this town is smaller than a baby bird's backside, and traffic is a yearly highlight —not a minute-by-minute inconvenience—I don't even have to look beyond the closest parking slip to find my car.

"You don't have to do that." I stomp closer and wedge myself between the frame of my rental and his hand, so when he reaches for my case, I slap my palm to its shell exterior and harden my gaze. "I've got it."

"Let it go." He yanks on the handle, though he doesn't use *all* of his strength. If he did, I suspect he could knock me clear into the street without even trying. "I'm doing it."

"And I said I've got it."

Irritated, he grabs my wrist and jerks me out of the way, sending me spinning without a word, which could be considered ballerina and cutesy, if not for the way my temper flares.

"Listen here, jackass!" I rush back in and hip-bump him aside. Or, well, I hip-bump him nowhere. But I try. "Don't touch my things. Don't look at me like I'm shit stuck to the bottom of your shoe. And stop acting like I've done something to deserve your shitty treatment. Existing doesn't count, since I never even asked to be here."

"Whatever you think I think of you, that's on you." He presses one hand to my chest, his fingers splayed wide and his long reach forcing me back. With the other, he tugs my smaller case free of the car and sets it on the ground. "In most circles, a man helping a woman with her luggage is cause for thanks. Nothing more, nothing less. Throwing a snit about it is honestly kinda weird."

"Uh-huh." I punch upwards and buckle his elbow. "In most circles, a woman visiting with her best friend, babysitting her kid, and helping her run her shop, is met with thanks and how-do-you-dos. Nothing more, nothing less. Hating my guts for something I literally haven't done is honestly kinda weird."

"You flatter yourself thinking I hate you." Scowling, he rubs his elbow and watches while I get what I wanted—*to pull my own suitcase out*—so when the fifty-pound monstrosity drops to the ground and crushes my toe, his eyes glitter with arrogant amusement.

I heave fresh air, breathing through the pain that began at five o'clock this morning. *Motherfffff!*

"I don't even know you," he continues. "But it took all of five minutes to figure out that you can't stand this town, you don't want to be here, and you have no desire to be nice to any of the locals."

"I'm a nice person!" Shouting. In the street. *Super nice.* "If people have a problem with me because I... sorry, let me check my notes: *exist*, then there's not much I can do about that. This town isn't intolerant of *me*, Christian, it's intolerant of *anyone* who isn't a fifth-generation hillbilly with a small mind and a little bit of inbreeding."

"Inbreeding?" He sets his hands on his hips. "But you're the friendly one?"

"You're being mean to me!" *Good lord, just shut up already!* "I'm here to see my friend. I'm on day two of forty-two, and if you try *really* hard, you could probably go this whole time without seeing me at all. Soon enough, I'll be on that plane, and you'll get your little family back, *all to yourself.* Jesus." I tear the handle up and drag the heavy suitcase from the road to the sidewalk. "Forty-two days, Christian. That's all I get. Your inability to be a decent human being for six fucking weeks, when Alana *specifically* asked me to be here, is ridiculous."

She wants me to be nice to him. She wants to spare his feelings. But fuck him! Why doesn't he get *the talk* about being nice to me?

Only one of us gets to be an active participant in Franky and the baby's lives. The other will be on the other side of the country, right where Alana left us.

If I'm lucky, I might get text updates and photos whenever she thinks of me.

Somehow, Chris gets to be the uncle, the next-door neighbor, and co-owner in the gym with Tommy, but he's convinced them all that *he* needs special treatment.

"She told me to be nice to you, you know that?" I meet his scorn-filled eyes and burn him with my ire. "She told me that you need gentle hands and sympathy because you're *oh-so-fragile*. What you actually need is a lesson in boundaries. Stop pretending I'm your own personal villain when I've never done a damn thing to hurt you."

Angry—at him, and at me, too, because I already broke my promise to Alana—I jerk my suitcase onto the sidewalk and stalk back to get the second, smaller case. My movements are jerky and uncoordinated, forcing the case off balance and stoking the flames of my temper.

"Maybe I deserve gentle hands, too," I growl. "Maybe I'm sensitive, but not nearly as whiny about it as you are." I get the second case onto the sidewalk and position them, one on each side of me, before drawing a deep breath and bringing my eyes up. "My *only* concern, from now until I'm on that plane heading east, is Alana, Franky, and the baby. My job, as Alana's best friend, is to honor her wishes and make this time as stress-free as it can be. So I'm going to be around, and I'm going to do the things she asks of me. I will be in their lives, and even when I'm gone, I'll *always* be the one they needed when those Watkins boys were hateful and mean."

"We didn't know the truth of what happened!" He throws his hand up in frustration. "We thought she left for no reason. Or worse, that she took Tommy's son and kept him away to be cruel. Or doubly worse," he snarls. "That she cheated and had someone else's baby and was too fucking scared to own up to it."

"And all along, she was a victim of something incredibly horrible. And you and Tommy sure were comfortable hating her. Some folks might consider that a learning experience and a chance for personal growth. But nope, you're out here embracing your hate like a good little small-town, small-minded douchebag." I turn on my heel and tug my suitcases along, but then I stop again and toss a pithy sneer over my shoulder. "It's telling, by the way, that you rate cheating as worse than the possibility of Tommy losing ten years with his own son. Neither is true, of course. But your priorities are clear. You value control over love. That's not cute." I bring my gaze back around and stride toward the shop door. I tear it open and make a hell of a ruckus, rolling the suitcases closer and stepping onto the threshold to bar the door from closing before I'm through.

Grumbling and scraping, dragging the stupid overweight cases through, I emerge on the other side and pretend not to see the dozen stares pointed back at me.

They don't care about me, and they sure as shit don't care to defend me to the asshole outside—why would they? They agree with him!

Screw them all.

"You need a hand, Aunt Fox?" Franky places his pen between the pages of his book and pushes his glasses along his nose. "I could help you if you want."

"No, I'm okay, buddy. I need you to run the shop for five more minutes until I can get these squared away. Can you do that?"

"I've got it." Chris sweeps past me, grabbing the heavier case and steamrolling across the store too fast for my brain to register what he's done. But when he reaches the base of the stairs, he stops and glances back, softening his expression.

Though I know it's fake.

How do I know? Because I have ten years of experience with Franklin Page, and those boys are damn near carbon copies of one another.

"You go first." He waits for my slow approach and gestures up the stairs. "I'll follow."

"Seems your default behavior is *dick*. But when you have an audience tapped into the town grapevine, you sure know how to act right again." I shoulder check him on the way past–since I can, and obviously, I still have a bunch of anger to work through–then I heft my suitcase up each step —*climb, thud, scrape, climb, thud, scrape*—and keep going until I get to the door that couldn't possibly be confused for anything except an apartment.

I snag the handle, pray it's unlocked, and growl when it's not. So then I have to wait—*climb, thud, scrape, climb, thud, scrape*—for Chris to join me on the tiny landing, made smaller by my luggage crowding us in.

He leans around me, his chest touching my back and his arm brushing my hip. I can't even call it a smooth move. The kind guys pull at the clubs in New York when they want to test a woman's tolerance.

Here, at this moment, it's nothing more than a necessity.

There simply isn't enough room for anything else.

He twists the key and releases the lock, then shoving the door open, he extends his hand forward, like I'm some kind of simpleton who needs direction.

"I installed a new lock this morning." He follows me in and rolls my suitcase just past the threshold, setting it out of the way. "Alana hasn't lived up here, obviously, and the lady who owned the place before had sixty grandkids and had given out too many spare keys to trust the place to be secure."

"Sixty?" I wander into the living room, which is also the bedroom, which is also the kitchen. Honestly, it's cute as hell. "Don't exaggerate for the sake of exaggeration, Christian."

Finally, perhaps for the first time since knowing him, his lips curl into a ghost of a smirk. "I wasn't exaggerating. Small-town folk with small minds only have two things to keep them busy. Gossiping is one of 'em."

Screwing is the other.

"I left a key for you on the counter," he gestures toward the glistening silver, "and I fixed the shower 'cos it was leaking. Alana brought linen and stuff over a few days ago and made the bed, but with all the work I've been doing, the covers got dusty, so I replaced all that this morning for you, too."

"You changed the sheets?" Swallowing, I look past him to the bed that looks… *amazing*. Military corners, but with thick, plush covers and heavenly pillows artistically scattered.

Not in a million years would I guess Chris was the type to create something *pretty*.

"You didn't have to change it all. You could've left the fresh linen on the end of the bed, and I would have dealt with it."

"Just say thanks," he grits out. "It's easy once you get used to it."

Smarmy bastard. But I'll be damned if I don't smirk anyway. "Thanks."

"Franky and I went grocery shopping yesterday, but we didn't go nuts, since I figured you'd spend most of your time at the house. Got you yogurts and fruit and stuff. Make sure you eat the bananas first, or they'll go bad."

"If they go bad, I tend to put them in the freezer until, *like magic*, they turn into banana bread." I drag my suitcase across the room and deposit it beside the first. "Or, well, they used to. When Alana was in New York. Now, I just have a bunch of bananas and no bread."

His eyes flicker with… *something*.

So maybe he's not Franky's carbon copy exactly. Because I can't read this look before it's gone again. Instead, I twine my fingers together and nibble on my bottom lip. "Thanks for setting the apartment up for me. I appreciate it."

"You're welcome." He exhales a heavy breath and drops his gaze. His jaw hardens, the muscles in his cheeks firming and releasing. For every moment of silence he allows, the dread in the base of my stomach grows heavier. And when he starts toward me, measured steps and twitching nostrils, my pulse skitters just a little faster.

Finally, he stops just two feet away and brings his gaze up to mine.

Self-conscious, I look down at myself. My clothes. My shoes. My existence, really. "What?"

"I'm sorry Alana left you. And I'm sorry for treating you like an enemy." He scratches the back of his neck. "I look at you, Fox, and I see a threat. Someone Alana might choose over…"

"You?"

Warmth settles in his cheeks, a gentle blush I'm not sure even he knows he's rocking. "Plainview. She might leave, which means I'll have to hold my brother through his grief again. Or he'll leave, too, and I'm honestly not sure who will hold me. Which, you're probably thinking I deserve; a result of my shitty attitude."

"I didn't say that." I dig my hands into my pockets and relax my shoulders. "Might've thought it here and there, but I wouldn't say so out loud."

He chuckles, exhaling a soft, mint-flavored breath that feathers against the hanging tendrils of my hair. "I was so focused on *me*, that I didn't consider you've lived the same life. I had Alana's childhood, and you had her twenties. We both know what it's like for her to hit the freeway and leave us behind, and dammit, I was so determined not to feel that way again. I wanted to hate you and hope you'd walk away."

"There's no rule that says we have to compete. She made her choices, and even if I think this place is a dump, I want her to be wherever she's happiest. That's what love means."

"Makes you a better person than me."

"Yeah. But I already told you that." My phone vibrates in my back pocket, buzzing against my butt and drawing my hand around to grab it. But I search Chris' eyes first. I don't dare pass up an opportunity for a truce. "She's not coming back to New York unless Tommy and Franky agree to do the same. And believe it or not, but word on the street is that Tommy ain't going anywhere without you. So you could probably chill on World War III. I'm only here to visit, and eventually, I have to leave again." I spy my phone screen and Tommy's text:

> 3cm! It's taking foreverrrrrr!

Lowering it again, I shrug. "If this was a competition, it's pretty safe to say you've already won."

"I'm sorry I was a dick."

"No, you're not. You meant every word you said, and you *definitely* can't wait for me to leave. But you feel kinda bad about it now that you realize you won." I bring my phone up again and show him the screen. "You wanna call Tommy and talk him down before he tears the walls off the hospital?"

He scans the words on my screen and smirks when he gets to the end. Concentration makes way for relief, and fear is replaced with contentment. Then he shakes his head and wanders to my fridge. "You call. Put him on speaker. We've got five minutes before Barbara makes a report to child services about Franky's neglect."

Snorting, I unlock the phone screen and swipe to my call log, but before hitting dial, I walk back to the door and onto the landing outside. And since I don't actually give a single shit about the people in this town and their judgment of me, I cup my mouth and shout, "Franky!? You okay down there?"

Scandalized, Chris straightens at the fridge and spins in my peripherals. This, at least, is entirely predictable. I consider it exposure therapy. Which is exactly how I got Franky used to my shouting.

"Franklin?!"

"Don't shout." Chris rushes across to the door. "He's never going to answer to—"

"I'm okay!"

Smug, I turn back and stare up at a man whose mouth hangs open in shock.

"If you do something often enough, even those who struggle with regulation and public nervousness tend to adapt. The first time, we were in a department store in the city, so I played Marco Polo just for fun."

"He would've hated that."

You would hate that.

"He did. At first. But he got used to it. Now, he knows the sooner he responds, the sooner I stop."

"Child abuse."

I choke out a laugh and shimmy around the man who takes up most of the doorway. Slipping under his arm, I stroll back to the fridge he left open. "Oh, you got the fruity soda. Franky, for sure, told you this was my favorite." I tap on Tommy's name and tap again on the icon to set the call on speaker, then I toss the device to the counter and snag a soda.

One for me. One for Chris.

"Is everything okay?" Tommy answers in a panic. "Please tell me you haven't lost Franky. Lana can't handle that kind of stress right now."

"You think so little of me." I pull up a chair at the counter and crack open my drink. "Franky's fine. I'm fine. Chris is a little out of sorts, so I figured he could do with hearing your voice."

"Chris?" His tone hitches on the single word. "Where is he? What'd you do to him?"

"What did *I* do? Jesus. What on earth have I done to earn this reputation? I'm a nice person!"

"I'm here," Chris rumbles, stalking to the end of the counter. He bends and rests his elbows on the faux-granite top, running a hand through his hair before he cracks the seal on his soda. "I was helping her bring her suitcases upstairs when you texted. So she called to check in."

"Called to give the man-boy a taste of home," I murmur under my breath, earning a side glare from said man-boy.

"Are you…" Hesitant, Tommy pauses. "You guys are getting along now?"

"We never *don't* get along." *Lie, lie, big fat pumpkin pie.* But I sip my soda and smirk behind the lip of the can. "Alana needs us to be friends. Thus, we're friends. I have no clue why you're so pressed about it."

"How's she doing?" Chris counters. *Change the subject, man-boy. It's okay. You miss your momma.* "She in pain?"

"She's frustrated and tired. And sweating a little bit."

Tommy mustn't be *with* her, since he wouldn't dare mention the sweat where she can hear.

Which, I suppose, is something Chris notices, too. "Where is she? Where are you?"

"I'm in the hall, Lana's in her room having her blood pressure taken. I saw Fox's name on my screen and figured she'd either lost Franky or killed my brother. Neither of which is something the mother of my child needs to overhear right now."

"Ye, of such little faith. In fact, Chris and I are basically best friends at this point." I glance across and beam because, of course, his eyes narrow to slits. *Something about lying really pisses him off.* "He helped me with my suitcases, and now we're having sodas. We're heading back downstairs in a sec, to make sure Franky hasn't been tempted by a pedo-van filled with puppies. Oh, and Barbara needs to have her bookstore membership revoked. She comes in here, reads books she didn't pay for, consumes the free coffee, and counts out her pennies for the pastry she wishes she could have at a five-finger discount. Who needs judgy, narcissistic mothers when you have customers like that?"

"Tell us how you really feel," Tommy drawls. "Are you pissing people off, Fox? Because I'd really like the store to still be operational by the time Alana gets back."

"I could light the old twat on fire, and the shop would still be functional. They come here for the gossip, Thomas, not the books." I set my soda on the counter and scrunch my nose, because Chris' controlling gaze follows my every move. Every breath. Every single word I utter. Sliding off my stool, I head back to the apartment door and cup my mouth. "Franklin? You okay?"

"Jesus fucking Christ," he growls. "This is how she parents, Tommy. Marco Polo is the extent of her protective measures."

"I'm okay!" Franky calls back.

Smug, I turn on my heels and enjoy that extra buzz of satisfaction when I find Chris's eyes glued to my legs.

Lord knows he doesn't mean for them to be.

"You sure whine a lot for a guy *not* parenting that kid. You could be downstairs right now, watching over him and beating child services off with a stick. Instead, you're up here, crawling out of your skin because you need your big brother to pat your head."

"This is gonna be a wild six weeks," Tommy sighs. "I'm hanging up."

"Wait!" Chris snatches my phone and holds it near his mouth. "She's okay? Does she need anything? Do *you* need anything?"

"I need to get back in there so I can take care of Alana and my baby girl, but I can't do that till you two knuckleheads stop bickering. Are we good?"

"We're good." I slide past Chris, brushing obnoxiously close purely to annoy him, and steal my phone and soda, walking away again. My suitcases are upstairs, and my favorite little guy is downstairs. Thus, it's time for relocation. "I'll keep the guys on a tight leash and the external stimuli to a minimum, lest we have a meltdown."

"You mean Franky?"

I saunter through the door and smirk at the thunder of Chris' stomping footsteps. "Sure. You go do the Alana stuff. Tell her I love her to bits, and I need her to bake me banana bread just as soon as she's up to it."

"Not gonna tell her that last bit."

"Bummer." I don't bother checking that Chris locks up behind him—despite my expensive laptop and the horde of snacks I packed—because I *know* he's that kind of guy. He wouldn't dare leave someone's living quarters exposed to the public. "Make sure you mention the love then, and send progress texts whenever you have time to breathe. If she's only at three centimeters, I expect that baby will be here somewhere between dinnertime and next Christmas."

"Helpful," Tommy grumbles. "Doctor said we still have a while."

"Like I said. We'll hang out here and lock up at five, then we'll get Franky fed and settled in or whatever. When it's time, it's time. You'll call when she's up for visitors."

"Yeah, I guess—"

"Oh! I meant to ask. Chris wants to know if he can be in the birthing suite? He wants to see Alana poop."

"What?"

Chris spasms, almost tumbling down the stairs behind me. "What?"

"No!" Tommy snarls. "He doesn't get to come in here for that. What the hell is wrong with you, Chris?"

I peek over my shoulder and swallow the bubbling laughter, desperate to escape. "Sorry, little buddy. I asked, but he said no."

"Chris!"

"I didn't ask that!" Chris grabs the phone and takes the call off speaker, then he shoves past me, crushing me to the wall because there's simply not enough room for us both. "I did *not* ask to see anything. She's full of shit."

He strides between book stacks and moves toward the front of the shop, nodding to whatever Tommy says and grunting at other things. Finally, he reaches the desk—no child-services officers in sight—and offers the phone. "You wanna talk to Tommy for a sec?"

Elated, Franky takes the phone and brings it to his ear. "Tommy! Is the baby here yet?"

While he chats, Chris turns with a snarl and stalks back in my direction, meeting me halfway through the long store and stopping only when our toes almost touch. He gives me no choice but to fold my neck back to maintain eye contact. Despite his formidable rage, I can't help the teasing upturn of my lips. "Problem, Christian?"

"We were getting along."

"Huh… Guess we were."

"And then you went and pulled that shit."

"You call that *shit*." I suckle on my bottom lip and snicker. "I call it comedic genius." And since his eyes drop to my lips, I decide I'll dig at him a little more. "I saw you checking out my ass, by the way. And my legs."

His cheeks turn a deathly white.

"You're an adult, I'm an adult. You're single, I'm single. We're healthy, attractive human specimens. It makes sense you'd look."

"I wasn't looking!"

"Really? You weren't?" I twist and peek back at my bum. "We were getting along, Christian. But here you go, defaulting back to being unkind." I exhale a dramatic sigh and pat his chest, before stepping around him and moving toward the counter. "Hurts my feelings. Hurts *all* my feelings!"

Still, I glance over my shoulder and catch him, deer in the headlights, staring at my ass.

"Mmhmm."

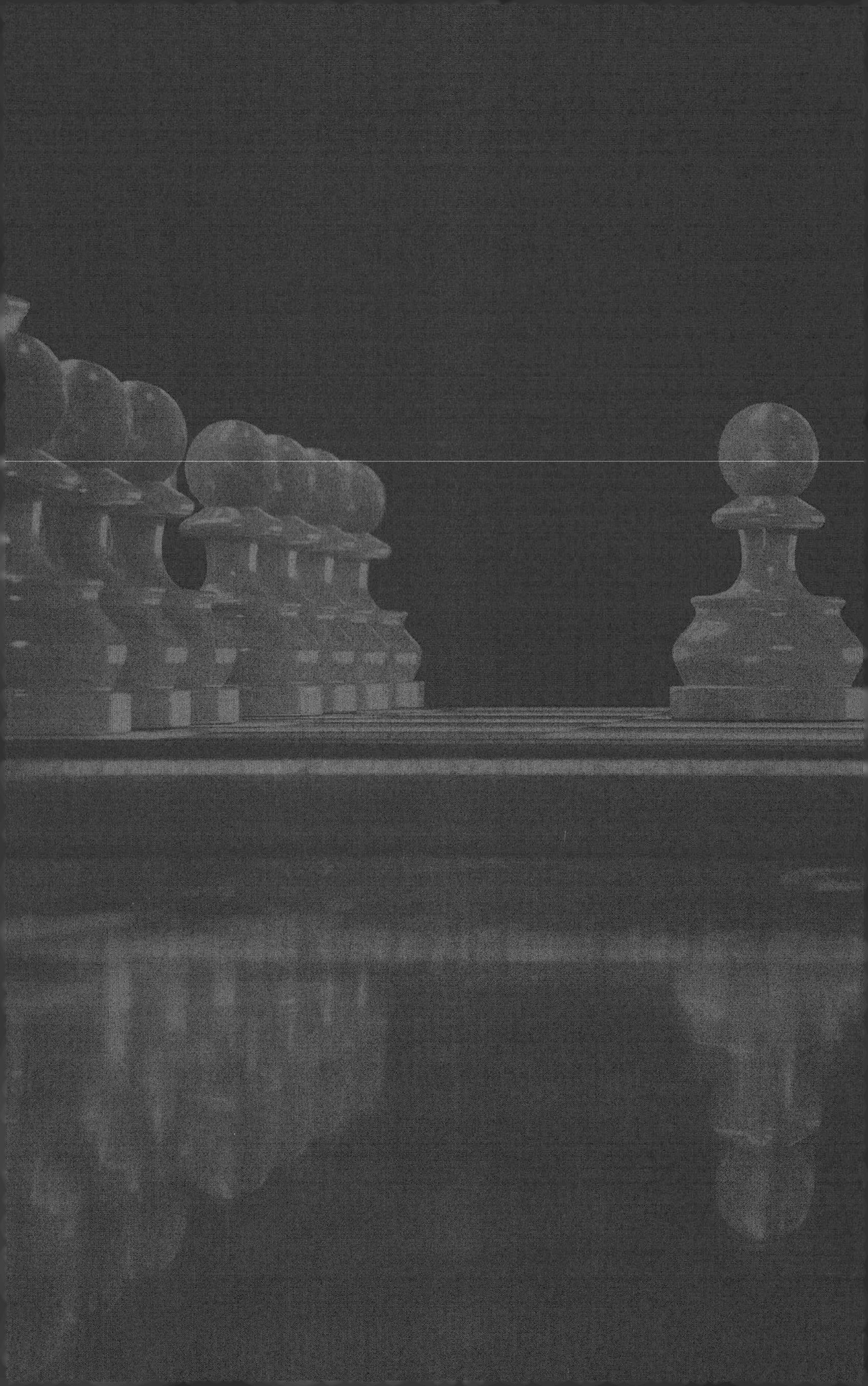

ROUND EIGHT
CHRIS

It would be a lie if I said Fox's constantly chirping phone—while mine remains silent—doesn't irk me a little. That Tommy chooses to update her, assuming she'll update the rest of us when, dammit, he could text me!

But those are thoughts I lock down. Those are feelings I trap inside. Because we came to an agreement... sort of.

Didn't we?

About how we would get along and stop picking at each other. About how, although Alana loves Fox and Fox is loud enough to always demand attention, the understanding is that at the end of the day, Alana lives here in Plainview.

Which translates to: *Chris wins, Fox loses.*

I should be happy when I think these thoughts. Fuck knows, I've over-analyzed this shit for months, and dropping Fox off a cliff when no one is looking has, admittedly, been a repeated consideration in the back of my mind.

But now, all I feel is an annoying ache in the pit of my stomach. Because I know what it is to hurt. To love and lose. To feel abandoned by someone as special as Alana Page.

Dammit, I sympathize with my enemy. Worse, I feel kinda guilty. So I cook a couple of steaks on the grill on Tommy's porch, watching the juicy cuts sizzle while Fox and Franky sit at the patio table and argue over a game of chess.

"You can't make that move!" Franky snatches up Fox's queen and puts her back where she belongs. "That's an illegal move, dummy."

She gasps, extra dramatic, and presses a hand to her heart. "Dummy? Excuse you, child. She's the queen. She can move wherever she wants."

"She can't move *anywhere* she wants. She still has to follow the rules." He's getting pissed, scratching the back of his neck and huffing through his anger. Which is exactly how he gets when he plays against Tommy. "You should move your knight." He picks it up and does it for her. "That would be a good move, because then you cut off my pawn and stop my attack."

"Really?" She settles back in her chair and swirls her wine—just one glass, she declared, so she can still drive to the hospital when we need to. Sipping, she hides her smile and masterfully manipulates the kid into playing against himself.

It would be genius, if it wasn't so fucking infuriating.

"How do I know you're not putting my knight there so you can take it later? Sounds like a conflict of interest to me."

"You can trust me not to trick you." He takes his turn—would have been a pawn move, had he not trapped himself with her knight—selecting his bishop instead. "It's not winning if I'm cheating. I like to win properly, Aunt Fox. You know that."

"Yeah, but…" She folds her legs, entirely too at ease. And because she's determined to fuck with us both, she spins the silverware Franky already set out for dinner. "I wonder if, as you're getting older, and especially now that you've got a baby sister on the way, maybe you're less about winning fairly and all about winning, full stop."

She sets the fork back where she found it… but upside down.

"You know that's not true." He leans across the table and puts the fork back the way it was. "Take your turn."

"Can I move this knight?" She pinches her king between her fingers and waltzes him five squares forward. "That's a good spot, right?"

Frustrated, he puts the damn king back and moves her castle instead.

"Have you received any updates since the last one?" Relaxed, she folds her neck back and flashes a taunting smirk my way. "I guess things are getting a little more serious, since Tommy's been less text-y."

"Nothing since five centimeters." I peel one end of my steak up and check underneath, so when I find it browned to perfection, I kill the gas and plate each cut up. "You were there for Franky's delivery, right? How long did that take?"

Piqued, Franky's eyes swing to his aunt.

She takes a long, easy sip of her wine and savors the flavor on her tongue. "I was there for every single minute of it. I even saw her poop." She grins, but that grin turns to a snicker in response to Franky's reddening cheeks. "Took about seventy-two hours from start to finish. It felt like an *eternity*."

I grab the salad bowl and move to the patio table, setting it in the middle. Then I head back for the potato salad Fox insisted on putting together. "Exaggerating for the sake of exaggerating is dumb."

"Cute. Except I wasn't exaggerating." She brings her eyes around to Franky and trades her wineglass for the fork on her left. *Mine*. "She went in on Monday, around dinnertime, and your slowpoke butt didn't turn up till Thursday. It was the longest three days of my freakin' life, and though I rarely, *rarely*, feel bad for men, those recliners they get to sleep in are rough."

"Was Colin there?" Setting the potato salad down, I snatch my fork from between her fingers and put it back where it belongs, before returning to the grill and grabbing our steaks. "Wouldn't he have been the one sleeping in the recliner?"

"Sure, he was there, and he was honestly the kindest, calmest, most thoughtful dude ever. He brought us food and drinks and blankets and such. But he wasn't her ride or die. I was."

"He was her husband."

"He was her *friend*. A man who saw a woman in need and knew it was within his power to help." She snags my fork again and turns it in her fingers. "Alana had no health insurance and no fixed address for state care, but she had a baby on the way. That's a dire situation to be in and one that could have been exceptionally dangerous if things had gone badly. Thankfully, before we even had to consider birthing in a back alley, Colin had a marriage certificate in hand and a health insurance policy drawn up. He was a good, good man, and any woman would be lucky to marry him. But they never…"

I toss her plate onto the table and steal my fork back.

In response, she chokes out an irritating laugh and rubs her hand, like my fast swipe hurt her.

It didn't.

"They never consummated their marriage, if you're picking up what I'm putting down."

"Subtle." I place Franky's plate in front of him, and then I head back to the grill to get the third for myself. "You're seriously telling me he did all that purely out of the goodness of his heart?"

She shrugs. "I doubted him, too. But it's been ten years, and he's still a perfect gentleman. Oh," ignoring me while I sit, she swings her eyes back to Franky, "but that brings me back to topic. Your mom's water broke on Monday, so we were living it up in luxury for a couple of days while you took your sweet time. Which was kinda nice, since, back then, we were just a couple of hooligan teenagers who'd never lived so comfortably before. Colin was at the hospital pretty much the whole time, helping when I told him what we needed. But when we got down to the business end of things, *I* was the one who got to hold you right after your mom. *I* got to cut the umbilical cord, too. It was like," she makes a show of gnashing her teeth and squeezing her hands. "Toughest sausage I ever cut through in my life."

I press a hand to my mouth, sweat beading on my brow. And when I glance across to Franky, I find him in a similar state.

He gags, green in the face. "That's so gross, Aunt Fox. Don't say things like that."

"Sorry." Not sorry at all, she lays her chin on her shoulder and looks me up and down. "You got a weak stomach, too, Watkins?"

"Not weak. I just expect a certain decorum at the dinner table. Discussing such topics while we're eating is hardly—"

She pats my back. "Sorry, little buddy. I didn't mean to upset you. Seventy-two hours," she concludes, grabbing my fork and her knife, and cutting into her steak. "It was the longest three days of my life, but it turned out alright, since we got the cutest little purple alien baby ever at the end of it. Tommy's in for a hell of a night, but he'll come out better for it."

"Why'd you take my fork?"

Unbothered, she cuts a chunk of steak and places the morsel on her tongue. "What?"

"My fork." I look down at where it *should* be, then up to where it *is*. "Franky set out the utensils."

"Okay..."

"So that was my fork. Was there a problem with the one he gave you?"

"Uh... no. Here." She elbows her unused fork in my direction. "Use this one."

"If I wanted that one, I'd have grabbed that one." I hate that my chest tightens. That my arms flex. My stomach hardens, and my jaw sets. "That's my fork. You took my fork when you had your own."

She chews and swallows, grinning around her meal. "It's just a fork."

"It's not just a fork," Franky rumbles, clinging to his like he's terrified he'll lose it. "These ones have a diamond design on the end, see? Diamonds."

"And this one—" I don't even touch the offending utensil—"It has no diamonds."

"You realize the pattern is not what makes the fork, right? The pokers are."

"They're called tines!" It's like The Hulk lives inside me, readying to explode. Waiting to spew green all over the place. And Fox is completely fucking incapable of not enraging me.

Luckily for her, I've had nearly three decades of practice keeping that fucker under control. So I breathe in through my nose and out through my mouth. Just like we teach at the gym.

Then I swallow and meet her eyes. "They're called tines. And I like the fork with the diamonds on it. It doesn't have to make sense to you. You just have to respect the way we do things around here."

Her eyes glitter with taunting, dancing menace. And since she's a cold-hearted, callous monster, she stabs her steak and cuts a little more off. "Why don't you ask Franky for his fork?"

Startled, he slips his hands beneath the table and hides the cutlery with them.

"I don't want his fork," I grit out. "I want mine."

"This one?" She drags her tongue along the silver, trapping the morsel of steak between her teeth and pulling it off to chew. "You'll ruin a perfectly good dinner because of a fork, when you have a suitable alternative sitting right there?"

I drop my gaze to the offending fork and sneer. I don't mean for my lips to peel back or for rage to build and bubble in my stomach, but when Fox breaks out in irritating little giggles, I know she knows she's fucking with me.

"I've already slobbered on this one." She lowers her lips into a fake pout. "And sharing spit germs is just… it's way too friendly for a couple of people who don't know each other, ya know?" She cuts a little more and stares straight into my fucking eyes as she places the tines between her lips. "Don't wait too long. This steak is delicious, but it won't be nearly as nice once it's cold."

It's a standoff. Her looking at me, and me looking at her. *My* fork, pinched between her fingers, while her fork sits unused between us.

Teasing. *Useless*!

"Why even have forks that you don't like to use? Seems kind of odd, don't you think?"

"Because this is not my house." My stomach grumbles with hunger, and my hands wrap around the armrests of my chair. If I squeeze, I might just snap the wood and stab someone with it. "There are appropriate forks at my house. While I'm here, everyone has the good fucking manners to let me use the one I want."

She scrunches her nose and leans just a little closer. "You're not supposed to say *fucking* in front of Franky. You're gonna get in trouble for that."

"If you wait a few minutes, you can use my fork." Franky pushes his glasses up his nose. "Wait till I'm finished."

"Fuck's sake." I grab my steak in my fist, like a common fucking neanderthal, and chew off a chunk using the teeth my cave dweller ancestors gave me. And when Fox throws her head back, laughing, I glower out at the lake and *chew, chew, chew* with the rage of a thousand angry little men. "Truce was fun while it lasted."

"Aww, don't get it all twisted." She sets my fork down and pats my shoulder instead. "You're gonna be okay, little buddy. You're gonna be just fine."

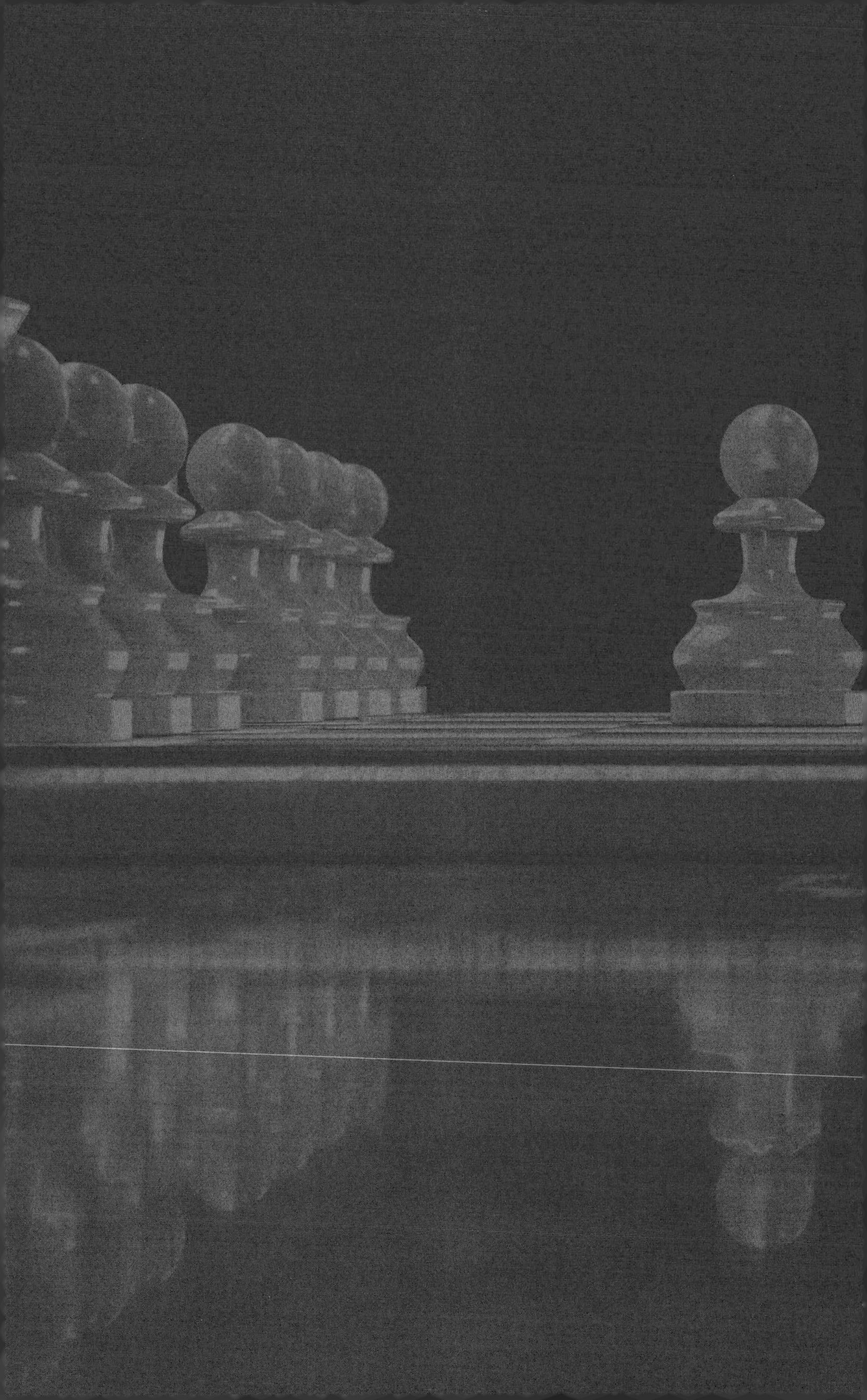

ROUND NINE
FOX

Is it cruel to taunt Christian Watkins using the tools I gathered throughout nine-ish years of co-parenting Franklin Page? Or am I doing him a favor, seeing as how no one else seems to want to help the dude grow out of his tight-fitting, overly controlled life where Tommy protects and Alana mothers?

Jesus. It's not like eating without his favorite fork will kill the guy.

"I've just turned the TV on and settled Franky on the couch." I meander into Tommy and Alana's kitchen and pause against the doorframe, folding my arms and dialing in on the show an aesthetically pleasing man puts on, not only cooking my dinner, but cleaning the dishes, too.

He bends over the sink, running his hands through hot, soapy water, and washes each piece one by one, despite the perfectly good dishwasher situated just five feet to his left.

Hell, maybe he needed a little more time with his beloved fork.

"Franky's doing Murdles and watching a show."

"Did he have a shower and change into pyjamas?" He peeks over his shoulder, though he doesn't turn all the way around, and pins me with a pair of too-intense eyes. He feels too much, I think. He gets caught up in anger too quickly, and sadness way too easily. Love—*as with Alana and Franky*—too completely, and worst of all, worries about the *what ifs* too freely. "He's normally in bed by now. We ran a little late outside."

"Nine o'clock is his regular bedtime. It's not even ten yet. It's the weekend, and this is a special occasion, so I doubt it matters."

"It matters to someone who relies on routine and predictability."

"You mean you?" I drop my arms and wander around to lean against the counter, and since I'm a nice person—*I keep saying so*—I grab a towel and select a plate to dry. "Believe it or not, but Franky is able to deviate from routine sometimes. It might be uncomfortable, but he can do it."

"Why would you *want* to make him uncomfortable? You say you love the kid. If that were true, you should want him to be happy."

"It's about short-term versus long-term goals. Being comfortable is fun and all, but growth is achieved when we're out of that comfort zone. Either he steps out voluntarily, or I'll shove him out. Regardless, the long-term benefits far outweigh the short-term crankiness."

I'm talking about you, too, jackass.

"You never think to expand your horizons and grow?"

"My entire childhood was uncomfortable." He focuses intently on his task, scrubbing a plate, though the damn thing is already clean. "I no longer wish to feel *uncomfortable*, like my blood is on fire or my skin is too tight. I've done my time. I'm an adult now and in charge of my own life, so I figure comfortable is exactly where I'll park my ass for the next eighty years."

"Shame." I click my tongue and run the soft side of the towel over the back of my plate. "My fondest adventures were had while I was uncomfortable as hell."

Unimpressed, he purses his lips. "Which ones?"

"Like, meeting a scared girl with a baby in her belly who needed a friend. I could have easily sent her packing, since that's a hell of a mess I didn't need to get involved in, and God knows, I was already kinda overloaded with my own bullshit. Still, I chose to jump in and create a family with that girl and her baby boy. Now look at me..." I flash a mischievous smirk, "rewarded with this conversation."

He rolls his eyes.

"I clawed my way into a college I couldn't afford, with a brain I wasn't sure could keep up, and begged for every scrap of financial aid I could find. Hell, I *invented* scholarships, pitching myself to businesses until they gave me money. *Comfortable* would have been to become just like my mother. Instead, I busted my ass studying until I wanted to scream and raised a baby with my best friend, so when I walked that stage, I was rewarded with both of them clapping for me. After graduation, I took a leap of faith and nagged a friend for a job, which was pretty *uncomfortable* for both of us, but I was relentless in my desire for a better life, and I'd already had practice making shit up. They didn't need a new team member in marketing, but morale at

Gable, Gains, and Hemingway was pretty low, and being on the fifty-first floor was a recipe for disaster. So I invented a whole new job and vowed to make it work."

"Chief happiness officer," he drawls. "Just because you keep saying it doesn't make it real."

"Dude, you wrestle with sweaty men for a living! If you insist on throwing stones, I suggest you don't be the guy performing soft-core porn."

"You— He—" His face burns a dangerous, angry red. "It's not soft-core porn!"

"I'm not judging your life choices," I tease. "I just wish you'd be more open about who you really are. True happiness begins with self-acceptance."

"My gym is a world-class training center!" He's horrified. Indignant. Sooooo offended. "We produce world champions, Fox! And what the hell kind of name is that, anyway? Made up job, made up name."

He's so ridiculously easy to goad.

I finish with my plate and move on to the next. "My name was picked by people who may or may not have been strung out on crack at the time. Fortunately, I don't hate it enough to change it. And my job—while I admit to pulling it out of my ass and hoping for the best—comes with data that proves my efforts matter. Staff morale is up, and GGH is not only a wildly successful company with an annual turnover of two hundred million smackeroos, but it's viciously sought after by applicants searching for employment. They line up out the door and around the block... on a Tuesday, when we don't even have a position available."

"It's a made-up job!"

"Kind of like professional fighting, I suppose." Smiling, I study his eyes. "If we were in Rome and the Colosseum was operational, then maybe you'd have a reason to train. Or if you were a stuntman in Hollywood, I suppose that would validate what you do. But there are no kingdoms to fight for anymore. You won't conquer a country in the octagon. You won't win a princess's hand in marriage."

"What are you even talking about?"

"*Why* does fighting exist? It's no longer a skill we need, and there are no wars that'll be won by hand-to-hand, rolling-around-on-the-floor combat. If you insist on throwing stones and picking at my job, then be prepared to admit the same about yours."

He's like a bull filling with rage, expanding with hot air and a need to explode. But all he manages is a grunt of exasperation. "You're infuriating!"

"I know. I'm pretty proud of it, actually."

"You took my fork on purpose to annoy me."

"Yeah." I select the fork from the drying tray and run the towel along its smooth edges. "I did. You could've taken it back by force, or you could've walked to your house and gotten another. You could've used the one I gave you, or stolen Franky's." I lean closer and whisper, "I have it on good authority that he can't fight for shit."

His eyes shoot toward the living room doorway, then back to mine.

"You had a million options tonight at dinner. I wanted to see which one you'd choose. Gotta say," I smirk, "I didn't expect you to eat with your hands."

"You call a truce, but irritate me anyway?"

"Truce, in that I won't push you in front of a speeding train. Irritating you is for my own personal enjoyment. But don't get your feelings hurt, because I irritate Franky, too. Growth is a good thing."

"I don't want to grow! I don't want to expand my horizons or become a better person or be schooled by some made-up chief happiness officer bullshit. I'm happy exactly how I am."

"Which brings us right back to where we began: some of my best adventures were had while I was uncomfortable." I tilt to the side and tap his shoulder with mine. "Being in Plainview is uncomfortable for me. My welcoming party would have had me back on that plane before I could take a whiff of the cool mountain air, my driver consistently and *only* expresses scorn, my best friend's future brother-in-law tells me I'm unwanted—"

"All of those people are me."

"I know." I set his special fork down and move on to the next. "The townspeople treat me like I'm less welcome than a puss-filled pimple on their backsides, constantly asking when I'm leaving again. And the town *itself* seems intent on destroying my toes with every door jamb, set of drawers, and curb it owns. Personally, I'm accustomed to late-night dining and shopping until my heart is content. I'm literally the only white person in my building in New York, and every building surrounding mine is the same. Yet, I haven't seen a single human since being here that didn't look like they came from the same set of grandparents."

He stares down his nose and into my eyes. "You think Plainview isn't good enough for you?"

"*Think?* Plainview is the butthole on the front of Satan's chin dimple, and nothing will ever change my mind on the matter. I get that this town is set in its ways, and those ways were set in stone a hundred years ago. You're male, an adult, a successful business owner, and an influential citizen, which makes existing pretty damn *comfortable* for you. You live with privilege, Christian, and that privilege could mean good things for this town. Sadly, that makes your abhorrence for change especially tragic. But..." I shrug and start working on the knives. "You know how I feel about *my* discomfort. I wonder what good will come of this visit?"

He raises a single, arched brow.

"The answer is easy, really. Alana and Tommy's baby girl will be here soon, which, in itself, is amazing. *Plus,* I get to spend six weeks of quality time with Franky. I know how you feel about all this, and God knows, you hate having to share. But before he was yours, he was mine." I slide the soft material along the dull side of the blade. "It's like Alana and I got a divorce, except no one really cares that I'm missing the baby I helped raise."

"Have you said any of this to Alana?"

"And break her heart?" I scoff. "I have no desire to cause that woman even a single shred of pain when I know she already carries so much. Besides, I know his life here is amazing."

"He hates the rooster. *Loathes* that motherfucker."

I cough out a laugh and place the dried knife on the counter. "Besides the chicken, then. Wherever Alana is happy, he's happy. And as long as they're happy, I'll deal. Though I sure as hell intend to soak up my six weeks and enjoy that little boy. And when the baby's here, I'm gonna snuggle her, too. When Alana's feeling better, I'll tackle her to the ground and hug her until she begs me to stop, because *that's* how fiercely I miss her. I intend to take these six weeks to get to know Tommy better, since I only really know what Alana has told me. And then..." I draw a long breath, filling my lungs. "Well..." I exhale again. "Then there's you."

He pulls back and blinks. Blinks. Blinks. "Me?"

"I look forward to irritating the ever-loving shit out of you over the next six weeks, Christian. Because you're a really fun, easy target, and you could do with a little discomfort. Who knows, I might annoy you just enough to force you to use your powers for good. Making a change, even a teeny tiny little one, could help this town move toward the twenty-first century." I set my towel on the counter beside the dry plates, then I brush my fingertips across the ball of his shoulder and thrill in the way his arm locks up, and the muscle turns rock hard. "If you won't step out of your comfort zone for you, consider doing it for those who aren't white, male, and successful. Who knows? If Plainview wasn't so ass-backward ten years ago, maybe an eighteen-year-old Alana could've stayed, supported by a community who had her back, instead of running away, terrified of what had been done to her."

I drop my hand and leave him to finish the dishes on his own. Sauntering into the living room, I find Franky exactly where I left him, his hair still wet, and his oversized pyjamas drowning his body.

He's not a baby anymore—though I think I miss that most of all—nor is he a full-grown man. He's just a boy, caught in the middle where he still needs adults to help him along, but with a brain of someone far exceeding his age. I flip the living room light out in silence, startling him from his book and earning a scowl, then I crawl onto the couch and drag him into my side until he comes, languid and loose, draping his arm across my stomach and resting his cheek on my chest.

"I didn't finish my Murdle yet, Aunt Fox."

"I miss you, even when you're in the other room." I kiss the top of his head and suck down the emotion set on making me out to be a fool. *He's not my child. And no matter my feelings on the matter, I don't get to keep him.* "Did you have a fun day today?"

"It was okay." He pushes his book away and peels his glasses off, then he fingers the frayed hem of my shorts, exhaling a long, lazy sigh. "You made Chris really cranky with that fork. Did you know?"

I snort and rest my lips on his forehead. "Yeah, honey. I know. I did it on purpose."

"I would get mad if you took my fork."

"I know." I slide my hand over his hipbone and bring my focus to the television. He's watching MythBusters. "But you would still love me, even if I annoyed you."

He nods, though the movement is subtle. "Is that a question?"

"No. Family loves each other, no matter what. Well, ours, anyway. And luckily for me, family doesn't always have to share DNA."

"Like us."

"Exactly like us. And honestly?" I inch back and search his tired eyes. "I love you *more* than every single other person on this planet whose DNA matches mine. I love you more than all of them combined."

He exhales, smiling and sighing until two deep dimples pop in his cheeks. And because it's late, his eyes flicker closed. "I love you, too. I'm glad you're visiting."

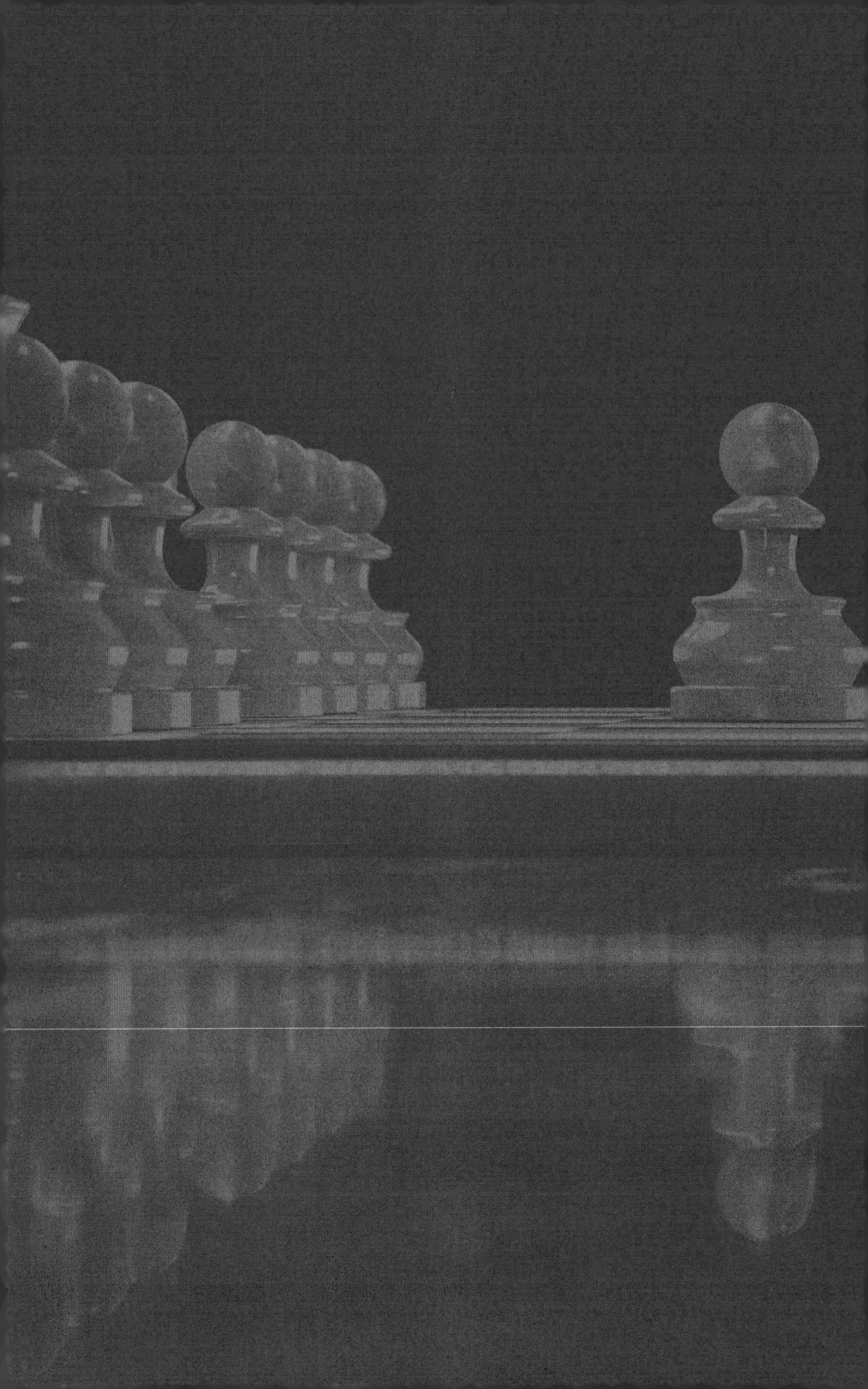

ROUND TEN
CHRIS

I don't begrudge Franky and Fox their ability to fall asleep, curled in each other's arms and draped across the couch in an odd pretzel shape that would leave me damn near broken by morning.

But I don't understand it, either.

I can't fathom how easily they rest, knowing Alana is at the hospital right now, her body stretching and tearing. Her life, in the hands of someone else while her baby claws its way into existence.

Everyone says that childbirth is beautiful and special. Magical. *Whatever*. But all I can focus on are the maternal mortality statistics my stupid fucking brain latched onto somewhere around Alana's fifth month.

Because that's what it does. It searches for facts and data. Statistics. When the world is upside down, and my normal, sensical routine is shoved off-kilter, I reach for literature, digesting the details as eagerly as a starving man feasts on his next meal.

Sometimes it helps.

In fact, most of the time, it does.

But not this time. Because instead of remembering the nearly six hundred babies born *safely* across the world every two minutes, I think about the one that dies.

Mother. Baby. Or both.

Instead of reminding myself of the advances in modern medicine and acknowledging how safe Alana and the baby truly are tonight, I think of the things I can't control.

Which, of course, is my fucking curse.

Why was I born like this?

Why, when Tommy and I shared a womb, did he come out with a normal brain. And I'm... fucked up?

It's my punishment, I guess.

The sky outside is pitch black, and the clock on the mantle reads three fifty-three. Frogs swim in the lake out back, while the cicadas, thankfully, sleep. Mosquitos buzz, hungrily hunting for a crack in the window screens surrounding Tommy's home. They know there are people inside, exposed arms and legs and blood ripe for suckling. But we learned long ago to make sure that shit is taken care of.

Franky and Fox sleep soundly, soft breaths inhaling and exhaling in sync. Franky rests with his face on Fox's chest, his long lashes folded down to kiss his cheeks, and his lips pushed forward in the pout he got from Alana.

Lucky kid.

Fortunately for him, he didn't get too much from the Watkins side of the family, besides his eyes—the same green sparkle as mine and Tommy's—and his over-analyzing *'why am I like this?'* mind—which only he and I have in common.

Fox shifts in her sleep, smacking her lips and exhaling a soft sigh. She curls tighter into the couch, pulling her feet up and resting her knees against Franky's hips, and because of her new position, her shorts ride up and reveal more than she probably means to. A fraction of her swollen ass cheek—just one side—and a flash of red underwear.

I should put a blanket over them.

Jesus, I should stop being a fucking creep. But knowing and doing are two entirely different things, and for as long as she's dreaming, she's not taunting me.

Which is a nice break, honestly. To see her like this, to appreciate the fine lines of her cheekbones and the long, cascading mahogany hair she tied up hours ago. She uses a thick scrunchy that I know, I can just tell, is made of smooth silk that would create the perfect sliding friction when rubbed between a man's fingers.

Her shirt rides up, exposing the bottom half of her ribs and delicate vines with draping flowers expertly inked into her skin. The designs sneak from her back to her belly, proving she didn't go with a small, spring-break tattoo like most girls get. No. She decorated her body with an entire piece that would have taken hours and hours, days, extended across several weeks, sitting in an artist's chair. It would have meant layers and careful planning and, when it was all done, a hell of a lot of money exchanged from one hand to the next.

I *really* should put a blanket over them.

I settle back in my recliner and tap my phone screen for the millionth time since the sun went down, a long white cord snaking from the wall to my device, because fuck knows, without it, I would've drained the battery hours ago.

No texts. No missed calls. No baby.

I peek toward Fox's phone, dumped on the couch cushion by her feet and seemingly forgotten, but her battery remains intact, the time glowing on the screen proof that if the baby was here, we'd know.

One of us would have been alerted.

Groaning, I drop my head back and stare up at the ceiling, as minute by minute, time passes through a sieve at the speed of... insanity. Sixty seconds never felt so long, and even when they pass, I merely start again and count the next. Then the next.

Two minutes feels like two hours, which gives me all the more time to obsess over the mortality rate data I tried eons ago to expunge from my mind. For every elevated breath sound Franky or Fox expels, time seems to go slower. Because their ability to sleep is as cruel as eating a meal in front of a hungry man.

Hell, if Fox hugged me the way she hugs Franky, maybe I could close my eyes, too.

"Jesus." *What the fuck is wrong with me?* I press my hands to my face and my fingers to my eyes, forcing them shut and holding the lids down, if only to force a little darkness, like that might help me sleep. But then my phone vibrates against my leg, silent, really, but right now, in the state I'm in, it could be a cannon blast piercing my thigh.

Startled, I fumble my phone, spinning it around, then spinning it again, and because the cord tangles, I yank it free of my phone and toss it aside.

Finally, I spy Tommy's name on the screen. A text, not a call.

I hurriedly open our chat and am met with a beautiful, soul-cleansing, heart-squeezing photo of a baby girl's foot.

Just her foot.

Air explodes from my lungs, collapsing my chest and drawing tears to my eyes, but I look at the speech bubbles popping up at the bottom of the picture, so I wait. And wait. And wait some more, and when the bubbles continue, but the words don't come, I consider smashing my fucking phone against the wall.

But then he hits send.

> She's here. If you guys are awake, come on over. Alana's begging to see you all. If you wanna wait till morning 'cos Franky's asleep, she'll understand.

Then he sends another.

> Don't call me. I don't wanna spoil her for you. Come meet your beautiful niece face to face. You're gonna be obsessed like I am.

Wait till morning?

Is he fucking insane?

I bound off the chair and shove the phone into my pocket, and though I *could* leave these two here to sleep, sucking in a few hours of pre-dawn baby snuggles all on my own, I know it wouldn't be the right thing to do.

It takes every ounce of willpower I possess not to turn on my heels and bolt out the front door. Every scrap of decency I've ever owned not to blame my actions on '*but I didn't want to wake you.*'

If I bring Fox and Franky to the hospital, I risk Fox grabbing the baby and claiming first rights. *Best friend. Aunty. Loud as fuck. Blah, blah, blah.*

I could just go. They'll get over it eventually.

Fuck.

I walk to the couch and slow my breathing. Calm my thoughts and regulate the adrenaline pulsing through my veins. It's like I'm readying for a fight. Bursting with bloodlust. Prepping to go toe-to-toe with someone bound to leave me busted and bruised.

But none of that is true. There is no threat.

There's just a woman who deserves to meet this baby as much as I do, and a little boy who deserves it a million times more than both of us combined.

Swallowing, I set one hand on the back of the couch, to prop myself over the duo so I don't fall on them, and then with the other, I gently shake Fox's shoulder. "Hey?" I whisper, barely loud enough for the sound to register in my own ears. Then I shake her again and watch as she slowly, dazedly, meanders toward consciousness. "Fox? You awake?"

Her eyes move behind her eyelids, but her lashes remain on her cheek.

"Fox? Can you hear me?"

"Screwing with my sleep is unforgivable." She snuggles into Franky and smacks her lips. "If this is payback for the fork, I'm gonna stab you with it."

I choke out a soft, barely there chuckle. And because I can, because fuck it, it's four in the damn morning, and she's all lazy and relaxed; I lean closer, resting my lips just an inch from her ear. "The baby is here."

Her eyes snap open.

Lowering into a crouch, I move to her level and brush messy locks of hair from her cheek. "Tommy texted and said we could meet her whenever we're ready."

She doesn't move. From deep sleep to completely alert, her brain switches on, but her body remains totally and severely still.

Her ability to control her movements this way is admirable.

Concerning, too, when I think of how she grew to conquer such skills.

She stares into my eyes, searching for the world's longest minute of silence. Then her lips curl into a devious grin, and her cheeks warm.

Fuck, why is she pretty at four in the morning?

"She's here?"

"That's what I heard."

"And we can see her?"

"He said Alana's bugging out for a visit. Which means she's okay." I scrub my free hand over my face and breathe again for the first time in a while. "I didn't ask questions, and he said not to call, since he wants us to meet her in person. But that implies Alana's doing good, too, dontcha think? Because she's the one who wants us to visit."

"Yeah. I think." She carefully straightens on the couch, slow movements and clumsy support while she tries to stop Franky from jolting awake.

My palm itches with: *do I, don't I?*

Stay the fuck away, or make this easier for her?

The darkness somehow makes everything just a little less... scary, the time, a little more whimsical, so I offer my hand and swallow my fiery exhale when she accepts, her fingers wrapping around to touch my wrist. She smiles in appreciation and uses me to stabilize herself on collapsing cushions until, finally, she extricates herself from beneath Franky's weight and lays him back down.

"You got it?"

"Yeah. Thanks." She fixes her shorts and drags her shirt down to cover her belly, then scrubbing her hands over her eyes, she blinks, blinks, and blinks again. "What time is it?"

"Nearly four. Which is basically six, your time, right?"

"Mmm." She pushes the hair off her face and turns to me with a megawatt smile. "She's actually here?"

"Unless Tommy's punking us."

Fuck me. She does a little dance, pumping fists and skipping feet. Then, like a light switch, she turns it off and strokes Franky's cheek instead. "Hey, buddy. Wake up."

He grumbles and pulls away from her touch.

"You have to get up, honey. We're going for a drive."

"You could probably stay here if you want." I fake a smile and pretend her rolling eyes aren't explicitly for me. "I mean, if he wants to sleep or whatever."

"Nice try." She bends over the couch, much like I did, with one hand on the back to support her weight, while she runs her fingers through Franky's hair with the other. But dammit, her shorts are still a little high, and the swell of her ass is just... it's right there. Right in front of my face. "Did you sleep?" she murmurs. "You look pretty alert for four in the morning."

"Got a few hours," I lie. "It's probably gonna be chilly out there. Do you have a sweater?"

"Oh..." Frowning, she glances over her shoulder. "No. I didn't bring one from the apartment. Shoot."

"Wake him up, and I'll get you one of Tommy's." I hold her gaze for a moment more, absorbing her early-morning niceness, since I know she'll return to her regular pain-in-the-ass self soon enough. Then, straightening my legs and maneuvering the gap between her, the couch, and the coffee table, I come out the other side and turn my slow walk to a sprint.

Sweater. Coffee. Car.

I race through the house and collect the things we need, draping a hoodie over my arm and pouring a to-go cup of coffee for the road, then returning to the living room less than a minute later, I stride in to find Franky still asleep.

Fuck it.

I flip the lights on and clap my hands.

"Wake up, Page!"

He shoots straight up on the couch, wild hair pointing in every direction and a nasty, mean scowl folding his lips down. "What the heck?"

"You're a big brother, kiddo! Let's go."

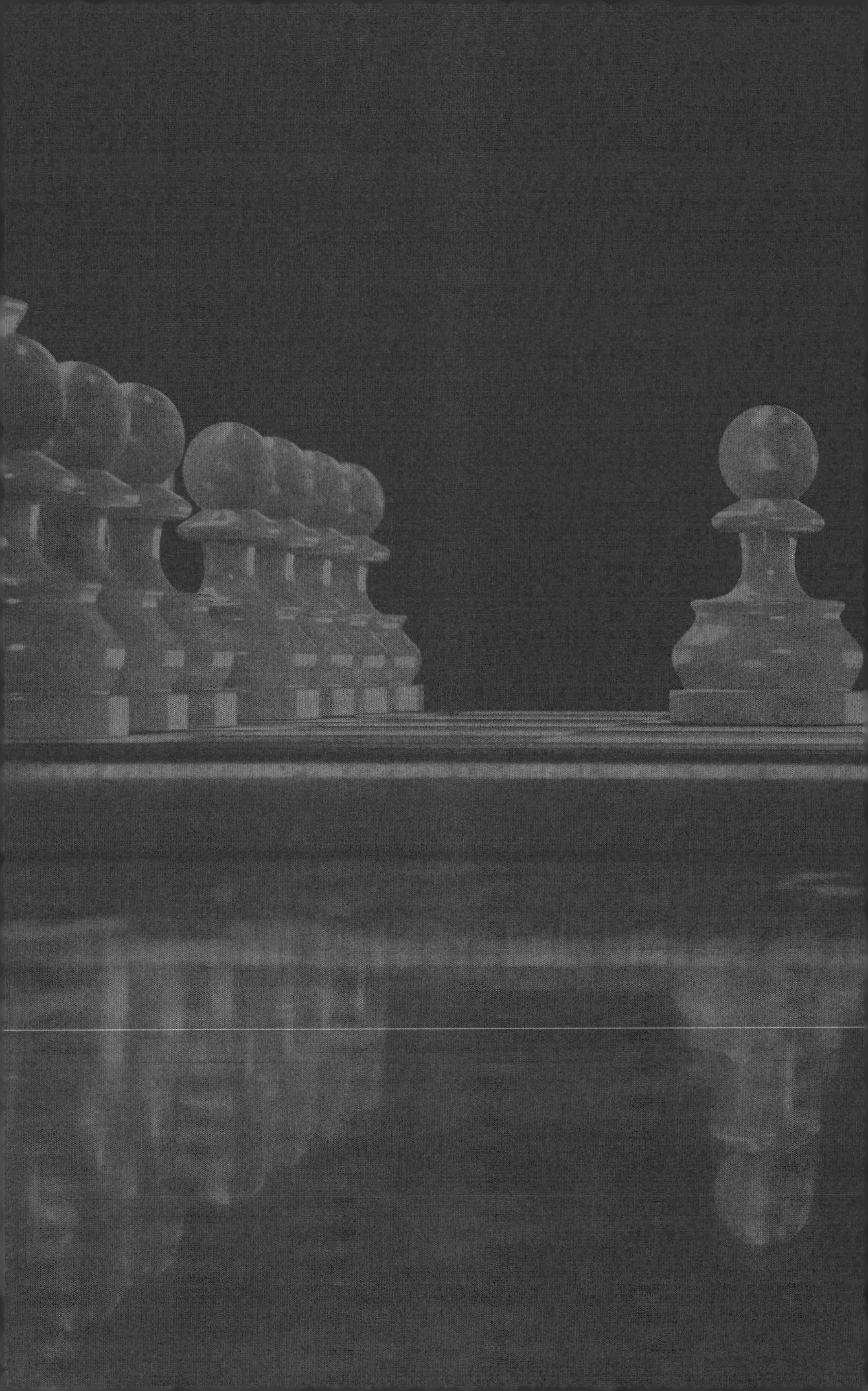

ROUND ELEVEN
FOX

"You doing okay?" I glance across in the dark, but for the streetlamps above, as Chris pulls his truck off the road and into the hospital parking lot. We hit potholes and bounce, the squeak of the truck's chassis the only sound we hear besides Franky's mouth-breathing.

He's nervous as hell, clutching the cute pink teddy he picked out for his sister with shaking hands and eyes that swing in every direction at once.

I *know* he's anxious. That much is expected.

But Chris... well, while I fully expected a mental breakdown due to his routine being tossed out the door and *different* is in, he merely presents as cool and collected. He's relaxed, if not a little eager and fidgety.

He grabs the keys from the ignition, fists them in his hand, and meets my eyes. Then his lips curl up, and his gaze drops to the hoodie he tossed in my face not ten minutes ago.

It's wildly too big, and comfortable as hell, but best of all, the fabric on the inside is neither pilly, nor cheap. This is a *nice* hoodie. Quality threads and an expensive finish. Which seems almost counterintuitive, considering it's a Love & War gym-branded hoodie.

Surely, there was a cheaper option for them to offer their customers.

"I'm doing okay," he murmurs over the top of Franky's head. "Kinda excited to meet the baby. Do you know her name?"

"The baby's? No."

"Tommy and Alana said they picked it out ages ago, but they're keeping it a secret."

Together, we peer down at Franky.

He only shakes his head. "I don't know it either. She's just *'the baby'*. Do you think she'll like the teddy I got her?" He lifts the stuffy, thoughtfully staring at its little black-thread eyes. "It's kinda dumb, don't you think?"

"No, honey. I think it's wonderful." Carefully, I take it in my hands and brush the silky fur back. It's softer than a brand-new baby's peach fuzz hair. And since I get the feeling Franky isn't moving until I do, I turn and push my door open. I slide onto the blacktop and tuck a fraction of the bottom of Tommy's hoodie into the top of my shorts.

If I don't, people will think I forgot my pants.

"I think this bear is the greatest, most special gift your baby sister will ever receive." I lean back into the truck and take Franky's shaking hand in mine, gently tugging him my way, while on the other side, Chris opens his door and climbs out with a frown. "She'll cherish it. I just know it. Not only because it was given to her the day she was born, but because it came from *you*."

"Maybe she won't even like it." Dropping to his feet and closing the door, he takes the teddy again and stares down at it. "Maybe she'd prefer a different bear."

"Or maybe she'll be as obsessed with you as you already are with her?" I slip my fingers into his hair and tug him in until his shoulder tucks beneath mine and his cheek rests against the top of my ribcage. "When she's the age you are now, you'll be all grown up. Doesn't that sound crazy?"

"Maybe she'll think I'm too old to hang out with."

"Or maybe you get the best of both worlds because you're old enough that you get to help your mom raise her. You get to feed the baby if you want to and hold her while she sleeps. Regular brothers and sisters are usually younger when they get a new baby in the family, so they're not big enough to help. You're lucky because you're old enough to remember the early days but young enough that you get to play with her, too. And when she's two or three years old, running around and getting into all sorts of things, she'll look for her Franky first. Even before she looks for your mom or Tommy."

While Chris walks ahead of us, leading the way with his hands in his pockets and his shoulders bowed forward, Franky peeks up, sliding his glasses along his nose. "You think so?"

"I *know* so. Honestly, there'll probably come a point when you think she's a bit annoying, so try to remember *this* moment right now, where you're excited to meet her and kinda nervous, too. Later, when you're cranky because she's noisy or messy or whatever, remember how much you love her."

"This way." Chris strides through the hospital's front doors and grabs the loose-fitting sleeve of my hoodie, drawing me and Franky around a corner. "We don't really have a maternity ward."

"There's no oncology ward. Or *any* kind of ward," Franky adds. "There's just *a* ward, since our hospital isn't very big."

"That means everyone gets to hang out together." Silver linings and all that. "Separation is fun for no one."

"Unless you have meningitis," he quips. "Then you *should* be separated away from the babies."

"Right." I massage the back of his head, right where his skull meets his spinal column, and follow Chris around another corner and through a password-protected set of doors—not sure how he got the password. "She's going to love her gift, honey. As long as you give it to her with love, she'll feel that love for the rest of her life. That's the true gift, don't you think?"

"So I could've given her a bottle cap? If I gave it to her with love and all that..."

"Sure. But a bottle cap is a choking hazard, so I'm glad you chose the bear." Snickering, I make a silly face and hope it helps the kid whose entire body trembles. But then Chris grabs my sleeve again, drawing my eyes up and dragging us to a stop.

Then he lifts his chin. "Next room along," he whispers. "They're in there."

"Why are you whispering?" I tease, *whispering*. "Don't tell me you're getting cold feet now."

"No, I—" He gnashes his teeth. "Of course not. I figured you'd—"

"Take over and steal your thunder?" I set my hand on his hip and gently nudge him forward, forcing him to move one step, then another. He and Franky are too alike, too excited and yet, horrifyingly nervous to meet their newest family member. So we become a chain of humans, where I push one and pull the other, and I'm just the idiot stuck in the middle. "She won't bite." I keep my voice low, since the other rooms beep and hum with life, too. "I mean, she won't bite *yet*. Not until she's about a year old and getting her new teeth."

Stunned, Chris whips his head back. "What?"

"You'll be fine. It's Alana and her boobs that need to worry." I hook my hand around the back of Franky's neck and dig my thumbnail into Chris's hip—tactical encouragement—and moving them along the all but silent hallway, I work on slowing *my* pounding heart. My cartwheeling organs.

I don't have the luxury of freaking out.

I bring them all the way to Alana's door, holding on when I know they want to turn and run. But I feel the tension drain from their bodies. Rigid muscles, softening in the very same moment Alana sits up in her bed and looks this way.

Messy hair, rosy cheeks, and a hospital gown that falls from her shoulder.

She's never been so beautiful.

"Hiii." Her lips quiver and her eyes glitter with happy tears. The bright blue orbs latched onto her sweet Franky and the bear he clasps between his hands. "Oh my gosh, honey. It's so good to see you."

"Are you okay?" He steps into the room, ignoring Tommy while he holds his bundled baby to his chest. The new dad stares down at her face, smiling and smitten, but when Franky stumbles on his way in, Tommy still manages to catch him. It's a silent exchange, a hand on the boy's shoulder until he's steady, a wink when their eyes meet, then Franky releases a hiccupped breath and runs the rest of the way, pressing his face to Alana's chest and hiding the tears that sparkle against his cheeks. "Are you hurt?"

"I'm okay, honey." She shifts to the side and makes room for her first baby to climb up, so when he does exactly that, she wraps him in her arms and kisses his temple. His cheek. His head. "Everything is okay, I promise."

"We named her Hazel." Tommy's eyes come up to mine. Then Chris's. Then, strolling across the room, he stops in front of us both and lowers his arms to reveal the sweetest, chubbiest, most beautiful baby girl that ever lived.

Damn if his hazel eyes don't glow with pride. "Alana insisted," he rasps. "She figures me, Chris, and Franky, being men, got the green eyes. So since she has blue, and the baby, being a girl, might also get blue—"

"She wanted to honor you with the name." I move onto my toes, all so I can get a better view of the beautiful girl. "I think *Hazel* is an amazing name. It totally suits her."

"Hazel Fox Watkins."

Oxygen stops in my throat, collapsing my lungs until I'm not sure they'll ever expand again. My stomach swirls, and my heart kicks painfully inside my chest, but I swing my eyes up and stop on his beaming smile.

"What?"

"Hazel Fox." He kisses her chubby cheek. "We wanted to honor you, too. Of all the women on the planet and all the allies Alana could've met when she needed one the most, she met a strong, confident, independent woman who loves without reservation and gives her heart to those who deserve it. You're kind..." But then he pauses and chuckles, "except to my brother."

"I'm not unkind to him! I'm just..." Frantic, I search for the right word. "It's a growth exercise."

"You're gracious," he continues. "You're silly and fun and smart. You're all of the things I wish for my baby, so when Alana wanted to honor me and Franky and Chris with the first name and to honor you with the second, I couldn't see a single reason to say no."

"Hazel Fox." I sniffle my tears back and steel myself, because I don't dare blubber on a brand-new baby, but I can't help the tremble of my jaw as I bring my arms up, nor my choked breath when he transfers her from his chest to mine. "Oh my gosh. Hazel Fox is a totally badass name." I'm not nervous the way I was when Franky arrived. I don't fear dropping her or panic at her floppy neck. I merely cradle her in my arm and slide the tips of my fingers over her rounded jaw. "She's going to have an amazing life. I just know it."

"Eight pounds." Alana sighs, stroking Franky's hair. "Nine ounces."

"Chonky baby." I bounce ever-so-gently, swaying just enough for my shoulder to brush Chris' chest. "You grew to be nice and strong before you came outta your momma, huh? You knew you'd need that extra bulk for your first pro-fight."

Snickering, Tommy claps Chris' shoulder. It's a brotherly thing, a hug and a hello. An *'I'm glad you're here'* and *'I'm probably gonna lose my shit soon and need a cry. Wait around for me.'* "She arrived just after three o'clock. Which was the exact right time, because they were talking about surgery if she didn't get her act together."

Chris tenses behind me, his entire hulking frame hardening at my back. "It was getting dangerous?"

"It was getting tedious," Tommy answers. "Alana was tired, and Ollie was worried because things weren't progressing."

"We were stuck at five centimeters for ages." Alana lays back comfortably, pulling Franky against her side and combing her fingers through his hair. "I was ready to tear her out myself."

"But then things happened *fast*," Tommy adds with a shrug. "Lana jumped from five centimeters to ten in a matter of minutes."

"Hurt like hell," she grumbles. "Like being tied to the back of a bus and dragged down Main Street."

Horrified, Franky pushes up to his elbow. "Not really, though, right? You didn't get dragged?"

"Not really." She swipes her thumb beneath his eye, shifting his glasses and wiping moisture from the top of his cheek. "I just meant it hurt a bunch. But it was totally worth it, don't you think?"

Chris steps around me, bristling and throbbing with anxiety, and crossing to the bed, he presses a long kiss to Alana's forehead. "I'm glad you're okay."

"You weren't worried, were you?" She squeezes his wrist, smiling up at her *first*-first baby. The one she had even before Franky. "Having babies is pretty safe nowadays. Hundreds are born every single minute."

Shaking his head, he backs up and falls to the visitor's chair with a harrumph. Tired, he opens his legs, tilts his head back, and though he tries so friggin' hard not to, his eyes swing across to me and the baby.

He's exhausted. But more than that, he's sad.

His heart breaks for every moment I hold Hazel, and he doesn't.

"I wasn't worried," he lies, peeling his eyes away and looking at Alana instead. "I was busy dealing with that menace over there and her terrible house manners."

"She stole Chris' fork," Franky snitches proudly. "Even when he asked for it back. She took it and licked it, so then Chris ate with his hands."

"Since when are we dirty little tattlers?" I roll my eyes and circle away from Tommy—breaking *his* heart, too—then I saunter to the bed and lean close enough to kiss Alana's cheek, just half an inch from her lips. "Congratulations, Momma. She's the cutest little stinker you could have ever conjured."

Her eyes glitter, emotion and exhaustion warring for dominance. "I think so, too."

I turn quickly, catching Chris' mean-man scowl just half a moment before he remembers to wipe his face clear, and because I know it would mean the world to him, I settle on the arm of his chair and offer the baby.

He startles and jerks up straight, flapping his hands because he has no damn clue what he's supposed to do with them. "Wait, wait, wait, wait," he panics. "I'm not ready."

"Make a cradle." I hold the baby in just one arm—horrifying, according to his expression—and use the other to position him correctly. Then I inch closer and gently place her against his chest. "See how she fits right there over your heart? She was made to fit exactly like that."

"She's so small." His heart races visibly against the side of his neck and in the rapid lift and fall of his chest. His cheeks flush warm, which is oddly and annoyingly charming, and though his eyes remain glued to Hazel's sweet face, he wiggles on his chair for a new, better, safer baby-holding position.

I'd hate to break it to him, but he'll never find it. Because his discomfort isn't a result of his butt or the chair. It's him, freaking the hell out. "Holy shit," he breathes, choking on a garbled laugh. He folds his legs, then unfolds. He tries again. Then straightens them out. "Hoooooly cow. Hi, Hazel. Hi."

"She looks good on you, Uncle Chris." I set my hand on his shoulder and earn a long, lazy grin from the man who looks damn good wearing one. *He should try it more.*

Confident his mom is okay, Franky slides off the bed until his feet touch the cold linoleum floor, then he wanders across and perches on Chris' other side to finally take a peek at the little girl he'll go to war for when he's older.

So, while they're busy, I push to my feet and crawl onto the bed instead. *Exactly like I did ten years ago in a hospital in New York.*

I'm careful, climbing up and lying on my side while she shifts and does the same, then I use my hand as a pillow and stare into her bright, blue eyes. "You did so good, beautiful girl. I'm so proud of you."

"Thank you." She suckles on her bottom lip and *blinks, blinks, blinks* fresh tears until they fall into her lashes. "I have stitches," she snickers, "Like, a *lot* of them. And I'm coming to the realization that Ollie—who was my high school friend—knows what the inside of my vagina looks like now."

I snort. "I'm sure it's pretty, as far as vaginas go."

"Part of me wants to freak out. But the other part doesn't care. I'm glad he was here." She swallows and studies my eyes. "He kept Tommy sane when things were getting kinda dicey."

"Eh." I bring my free hand up and gently tap the tip of her nose. "That guy probably wanted to see you all along, so he pursued a medical degree and did years of residency, all on the off chance you'd have a baby someday, and he could get a peek."

"It was a long game," she happily sighs. While the Watkins men ga-ga over sweet baby Hazel, and Franky gifts her his little bear, Alana scans my face, long sweeps of her pretty eyes and a flattening of her lips that *always* precedes a lecture. "You took his fork?"

I choke out a cackling giggle that startles us all, then swallow it back down again until I'm bouncing and bursting. "He survived! He's fine."

"Your job was to help!"

"He needs to loosen up. He adapted, and we even became friends... *sort of*. He still ate his dinner, and he didn't stab me with a steak knife, so really, it all worked out exactly how it was supposed to." My cheeks ache from smiling, and inside, my heart skitters with happiness. "Hazel is safe, momma is safe, and the boys have arrived in one piece. I did my job."

"You could've just given him a relaxing, non-dramatic evening in front of the TV like you did with Franky."

"Bold assumption to make," I tease. "I messed with the little one, too. Turns out you're not allowed to move the queen *anywhere* in a game of chess. There are *rules*," I drawl. "And *guidelines*. Honestly, I feel he was less anxious when I still had daily access."

"He was stressed," she growls. "He's *allowed* to follow the rules that make his life more comfortable."

"Are you talking about Franky? Or Christian?"

She narrows her eyes, so I wrinkle my nose in response. "They're fine. Let's talk about your vagina some more."

"Let's talk about your hoodie," she counters quietly. "Looks good on you."

"Oh, yeah." I look down at the fabric swimming on my body. The slate gray material and the perfectly measured strings that hang from the hood. "I hope it's not weird. I left all my luggage at the apartment. Chris figured I'd get cold on the drive."

"So he offered you his hoodie? And you accepted?"

"No, he…" I peek at the too-long sleeve cuff. "Tommy's hoodie."

She makes a sound in the back of her throat, a *nuh-uh* that sends my pulse skittering. And like she knows it, her lips curl higher with every thunderous beat of my heart.

"Chris's." She smirks.

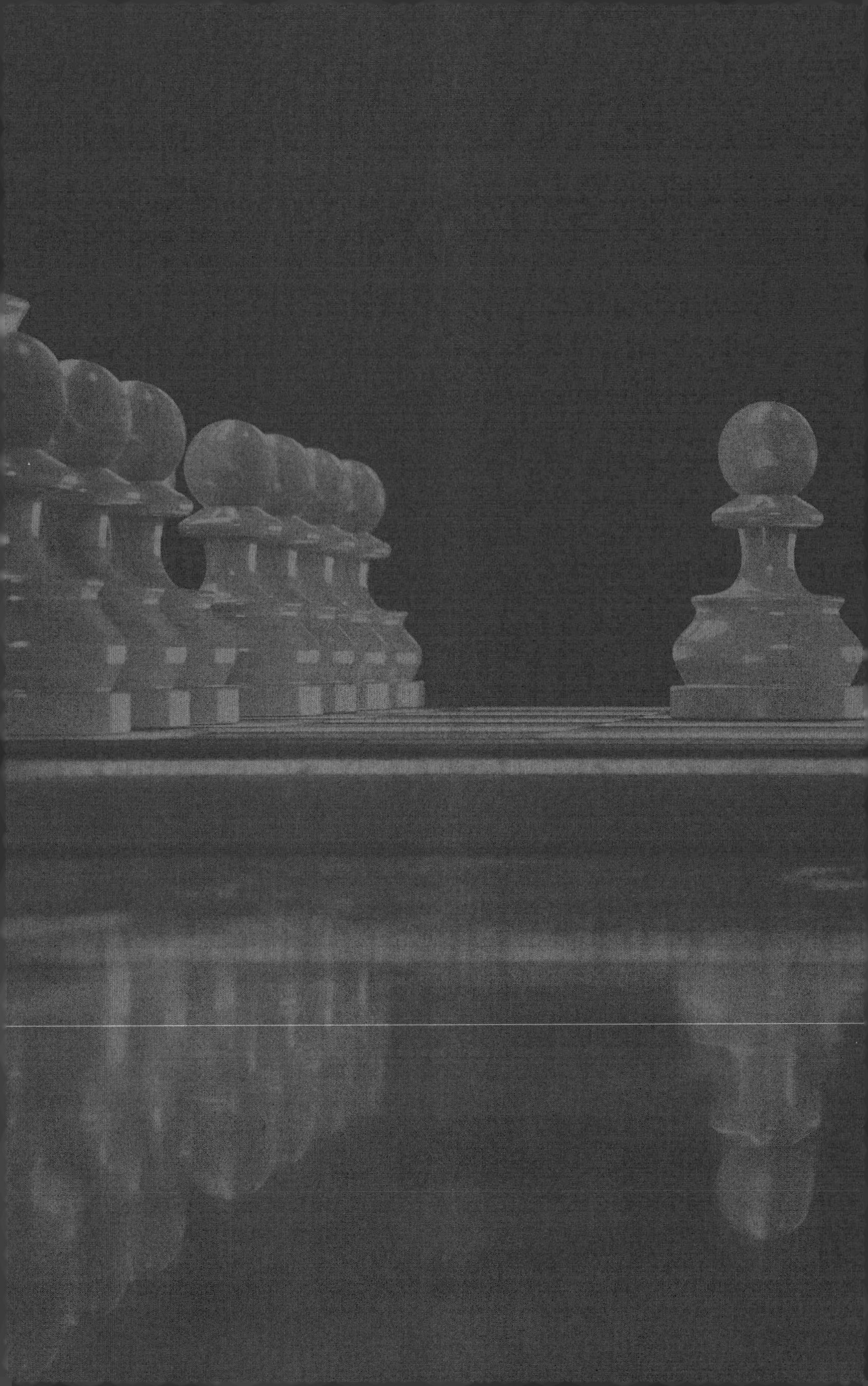

ROUND TWELVE
CHRIS

Ten little fingers, and ten little toes. I count every single one of them ten times over in the hours after we arrive at the hospital, and when I'm done with those, I move on to her chubby cheeks, the dark tint to the wispy curls stuck to the top of her head, bow-lips straight from the Page family tree, and a pert little nose.

She's perfect.

"She hasn't woken up yet." I don't bother looking at the clock on the wall, and I haven't taken my phone out of my pocket since we arrived. I merely slide my thumb into Hazel's little fist and take a guess, factoring in the sun high in the sky outside the hospital windows. "It's been hours. Is that normal?"

Fox crosses to my chair and drops into a crouch, resting her arms on the armrest and her chin on her hands. Smiling—*fuck, she's kinda pretty today* —she studies us with dancing eyes. "I admit, my baby knowledge extends only as far as that one, itty bitty baby that came screaming into the world ten years ago, but Franky slept for, like..." Questioning, she peeks over her shoulder at the duo perched on her bed, crisscrossed legs and a mini magnetized chessboard set up between them. "It was almost twenty hours, right, Alana?"

She shifts and grits her teeth, hiding her pain from the other two who've made a habit of jumping anytime she so much as breathes funny. Glancing across, she considers and nods. "I was getting pretty worried by the end. Babies are supposed to cry and eat and stuff. But Franky was totally chill for almost the entire first day."

Smug, Fox brings her eyes back around. "He was fine. Hazel's only half a day old, so she might be out for a little while yet."

"You wanna hold her yet?" I don't want to give her up. Fuckkkk, I don't want to hand her off and risk not getting her back. But this woman, this person I was *convinced* would take over, has been insanely patient all morning. More patient than I could ever be. "You could have my seat and hold her for a bit."

"It's okay." She lays her arm over mine and strokes Hazel's little chin with the tip of her finger. "I don't mind. I got Franky's first ten years, so you can probably have her whole first day and it still wouldn't be a fair exchange. Besides," she pushes up straight, arching her back and groaning in response to the loud pops that become audible. Then she turns to Franky but backs up and leans against my chair.

She's tired.

"We missed breakfast, and the lunch ladies came around a whole hour ago. We made sure Mom ate but forgot about us. You wanna come with me to get something to eat, buddy?"

"No, thanks." He concentrates on the board, nudging his glasses higher and selecting a pawn to charge forward. "I ate some of Mom's sandwich, so I'm not hungry anymore."

True, I'm sure. But what he actually means is he missed the shit out of his mother, and he's not letting her out of his sight until he has to.

"Thanks, though."

"Why don't you go back to the apartment and chill?" Tommy offers. "You're still wearing yesterday's clothes, so a shower and a meal will set you up for another night at the house. We're good here for a while."

"I suppose." Thoughtful, she rolls the sleeves of my hoodie up her arms and reaches back to fix her messy ponytail. "Franky, you wanna come to the apartment and—"

"No, thanks."

"Leave him here with us," Alana murmurs, meeting his worried eyes with a playful wink. "Tommy can get us snacks, then we'll settle in for a quiet afternoon. Ollie said he'll check on us in a little bit, and I kinda want a nap before then."

"Family time." Tommy presses a kiss to Alana's knuckles. "Sounds perfect."

"Yeah. Family time." Fox takes out her phone and stares at the screen like it holds the world's secrets. But fuck if I don't see the flicker of hurt passing through her eyes. The ache she won't verbalize. *Family time. Without her.* "Heading back to the apartment sounds like a great idea, actually." She puts her phone back and pats her pockets. "I guess I'll give credit where credit's due—" She rearranges her expression, pasting on a fake smile, then she spins and beams for her best friend, "Plainview being so small means I can walk anywhere in a matter of two blocks and five minutes. If I was in New York and forgot my car at home, I'd need two trains and a sacrificial goat."

"I'll drive you." Hugging Hazel to my chest, I stand and earn Fox's surprised gaze as she swings back around. Then I brush past her and cross the room. "They want family time, and I drove us here in my truck."

She wrings her hands together and tracks my every step. "Family means you too, Uncle Chris."

I kiss Hazel's forehead and gently lay her bundled body in Tommy's waiting arms. Then, I meet Fox's eyes and feel a little bad for her.

For the first time ever.

"It means the four of them. Not four and a hanger-on-er."

"You could stay if you want to," Alana counters. Explains. *Overexplains.* "I didn't mean to push you out. That's not what I meant—"

"I don't feel pushed out." I cross to her and drop a kiss on her cheek, then I ruffle Franky's hair and murmur, "Castle to D5. Take his queen and destroy his attack."

"Chris!" He slaps my hand away. "Don't tell her how to win! That's cheating."

Snickering, Alana moves her castle and decimates her son's defense.

"Come on." I turn again and hate how annoyingly pretty Fox is when she's not the loudest, cockiest rooster in the room. Confidence is sexy, and the fact she's no pushover is delicious—beneath the irritation, anyway—but when she's not quite sure where she belongs, hasn't slept as much as she'd like, and she's not as perfectly presented as her corporate Barbie preference, she's vulnerable and cute and bordering on sheepish.

Jesus save me. I don't want *to think of her as anything except untouchable and a little bitchy. Life is safer that way.*

I stroll across the room, and grab the hem of her hoodie—my hoodie—and give it a gentle tug. "I'm starving, my body's eating itself, I haven't stretched my legs yet today, and you're looking a little—" *adorable* "—messy."

Predictably, her eyes narrow to slits, and her hands fly up to flatten her hair. "I'm not messy. I look fine."

"You look like you're doing a walk of shame. Everyone's thinking it."

"I'm not doing a walk of shame! You know exactly where I was last night, jackass." She follows me out of the hospital room, dogging my steps and crashing into my back when I stop and wait for the security doors to let us out. "You poke at me because you *want* us to fight, Christian. You *want* me to be mean to you."

"Do I?" I slip my hands into my pockets and spy her bulldog nose scrunched with viciousness. "I guess I picked that habit up from you. Fighting with you is easy. It might even be fun sometimes."

"I can walk to the apartment." Two deep lines cut between her brows, furrowing and frustrated. "I don't trust myself to be kind when I'm tired, and your feelings are too easily hurt."

"I think I'm gonna be okay." I cut left and snag her hoodie, pulling her along with me. "You can have a shower, and I'll relax in front of the television while I wait. Twenty minutes of quiet would be nice, then we can grab something to eat before I die of starvation."

"Alternatively," she grumbles. "I think I'll walk home and leave you to find a TV and food somewhere else. *Alone*."

"You get cranky when you've spent the day trapped in a small room, and you haven't had a chance to run your mouth. Alana being there kept you on your best behavior."

"No shit! I have all this negative energy just sitting here in my chest, loaded and ready to go." She stomps out of the hospital just two steps ahead of me, but when I expect her to take off and charge toward the street, she stops instead and lifts her face to the sky. It's what she did yesterday morning, too, when she thought she was alone. It's a compulsion, maybe. As natural as drawing air into her lungs and accepting the sun's hit of vitamin D.

Her bad mood makes way for serenity, and her scowl transforms into a smile.

Damn her for being cute.

"Why do you do that?" I stride around and stand over her, blocking her from the sun until her eyes snap open. "It's like you're saying good morning to the world."

"Why not?" She sidesteps me and struts away, cutting through the hospital driveway and angling toward the road. But the woman I thought was wild and unpredictable is, it turns out, the complete opposite. And it only took minutes for me to figure her out.

I snag her sleeve and drag her the other way.

"Chris!"

"You're riding with me. We're not negotiating this, and I'm not gonna stand here and let you choose otherwise." I sling her forward, release her sleeve, and watch her sail toward my truck. "You've spent all this time picking at me, because you knew it bothered me. But it looks like I've figured you out, too. You don't like controlling your sassy bullshit for twelve hours, and you sure as shit don't like being woken up before the sun. It makes you cranky."

"And even knowing that, you insist on driving me around." She trudges to the passenger side door and yanks it open. "If you let me walk my mood off, you could drive a different way, still get your TV and quiet time, eat whatever you want, and *not* get chewed out for any of it."

"Or maybe you're not upset about being locked up at all." I slide into the driver's side and slip the key into the ignition. "Maybe it's because Alana said she wanted family time, and for a moment there, you felt like that meant everyone except you." I turn the engine over and set my foot on the gas, revving the old motor. "That rejection stung. And even if you know that wasn't her intention, it still hit a nerve."

"Well shit, Dr. Phil." She tears the seatbelt across her body and stabs the metal into the catch. "You're probably right. You're a genius."

"Hurt your feelings." I turn the radio up, just loud enough to cover the noise of my engine, and driving away from our parking slip, I angle for the exit and hit one or two—*dozen*—potholes in the blacktop. "You went out of your way to let me hold the baby all day 'cos you didn't want to hurt my feelings. Then *family* was mentioned, and it felt like a bit of a slap to the face."

"Uh-huh. And my niceness was for naught, because you're still here, badgering me when I could be wandering in the middle-of-the-day sun."

"You can go for a walk later." I amble onto the road and settle in for our thirty-second journey. "There are some really pretty trails that cut through mine and Tommy's yards. They wind around the lake and lead into a few hidden spots we didn't even know existed until we bought the land. Alana will be in the hospital for another day or two, which means you're sleeping at Tommy's until she's back. Save your walk for later."

"You almost sound genuine, but my spidey-senses predict a hike where, eventually, I die from exposure and a mass-mosquito buffet. You'd stay inside with Franky, so when I'm gone and out of the way, you can be his savior and never have to deal with me again. I'm not stupid."

"Right. 'Cos killing Alana's best friend and Hazel's namesake would go completely unnoticed."

"Oh my gosh!" Like the flip of a switch, she transforms from night to day, slapping her hands to her mouth and twisting to place her knee on the bench seat. "I'm her namesake! Isn't that amazing?"

"It's pretty amazing."

"I get to be *the* Fox from Hazel Fox. Like, what?"

I tap along to a Kane Brown song and smile. Dammit, I don't want to smile. "It's very cool."

"And sure, *you* get to claim the Watkins thing, since you all have that name now, and eventually, Alana and Franky will, too. And Hazel is Hazel because of your eyes. But *I'm* Fox. I'm *the* Fox!"

"You're *the* Fox."

"I'm gonna have a couple of kids someday and call them Alana and Tommy, just so they can understand how *amazing* this feels. There's a whole new human in the world, Chris, and she was named after me!"

I peek at her from the corner of my eyes and shake my head because she's no longer cranky and mean. She's jittery and beaming. Wriggling with excitement and clenching her fists.

"I never knew that was something I wanted. I didn't even know it was something I'd care about. But she's named after me! So for the rest of her life, when people meet her and ask about her name, she can point at me like, '*yeah, that cool chick over there. She's the OG Fox.*' I don't have to be Uncle Chris, sharing DNA and a surname when I can be Aunty Fox. *Fox!*"

"You're kinda excited, huh?" I pull into a parking spot outside the bookstore, recently named *Happily Ever After*, and dragging the key from the ignition, I glance across and study her giddy grin. "Did you have suspicions they were gonna do that? Did Alana give you any hints?"

"No! Did she tell you?"

I shake my head. "They were firm on keeping it under wraps till she was here. Though I reckon Alana probably worried about my feelings. I'm hearing rumors that I'm kinda protected and whiny when it comes to them."

"At least you admit it." Laughing, she turns to her door and shoves it open, sliding out until her feet touch the road. Then she slams it shut again and waits for me to do the same. "It's clear Alana spent her entire youth mothering you, and hell if you didn't come to rely on it." She wanders to the shop door and pats her pockets. Searching. Panicking. And then realizing. No keys. No purse. Nothing but the phone in her pocket and hopes and dreams—and puppy dog eyes glittering up at mine. "Can you…"

"Bet you're glad I drove you now, huh?" I unlock the door and push it open, then I hold it wide and wait for her to pass under my arm before I follow and close up behind us.

Fuck knows, Barbara will waltz on in if she sees the place unlocked for more than three seconds. "You would have walked your cranky ass across town, kicking stones and cussing me out for no reason except your own bad mood, then you would've arrived and realized you couldn't get inside."

"Lucky me." She tears the scrunchie from her hair and cuts a line through the store. "You get to be my knight in shining armor. Oh, Sir Lancelot. They were right to dub you the most perfect knight."

She swings her hips and traverses the stairs, and coming to a stop on the top landing, she peeks over her shoulder, doe-eyed and sugary sweet. "Please, my sweet knight. Putteth the key in the locketh."

"Pretty sure that's not how they spoke back then." I unlock her door and knock it wide to allow her entry. I open my mouth to tell her which way to walk, but then I snap my lips shut again. There's no need for a tour of her new digs; the place only has one door beside the one we just walked through.

I close up behind me and set my keys on the counter, my phone right after them. Then, bending at the hips and pressing my elbows to the countertop, I drop my head and run my fingers through my hair. "I haven't pulled an all-nighter in a good long while. Turns out I'm not twenty-one and buzzing with teenage energy anymore."

"Yeah, because being twenty-nine and an athlete means you're not literally in your prime right now." She strolls through the bathroom door and closes it most of the way, and tossing her hair tie to the basin, she peels the hoodie up and lobs it to the floor. But I guess the fabric is kinda heavy, heavier than she's used to, because it hits the bottom of the door and knocks it a few inches wider without her realizing.

Fuck me. I catch her reflection in the vanity mirror, the perfect view of her smooth skin and muscular shoulders as she peels her shirt up. She reveals a flat stomach and a glittering belly piercing, and higher up, a lacy red bra that matches her underwear perfectly.

Her spine creates a deep valley in the center of her back, and the ink I glimpsed earlier turns out to be a million times more detailed than I even guessed, stretching all the way around her hip and up to her right shoulder blade.

She didn't touch her arms. Not her neck. She didn't even mark up her stomach, except the very lowest section.

I lick my lips and watch, a prisoner to the show she unknowingly puts on, as she unbuttons her shorts and wiggles them over her hips. They're wide enough to create the perfect hourglass shape. Her backside, just thick enough to force her to work the denim down instead of letting it fall.

Turn around, Christian.
This isn't a peepshow, and she hasn't invited you in.

She slides the shorts all the way to her feet and steps out of the denim. Her sinfully long legs are made longer now that she's almost completely in her skin, then she reaches back and unsnaps the catch on her bra.

God save me. Please. Because maybe she's infuriating, and perhaps we're destined for a lifetime of bickering. But she's fucking beautiful, and I'm just a man who hasn't touched a woman in too damn long.

She releases the straps of her bra and shucks the lacy material down, until all she has left is her and her panties, and damn her to hell and back, but they hug her ass and provide me a challenge; *see if your hands can do the same.*

I'm not sure I breathe. I'm not sure I even know how.

But I stare and consider. I hungrily study her long limbs and delicate ink. Her thick thighs, the kind I'd assume belonged to an athlete. And then her eyes, when they come to mine in the mirror.

"Shit." I drop my head and clamp my eyes shut, squeezing them tight and gritting my teeth. "I'm sorry. I didn't mean—" I shake my head. "I meant to tell you the door was knocked open, and I—"

"I'm not mad." Her voice is stunningly husky, and fuck if it's not needy enough to draw my eyes open again. Swallowing, I glance across and watch her hide on the other side of the door. She rests her cheek on the wood, her bottom lip between her teeth. "Not sure if inviting you in would be the most satisfying thing I've ever done," she murmurs. "Or if it would be opening a can of worms I'm not entirely sure I could manage."

Beautiful brown eyes search my face, her gaze, as warm on my skin as her touch would be… if only I allowed myself to walk closer. I push off the counter and turn, dangling my hands by my sides, but that might be a mistake, too. Because she lowers her eyes, trailing them over my thundering heart, my swirling belly… finally, my crotch.

"At least I know what you think of me."

Groaning, I press my hands to my cock and cover the tent it makes of my pants. "I'm sorry."

"If I go to bed with you, are you gonna be a control freak, like the fork thing?" She plays with me, teasing as she runs her tongue across her lips. "Or a control freak, like *you're* gonna decide when I get to breathe and how often I get to come?"

Fuckkkkk meeeee. My cock throbs.

"Because if it's the first, I'll tire of you really fast. No woman ever wanted to be screwed by a man who never quite grew out of his ten-year-old dysregulated phase."

"Fox—"

"But if it's the second," she hums, suckling on her bottom lip. "I can't say I haven't thought about it. Six weeks can be a really long time if all we're doing is swiping at each other."

"So you wanna fuck instead?" *Shut up, shut up, shut up!* "You think instead of fighting, we could direct our energies elsewhere?"

She lifts her shoulder in a lazy shrug. "I think we know how to annoy each other. It comes instinctually. So perhaps we could extend those skills and figure out how to please each other, too." She nibbles on her plump top lip. "I've never been one to shy away from a little hard work, and God knows, I love an opportunity to learn something new."

"You can't argue with me if your mouth is filled with my cock."

She trembles, her pulse pounding against her throat and her smile curling up in challenge. Finally, she nudges the door open another inch. "Prove it."

Heaven help me.

"Fox..." I flex my hands by my side, locking my feet to the floor and my racing heart into a cage I don't dare open. "This isn't something you can play with. This isn't—"

"Are you not up for it?" She trails the tip of her finger over her chest, across to her inked ribs, and down until she knows she's got me, body and soul. "Even if I'm daring you?" Taunting, she peers up at me from beneath thick lashes. "Even if I'm begging you?"

Fuck it. I cross the apartment and shove my fingers into her hair, fisting my hand and tilting her head to the side until a whimper of surprise ricochets along her throat. And because I want to look, I drag her half a foot to the right, out of the way of the door, and kick it open to reveal her body, my visual wonderland. Her chest lifts and falls, racing for fresh oxygen, and her pulse skitters against her neck.

But her tits... fuck me.

Her tits are perfect and swollen. C-cups, with rosy pink nipples peaked for my pleasure. "I didn't mean to see you." But I study her now. "I didn't mean to look when the door was knocked open." But I wouldn't change it now. My cock aches, trapped behind the zipper of my jeans. The desire to press her to her knees is almost crippling.

Soon.

So fucking soon.

"I didn't mean to look," I rasp. "But now I want to tie you down and force you to stay still, because I want to see all of you. In my own time. At my own pace."

"You—"

"If you argue with me, I'll fill your mouth and shut you the fuck up." I want to taste her. To savor her. I want to bite her, and *fuckkkk*, I want to own her. If only for an hour. "You have time to say no."

Please say no.

Please *don't* say no.

"We haven't touched yet. So if you want out, say so before we cross the line and make a mess of what doesn't have to be messy."

"I like messy." She moves onto the tips of her toes and presses her supple chest to mine. "It's you who struggles with that sort of thing. You like order. And rules. Routine and normalcy. Me?" Her eyes are like molten lava, burning as she shakes her head gently from side to side. "I'm okay with jumping out of repetition and into bed with a man who knows how to command my body."

She sets her hands on my chest, walking her fingers over my pecs and up to my neck, and then with a wicked smile, she places two fingers past my lips and onto my tongue. "I have always, *always* been a fan of the things men can do with their mouths. And I don't mean talking."

"You think you're in charge, don't you?" I capture her wrist and fold it back. But I don't toss her away. Instead, I nibble on her throbbing pulse, biting just hard enough to taste her. Suckling until her skin turns a pretty pink. "You think because I like things a certain way that I'm a fucking idiot." I tighten my grip on her hair. "I'm not incapable, Fox. I just know what I like and rarely look for something else." I release her wrist and grab her hip, peeling her panties down a half inch because I want to see where her ink begins. "Did you fuck whoever put this on your body?" I glide my palm over her garden of Eden. Apt, I suppose, considering how close it is to her pussy. "No way he got so near and didn't want a taste."

"Sadly, I don't relish the idea of eating kitty, and my tattoo artist has one of those." She steps closer, stealing my view of her perfect body and resting her nose against my chest. She inhales, humming in the back of her throat and grinning when she's done. "I wasn't gonna tell you, since it sounds kinda weird. But I caught a whiff of your aftershave that first time I met you." She pulls back and searches my eyes. "We were at a funeral, which made things a little icky, but if we'd met in a dark club and I was led only by how you smelled, I'd have done anything you wanted right there and then."

"You like how I smell?" I bring the front of my shirt forward and inhale. "I wasn't wearing aftershave at the funeral. Or now."

"Guess it's just you, then." She trails her fingers over my jaw, stroking the bone. "You can kiss me, Christian. Do you need direct instructions? Because I'm standing here, buck ass naked, and you're not slamming me against the shower wall yet."

"You want me to slam you?" I slip my hand into the back of her panties and massage her ass. So thick. So malleable. "You don't want this to be slow and gentle?"

"Not even a little bit." She pulls me closer and nips at my lip, biting until electricity sizzles in my veins. "I like it when it hurts. I love it when I'm still a little sore the next morning." She dips her tongue forward, soothing what she hurt. "I like it when, even after we're done, I can touch any part of my body and remember exactly how you grabbed me."

She reaches back and wraps her hand around my wrist, and staring into my eyes, she pulls me to the front and gasps when my fingers brush over her pulsing clit. "Shit." She drops her head back, the ends of her hair tickling the middle of her spine. "I wasn't even going to tell you I've thought of you. No way did I plan to admit that I wanted the guy who annoys the shit out of me."

"But then you went ahead and undressed in front of me. Now we're stuck." I cup her tit and fold my neck, suckling the supple peak between my lips, and because she arches closer, feeding me, I slip my fingers into her soaked pussy and hold on when her knees buckle. "What do you taste like, Fox? Your wrist is nice. And your tit is better." I pump my hand and dig deeper. "But how do you taste where it matters?"

"Probably a little salty, to be honest." She chokes out a desperate snigger. "I haven't showered since last night."

"Exactly how I like it." I lower to my knees and peel her panties down. *Fuck it.* "I don't wanna eat when you've just come out of the shower. That's bland." I circle her clit with my thumb and nip at her hipbone. "I want to feast on *you*."

I drag her panties to the floor and help her step out of them, then I grab her thigh and drape it over my shoulder, reveling in her cry of surprise and the perfect view of her needy pussy. "Hold on to me." I slam three fingers upwards, stretching her out without a single shred of caution, then I lean forward and trap her clit between my teeth.

"Oh God!" She throws her head back, slamming it against the doorframe and tangling her fingers in my hair for balance. "Jesus, Chris!"

"You don't know me well enough to know I like to savor." I slide my tongue along her drenched slit and taste her at her best. "I take my time, and I make damn sure to milk you for every last drop you have."

"I'm more of a slam and bam, fast and nasty." She juts her hips forward, feeding me, though I need no help. "I get bored easily and don't have time to waste."

"You won't be bored while I'm with you." I slide my free hand around and up the back of her thigh. And because she wants to test me, I slip my thumb between her ass cheeks and deep into her asshole without asking.

Without waiting.

I give her no time to adjust, and fuck it, I feel no remorse when she chokes in pleasure and pain.

"I'm all about making you feel good." I grab her other thigh and lift her, stealing her foundations and holding her up on my own, then I push her against the wall and straighten out until I'm standing, creating a vise-like grip on either side of my head.

And yet, I know I won't fumble her.

"I'm gonna make you come until you want to scream, and then I'll make you come some more until you tell me you have nothing left."

"Chris—"

"And then I'm gonna make you come some *more* because, damn it, Fox, I won't be finished with you yet." I bury my face between her legs and drink her down, guzzling her release and groaning when I have her smeared all over my lips. Until she's dribbling down my neck and into my shirt. "You mock my need for control, but you'll find a new appreciation for it when I'm fucking you into insanity, and still, I'm not finished."

"Oh, God." She fists my hair and pulls me closer. Closer. "Make me come. Please."

"You're okay with ass play." I draw my thumb out, then back in again until she rewards me with an animalistic groan. "You like that."

"I like it." She crushes her back to the wall and pants. "Yes."

"So I'm gonna fuck your ass, too. I'm gonna own all of you."

"Yes, please."

"And if you cry because it hurts…" I inch back and wait for her eyes, jutting my hips forward because I want her. God, I want her. "If you cry, I'll fuck you harder. Because I got the screwy Watkins DNA no one likes to talk about. I keep most of it locked away. But not this one." I bite her clit and thrill in her scream. "I feel like a god when I make you hurt."

"I don't want you to feast anymore." And yet, she crushes my face between her legs. "I want you to fuck me."

"Not until I say so." I press three fingers into her pussy, slamming her backward and pinning her to the wall—*if I step out from beneath her, will she still stay put?*—and when she likes that, I pull back, then in again until she's eating three fingers and my knuckles.

I could make her swallow my fist if I keep going.

Because she wants it.

She wants me.

"You're a hungry one, aren't you?" I bring my hand back and push it in again, stopped only by my pinkie knuckle and her desperate cry of pleasure. "You want me to fuck you, Fox?"

Her breath comes out on an explosive "Yes!"

"You want me to tear you open and put you back together again?" I swap my thumb for two fingers and drink her down. She doesn't just come. She floods, filling my mouth and tickling my insides. "I could make you my fuck doll, molding you to the perfect fit for *me*, and never again will you go to bed with another man and believe he stacks up."

"Chris—"

"I like it when you beg." I brush her leg off my shoulder and catch her, despite her panicked cry. Wrapping her around my hips, I consider the fact I'm still wearing jeans the *only* reason I'm not already filling her up. "I want to see you cry." I crush her against the wall and capture her lips with mine. Make her taste herself. Prove to her that she's delicious. "I want you to beg me to fuck you. Because I'm a proud man, and you've been poking at me for way too long."

"Please fuck me." She grinds against my belly, searching for friction. For fulfillment. "I'm begging, you see? I'm already begging."

"Nuh-uh." I set her on her feet and take a step back, releasing her and forcing her to stand on her own, heart pounding, knees shaking. She's naked and beautiful. Deliciously deranged and desperate for me. *Exactly how I like her*. "I'm not the bam and done type, remember?" I slip my hand into my jeans and circle my cock. It's like touching electricity. It's like grabbing a live wire and hoping not to get burned up. But then I charge forward again and spin her around. I crush her chest to the wall, her hands beside her shoulders, then I draw her back until she figures it out.

Show me.

"Your asshole is throbbing for me." I peel her cheeks apart and groan because she's tight and forbidden. But she'll take me. Even if it hurts, I'll make sure she takes me. "Have you ever wanted to be fucked in the ass before, Fox?"

"Yes." She chokes for air. "Yes, I want to."

"You ever been fucked in the ass before?"

She shakes her head, swallowing and trembling. "Not by a cock, and not by someone else."

Curious, I spit on my hand and rub my thumb over her asshole. "What do you mean?"

"I use toys on myself." She shudders and attempts to sit backward. She's hungry for my thumb. Desperate for my touch. "I use toys on myself often. More often since I met you."

"You think of me while you're fucking yourself?"

She whimpers in frustration, wiggling her hips in search of more.

But she doesn't answer, so I bring my hand back and slap her ass with a loud, resounding crack.

"Ah!" She startles forward to escape the pain. But hell, if she doesn't override that instinct and drive herself back again.

"I asked if you fuck yourself and think of me."

"Yes." She drops a hand from the wall and touches herself, too impatient to wait. Too anxious for more. "Yes, I fuck myself and think of you. I've been touching myself and thinking of you since we first met in the summer."

"Seven months of practice." I hum my appreciation and slip two fingers into her asshole.

She cries out at the intrusion, her legs quivering and her fingers still fucking. So now we're both working.

"How big are your toys? As big as me?"

"No."

"How do you know?" I drive my hips forward and slide my zippered cock against her clit. "You don't know how big I am."

"Educated guess." She gushes onto the floor, drawing me closer. Closer to taking her. Closer to destroying her.

Closer to owning her.

"I only had a bullet-sized plug before. But now..." She gasps, panting and moaning. "The one I use now is much larger."

"Because you think of me?" My heart thunders, and my lungs seize. Fuck me, I might not survive her. But I'm determined to accept my death and ride her all the way to hell. "You got any lube? I might not get another chance with you, Fox. So I'm having you. All of you. Right now."

"Lube?" she questions, breathless, and a little confused. "What?"

"For the first time? You want lube." Desperate, I bend and bury my tongue between her ass cheeks.

"Argh!" She comes again, spraying the floor and soaking her thighs. "Chris..."

"We need lube. And condoms. And the fucking bed."

She heaves for fresh air, crying with needy anticipation, and glancing over her shoulder, she meets my eyes and gulps. "I saw a drugstore three doors up. Run."

"What?"

Like the vixen she is, she pulls forward, disengaging, closing her legs, straightening her spine, and stealing from me the things I've already laid claim to. Then she swallows and grabs the bathroom door. "I said run."

"Fox—"

"I noticed the brand-new showerhead in here. I was gonna use it for my pleasure, even before you started this fun little game. I planned to make myself come with you right there in my living room. But now you have an invitation to join me."

"Fox..."

"Run." She tugs the shower door open and flips the taps on, and to drive her point home, she slips her fingers between her legs and moans. "If I'm finished before you get back, I guess you miss out."

"Fuck."

I spin on my heels and bolt through the apartment, slamming my way through the door and sprinting down the stairs. A dull headache pounds in the base of my skull, and my thundering heart is like a bass drum between my ears.

I risk breaking my ankle.

My leg.

My fucking neck.

But I skip half a dozen steps and stumble to the main floor, and pumping my arms, I cross the bookstore and crash into the front door with a heavy exhalation of air.

Only now, I remember I didn't bring keys. Or my phone. Or fuck, my wallet. So I spin back and sweep up the petty cash container Alana keeps under the front desk. I tear the damn thing open and steal a fifty, then I circle the desk and crash through the shop doors. I leave them unlocked—I don't have a choice. I drop my head and pump my arms harder, clinging to the cash I stole, the robbery I committed, all in the name of sex with the one I never thought I'd get to taste.

I drag my shirt up and wipe my face on the run, since going out in public with Fox Tatum's pussy on my lips is a tad uncouth, and sidestepping a little family on their way to fuck-knows-where, I burst into the drugstore with enough noise, that every soul inside stops to study me.

Good lord, they're all watching me.

"Oh, hi Chris." Barbara bustles closer. "I'm glad I saw you today. I wanted to check in about the—"

I point to my ear in that universal '*I'm wearing headphones*' way, blatantly lying and shoving past the old lady. Shamelessly, I make a beeline for the condoms and use every ounce of willpower I possess to ignore the eyes that follow me.

"Chris?" Eliza Darling waves from the other side of the store. "Hey, wait up—"

"Can't, sorry!" I don't stop to study brands. Or prices. Flavors. *Ribbed for her pleasure. What?* Fuck me. I grab the first bottle of lube I find and the first box with a trojan soldier on the packaging. Sprinting to the front counter, I slap the fifty down beside an ugly belly dancer ornament the owners put on display after their honeymoon—thirty something years ago—then I lean across the desk and snatch a paper bag. I meet the eyes of the little old lady working her once-a-month Sunday. "Keep the change. I don't even care."

"I have to scan those first—"

"No, you don't. I was never here." I bag my own things and charge toward the front door, only to skid to a stop when Mrs. Tower, an old teacher from my godforsaken high school days, steps in with her husband.

She hated me back then, but now she smiles. "Oh, hi Chris—"

"Nope." I circle on the fly, bursting through the doorway and onto the sidewalk outside, and because one of Alana's mother's friends waves from her little bench seat on the other side of the street, I shake my head and avert my gaze.

"Chris, I was hoping to talk to you about—"

"Stop talking to me! Everyone, shut the fuck up!" I crush my semi-stolen goods against my chest and sprint toward the shop, and when Ollie Darling's getting-older father grabs the door and attempts to step inside, I blow past him and flip the *open* sign to *closed*. "Sorry. We forgot to turn this yesterday. Store's not open on Sundays."

"But, I—"

"Catch you tomorrow!" I slam the locks into place and lower the blinds on the inside of the door, and crossing the store at a sprint, I listen for the sound of the shower still running.

The rattle of the old pipes in the wall.

I scramble onto the steps, missing the third and stumbling on the way up, but fuck, I use my free hand to help my trek. Sweat beads on my brow, and my heart threatens to give out on me. I swear to God, if she's changed her mind about this, I might drive on over to the house I was raised and abused in and shoot myself in the head.

But I run to the top of the stairs and crash through the apartment door, locking it up to keep intruders away, then I peel my shirt off and find Fox's suitcase lying open on the floor.

It wasn't like that just two minutes ago.

"Fox?" With my heart in my throat and the blood in my veins hot enough to burn, I stride to the closed bathroom door and pray. Fuck, I plead and bargain and prepare to beg. "You okay in there?"

"Yeah." She releases a groaning whimper. "Come in."

Thank fuck!

I whip the door open and skid to a stop, my pulse skittering at a dizzying gallop, but my cock sings in response to what I see. It throbs and tries to break through my zipper.

"You brought your toys to Plainview?" I toss the bag of contraband to the sink and walk straight into the shower. I don't fucking care that my shoes get wet. Or my jeans. Or my soul, really. Because she prepared for me, pressing her chest and cheek to the shower wall, the detached shower head between her legs, and a big fat plug nestled neatly in her ass. "You're a thirsty, thirsty girl, aren't you?"

I lower to my knees and cop a face full of shower water. But I don't give a single shit because her ass throbs, and her plug is big enough to almost compete with me.

Not really.

But it's a start.

"You're the most delicious slut I've ever met." I bury my face between her legs and slide my tongue along her slit. "Jesus, Fox. You want me to destroy your pretty little cunt, don't you?"

"I'm waiting for you." She pushes back and sits on my face. "I'm so desperate for you, Chris. So needy."

"I got what we needed." Pulling back, I slowly drag the plug from her ass, breathless at the sight of her body clinging to it. Her asshole, begging to keep it in. And then her knees, knocking when I take it away.

I consider myself a forward-thinking man, so I pump a little soap onto the plug and give it a wash. Rinsing the bubbles away. The bacteria. The danger. Then I press it into her pussy and elicit an electric cry of surprise.

She scrambles forward, crashing against the wall.

"I'm gonna fill you right up, beautiful. Split you in half and have you thank me for it." I back up out of the shower, unsnapping my jeans and shoving them down. Denim sticks to my legs, and I damn near break my bones when I toe my boots off.

But there's nothing more painful than *not* being inside her. So I kick my boots away and toss my pants and boxers, and tearing the paper bag open, I grab the box of condoms and the bottle of lube and take them back to the shower with me.

I slap her ass, right where my handprint already marks her skin, and tug the glass door closed behind me. Fuck knows, the rest of the bathroom is already wet and messy, and closing the door makes less room for me to stretch out. But my brain isn't quite where it needs to be. Not when all my blood is in my cock. "It's probably gonna hurt, babe." I reach around her and turn the shower off—because I'm an asshole, possibly. Or because I don't want it to wash away the lube—and ripping the condom packaging open, I take one out, tear the foil and glide the rubber over my cock. Then I grab her hands and place them on the handy-dandy handrails an old lady had installed at some point in the last two decades. "Hold on to these. Don't let go."

"Faster." She grinds backward. Searching. Needy. "Please."

"Keep begging." I flick the lid off the lube and squirt a liberal amount onto her ass, and because I fucking want to, I slam my finger inside and growl when she bucks with pleasure. "Cry for me, Fox. Tell me how much I'm hurting you. Tell me how cruel I am." I fist my cock and squeeze until the lights in the backs of my eyes darken, and my balls prepare to empty.

But no chance. No fucking way are we ready for that.

I slide the tip of my cock over her asshole instead, collecting lube and teasing her with what's coming. "You'll be my greatest conquest." I grab her pussy plug and slam it forward.

"God." She screams, crashing her forehead to the tile wall. "Fuck, Chris."

"You don't get to tell me to stop." I nudge inside her, before pulling back, squeezing more lube onto my cock, and reclaiming what I took. "You're extra tight because of the plug."

"Too tight." Panting, she rolls her forehead on the wall. "Too much."

"Too bad for you, you don't get to decide." I re-situate her weakening hands on the rails. "Grab on. I don't wanna toss you around and break a bone."

"Chris—"

"Swallow me down, beautiful." I steal more of her ass and fight the urge to blow already. "Take my cock. Then I'll take your cunt. I'm gonna have your mouth, too, and you'll know no one will ever compare again."

"Oh, God—"

"Not God. Chris. You'll pray in the kingdom of Christian Watkins from now on. And every time you open that smart mouth to fuck with me, know that I'll fill it again and make you eat my seed." I can't go slow. Fuck, I can't pace myself, so I push in a little more and fight with the solid plug taking up so much space. Hard rubber isn't like a cock. It's not as malleable, which means she crushes me half to death and whimpers at the tight fit. "You did good prepping for me."

"It's too much," she moans. "It hurts."

"You've wanted me for so long. Arguing with me was your foreplay."

"Chris! It hurts."

"Good." I slam forward and seat myself all the way to the base, and when she screams, I grab her neck and twist until her spine crackles and the tears in her eyes turn me on.

Finally, I take her lips with mine and suck her all the way into my soul.

"So perfect." I bite her bottom lip and inhale her cry of pain. "Now you're mine. I'm never gonna stop, and you'll always know who you belong to."

She chokes on her hitching breath, squeezing the railing until her knuckles turn white and her biceps bulge. Then she frees herself and turns to the wall, bending at the hips and presenting herself for more. "Please."

"Hungry, hungry little cunt." I grab her hips and drag her back to sit on my cock, then I push her forward and follow until her cry echoes from wall to wall. "I wish there was more of me. Fuck, I wish I could fill all of you, all at the same time."

"Chris—"

"Say my name, over and over and over again. Tell me how good I am."

"So good." She drops her head and whines. "So thick."

"I want to brand you all over." I don't bother with careful anymore —*did I ever*? Instead, I ride her like a stallion rides a broodmare. I grip her hips, bruising her flesh, and when the pressure builds between us, I pop the plug free of her pussy and thrill in the way she squirts all over my feet.

Then I put it back in place and keep going.

"You're so perfect." I fold over her back and bite her shoulder blades. Her spine. I mark her skin and know, if she swims in a bikini in the next six weeks, anyone within a hundred yards of her will see my claim. And I won't even be sorry for it. "I want you to beg me to fuck you until you've got nothing left." I still my hips and grin when her fiery eyes come around to burn me. Then I slam forward again and take more. "I want you to beg me to stop. I want you to think of me while you sleep, and then I want you to touch yourself until the ache goes away."

"Oh God," she groans. "Chris—"

"Better yet, I want you to climb out of your bed and get into mine. In the middle of the night, I want you to sit on my cock and wake me up that way."

She moans, animalistic and desperate.

"I can't get enough of you." It feels like I have lava for blood. Poison for cum, just begging to fill her. "You're a wonderland, and I'm overwhelmed by all I can explore. I'm tempted to rush from this to the next." But I pace myself, gliding out of her hungry asshole and back in again until there's nowhere left to go. "But I won't rush. I'm gonna make this last and prove you won't grow bored with me."

She reaches between her legs and twists the plug, the solid rubber turning against the side of my cock.

"Then I'll fuck your sweet cunt, too. I'm gonna brand every hole, so next time you lay with a man, he'll know I was here and that he'll never measure up." I bring my arm back and slap her ass. Then, reaching around, I smack her pussy, too.

She creams all over the plug, her delicious juices escaping around the intrusion and down to soak her thighs.

"Dammit, Fox. You're perfect." I twist the plug and push it as deep as she can take it, and rocking my hips back, I charge forward and fill her again. "Does it hurt?"

She heaves for air. "Yes."

"Good." I smack her again and hold my breath, so I don't come too soon. She's a siren luring me out to sea. A seductress intent on destroying me. But I can't think of a better way to die. "I'm so fucking hungry for you."

She throws her head backward, arching her spine and crying toward the ceiling. And because I want her so fucking much, I grab her throat and fold her back, until her ass crushes my cock and her air garbles to a stop.

I hold her captive, crushing her larynx and dragging my tongue along the side of her neck.

"You won't ever think down on me again, Fox Tatum. Your knees will forever tremble, begging you to get on them, which is where you need to be to please me." I swap her throat for her hair, fisting it and tilting her head around, and taking her tongue with mine, I walk my free hand down and torment her clit.

"Argh!" She explodes, crying out and popping her plug free, drenching our feet with her release. I swallow her cries and her tongue, and when her legs give out, I hold her up and contort her succulent body to my whims.

I flip the shower back on—freezing cold at first, then stifling hot—and finding the exact right temperature, I let her breathe again while I pull out of her ass and peel my condom off.

I toss it to the tile floor and grab another from the box.

"Jesus." She clings to the handrails. "Chris..."

"I'm absolutely not done with you." I set the condom between my teeth and bend to grab the plug, and giving it a quick clean under the shower, I jerk her around again with my hand in her hair, nibbling on her bottom lip and tasting the salt of her tears on her tongue. "Bend over for me."

"What?"

"I know you fucking heard me." I smack her ass and squeeze the column of her neck with my fingers. I take a step back to make room, then I shove her head forward until she's bent at the hips. "Gonna put this back where I found it." I lower to my knees, the shower water sluicing over her back, but before I slam the plug home, I surge forward and eat her asshole.

She screams out in pleasure, squeezing the rails between her fingers and bucking under my touch.

More. More. More.

"You have a nasty, hungry cunt, don't you, Fox?" I slide my tongue deep inside her asshole and thrill in how she grips me. So hungry. So receptive and needy. "You have three holes for me to explore, and goddammit, I don't want to give any up to move to the next."

"Chris—"

"I'm just one man. I can only have so much of you at once. But I promise, once we're done, I'll know all of you."

"Fuck!" She explodes again, frothing over until her sweet cream splashes against my chest. For the rest of my life, I'll run my hands over my heart and know she's branded me, too. "Sweet, sweet pussy." I slide my fingers inside, soaking them with her release and walking them to her asshole to taunt her.

"You're so needy." I set the plug in place and wait for her to swallow it up like a good, good girl.

She whimpers, dropping her head and letting it dangle. She steels her legs, though I know they'd rather quiver.

"You're tired." I play with her, tease her by twisting the plug and reseating it where my cock was only minutes ago. "You've already come, but I'm not done with you yet."

"Fuck me, Chris." She reaches between her legs and plays with her clit. "Please. Fuck me."

I push up straight and grab her hair, yanking her around until her cry makes me harder. Her pain makes my heart thunder. "I fucking *love* the sound of you begging." I fist my purpling cock, and because she's still bent at the hips, facing me this time, I slap her cheek with it and earn her feral growl. "I like knowing you're desperate." I slap again, watching as her lips pop open. She chases me for fulfillment. "You want to suck my cock, beautiful?" I drag the head over her bottom lip and stop myself from slamming all the way to her throat.

I could.

Fuck, she'd even thank me for it.

"You want to taste me, don't you?"

"Yes." She rests her ass against the shower wall, pleasuring herself with the plug jammed deep inside. "Yes, I want to taste you."

"You want me to cum in your throat?"

"Yes, I—"

"What if I let you eat my release, but I *don't* fuck your cunt?" I dip my fingers into her mouth and moan because she suckles. She's trained, just for me. Hungry, but only for what I offer. "I could leave you like this."

I tug my fingers free and feed my cock between her lips, cupping her head and pulling her forward until I feel the back of her throat. Until tears spring from the corners of her eyes.

And still, she stares up at me like the subservient perfection she is beneath all the sass.

"I could get off and walk away." I fuck her face, bouncing her against the wall so the plug fucks her ass and her release soaks her thighs. "I know you've come," I rasp. "And I know it feels good. But to finish without ever having my cock inside your pussy would be a disservice, don't you think?"

She sucks fresh air through her nose, desperately clamoring to fill her lungs. But because I'm a bastard, I pinch her nostrils and grin as her eyes flare wide with panic.

"You won't die." I charge forward, filling her throat, and slamming her to the shower wall. Retreating, I do it again and feel the shower door flex and groan under the pressure of my back.

I release her nose and lean over her back, twisting the plug until she creams anew. Foamy and delicious, so receptive to every move I make. "Fuck. You're amazing." My heart thunders faster than it does in the gym. Faster than when I'm sparring. Faster than it ran when I caught her on the dock yesterday morning.

And dammit, but it sprinted when our eyes met through the fog.

She scoops my balls into her palm and gently massages, hauling me relentlessly toward my own release. But I'm not ready, so I shove her back and break the seal she has on my cock.

"Do I taste good to you?" I set my fingers on her tongue, digging them to the base of her throat. "You keeping count?" I fist her hair and jerk her up, crushing her belly to mine. "That's five to zero so far, right?"

She wraps her arms over my shoulders and hungrily latches onto my lips.

"Five to zero, and you're a squirter." I bite her bottom lip. "Now I want you to squirt on my face. I wanna drink you down, Fox."

"So get behind me." She fists my cock, gripping tight enough to draw my heart to a dead standstill. Then she runs the pad of her thumb over the head, collecting my pre-cum before bringing it up and placing it on my tongue. "What's good for me is good for you, right?"

"You act like I don't wanna taste that." I tear her closer and suckle her tongue. "Babe, I will come in your asshole and eat it out again. I don't give a fuck."

She trembles in my arms, her cheeks burning a rosy red and her eyes glowing with hunger. Then she slides my hand around to her ass, hitching her leg on my hip and opening herself wider until I find her plug. "So do it." She quivers, not because of my fingers, but because of our new position and the head of my cock teasing her pussy. "I love it when you eat me," she purrs. "I've never come so many times in my life, but you know exactly what I need."

"Coming in you means no rubber." I take her nipple between my teeth, suckling and biting. "No rubber means no protection."

"You got anything I need to know about?" She angles back, resting her head on the shower wall and arching her spine to present her tits for me to feast. "Any diseases we should discuss?"

"No." Her fiery pussy summons my cock. Her tight folds, so fucking close. "I'm clean. You?"

"I'm good. I have an IUD, yearly screeners, and a clean bill of health." She reaches between us and fists my dick, and because she's a woman who likes evenly attended to nipples, she forces me across to the other. "Fuck me, Chris. Make it hurt."

"You're really bossy, you know that?" I shove her to the shower wall and follow her in, swallowing her exhale and cupping her tits in my hands. But I'm not done tasting her yet, so I crouch and dig my arms under her legs, lifting and burying my tongue between her thighs. She cries out in surprise, then pain, when her shoulder hits the shower spout, knocking it from the holder until the end snakes wildly out of control.

"I'm not gonna get enough of you today." I nip at her throbbing clit and drink her delicious nectar. I slide my tongue along her slit and play with her ass and the plug she doesn't get to remove until I'm ready to let her go. "I could make you come thirty times in thirty different ways, and I'd still feel like I didn't get enough."

Crying out, she fists my hair with one hand and places the other flat against the ceiling for balance. And because she's a thirsty girl, she grinds her hips against my mouth. "Jesus."

"I want six weeks of this." I suckle and draw her to a trembling, shivering mess, panting for air and bathing me in *her*. "Be mine for six weeks, Fox. Whenever I fucking want you. Wherever. No matter how often I ask."

She gulps and licks her lips, rewarding me with a jerky nod. "You want to fuck, we'll fuck."

"Even if you're annoyed by me. In fact," I drop her leg off my shoulder and enjoy her frightened yelp, then I lower the other side and catch her before she hits the tile floor. Finally, I look into her dazed eyes and smirk. "*Especially* when you're annoyed by me. Turn." I grab her by the throat and spin her around, and just like when we began, I place her hands on the rails and make damn sure she's holding on. "No condom. You sure?"

"Yes." She chokes out the word, grinding closer against my cock. "I'm sure."

"Plug stays in." I fist my length and find her cream-covered opening. "Hold on," I grit out. "I've waited too fucking long for this."

She re-fastens her grip, wrapping her fingers around the steel rails.

"You need gentle?" I nudge the head of my cock against her fiery opening, groaning at the instant tight squeeze. "You afraid?"

"Go slow the first time." She gasps for every inch I claim, hissing at the wide flare of the plug and its unrelenting intrusion. "Just for the first time until we—"

I fill her, cruel and careless, and bury myself to the hilt. Her scream is fuel for a man as twisted as me. It's pleasure for someone who knows nothing else.

"I'm not sorry." I draw back and tighten my grip on her succulent hips, then I slam forward and claim her again. "I could lie, but that would be dumb. I *want* you to know I'm not."

She gasps for air, choking and coughing in an attempt to fill her lungs. And because I love to be an asshole, I circle her throat with my palm and drag her up until her new stance squeezes me tighter.

"You're the most responsive woman I've ever known." I play with her clit and drive my hips upward. "Fuck, Fox. I gotta be careful, or I'm never gonna let you go."

She whimpers, bucking in my arms and wrenching on the handrails until the tiles surrounding them crackle.

"I want you to swallow my cum." I ride her, brutally aware I'll soon lose my battle against willpower. "I want you to leave this bathroom with my seed sliding down your throat and sitting heavy in your stomach."

"You want me to suck your cock again?"

"No." I walk two fingers away from her clit and down to where my cock enters her. Then I slip those inside, too, stretching her wider and earning a cry of pain from the depths of her throat. "No, I'm gonna come inside you. Then I'll eat it out and feed it back to you." I'll be done in a minute. Two at the most. "And twenty minutes from now, once we've caught our breath, I'm gonna start again and make sure I've tasted you all over."

"Chris—"

Thirty seconds before I lose all control.

"And later, I'll fuck you again. I'll come in your asshole and do the same. And maybe, for date night, I'll drive you to the next town over and we'll find you a new plug. A pretty one."

"Oh, god—"

"One with a remote control, so I can torment you even when I'm not fucking you."

"Chris." Her breath comes shorter. Choppier. And when I add a third finger, she tears the handrail clear off the fucking wall.

We stop, stunned, torn out of our pleasure for half a beat. Then I bark out a laugh and ride her all over again.

"You just bought us a little more time."

"I broke it." She heaves for new air, her chest and shoulders growing and shrinking with her lungs. "Holy shit. I'm gonna get in trouble for that."

"Focus on me." I grab her throat and cut her off, which has her pussy shuddering and her eyes whipping back to mine. "When I'm fucking you, you'll pay attention *only* to me. I don't care if the building is on fire." I slam my tongue inside her mouth and suckle. "I won't have it any other way."

"Chris—"

"Tell me you're sorry."

"I'm..." She pants. "What?"

"Tell me you're sorry for not doing as I want. For not paying attention to me."

"No, I—"

I pull out of her cunt and revel in her cry of torment. I slam her back against the shower wall, but I don't chase her in. I don't refill her sweet pussy.

Instead, I grab her throat and wait for her brain to realize no new air passes through.

"Tell me you're sorry. And that you won't get distracted again."

She drops her hand, desperately searching between her legs and bringing herself pleasure.

So I slap it away and groan at her cry of surprise. And pain.

"Tell me you're sorry, Fox."

"I'm sorry." She licks her lips and studies my eyes. "I'm sorry for not focusing on you."

"Now beg me to fuck you."

She shudders under my touch, her lashes coming down to kiss her fiery cheeks. But her lips curl with a deliciously tormenting smirk. "Please fuck me. I'm begging you to fuck me. Then eat me. Then feed me."

"Yeah." I pick her up and slam inside her, spreading her legs wide enough that I get to play with the plug too. "You'll remember this." I swing her around, too fast to be safe, then I crouch and set her on the floor, folding her knees over her chest until she's mine. A fucking buffet set out purely for me.

"Jesus Christ." I lower to my knees, broken shards of tile cutting into my skin, and yet, I ride her like a madman. "You're perfect, Fox." I watch her bouncing tits and desperately wish for her tongue in my mouth. But I'd have to trade her legs to reach, and I'm not willing to give up this view. "You got one more left for me? Cream one more time, beautiful."

"Chris—"

"One more." I slap her clit and throw my head back, roaring up at the ceiling and filling her cunt with my seed until it squeezes free and smears my crotch. "Yes." I twitch with every spark of electricity pulsing in my veins, and because my balls are keen, I cum a little more. "Fuckkkkk," I moan, my voice turning hoarse from the pain. "Such a good pussy."

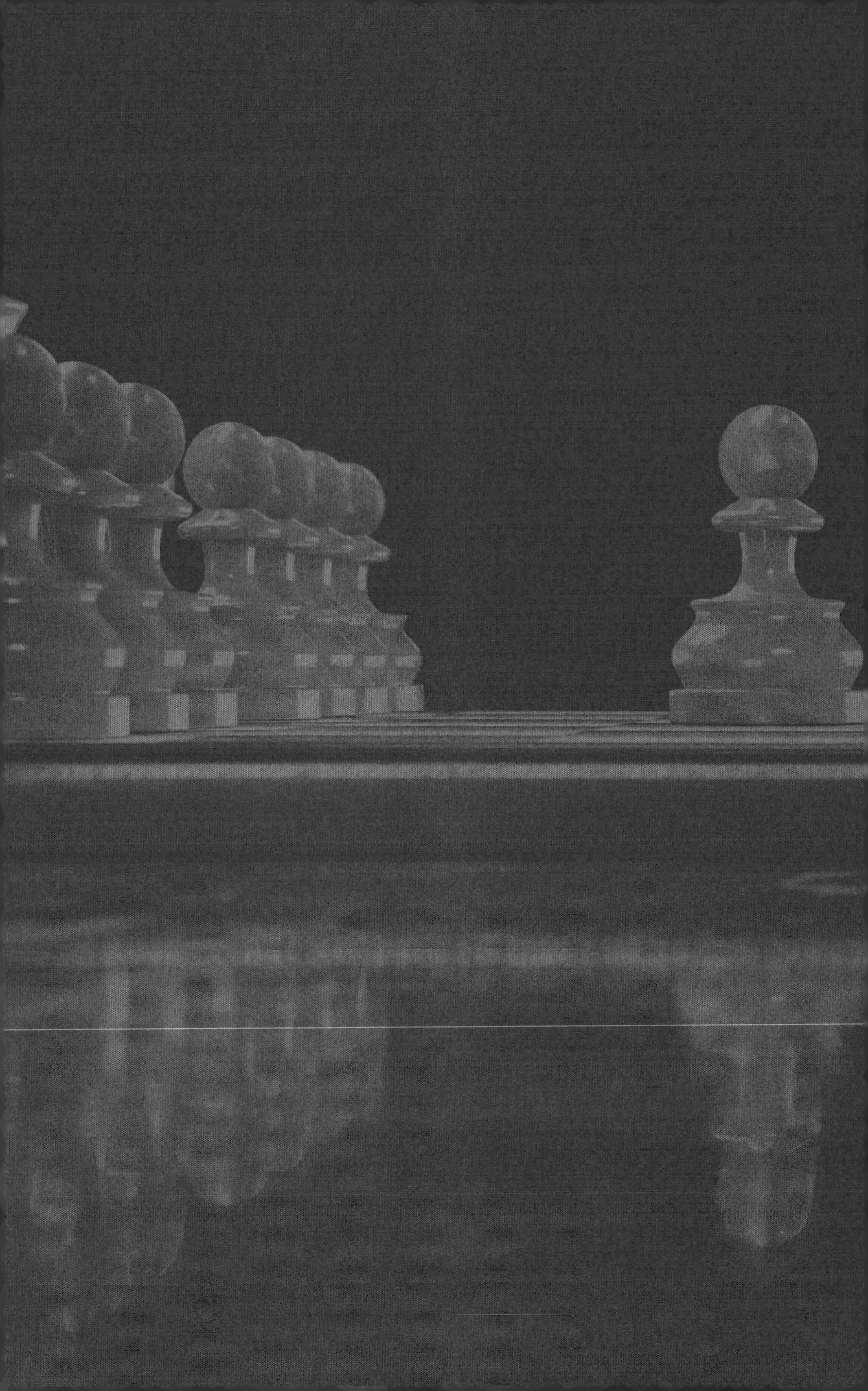

ROUND THIRTEEN
FOX

What have I done?

What epic lines have I crossed?

And hell, do I regret it?

Oddly, while I lie in the center of the bed Chris made up for me before I ever stepped foot in this apartment, the soft finish of expensive sheets tickling my skin, I look down my nose at his single pointer finger, tracing the ink that sneaks around my ribs and onto my back, and though I search for it, I can't find a single shred of remorse for what we've just done.

I'm still stuck on the mind-numbing effects of being fucked most of the way to death.

"This one?"

Lazily, I lift just my head and peek down at the cherry blossom hidden amongst my plethora of floral reminders.

"Japan." I flop back to my pillow and melt into the silky softness, running my fingers over the smooth finish while Chris runs his over my flesh. "I have chrysanthemums in there, too, to commemorate my trip."

"And the lotus?"

I exhale a contented sigh and hum in the back of my throat. "India. I already said: I've been everywhere."

He's so handsome in the afternoon light, his dark hair just long enough to dangle over his forehead and catch in his eyelashes. His lips are thick, plumper now because I bit them a time or two. But his eyes, the beautiful hazel I've seen in no one who doesn't possess the Watkins blood... those are my favorite.

"The iris?"

"France." I reach across and stroke his strong jawbone with my thumb. And like a kitten, he leans into my touch. "I've traveled a lot for work," I mumble. "Figured I'd get some ink to commemorate it."

"There are a lot of flowers here."

I breathe out a long, soft, satisfied exhale. "The world is a large place, and everywhere has something pretty to remember it by."

"I wouldn't know." He turns his face and nips at the heel of my palm. "Before I was eighteen, I hadn't gone further than the town I picked you up from the other day."

"And now?"

He grunts. "Now, I fly out only when I have to, depending on where we're fighting."

"Vegas only?"

He shakes his head and trails his lips along my wrist. Biting, then kissing. Pain, and then pleasure. "Montreal year before last. Thailand, the year before that. I prefer to stay here, though."

"You don't like to travel?" I can't relate, so I sink deeper into the mattress and enjoy the sensation of his teeth working along my hipbone. "It's one of my favorite things to do."

"I don't like planes. They're cramped and smelly and almost always come with nasty germs." He brings his eyes up, darker than usual, and grins. "Even first class: same plane, same germs. Just larger seats."

"Maybe you should buy a private jet," I tease, goosebumps sprinting along my skin because of his feather-soft touch. "Tommy makes enough, doesn't he?"

"Yeah. But we don't waste." He peppers his lips over my pubic bone and down to my thighs. "You done traveling yet? Since you got 'em all."

I tilt my head to the side and glance out the window at the far end of the room, the sun glaring right through now that afternoon winds toward evening. "I fly a couple of times a year for work, since GGH has offices in Paris, London, and Rome. It's especially fun when I get to travel on someone else's dime." Smug, I bring my eyes back to his. "Those business class seats are lush."

My stomach rumbles, loud enough to prompt him to turn and get up, but I grab his wrist and pull him back down again, drawing him closer until his lips naturally fall to mine.

"You're hungry."

"I'll get it in a second." Once we leave this bed and go back to the real world, I'm not sure either of us will know how to be who we are right now. Oddly, I'm shocked at how scared I am that we'll return to the Fox and Chris from earlier.

And then, of course, there's the part of me that *wants* us to return to that version of us.

It's safer. It's normal.

"I need to pee," I murmur, "then I'll grab a quick snack before we have to go back to the hospital." I press one last kiss to his lips, then I twist from beneath his weight and set my feet on the shag rug someone cared enough to put under my bed, so the first thing I touch each morning won't be buffed concrete floors.

Thoughtful.

Pushing up to stand, I wander toward the end of the bed, while behind me, Chris flops into my spot and turns to his back, his cock lying limp and thick against his hip.

"You pick those sheets out yourself?" I walk naked, since he's not done looking, and I'm not especially excited with the idea of fabric touching my sensitive skin anyway. Heading to the fridge, I tug it open and find a pre-made salad in an air-wrapped container with a use-by date ending tomorrow. I grab it and a bottle of dressing from the door. "It's not that I'm complaining about the sheets at Tommy's house, but these…" I set my things on the counter, peel the plastic off the salad, and crack open the bottle of dressing to pour on top. "These sheets are *far* superior."

"Tommy doesn't seem to mind what he's sleeping on, so long as Alana's in the bed with him. He wouldn't care if their mattress was made of broken glass and an itchy bale of hay."

"You, on the other hand?"

He sets his hands under his head and crosses his feet at the ankles. "I don't spend my money on much else but expensive fabrics…" Lazy and pleased with it, his lips curl up into a handsome grin. "That's where I draw the line. Cheap sheets would make it impossible for me to sleep. Cheap shirts would send me nuts by the end of the day. I buy quality for the important things."

"You use your world-travel budget for fancy linen instead." I drench the lettuce and croutons and robotically open drawers until I find the one with silverware.

Whatdoyaknow. I get to use the forks with little diamond designs here, too.

Snorting, I grab one and stab it into my meal, then picking the container up, I turn and shovel lettuce into my mouth. "I guess you supplied the silverware too, huh?" I chew like a cow out to pasture, noisily and with my mouth open, and while I saunter back toward the bed, I stack and stab more onto the fork. I set one knee on the mattress when I arrive, extending my offering with a smile. "You haven't eaten either."

Pleasantly surprised, he pushes up to his elbows and accepts his lunch with a seductive roll of his lips circling the fork. "Lettuce is not a meal," he murmurs. "You need meat."

"There's more than lettuce in this." I stab some more and shove it into my mouth, and while he chews his, I stand again and turn toward the bathroom. "I see carrot, sprouts, croutons. Bell peppers, too, and some weird seed-looking thing."

He reaches into his mouth and takes out whatever the seed is. "Nasty."

"Says the guy who eats ass without complaints." I come to the bathroom door, fully prepared to sit on the toilet and eat while I pee, but I stop at the threshold as a thousand glittering shards of glass bring me up short, the old silver hardware resting on top of the ruins. "What the hell happened to the shower door?"

"Broke it."

Stunned, I lean back and spy him lazily stretched across my bed, his hands behind his head and his ankles crossed once more.

"How?" I exclaim. "I was with you the whole damn time!"

Smirking, he shrugs and sends his powerful chest rippling. "I guess I slammed my knee against the door near the end. You were focused on me, so I suppose you didn't notice."

"How does someone not notice something like that? And oh my god!" I gasp, slamming my hand to my mouth. "What the hell do I tell Alana? We destroyed her bathroom!"

Snickering, he digs lettuce from his teeth with the tip of his tongue. "We'll come up with something. It'll be fine."

"Christian!"

"She had a baby today. She won't step foot in this place for weeks, and she'll be too sleep-deprived to care even when she does. Now come back over here and sit on my face so I can eat."

I roll my eyes and dig into my salad for more. "You need real food. Not pussy. And I need a shower—like, a *proper* shower—so I can get dressed and head back to the hospital."

"Put something on, and I'll take you to my house. You can shower there, and in the meantime, I'll have someone come out and clean up this bathroom, so it's safe again."

"How do I tell Alana I tore the rail off the wall and broke her door, without telling her I was having wild sex with her brother-in-law in there?"

His eyes glitter with taunting menace.

"I'm not telling her I was having wild sex with her brother-in-law in there!" Frustrated, and hungrier now than I was when I started eating, I scoop lettuce into my mouth and stalk to my suitcases laid out on the floor. "Also, I need meat. This salad isn't helping anything."

Chuckling, he sits up on the bed and looks me up and down with an appreciative gleam in his eyes. "Get dressed, and grab another outfit to change into. I'll take you to my place, you shower, I'll make you a meal with protein in it. Then we'll head back to the hospital."

"And pretend none of this ever happened." How does one bend over her suitcase, *naked*, without appearing ridiculously crass? "I made a promise," I admit. "Something about six weeks of banging whenever we're both in the mood."

"I don't recall mentioning moods. I specifically said you would become my fuck doll whenever I wanted you."

"However," I push on, dancing right over his words. "I don't want to tell Alana or Tommy about this. Alana, especially, is about to go through some shit with postpartum recovery and chronic sleep deprivation. The last thing she needs to worry about is her first baby—*you*," I add, peeking over my shoulder to confirm he's listening. "If she knows we're hooking up, she'll stress out about breakups and hurt feelings and all that jazz."

"We're gonna break up?"

"No. We're not." I poke through my luggage and select fresh underwear. "Because healthy, consenting adults having casual sex are not *together*, thus, there is no breakup to be had. There's just us, sneaking around every now and again, orgasming, and then moving on with our lives."

"Interesting."

"We're just two busy, intelligent, sex-starved adults with free will, who live a really, really far distance from one another but will enjoy five-and-a-half weeks of *that*." I point an accusing finger toward the bathroom. "More of that, please. At the end, you could probably drive me back to the airport and wish me good luck with the plane germs, and then it's done. Good terms, no mess, no fuss, and when I come back for Hazel's first birthday, maybe we'll pick up where we left off and destroy another shower."

"Sounds like you have it all planned out."

"I do." I snatch up a shirt and a pair of yoga pants that look kinda dressy when paired with a blouse.

Ish.

"The plan is to have no plan at all, except sex and orgasms and not stressing Alana out. That's what I'm agreeing to." I glance over my shoulder. "Deal?"

His lips curl into a smile, and his eyes glitter with something dark and dangerous. "Deal."

"Great. This salad is shit, by the way." I push it and the fancy diamond-decorated fork away, then I straighten out with my new clothes. "Let's go so we can get back to Franky before it's too late to feed him dinner."

"You're bossy, inside and out of the shower." He peels himself off the bed with a groan suited for an old man, then he wanders across the room, his well-hung dick lax between his legs. Unhurried, he stops behind me and drags my hair off my shoulder, before pressing a chaste kiss to the base of my neck. "Even if you didn't want to go to my place, we have to. My clothes and boots are wet."

"Sounds like you lack impulse control and a little button in the back of your brain that tells you to take your clothes off before you climb into the shower."

He grabs my ass and squeezes it in his broad, strong hand. "Bend over and show me that target, just like you did earlier, and I'll *always* choose impulse over sensibility. By that point, my dick is doing all the thinking, and even then, it's not thinking about laundry."

"You're needlessly horny." I step into my fresh underwear, pulling lace along my legs and up to sit on my hips. Then I work on my pants. "You're hot. You're successful. You're even kinda rich, which means you can buy an hour of a woman's time. Is there a reason you act like you haven't been laid in a year?"

"Dunno. Something about quality over quantity." He reaches around me and cups my boobs, chuckling when I drop my head back and meet his eyes. "Just holding them up for you. I like to be helpful when I can."

"Uh-huh." I smack his hands away and slide my arms into the straps of my bra. "Where can we get fast food in this shithole town? I haven't seen a single drive-thru in all the time I've been here."

"My house." He leans around and kisses my cheek. "I'll whip something up while you're in the shower. If you put your shoes on real quick, you can be sitting down to a meal fifteen minutes from now."

***

My stomach tingles, and my legs shake. My entire soul quivers at the knowledge of what Christian Watkins can do to my body. But I have a full belly and an encore performance playing on repeat in the front of my mind, but more than that, I have a responsibility to Franky and sheer determination not to let Alana know the craziness I've stepped into.

So I walk ahead of Chris into the hospital and pause by the locked doors so he can punch in the code to gain us entry into the inner sanctum.

"You smell nice." He walks a little too close for comfort, his chest brushing my back and his deodorant hitting my lungs for added impact. "You smell like my body wash now."

"I hope it's not too obvious." I paste on a fake smile and continue forward, only to stop again at the semi-familiar face that brightens when his eyes lift to ours.

"Ollie." Chris steps around me and pulls his friend in for a back-slapping hug. "I'm glad I caught you before you clocked out for the day."

"Clocked out?" He sets his hands on his hips. "Dude, I didn't even clock in yet. Or out. Or in." He shakes his head. "I've lost touch with reality. What day is it?"

"Sunday. You delivered my baby niece today."

"That was today?" Surprised, he scrubs his hands over his eyes. "Feels like a lifetime ago."

"You did good." Chris settles back on his heels, his shoulder brushing mine. "Thanks for taking care of them."

"No problem. And I won't even send them a bill, since I kinda screwed up their lives once already." Delirious, he brings his gaze across to mine. "Fox, right?"

"Right." I accept his hand and hold on to his jerky, almost painful shake. "Fox Tatum. We met at Alana's mom's funeral."

"Yeah, I remember. Good to see you again." He releases me and yawns. "I'm just finishing up my charts, then I was planning to head in and see them. Nurses say the baby is doing well."

"We've been out the last couple of hours," Chris murmurs. "But I got a bunch of time with her this morning. Healthy as a horse, chunky enough to boast extra chins, and Alana looked good, too. She looked better than Tommy."

Ollie snorts. "That's 'cos Tommy was freaking the hell out and would've ended up with a concussion if I wasn't so busy catching his baby." He looks at me. "Was Chris as ridiculous on your watch? Because I met a new Tommy last night, and I'm pretty sure I wanna put him in a ditch because of it."

"I wasn't acting like—"

"Total whine-fest," I cut in. "He was pacing and panicking. Chewing his nails and eating his dinner with his hands. I had higher hopes for Tommy, seeing as how he was right here with Alana, and, well…" I scrunch my nose. "He's not Chris."

"Pacing is allowed! Pacing is a completely reasonable reaction to worry."

"Figured." Ollie runs a hand over his stubbled chin. "Kinda cute how Chris thinks he's on Franky duty, when really, you're on Chris *and* Franky duty."

"Dude!"

"We know what's really up," I snicker. "But I'm told saying so out loud *hurts feelings*."

"Fuck this." Chris grabs my wrist and stomps past his friend. "If I'm going to be insulted, I'd rather take it while holding my niece." But then he stops and spins, waiting for Ollie's dazed eyes to come to his. "You didn't screw anyone's lives up, by the way. Stop with the shit."

"Pretty sure I did," he yawns. "I'm the reason Tommy left her that night. I'm the reason that prick got access and did the things he did. And then *I* dared to lecture *her* about leaving?" Disgusted, he shakes his head. "Jesus. Could I be more of a cock?"

"You didn't hurt her." I drag myself free of Chris' tight grip, and meander back to stand in front of Ollie. He's taller than me by several inches, muscular like Tommy and Chris, but he comes with the added bonus of no sleep since… the night before last. "I knew her after Plainview. I met the girl who ran away from this mess. The one who needed to find the good in humanity again."

"Don't. Please," he groans. "I don't wanna—"

"I had her for ten years, which means I'd met you all *long* before we ever came together in the same space. She told me about Tommy. And Chris. Raquel. Grady," I sneer. "The feral pig bastard."

"Deserves worse than he got," he growls. "Deserves *so* much worse."

"She told me about you, too, Ollie. The friend with two baby sisters he'd protect to the death. She told me about the guy who was always overly empathetic and kind, and she cried, terrified you'd find out how everything came to be. She *knew* you'd shoulder that blame, even though none of it was your fault."

"I was the key to what happened to her." He runs his fingers through his hair, tugging the locks until they stand on end and glow under the hospital hallway fluorescents. "She was assaulted, Fox, and a little baby boy was the result. If I'd behaved that night, or if I'd called literally anyone else, none of this would've happened."

"If you'd changed anything about that night, we wouldn't have Franky." I gently pat his shoulder. "It sucks, I know. But we're here now, and we wouldn't trade that baby boy for anything. If you're struggling to overcome your guilt about all this, I suggest you talk to someone. For your own mental health. Alana has *never* held a grudge, and I have no reason to lie to you about that. Ask your sister," I wink. "She knows I say what I mean, and I punish those who mess with my family." I squeeze his muscular arm and wait for his tired eyes to come back to mine.

Doubt. Devastation. Hope, maybe. A tiny sliver of it.

Then I turn on my heels and wander straight past a watchful Chris. "I need to see my babies." I cup my mouth and speak barely above regular volume. "Franklin Page? Aunty Fox is looking for you."

Like I knew he would, he pokes his head out of Alana's room and stares me down, his glasses perched on the end of his nose and his lips flattened into unimpressed lines.

Because I'm embarrassing him.

"In here." He rolls his eyes and brushes my hand away. "Hazel's sleeping. But Mom said we can make any noise we want 'cos she's not gonna wake up from it."

"You were like that when you were a baby, too." I set my hand on the back of his neck and walk him in, only to find the exact scene I've imagined for most of a year already.

I'm a romantic at heart, and living through Alana's heartache for a decade left me wishing for better for her. So when I find Tommy laid out on Alana's bed, his shirt gone, his baby girl resting on his chest, and Alana's cheek on his shoulder, I feel like it was all worth it.

All the pain. All the tears and fears and the complete and utter devastation Alana carried for so long, worth it now that she has her family together.

In the quiet, Tommy lolls his head to the left and meets my eyes.

"Hey." Alana scans me up and down, her lips curling into a sweet smile. "You were gone awhile. Started to think you'd jumped on a plane and left me for New York."

"No chance." I release Franky and stroll toward the bed. *How many boundaries do I disrespectfully dance upon now that I'm in the same room as a shirtless Tommy Watkins, while my body still tingles after being destroyed by Christian Watkins...*

So many boundaries. So much disrespect.

"I'm not leaving a single day before my six weeks end." I place my fingers on Hazel's chubby cheek and stroke. "I've been counting down to this vacation. No way I'm giving any of it up."

"Kinda worried you and Chris had turned on each other," Tommy jokes. *Oh God, if only he knew.* "Not sure who would win that battle, but seeing as how we don't wanna lose either of you…"

"You should *definitely* worry about him most of all. I've got street smarts and a lead foot that's known to run men down in broad daylight."

"She's talking about you," Franky mumbles.

I twist and glance over my shoulder to find Chris standing in the doorway, his shoulder resting against the frame.

"That was a threat," the boy continues. "Don't give her the car keys."

Amused, Chris folds his arms and smirks. "I think I'll be okay. I'll keep an eye out for speeding cars, just in case." He lifts his chin. "Hazel still as cute as she was a couple of hours ago?"

"Cuter," Tommy hums, patting her butt. "She's pretty perfect."

My mind obsesses over the sound of Chris' footsteps on the linoleum floor. Then his warmth, his chest almost touching my back as he comes to a stop behind me. He places a subtle hand on my shoulder, pushing me down when my nervous system would have me jumping clear off the ground. And though my heart thunders annoyingly loud between my ears, he merely smiles.

"Can I hold her?" His breath hits loose tendrils of hair that tickle my neck, his vulnerability a sweet reminder of who he is beneath that man I spent the afternoon with. He's sweet and sour, wrapped up in one human being. Hot and cold. Intensity and lazy days. "Just for a few minutes," he murmurs. "'Cos then we gotta take Franky home and get him some dinner."

"Only because I've had her for three hours straight." Carefully, Tommy peels the baby off his chest and maneuvers her into Chris' arms, and because Chris happily plays along with my *let's not tell Alana* ruse, he practically knocks me out of the way to get a better position with his baby.

"You *are* cuter than before." He brings her higher and presses a gentle kiss to her forehead. "Oh my goodness, Hazel Fox. You are the cutest niece in the world."

Hazel Fox.

"I forgot you did that." Pleasure ripples through my blood and out to the tips of my fingers, so when Tommy sits up and shrugs on a shirt, climbing off the bed because he's a good guy who knows his place within this dynamic, I slide into his place and snuggle in with my best friend. "Holy shit, Lana, you named your baby after me."

"It sounds good, huh? Hazel Fox." She yawns, turning to her side and using her hand to prop up her face. "I knew right away what her name would be."

"I'm honored." I turn to my side, too, giving the guys my back, and take her free hand with mine. "There's nothing on the planet anyone could gift me that would mean more than this."

"Really?" She searches my eyes, though bags sit beneath hers and create deep shadows that tell me how truly tired she is. "Because I was meaning to ask if you'd be her godmother, too." She smacks her lips, lazily exhaling. "But if you're not interested, since the name thing is all you—"

"Wait. What?" Frantic, I squeeze her hand. "Alana! What?"

"We wanted to ask you both," Tommy explains from across the room. "Alana chose Fox, and I chose my brother. Two sides to the family, so we know our bases are covered, and Hazel will be with people she loves if the worst happens."

"I'm already Franky's guardian." Tears swell in my eyes and leave my cheeks burning. "I get Hazel, too?"

"My babies are staying together. Forever."

"What does it mean to be someone's godfather?" Chris' deep voice rumbles differently than how I heard him *before*. Now, I feel less '*I want to mess with him,*' and more '*damn, his voice makes my stomach dip.*' "Specifically, what does it mean?"

"We mean it more along the lines of guardianship," Tommy clarifies. "Godparent is a religious thing, but our intentions are that if anything happens to us, we know the kids will be with people we trust. You'll send each other crazy trying to figure it out," he chuckles. "But we know every argument you have will be because you're fighting for what's best for the kids."

"Unless I'm eighteen," Franky inserts smugly, pulling his feet up on the chair and resting a book on his knees. "If I'm eighteen when they die—"

"Not that we're planning for anything to happen to us," Alana drawls. "Don't get too far ahead of yourself, honey."

"*If* something happens and I'm already eighteen, I become Hazel's guardian. 'Cos she's *my* baby sister."

"You'll help him," Alana whispers. "And you're not allowed to kill Chris."

"I'm honored." I crawl closer and press a smiling, noisy kiss on her forehead. "I accept. And I probably won't kill Chris. Unless he makes a big deal about silverware again, in which case, I'll use my fork to puncture his leg."

"She's all talk." Chris rocks the baby and wanders around the room, smirking when he's on Alana's other side and winking when I'm the only person in the world who can see him. "I'm ready for your attacks, Tatum. Though I'm starting to think you're nothing more than a kitten."

"Excuse you?"

"You got the claws, and you make the noises. But ultimately, you scare no one."

"Listen here." I shove up to my elbow and point a jabbing, dangerous finger in his direction. "You're just a—"

"No." Alana pinches my lips and drags me back down. "No bickering. It's my baby's birthday." She releases me and settles against her pillow, closing her eyes and exhaling a soft breath. "Also, you smell kinda nice. I told him to buy the frangipani soap when we were shopping, but I guess he bought his favorite instead."

"Samoa." He strokes Hazel's double chin and smirks, knowing Alana can't see him. "They have frangipanis in Samoa."

"They have frangipanis in lots of places," Franky adds dryly. "Like Hawaii, Australia, and The Solomon Islands. And Papua New Guinea. And The Cook Islands. And—"

"And Samoa," Chris counters. "I was just saying, is all."

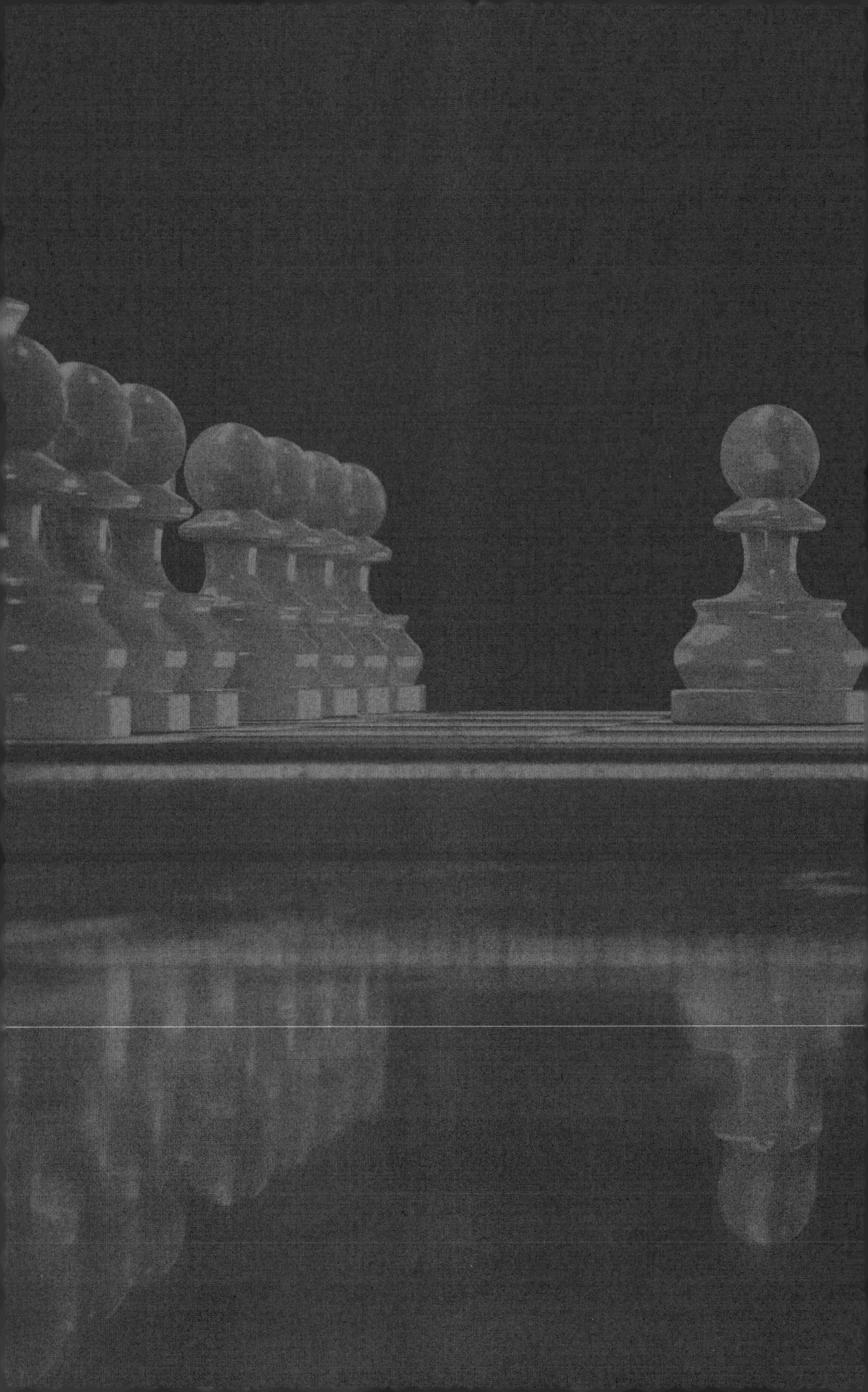

ROUND FOURTEEN
CHRIS

"Where the hell is it?" Fox searches her purse, pulling things out and dumping them on my kitchen counter. Lipstick rolls toward Franky's elbow, his face buried in a book, while a homemade pizza sizzles in the oven behind me. "Did you see Aunty Fox's pen, honey?" She slaps a stack of Post-its to the counter. "It was in my bag, but now I can't find it."

He clings to his pen, afraid she'll take it. "Nope. I've got my own."

"So where's mine?" She dumps a box of tampons beside everything else, then a notebook and a small diary with wrinkled pages and dog-eared folds. "Why is this so difficult?"

"It's just a pen, right?" I open my junk drawer and take out a spare. Blue. Boring. A perfect replacement for the one she lost. "Use this one."

"But I need to find *mine*. It has my teeth marks on the cap."

I set it on the counter and dig my hands into my pockets. "You want it back *because* of the teeth marks? Why not accept a new one and chew it to match?"

"Why not just mind your damn business and help me find *my* pen?" Yet, she snatches up my offering, grips it between her teeth, and goes to work packing away her mess. "I bet this one doesn't even feel good to write with. Comfortable pens matter, ya know?"

"You sound awfully cranky for a *chief happiness guru*."

Franky chokes out a silly giggle and hides within the pages of his book.

"Chief Happiness Officer," she snarls. "It's a real job."

"So use the skills you made up to get that job and apply them to your pen situation." Smug, I turn and make myself busy checking on our dinner. "What do you need to write down? There are electronic devices for that stuff nowadays anyway."

"I'm planning Alana's baby shower, and I don't have a bunch of time to get everything done."

"What baby shower?" Closing the oven, I straighten out and peek over my shoulder. "Hazel's already here. Showers are typically for *before* the baby arrives, no?"

"Typically." She flicks the cap off her new pen and whips open her notebook. "But Alana and Tommy aren't really the '*do things in the correct order*' kind of people, and if anyone wants to complain about celebrating Hazel's existence, then I'll introduce them to my fists."

She's cute. Fuck, she's cute.

I set my elbows on the counter and wait for her eyes. "Ever thrown a jab before in your life?"

"Not recently. But I have an arm and ten knuckles. I figure throwing is throwing, and the rest will take care of itself. Also, we need a venue: we're commandeering the gym for the party."

"Uh, hold up." I slap my hand over her notebook and earn a feral glare. "You're planning a party? And you're taking over my gym?"

"Tommy's baby, Tommy's portion of the gym." She flicks my arm away and goes back to writing. "Your niece. I'm certain you'll understand and realize sharing your portion of the gym will be okay."

"It's not so much about sharing anything and more about the fact you're planning a party I had no clue existed three minutes ago."

"Did Alana have a baby shower?" She glances at Franklin and arches a perfectly sculpted brow. "Did your mom have a party while Hazel was in her tummy, where people came and gave her gifts?"

Disinterested, he shakes his head. "No."

"See?" She hits me with a look. "She's had *two* babies and no parties. She deserves this."

"But she already has everything she needs. It's not like she can fit three more cribs in Hazel's room or another stroller in the trunk of her car. Tommy made damn sure she's set."

"It's not about the *things*. It's about *who* celebrates with you. It's about letting her experience something good in this podunk godforsaken town, and even if it pains me to know we'll have to include the gossipy Judgy McJudgersons who hang around Main Street all day, I hold out hope that you and Tommy will know some *other* people, too."

"No, I—"

"If you contribute nothing, and no one comes, and Alana feels unloved, *especially* after everything that happened last time she lived here," she looks into my fucking soul, narrowing her eyes to push her point home, "I'll make sure you pay in an extremely painful way. If, for any reason, Alana Page is made to feel less than wonderful for this one day of her life, I'll hurt you."

"You're mean." I back away from the counter and switch the oven off. *It's time to eat.* "You want a party? You can have a party. My gym, your gym."

"That's what I thought." Snarling, she grabs the pen and goes back to jotting down her notes. "So now that Hazel is here, she's a she, and we have a color scheme, we can talk about ordering a cake and decorations."

"Can get a cake from the place that does the shop pastries," Franky inserts in monotone. "Also, do I have to go to the party?"

"Yes. Name of the bakery?"

"*The bakery.*" I don an oven mitt and slide the pizza stone from the middle rack. "Plainview is a small town, Fox. *The bakery* is the only bakery. Head in and ask to speak to Pedro. He'll figure you out easy peasy."

"Great. And since it's so *easy peasy*, I'm officially putting you in charge of the cake."

Unimpressed, I straighten and turn to her with a sneer. "Seriously?"

"Yep. And before you ask, yes, you have to go to the party."

"Wasn't gonna ask." *I'll just hang out in my office and go on with my life.* "Color scheme is pink?"

"Color scheme is green," she drawls. "Pink is small town, small minds. Green will match her name, if not her eyes."

"Silly me." I set our dinner on the stove and come around to the silverware drawer, yanking it open and snatching out the pizza slicer that *tings* against the countertop when steel meets stone. "I can't believe I assumed pink was an appropriate color scheme for a girly party. When is it? Also, have you told Tommy?"

"The Saturday a week before I leave. That gives Alana time to settle in with the baby, and it allows for your invitees to RSVP and plan their travels."

"Travels?" I move back to the pizza and roll the slicer through. "Where the hell are they traveling from? We don't know people outside of Plainview."

"Alana knows plenty of people outside Plainview, and if you tried really hard, I bet you could think of some, too."

"You know fighters," Franky drawls, his tone as bland as if we were discussing dirt. *Actually, dirt would be more interesting.* "You know loads of fighters."

"And remind me again why the hell I would invite fighters from outside of Plainview for a baby shower for a baby who is already born to a woman they've never met?"

"Because if you contribute nothing, and no one comes, and Alana feels unloved, *especially* after everything that happened last time she lived here…"

"Fine." I wave her off and wish for bedtime-Fox. Sexy-time Fox. I'd even take sleepy-time Fox. Because any of those are preferable to rest-of-the-day Fox. "I hear you. I'll think of some folks and figure out a way to invite them without looking like a total fucking idiot."

"Thomas Watkins is the current world champion," she huffs. "I'm certain you could fill a stadium if you simply *spoke* to another human being."

Sleep escapes me for the second night in a row while frogs croak outside and the cicadas scream from the trees. A soft breeze knocks on the windows of Tommy and Alana's house—Franky wanted to sleep here, in his own bed, but only if Fox went upstairs with him—which means I sit on the couch, my body dug between the cushions and my legs spread wide apart.

I tap my fingers against the arm of the couch to a tune I don't even know, and while the clock *tick-tock-tick-tocks*, promising to steal my sanity, I simply… exist.

I fucking hate the nighttime.

"You look lonely." Fox's soft voice rolls through the dark, like a hug that wraps all the way around. A caress that touches a man's soul.

I tilt my head back and watch her, upside down, step off the staircase in a pair of tiny sleep shorts I'm pretty sure belong to Alana and a sports bra brandishing my own gym logo on it.

Fuck. Me. Please.

Smirking, she saunters around the couch with a seductive swing of her hips and a delicious arch in her back. She wears her hair in a messy bun atop her head and a spare scrunchie on her wrist, its stark blackness standing out against her pale skin.

"You often awake this late at night, or is it a new thing for you?"

"It's not uncommon," I grumble. *Despite my strict bedtime routine and the handful of melatonin I choke down every evening.*

She wanders around and stops between my legs, grinning and tilting her head to the side.

"Franky asleep?"

Nodding, she nibbles on her bottom lip. "Uh-huh."

"Are *you* often awake this late?" I surge forward and snag her wrist, then I pull her onto my lap, her excited exhalation, a sweet breeze hitting my face as I help her settle over top of me, her legs on either side of mine, and my hands on her hips. "How can you be a night owl and a morning person, all at the same time?"

"I'm not a morning person, typically. But the time difference makes it tricky to sleep past five." She grinds down over my cock. "I'm more of a stay-up-late kind of person, which is why I love my neighborhood. I haven't *not* discovered a new dessert during my middle-of-the-night explorations yet."

"That's not safe." I slide my hands along her bare thighs, drawing circles on her skin and creeping closer to find her warmth.

She came to me. Fuck it, I intend to claim what she so freely offers.

"You could get hurt doing that, Fox."

"And yet, I've never felt unsafe." She shudders under my touch, smiling in the dark like the vixen she is. "You told me to come to you."

"I did, didn't I?" I slip my fingers through the gap of her shorts and into her panties, only to find her wet and waiting. "You're still needy, even after today?" I slip my thumb into her pussy and elicit her explosive sigh. "Pretty sure I mentioned how hungry your cunt is."

"Funny, since I wasn't all that needy last week." She drops her head back and rides my digit, moaning with pleasure and swallowing, so I'm treated to a view of her bobbing throat. "Didn't realize how much I needed this until we started."

"Now you can't get enough." I unsnap my jeans with one hand, rolling the zipper down and freeing my cock. So full already. So hard and lined with thick veins. "Gotta keep it quiet this time. Making you scream is how we ruin a good time."

She reaches between her legs and drags my hand away, then she grabs my cock and pushes her shorts to the side, making room and lifting onto her knees. "Guess you're gonna have to be gentle this time." She brings hooded eyes down to look into mine, then she sinks and uses my hand to trap her cry behind closed lips. "Shit!"

I grit down on the yelp I want so badly to cough out. The shouted *fuck* bubbling at the base of my throat. And when she rides me, slow enough to torment us both, tight enough to play with my sanity, I simply sit back and watch the show she puts on.

Her stomach ripples. Her chest races, and her throat bobs. And because I want to see, I peel her sports bra up and allow her tits to fall free.

"You're so beautiful, Fox." I take her nipple between my lips and hold my breath, for fear of losing my load too soon. "So fucking infuriating."

"You mean infuriatingly beautiful?"

"No, I mean infuriating." I bite and slip my fingers into her mouth to shut her up. "You wanna know how many times you rolled your eyes at dinner?" I play with her tongue. "Six. I was counting. When we're alone, you're the most exquisite fucking creature I've ever met. But as soon as we're back in the real world and we have witnesses, you're a pain in my ass with a metric ton of sass and no '*off*' button when I need a little quiet."

She snickers, biting my fingers and suckling on the moist ends. "I could say the same about you. The *best* monster in bed, but an uptight, un-fun person in the real world."

"Better to be un-fun than a complete pest." I plant my feet on the floor and slam my hips upward, filling her pussy and stealing her breath. Then I take the scrunchie from around her wrist and tie her hands together behind her back. "When we're fucking, I lose a little of my soul to you. You're my siren, Fox, and I have no fear of death in the ocean. But when we're not fucking, you're my demon succubus, and I genuinely think you hope to send me to the asylum before you're done."

"I'm just me," she whimpers, creaming on my cock. "I'm the same, no matter where we are or who we're with."

I hold her bound hands and reach around with the other to play with her ass. So ripe and inviting. So delicious and swollen and tempting.

She tips her head back, moaning. "Jesus."

"Want me inside you?" I play with her asshole, circling the outside and holding my release captive before I embarrass myself. "Too bad I didn't bring the bottle of lube. I'd pay a lot of money to fuck your ass again right now."

"Please... just..."

"This?" I slip a finger inside and groan at her wild bucking, her squeezing pussy. "You like that, huh?"

She pants, frantically nodding. "Yes."

"I bet I could sleep better with my cock in your ass." I draw my finger out and replace it with two, taking her nipple between my lips and suckling. "Fuck, I want a whole night to sleep inside you. Just to test it out."

She chokes out a soft, almost silent laugh. "Okay."

"I haven't slept a full night my whole life." I switch breasts and bite down. "The dark was always too scary. There were so many fucking bugs just waiting to crawl on my face."

She slows her hips, bringing her eyes back to mine... they shine with sympathy.

Fuck.

"Ignore what I said—"

"I can keep watch while you sleep." She uses her core strength and leans forward, taking my lips with hers. "I'll protect you. I promise."

"Climb off." Surprising us both, I lift her off my cock and destroy a moment that could almost be considered beautiful, then setting her on her knees on the floor, I move around behind her and shove the coffee table back to give myself room. Finally, I fold her over the cushions and fist her hair in my right hand. "I like hurting you." I slam inside her pussy and crush her face to the couch to muffle her scream. "I like making you cry."

"Chris—"

"I like taking your power and keeping it all for myself."

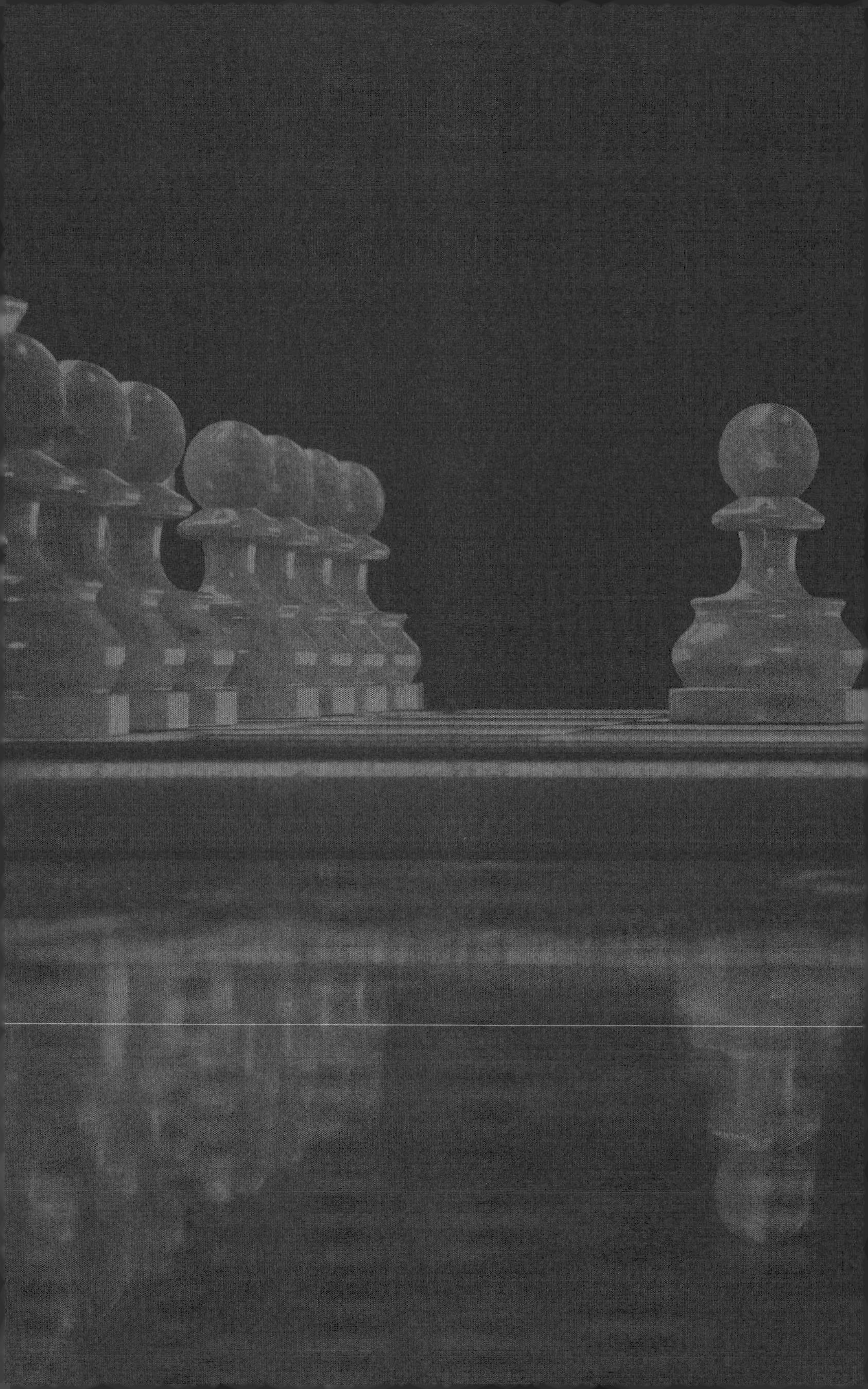

ROUND FIFTEEN
FOX

Plainview, in total, is about as big as a dozen New York City blocks, and most of the town itself is huddled within a three-block radius—the grocery store, library, police station, hospital, and Franky's school—all just minutes from each other. So although I have a car to use, I find walking from one destination to the next and enjoying the spring weather makes living here just a little more tolerable.

Snow stuck to the ground—according to Alana—all winter long. Several feet deep and heavy enough to make the old roofs creak. But spring is in full swing, and with it, beautiful flowerbeds and lush green grass.

I suppose, if I *must* acknowledge anything positive about this town, it would be that spring makes for a stunning backdrop, and waking on the lake, enjoying a coffee on the porch with fuzzy socks wrapped around my feet to keep them warm makes for a good way to start a day.

Those Watkins brothers knew *exactly* what they were doing when they graduated from boys to men, buying up all the good real estate before anyone else thought to slide in and take it.

Now that it's Monday, life restarts despite the woman still recovering in her hospital bed. Chris woke at stupid o'clock this morning, escaping Tommy's house before the sun truly came up, and went about his routine of tiring himself out before his *actual* job of working out begins. Franky whined about school and how he shouldn't have to go—*because he wants to see Hazel*—and I... well, I have a bookstore to manage, and I have to do it knowing I didn't listen the way I should have when Franky was teaching me the ropes.

But none of that really matters right now, because I doubt Mondays are particularly busy in the book world. I walk Franky to school and leave his pouty-butt behind with a smirk plastered across my lips and a skip to my steps, and wandering Main Street, I discover *the bakery* by following my nose.

Curious and desperate to taste the coffee that corresponds to the delicious scent of roasting beans traveling along the street, I step inside, only to smack my toes on the tiny lift in the tiles only a local would know about. I hiss and hold my breath, gritting my teeth and counting through the twenty seconds of pain that ricochets throughout my foot. Tears well in my eyes, and when I bring my gaze up, I find a bakery bustling with chaos.

And unfortunately for me, thirty stares pointed back at me.

Customers place their orders, some line up for service, and others sip their coffees. They gossip and smirk, whisper, and blatantly talk about me like I'm not here. Pastries exchange hands, and to-go cups are filled, and though my foot aches, I shake the pain away, determined to join the end of the long line that moves surprisingly fast. And though my heart pounds, I lift my chin and pretend that I don't care about the small-minded idiots who refuse to stand too near.

Do I have leprosy or something? Fuck.

I wait patiently and move closer to the front counter, and when it's my turn to be served, I smile at the attendant and note her youthful face. *She can't be more than a teen, surely.* "I'll have whatever that garlicky-smelling pastry is, please. And a cup of coffee."

"Sure thing. You're Fox Tatum, right? Alana's friend."

"I am." I cock my hip and rest against the stainless-steel counter. "People usually say it like '*you're that Fox Tatum, aren't ya? From New York.*'" I add a nasally drone to my voice. "'*We don't like you, 'cos you're not from 'round here.*'"

She snickers, bagging my breakfast with a fast flip of her wrists. "People around here can get a little funny about city folks." She sets my pastry on the counter and slides across to begin steaming milk at the industrial-sized machine. "I'm not eighty-seven years old, though. And I'd *kill* to live in New York. There's a saying about attracting flies with honey, no?"

"How old are you?" I snag my breakfast and tear off a little of the garlicky bread. "High school, right?"

"I'm in tenth grade." Her eyes swing to the clock above the door, her cheeks warming because we *both* know she's late. "I have a study period first thing on Mondays, so I stay here a little longer and help my mom and dad. I'll walk to school soon."

"What do you want to do when you get to New York?" Screw anyone still waiting to be served; this kid might become my only friend inside this town other than Alana, so I settle in and nibble while she works. "Will you go to college?"

"I would *love* to get into the Fashion Institute so I can design clothes."

"For the runways?" I take another look at her outfit, all but hidden behind a flour-covered apron, and find cute black cargo pants with silver chains hanging from her pockets and buttons pressed along the legs. She wears a chunky belt, almost two inches wide, and a form-fitting black shirt that leaves an inch of her stomach showing and boasts what I think might be a unicorn riding a rainbow right across her chest.

She's got a rainbow-magic goth look going on. And hell, maybe it's not *my* kind of look, but I'll be damned if it isn't *a* look.

Like her, it's cute as hell and makes a statement.

"I think you already have a firm stance on fashion," I decide, "and you should totally explore that more."

"My parents don't like what I wear." She speaks, not with a disappointed lilt in her voice, but with the clear, concise repetition of facts. Seems she's accepted their opinion. "They think I should stay here and take over the bakery so they can retire. But I dunno." She shrugs, switching off the steamer and pouring hot milk into a to-go cup. "I appreciate getting to work here because I've been saving my money. But it's not what I want forever."

"I understand that." I tear off a little more pastry and set it on my tongue. "I think everyone should experience life outside their small town at least once."

She scoffs. *Not my parents.*

"That doesn't mean you have to stay away. But there's a whole wide world outside of Plainview. It would be a shame to never see it. I feel kind of lucky because I've traveled almost *everywhere* in the last few years."

Her eyes widen, brimming with excitement.

"It's beautiful out there," I sigh. "I cherish my memories and the photos stuck in my cloud storage I'll probably never look at again."

She snorts. "You're kind of my hero, and we hadn't even met five minutes ago."

"Well, you know my name, and you probably know where I'm staying. I'll be at *Happily Ever After* from nine till five, five days a week. I bet there are books there about the Fashion Institute of Technology. And France," I tease, since any aspiring designer dreams of visiting Paris in the spring. "You should drop by, since you're literally the only nice person I've met here besides my best friend."

She sprinkles a little chocolate on top of my milk froth and caps the cup, then she slides it across the counter and taps my purchase into the register. "My name is Raya. Collins," she adds as an afterthought. "I might swing by the bookstore sometime."

"Good." I wave my card over the reader and wait for it to beep and take my money, then I set everything back in my bag. "Oh, and since you're nice and all that, you should know about the party I'm planning for Alana."

"A party?"

"Mmm. The baby's here, and it serves as no surprise whatsoever that those Watkins boys didn't even consider a baby shower to honor her. So a month from now, I'm having a little shindig over at the gym, and since I don't hardly know anyone, I'm inviting you."

"At the gym?" She squeaks. "The war room gym?"

"Uh…" I wrap my hand around my coffee and carefully drag it closer. "I thought it was called Love & War?"

"It is." She waves me off. "But locals call it the war room. You're having a party there? Where the Watkins twins will be?"

"Well, one of the Watkins twins is the baby daddy, so… sure." I flash a teasing smile. "It would be best if he were there. And while we're on the topic, Chris Watkins is in charge of ordering a cake. I'm told this is where he'll come, and he *swears* he'll take care of it. But if he fails to do what needs doing by the end of next week, maybe you could let me know?" I lean against the counter and roll my eyes. "He's allergic to talking to other human beings, I think, and he might let this detail slip. I'm not his mother, which means I refuse to nag him. But if he fumbles, give me a head's up so I can take care of it."

"Sure." She brushes flour off her apron and massages her bottom lip between her teeth. "I'll keep an eye on the situation."

"Excellent. Oh, and do you know any handymen around town?"

She frowns. It's entirely possible she considers me insane, jumping from topic to topic. "Uh, I guess I'd have to know what exactly you need help with."

"A mini-bathroom renovation." My stomach tumbles, and my pulse quickens because, damn, I still feel Chris Watkins between my legs. I feel his cock filling me all over. His hands on my flesh. I feel the bruises he left behind, and, more importantly, the absolute knowledge he knows how to destroy me in all the best ways. "I need tiling repairs," I mutter, brushing a hand over my lips to muffle my words from listening ears. "And a new shower door installed. The sooner, the better."

"Well…" She nibbles on her pinky finger. "I'm not sure. But I'll have a think about it and let you know."

"You're the best." I glance over my shoulder and find a long line of customers tapping their toes and not-so-patiently waiting for their turn to be served. So I grin and bring my eyes back to Raya. "Thanks. Do you work here every morning?"

"Seven days a week. I have class earlier on Tuesdays and Thursdays, but every other day, I stick around till about nine-thirty."

"So maybe I'll see you every other day." I dig a hand into my purse and search for some cash, and when I find it, I slide a ten-dollar bill across the counter. "For such good customer service, and hopefully the start of a Raya-goes-to-New-York fund."

"Thanks." She slips her bounty into the pocket of her apron and blushes. "I really appreciate it."

"No problem. Don't forget the cake situation. I'm begging you."

She giggles. "I won't."

I take my things and meander toward the door, passing curious stares and beady-eyed scrutiny. Some of the dozen in line watch me with obvious distrust. Others look down their noses despite the fact I'm physically taller than them. One even drops his chin and avoids meeting my eyes.

And *none* show any concern when I slam my toe on that fucking step, as the pain steals my breath and draws me short. "Shit!" I skip through the doorway, spilling my coffee and burning my hand. "Dammit!" Limping onto the sidewalk and wiping the spilled coffee onto my pants, I turn right and trudge my way toward the bookstore.

I could grumble under my breath, growling about this shitty town. I could mass-text my friends and tell them this place sucks. Hell, I could scream in the middle of the street, confident I wouldn't even get hit by a car, since traffic here is less common than a horse-drawn cart.

But then again, Plainview seems to be on a mission to break me, and knowing my luck, the moment my feet touch the tar, a fleet of carts is apt to run me down.

Instead, I eat my pastry and continue toward the bookstore, and when I remember I didn't spill *all* of my coffee, I sip the deliciously rich beverage and arrive at *Happily Ever After* in a fractionally better mood.

Chief Happiness Officer, indeed.

Juggling my breakfast and slipping a key into the lock, I push the door open and step inside, a broad smile stretching across my face, my mood soaring and my stomach tumbling, all because I cross the threshold and smell… us.

Me and Chris.

Not an overwhelming, nasty sex smell. But a sweet tang of body soap and excellent linen. It's salad dressing and long, drawn-out pleasure.

Jesus, it's nice. And if I'm not careful, that niceness will kick my ass and send my heart pitter-pattering all the way to the edge of a cliff just as soon as I'm back in New York, out of reach for the man whose hands worship. Whose eyes consume. Whose voice commands.

Shaking my head, I shut the door and leave the closed sign turned toward the street, then placing my coffee and half-eaten pastry on the counter, I cross the store and continue up the stairs and into my apartment, where the smell of us is richer. More concentrated.

I'm certain we left my bed unmade when we left yesterday, and I *know* I left my salad uneaten, with a fork still in it, sitting on the floor. But as I cross the threshold and wander through my kitchen, I come to realize Chris' early departure this morning might've led him here.

Curious, I set my bag on the counter by the sink and quickly grab the things I need for today—my phone and keys, plus my little notebook and Chris' pen—and digging them into my pockets, I stroll toward the bathroom with the memories of shattered glass playing through my mind. But reality leaves me with something far less hectic. The shower door is missing, of course, and the handrail sits on the floor. But the glass is gone. The shattered remains, swept up, so the danger is gone, and my ability to pee in my own bathroom, restored.

Did he come by because he's a clean freak? Or because he wanted to do something nice for me?

The former, probably. But the fact he could walk away from it all yesterday was, in itself, a surprise I didn't dare vocalize for fear of ruining an amazing afternoon.

Christian Watkins is the perfect lover. Determined to please and demanding in all the best ways. When his dick is hard, and his hands are grabbing, he's the kind of man I could get used to spending my time with. But when the sun is out, and the real world encroaches, he's a different person entirely. Nitpicky, cranky, unbending, and not really all that nice.

All because of parents who hurt their sons and a life that chose to be cruel, when those boys deserved so much better.

"Ah, well." Exhaling, I turn on my heels and make my way back through my apartment, through the door and pulling it shut when I'm on the other side, then down the stairs so I can honor Alana's need for her store to remain functional while she's out of action.

I open a few windows and turn the *closed* sign around. I power up the computer and switch on the coffee machine, and passing by the stereo, I flick it on, too, so music plays through the speakers perched in every corner of the store.

Not loud.

Merely present.

By nine-fifteen, the pastries arrive from the bakery, and by nine-thirty, I have the fridge stocked and customers perusing the shelves.

I've got this business on lock.

I spend a few hours serving and dropping cash into the register, but it takes just half a day to realize they come for a social life and not for the literature. Little old ladies create a book club, each of them balancing a tattered novel on their knees and a cup of coffee in their hands, and yet, the conversation is one percent about whatever Tolstoy wrote about and ninety-nine-point-nine percent whatever everyone else is doing around town.

I hear snippets about a doctor who lives in *the city*, who, according to Barbara, isn't really a doctor at all, but *we don't say so in front of her father*, because that creates rifts amongst the social circles. And I catch whispers about Alana and Tommy and how they *really should be married before making babies*, though the old bitches shut their traps when I *accidentally* slam their ankles with the vacuum cleaner.

Which makes me the *clumsy Yankee bitch.*

Proudly.

Eliza Darling is apparently dating someone named Roger—according to Betty. Ollie Darling is helplessly single—according to Gloria. And Christian Watkins is probably still a virgin—according to Henrietta.

Jesus Christ take the wheel. If their information on Chris is anything to go by, then Eliza is probably dating someone named Greg, and Ollie is probably set to marry a hooker.

My phone trills around two o'clock with a New York area code and a picture that leaves my cheeks aching, so I answer on the fly and keep my voice low enough that the book club from hell can't listen in. "Booker?"

He breathes out a satisfied, smiling exhale. "There she is. Tell me, Fox. How can it only be Monday, and you left on Friday, yet it feels like I haven't seen you in weeks?"

"It's only been two days?" I stop between two bookshelves and stare up at the ceiling in wonder. And confusion. "Really?"

"That's what I'm saying! Time has slowed down, and morale is plummeting. Even the stock market is crashing. We *need* you back."

"Oh, please." I lower my gaze and wander toward the back of the store. "You're being a little OTT. How are things over there in the land of the sane?"

"I'd much rather hear about you," he counters, laughing. "How's life in the middle of nowhere? What do you even do with your time? That's why it feels like forever, by the way. You have nothing to do and twenty-four long hours a day to do it in."

"My days are going fast and slow at the same time." I put the vacuum back on the charger and lean against the wall, taking a moment of privacy back here by the World History textbooks. *No one cares to read those*. "The baby arrived."

"Already? Alana's okay? And the baby?"

"Everyone is good. Alana was already having contractions by Saturday morning, was in labor all day, and then spat that baby out by three o'clock Sunday morning."

"Girl or boy?"

"Girl," I happily sigh. "And get this! Her name is Hazel Fox."

"No shit," he exclaims. "Awesome name to honor an awesome woman. Bet you cried, huh?"

"No. Misty eyed," I clarify. "I was surprised and got in my feels a little bit, but I didn't sob or anything weird like that."

He chuckles. "Strong name from a strong woman. Mom and baby are healthy?"

"Uh-huh. I spoke to Alana this morning before dropping Franky at school, and I'll take him over to the hospital this afternoon once I close the shop. She said Hazel's starting to wake a little bit more, and breastfeeding is going well. They expect to be able to come home either tomorrow or Wednesday at the latest."

"Why Wednesday if they're healthy?"

"Hazel's a little yellow," I shrug. "Doctor said it's normal and expected. And Franky was the same, so they're just keeping an eye on it. Otherwise, everyone is passing their tests and doing amazing."

"Send me an address." I don't have to be in his office to know he sits in his chair and grabs a pen. "I wanna send a gift."

"Or…" I tease. "You could hop a flight and visit. I'm throwing a little party for Alana and Hazel in a few weeks, and seeing as how I have no friends and could do with fattening the guest list a little…"

"What date?"

"Uh…" I pull the phone from my ear and quickly flick to my calendar app. "June seventh. I'll send you a formal invitation once I've designed them."

"Don't bother." His voice turns sad in an instant. He clicks his computer mouse, checking his schedule. "I have Rome on my calendar for the week leading into the seventh, then London right after for the Maher Conference. I have no room to sneak over to Bumfuck Idaho, not even for a day."

Disappointed, I flatten my back against the wall and exhale. "That's shitty. How dare they plan an annual event that clashes with my hastily put-together baby shower for a baby who has already arrived?"

He snickers. "Those inconsiderate bastards. Send me her address so I can have something delivered. Let me buy her forgiveness."

"Fine. But don't mention the party while you're asking for mercy, since she doesn't actually know about it yet." When the silence of the bookstore grows heavy, and that silence taps at the side of my brain, I snap my lips closed and angle away from the wall. Just like I knew I would, I lock eyes with the book club bitches and send them scrambling. They spin and whip books open, plopping back into their seats and juggling coffee cups.

"She'll know soon." I roll my eyes, bringing my attention back to Booker. "Since the gossip vines here are more active than *anyone's* sex life. In fact, she probably heard about it before I even thought it."

He snorts.

"But if, by some miracle, she's too tired and hasn't been paying attention, I'd like to keep this a surprise for as long as possible."

"My lips are sealed," he promises, sitting back again so the groan of his chair announces his movement. "It's too bad you're not here for Rome, Fox. That's our tradition." He pauses before adding, "It's your dream."

"It's really inconvenient that Alana had sex when she did, *knowing* my butt had plans with those business class seats. She's rude and inconsiderate."

"Tell her we said so," he chuckles. "What are you up to today? Tipped any cows?"

"Not this week. But it's only Monday, and my schedule is wide open. I'm working at the bookstore today. It's my first day alone, and I haven't broken anything, so I guess I'm off to a good start."

Well… except for a shower rail. My stomach tumbles with remembrance. With nerves and a strong side-ache tinged with desire. *None of which I wish to experience while on the phone with my boss.*

"Sounds like you have a promising career in small-town bookstores if Gable or Gains ever tire of you."

"And I note that you didn't mention Hemingway growing bored. That guy is a total puppy dog. He won't ever fire me."

He laughs. "Not even when you accidentally set the office sprinklers off and destroy tens of thousands of dollars in technology." He reaches across with a grunt I know too well and grabs a cup of coffee. Next, he'll sip and *ahhhh*. "We learned a lesson that day, didn't we, Ms. Tatum?"

"Yes. The lesson was *not* to light too much incense in the office, and that hot yoga is better left for actual yoga studios. But ya know what? We live and we learn."

He snorts. "We sure do."

The bookstore bell jingles above the front door, silencing the horde of old women—and one man—and announcing a newcomer. And since the horde *remains* silent, I know whoever has arrived is not just another old bitty sliding in to join the gossip.

So I push away from the wall and wander toward the front.

"Sounds like you've gotta go," Booker murmurs. "Also, if you ever install a doorbell here at our office, I may turn homicidal. You've been warned."

"I've heard it approximately thirty-seven million times today already. I swear, I'm about to shove it straight up a cow's bum." I come to the end of the book stacks and step into view with my customer service smile firmly in place, but then I skid to a stop and tilt my head to the side, taking in the fighter who turns with a hat pressed over his chest.

He's *a* fighter. But not one of the ones I know.

He dips his chin and half-bows. "Ma'am."

"Woah," Booker exclaims in my ear. "He sounds like an *actual* cowboy. Like, the real kind out in Texas."

I study the guy's wide-brimmed hat and the buckle on his belt. The tight denim jeans hugging thick thighs and the *I know I'm handsome* smirk I *know* he uses as often as he can. "I'll talk to you later, Booker. Be good. Reschedule Rome." Then, pulling the phone from my ear and ending the call, I slip the device into my back pocket. "I know you're a fighter because you have broad shoulders and thick arms."

Pleased, he looks down at himself. "Is that how you can tell?"

"That, and the Love & War tattoo, right there on your forearm."

Humored, he brings his eyes up again. "Got me. My loyalty stands with that family, so putting them on my skin was a no-brainer. And you're Fox

Tatum. I can tell 'cos you're new around here, and I saw you at Bitsy's funeral last year."

I study my arms, smirking as I search for my fighter muscle. *Hint: I have none.* "Is that how you can tell?"

"Plus, you got that fancy accent." He takes a step forward, transferring his hat to his left hand, and offers the right. "I'm Cliff. I'm a fighter sometimes, though I'm not good enough to make a living or bring home a trophy."

"Oh, well... that's a shame."

"Means I have a job, too. And that job includes renovations and fixin' things. I was in the bakery just ten minutes ago and heard a rumor you needed some help down here."

"You *heard*?" I narrow my eyes until I feel that annoying wrinkle dig between my brows. "Shouldn't Raya be in school by now?"

He holds on to my hand a moment longer, tugging me just a little closer, and flashes a devilish smile. "You say something in this town, someone else is gonna overhear and repeat it. Bill was in line behind you at the bakery, so I guess he went and told Gavin what he heard. Gavin told me." He releases me and shrugs. "Here we are. It just so happens I *also* have ties to the war room, and *this* just so happens to be a business owned by the same family trust, in a way. I'm happy to come and take a look at what you need done, and I'd bet Tommy would vouch for me in a New York minute." His eyes brighten, dancing with humor. "See what I did there?"

"I see it." Snickering, I wander to the other side of the counter and turn to lean against the hard edge, and because Cliff is simply *different* from anyone else I know, I take a moment to study his milky brown eyes and the dark dirty-blond, shaggy hair that boasts a semi-permanent ridge where his hat sits.

"I guess I need a little tile work done," I decide. "Replace the handrails and match the tiles to those already there... or re-do the whole bathroom. Either is fine. The shower stall is old, which leaves me with little hope that we'll find a replacement door, so it may be necessary to put in a whole new shower, too."

"I can take a peek for you and let you know your options. I'll send the invoices to Tommy?"

"Oh, no." I cough out a snigger and cover what I damn well know are my heating cheeks. "I'll pay. I walked in to a perfectly functional bathroom, but now I want something fresh and new." *Sort of.* "I started the demolition already and realized I should've thought ahead, so if you could help me out and keep it on the down-low, that'd be cool."

"You're gonna finance a renovation for a bathroom you don't even get to keep?" He whistles and rocks back onto his heels. "Sheesh. Where do I get me one of those rich New York friends?"

"Leaving Plainview would be step one," I tease right back. "Visit New York, probably. Stick to Manhattan; that's where the money tends to gather."

"Solid tips." He hooks a thumb over his shoulder and tilts his head toward the back. "You want me to take a look while I'm here? Give you a quick estimate on what I think you need, how long it'll take, and how much it'll cost you?"

"Quick?" I check the time and cast a look at the watchful ladies taking notes and preparing to gossip all over town. Then I spy the only other customer *actually* looking at buying a book. Finally, I bring my attention back to Cliff and nod. "I have about two minutes. Oh, and I don't know if you heard, but we're having a little party at the gym in a few weeks." I dash around the counter and lead the way, since *'abandoned her post and was way too distracted by personal business'* is bound to be a performance evaluation delivered to Alana by the watchful committee of Plainview enthusiasts.

I'm not afraid of being fired—*ha! Alana wouldn't dare*—but I'd rather she didn't receive anything less than stellar while she's working through postpartum hormones. "Chris already knows about the party. I don't think Tommy does yet." I march up the stairs and push through the apartment door, stepping aside to let Cliff through. "I'm holding it at the gym. It would mean a lot if you came to celebrate Alana and the baby."

"I'll be there." He swaggers—true cowboy style—into the bathroom and frowns as my *'I started demo already'* lie frays at the seams. "What kind of gift does a man bring to one of those events?"

"Uh... you could probably bring her cookies."

Curious, he inches back and eyes me across the room. "Cookies?"

"Mmhm. Especially cookies with oats in them. They're good for her milk production."

"Oh, well..." Blushing, he ducks his head back into the bathroom and takes out his phone. To write notes, maybe. Or to snap a couple of pictures. "I wanna help her, Ms. Tatum, but I'm not sure that's an appropriate gift from another man. Tommy's my friend, and I don't relish the idea of him smashing my skull into the ground when he finds out I'm influencing her boobs... positive or not."

Coward. "Fine. You could get diapers. Buy them a box of the next size up, so when the baby grows overnight, and they're not prepared for that spurt, they'll be all set."

"Sounds perfect." He takes a picture. Then another. A third. Then, pulling back, his eyes swing to mine. "And just to confirm, what size is she now? And what size is the next size up?"

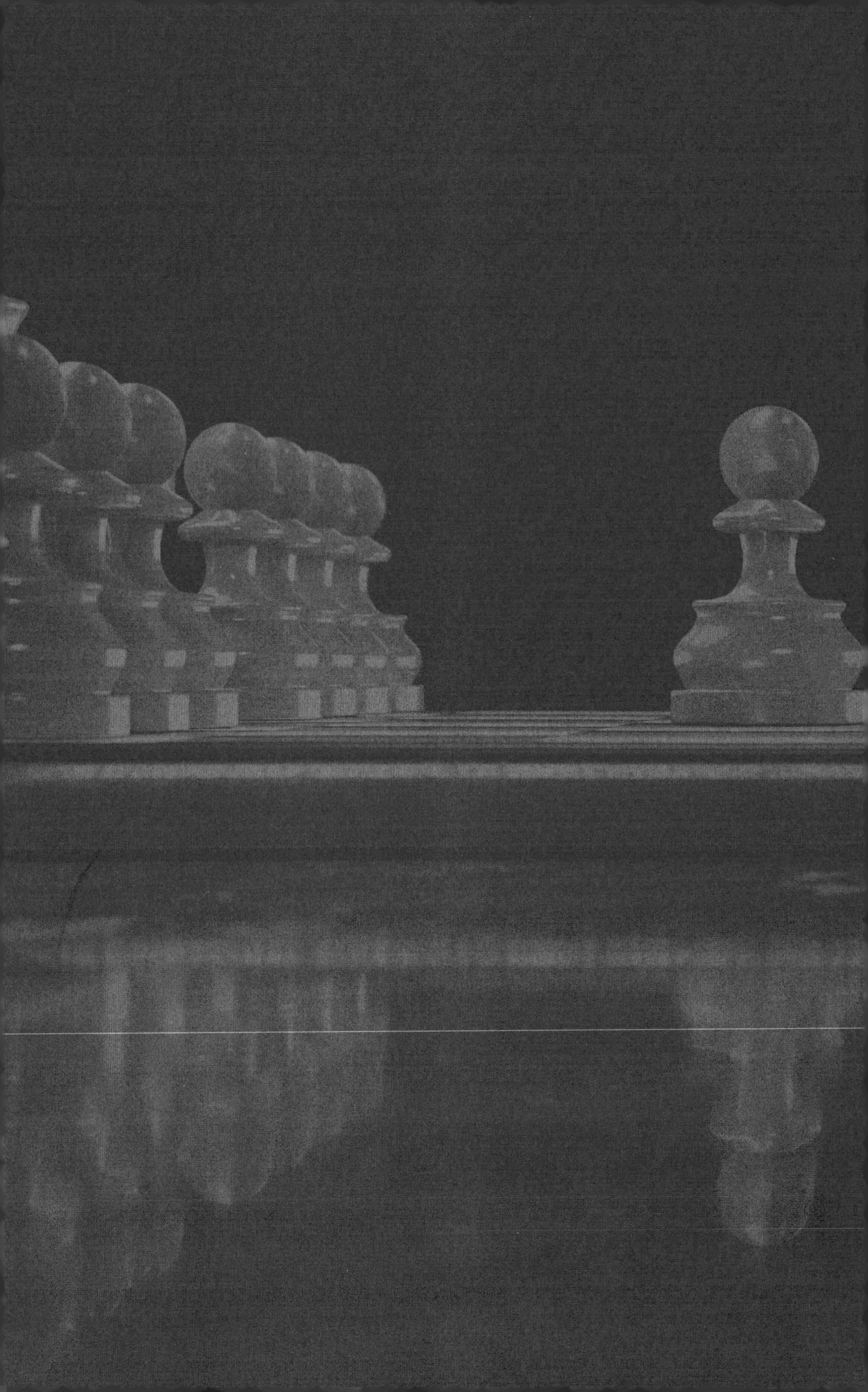

ROUND SIXTEEN
CHRIS

"It's dangerous to spar when you haven't slept in nearly three days." And still, I swing out with a powerful right hook and slam Ollie's jaw around. The fact his neck cracks means his chiropractor will have their work cut out for them over the next little while. "Rested-Ollie wouldn't have let that through."

He circles, his hands set at chest height instead of up where they belong, and a long dribble of blood trickles onto his jaw. "The good news is I can't feel the pain." He steps in with *what I think* is a fast one-two jab.

Too bad he misses me... by about three feet.

"Shit," he hisses. "Almost gotcha."

"I'm calling it." Laughing, Eliza Darling, Ollie's baby sister, an entire decade younger than he is, drapes her fourteen-percent body fat across the ropes and grabs his shirt before he can come for me again. "Dude, sit down before you fall."

"I'm fine!" He spins and stumbles, a goofy grin spread over his lips and blood coating his mouth guard. "He was gonna tap soon, Lize."

"You're delirious." She tugs him backward and sighs when he trips, falling to his ass and rolling to his back. She shakes her head, firming plump bow lips. "You're a mess. You know better than to go this long without sleep, so why the hell are you messing up now?"

"'Cos Alana was having her baby." He spits his mouth guard out, which mostly kind of flies *up*, then *down* again, smacking his chin and landing on the canvas by his ear. "I wasn't leaving her alone when she needed me."

"This is getting dangerous." Frustrated, I stalk forward and stand over him. "She's safe, dipshit. She's fine. And you're killing yourself over something you had no control over."

"She sacrificed herself and accepted all that hate because of *my* stupid ass actions."

"Because of the high school thing?" Growling, Eliza climbs over the ropes and stands on Ollie's other side. "You were a kid! Kids do dumb shit."

"Yeah, and my dumb shit led directly to Alana's rape." He sets his feet on the floor, bending at the knees. "My dumb shit changed everyone's lives. That's not regular dumb shit. That's excessive dumb shit, and no one even wants to punish me for it."

"So what do you want?" Eliza snarls. "You want Alana to hate you? You want Tommy to beat the crap out of you?"

He shrugs, extending his legs again and letting them flop to the canvas.

"If you accept this level of blame, all because you asked Tommy to come down to the station one time while Alana was asleep in his bed, then I suppose Tommy should probably feel just as guilty, huh?" I set my hands on my hips and wait for his eyes to roll across to mine. "Since he was the one who left her."

"No, I—"

"Or maybe *I* should feel guilty?" *I do. Fuck, I do!* "Because I was in the house. I stayed in my bed while Tommy came out to get you. So it's worse, isn't it? That I was there, and I did nothing."

"You were asleep," he slurs. "Not your fault."

"You got arrested for something entirely unrelated! Not your fault."

"Ya know," Eliza sets her elbows on her knees, bending to get closer to her brother. "Most doctors struggling with guilt and a troubled mind usually turn to drugs and alcohol. Claim a gym injury, prescribe a little oxy, and ride the wave into that happy little place where nothing hurts and memories blur."

"Dude," I scowl. "Don't give him ideas."

"But not you. You'd rather work yourself to the bone, then train with whatever energy you have left. And you don't just work out—like, running on the machines or hitting a bag. You step into the ring with another fighter, so they can punish you, and you claim it's sport."

"You feel you owe her something? Fine. We all carry a little guilt from back then, and now that we know the truth, we have to deal with the fallout of our actions. But you just delivered her baby, Ollie. You held her and Tommy through some pretty scary shit, and you kept Alana and Hazel alive. So maybe you can stop with the bullshit now and consider your debt repaid."

"Maybe she'll have another baby," he murmurs, half-asleep now that he's horizontal. "Maybe she can have another nine. One for every year she was gone. Then I can feel better."

"Fine." Eliza snaps. "I'll tell her to have nine more babies, just for you. Maybe she and Tommy can light some candles and include a framed portrait of you, to really include you in the baby making. Then you're gonna chill the hell out and come back to us as a normal, functioning human being again?"

"Yeah." He smacks his lips, drifting toward unconsciousness. "I think that would make me feel better."

"He's out." When a fresh set of fighters approaches the ring, gloves and mouthguards ready, I turn and shake my head. "This one's closed until he's done."

"Sleeping, Coach?" One of them leans to the left and spies Ollie laid out on the canvas. "We allowed to do that now?"

"He is. Which means this ring is out of commission until he's up again. If you intentionally wake him because you wanna train, you're on bathroom duties till my mood stabilizes." I pause, driving my point home. "You understand?"

He lifts his gloved hand and nods. "Understood, Coach."

"Good." I turn to Eliza. "You wanna be on babysitting duty to make sure he gets his rest?"

"I'll sit here for a bit. Kids classes start in a little while, so—"

"Gosh. Is this how fight gyms typically function?"

Her voice is like a sucker punch to my solar plexus. Her taunting smile, even before I see it, a jab to my throat.

I spin on fast feet and almost trample Ollie despite my orders to everyone else, and catching an eye full of Fox Tatum in a beautiful dress, the kind she might wear to the office, she becomes a feast for my senses, a feast I feel all the way to the base of my stomach.

"He's asleep?" With a seductive sway of her hips, she wanders forward and sets her hands on the ropes. "Are you charging him for this? Because if I knew there was money to be made for a group sleeping situation, I might buy a warehouse in the village and set up a few bunks."

"Fox." *Don't you put your hand on your heart, stupid. Don't you dare*! "What are you doing here?"

"Fox Tatum." Eliza meanders closer and stops with her shoulder brushing my arm. She's sweaty, with her hair tied in messy braids and washboard flat abs Fox's eyes inevitably drop to. "Heard you were in town. Figured I'd see you at some point."

She offers her fist and waits for Fox to return the gesture with a bump, and though I step forward to mediate, *since that's not really Fox's thing*, I snap my lips shut again when I'm proven wrong.

"Hey. It occurred to me today that I've only been in town for a weekend. Though I swear, it feels like it's been an eternity already."

"And, of course, I heard all about the baby." Eliza jabs a thumb back toward Ollie. "He's a very proud quasi-uncle, if not a little emotionally stunted and over-tired. You running the bookstore today?"

"Mmhm. Running it for the next six weeks. Do you have an outside job, or is this it?"

"Uh..."

"I only ask, because I realized today that not all fighters get paid for it. Some have regular jobs, and fighting is just a fun hobby on the side."

"This is my job." She slides her tongue over her lips, grinning. "Sponsorship deals pay my bills, and Chris and Tommy pay me a salary to run the kid classes five nights a week. You looking at joining up and hitting something?"

"I get to hit things?" She swings beautiful, bright eyes my way. "Do I get to choose *who* I hit? Because I have a list, and it only has two people on it so far. One of them is Chris, and the other is a little old lady. She's small and kinda frail looking. So I bet I could really mess her up."

Eliza laughs. "I get to hit Chris often. It's fun. And I've wanted to smack little old ladies my whole life. Which one pissed you off?"

"I'm actually not sure..." She drags her bottom lip between her teeth. "They all look kinda the same. But let's circle back to the hitting Chris thing?"

"Sounds to me like you got yourself a PT client." Eliza slaps my back and turns to her brother. "I'll keep an eye on this dipshit until classes begin."

"Where's Franky?" I climb through the ropes and move to the padded floors in bare feet. Bare chest, too, now that I look down and pay attention.

Fox's glittering eyes do the same, her not-so-subtle body tilt, allowing her a better view.

"Fox?" I clear my throat. "You didn't forget him at school, did you?"

"Oh shoot! Franky!" She claps a hand to her mouth. "I thought you were picking him up?"

"What?" My lungs squeeze flat, and my heart thunders, painfully bruising the inside of my chest. To be forgotten. Made to feel like he doesn't matter. *Jesus, I know what that's like.* "Are you serious? You were supposed to pick him up hours ago!"

She giggles. Belly rolling, chest bouncing, shoulder trembling laughter that travels all the way to her eyes. "I was kidding. Geez. He's at the hospital with Alana and Tommy and the baby."

"He is?"

"Yeah, I picked him up at three, exactly like I was supposed to. We had ice cream, discussed school politics, seeing as how he's headed for middle school next year. Then I offered to bring him to the bookstore or the hospital before training."

"He chose the hospital?"

"Uh-huh." She turns, forcing me to follow or remain left behind. So I dog her steps and go on a tour of my own gym through her eyes. "He misses his mom, which makes sense, seeing as this is literally the first time in his entire life he's been without her. Aunty Fox and big brother Chris are fun and all, but there's no one like Mom. So I took him there, stayed for ten minutes to hug my namesake." She glances back and smirks. "Then I returned to the bookstore to finish out the day. I locked up at five and realized I had nowhere to be. So…" She wanders to a hanging bag and taps it with her knuckles, only for her smile to turn to a frown. *Maybe she expected it to be soft.* "I started walking down Main Street, then I turned left, and then I turned again. Next thing I knew, I walked in here and found you and that chick standing over Ollie. I'll head out and grab Franky in an hour and bring him back here for class. Then…" She taps the bag again. "I guess we'll figure out dinner and settle in for his last night without his mom."

"She's coming home tomorrow?"

She turns her back to the bag, resting against its hard leather, and places her hands on either side. Fuck if I don't imagine binding her wrists and tying her to the bar above, all so I can fuck her in my own gym, knowing she'll claim the mats as desperately as she claimed the apartment bathroom.

And me.

God, how she claimed me.

"*They* said maybe Wednesday. *She* said for sure tomorrow. Franky's doing okay… barely," she clarifies. "But he's at the end of his tolerance. One more night, and he's done. So if Alana isn't a free woman by the school bell tomorrow, he's gonna set some shit on fire."

"And our job, I suppose, is to hide the matches and keep him calm."

A soft, seductive smile crosses her lips and ends in her eyes. *Her bedroom eyes.* "Basically. Why don't you go work out for a bit and let me watch? I'd like to objectify you, but discreetly. The way you're standing over me right now makes it hella obvious we have a secret we don't want Alana to know about."

"And we definitely don't want Alana to know." I take a step back. Just one, because she smells delicious, and testing boundaries can be fun. "Why don't you get changed and pay me ten dollars? We can call it PT, and I'll get to touch you in front of everyone."

"Only ten dollars?" Her left brow slings high on her forehead. "You're undercharging."

"It's usually a hundred an hour." I look down at my hands—my palms literally itching to touch—and keep them exactly where they are. *Not on her.* "Figured giving you a first-class-is-cheap discount is the gentlemanly thing to do. That's how we secure business, after all."

"Makes complete sense." She allows her eyes to slide along my torso and down to where my shorts sit low on my hips. "How many PT clients do you currently have? Five? Ten? Twenty?"

None. I run classes and get fighters ready for their titles.

"I have room for one more. And after tomorrow, when Franky's back with Alana, we could even have the gym to ourselves after-hours." I lean just a little closer, grinning when her pulse grows a little faster. "I'd hang you from the rack above your head—"

She looks up.

"—and fuck you until I got the itch out of my system. Unlucky for you, I'm itching a lot lately, so your arms are probably gonna get sore."

"*Unlucky* for me?" She scoffs. "Christian, I think you misunderstand how pleasant I find those experiences. Though, now that I'm thinking about it... if I pay you, whether it's ten dollars, or a hundred, that changes our dynamic. Makes you my purchased whore."

I choke out a laugh and inch back again, since I'm still in her space. "So don't pay me. Or do. Whatever gets me an hour of fucking you right here against *this* bag."

"It's a favorite of yours?" She pushes away, but only to circle the bag and drag her fingertips along the leather. "Looks just like all the others. What makes this one so special?"

"It's the one you walked to when you could've picked any of them." I settle onto my heels and place my hands on my hips. "You're making it awfully hard for me to stand here. My shorts aren't cut out for hiding a hard cock, and I'm already fucking you in my head. I've lost the battle against myself."

"Poor, poor impulse control." She wanders from this bag to the next, playing a game of peek-a-boo in the gaps between. "Are you capable of engaging with me now without making it sexual? Have we ruined our chances of being friends, too?"

"We were never friends." I step left, following her. Then I step again. "You have two modes, Fox. Irritating me and bringing me immense pleasure until my head wants to explode and my balls bring me actual, physical pain." I step again and pray the fighter on the bag at the end minds his own fucking business. "You're not irritating me right now, which means…"

"Sex." Faux disappointed, she shakes her head gently side-to-side. "Geez. That's where men and women differ. I can be turned on, and irritated, and mentally preparing my yearly taxes, all at the same time."

"You're trying to challenge me." I cast my eyes across the room and consider how far we have to run to get from where we are right now, to where we need to be—*in my office, behind a locked door*. "You say things like that to annoy me. Your taxes? Woman, when I'm with you, you can't count to three."

Her cheeks warm, and a soft blush spreads to her chest. It's not entirely obvious to anyone else, but I make it a damn point to know her body as well as I know my own.

"Would you like to step into my office, Ms. Tatum?" I clear my throat and give her my professional voice. "We could get your paperwork started and your membership approved within the hour, I reckon. Just in time for you to collect Franky from the hospital."

"You'd make me go get him?" She turns on her heels, rolling her eyes for show. "After all the hard work of filling in forms and such, you'd make *me* walk to the hospital?"

"I mean… I could do it." I follow her across the room and past the ring, and though most others might consider babysitting Ollie a time to sit and scroll their phone, Eliza skips instead, bounce-bounce-bouncing against the canvas, creating a repetition that probably helps him sleep deeper. "Fox is looking to join up," I explain. *Badly*. "I'm gonna get the paperwork sorted and stuff."

She watches me with a big fat '*dude, I don't give a fuck*' plastered on her face. Shaking her head, she closes her eyes and finds her zen. So I set my hand on the middle of Fox's back and nudge her toward the hall that leads to our offices. "This way, Ms. Tatum." And because I think to do it, I pass the stereo system and turn it up just a little louder than usual.

Anything to drown out the sound of me smashing her against my desk.

"We have pay-as-you-go, weekly, monthly, and annual payment plans. Personally," I open my door and allow her to stroll in ahead of me, "I prefer anal. I mean…" I follow her in and close the door at my back. "Annual. Taking care of the long-term stuff always makes for smoother times."

"I think I'm more of a pay-as-I-go kinda gal." Her eyes drop to my hands, my fingers flicking the locks to ensure we remain alone. Then she brings her gaze up and her tongue forward to trace the front of her teeth. "I don't know what power you yield, Christian, but I've *never* been an on/off switch kind of woman before. Yet, you mention fucking me, and immediately, my panties are soaked and my throat is dry."

"Because you like what I do to you. Suck my cock."

Surprised, her eyes flicker wide, and her heart pounds heavily against her throat. "I'm sorry. What?"

"You heard me." I press my back against the door and undo the knot at the front of my shorts, tearing the laces open and pushing the material down to reveal my hard length. "I've been working out. Sweating. It's gonna be salty, and you're gonna fucking love it."

She splays her hand over her stomach, shuddering. "I recall a promise of being fucked. Is this a bait and switch, Mr. Watkins?"

I fist my cock and tilt my head back, groaning when that alone makes my balls jump. "I'll fuck you, too. We have an entire hour, and I'm gonna make sure I have wet wipes in here next time. I wanna come on your face and rub it into your skin. I'm aware we're on a deadline, and you have somewhere to be after this, so you'll swallow my cum today. You'll wear it tomorrow."

"You're bossy." Sauntering back in my direction, she slides her hand up, cupping her breast and squeezing just enough to make it feel good. "I like it when you're bossy."

"I know." When she's a mere two feet away, I swing out just as fast as I do when I'm fighting, but instead of clocking her on the jaw, I grab her hair and force her to her knees.

She yelps, crashing to the floor and grabbing my hips for balance, then she glances up and meets my eyes.

She's all of my hottest dreams wrapped up in one woman who worships me with her lips.

She brushes my hand away and fists my cock, circling my shaft with her fingers and drawing me ridiculously close to completion. But my heart doesn't skitter until she takes the head of my cock with her lips and suckles, dragging her tongue over the very tip.

"Fuck." I groan. "You're a goddess."

She opens her mouth wider and takes me all the way to the back of her throat, cupping my balls in her free hand.

I slip my fingers through her hair and pull her back, killing myself while I deprive myself of her wet heat, then I slam her forward and thrill in her choked gasp. "Yes," I hiss, my knees turning weak and my flexing fingers curling tight in her hair. "Next time you come to me, have your plug in already." I drag her back, then slam her forward, fucking her face and sprinting closer to the explosion I refuse to indulge in until I'm damn well ready. "I wanna fuck your ass, Fox. Every single day from now until I'm dead. But you gotta wear the plug, so I know you're ready for me."

She garbles around my cock, sucking my soul straight out of my body and into hers. She's a witch out to collect immortality.

"Does it taste good, beautiful?" I peer down into her wet eyes. "Salty, but yummy. Do I taste good to you?"

She nods, choking on my dick and squeezing the base tighter.

"You want me to fuck your ass?" I jut my hips forward, abusing the back of her throat and enjoying every fucking second of it. "You want me to sodomize you again? Fuck you like we're animals. Because I like it when we do." I pull her away and drag her back in, controlling her every movement and the breaths she's allowed to take into her lungs. "Outside of this, I like to think I respect women. I hold doors and say nice things. But when my dick is hard and your pussy throbs for me, I lose all that respect and get off on treating you like a bitch dog made for breeding."

She shudders, gasping for air as I fill her throat again. And because I'm a selfish motherfucker, she reaches between her legs and plays.

"I should make you wait." I slam forward and grit my teeth, because my release threatens an early rebellion. Then I pull out of her mouth and pick her up, slipping my hand beneath her dress to find her soaked and aching.

But fuck, I find so much more.

I grab the back of her neck and march her to my desk, folding her over the stacks of paperwork I might never truly file and the bag of new merch we haven't put out yet, then whipping her dress up and her panties down, I find our surprise.

"*Fuckkkk* me." My lungs shudder, and my cock rages, pointing straight toward home. "You already have your plug?" I grab the end between my fingers and tug it just far enough to make her cry, then spinning it, I push it back in again. "You didn't go for a random fucking walk, Fox Tatum. You came looking for me."

Panting and trembling, she drapes herself across my desk.

"You talk to anyone else while you had this in you?" I smack her ass and grind against her soaked pussy. "You stop anywhere and talk to anyone?"

Breathless, she shakes her head. "Just you and Eliza."

"Because if you'd talked to a guy," I smack her again, "if you'd even *smiled* at a guy while you had this in you, I'd have to punish you." I fist my cock and tease her opening with the tip, giving her just an inch before pulling away again. "When you're wet and desperate, you fucking belong to me."

"Chris—"

"Tell me you understand." I give her two inches, then back away in punishment. "Tell me, Fox."

"I understand." She grinds her ass backward. "Please, Chris."

"Beg me."

"I'm begging you!" She reaches around and plays with herself, dragging her fingers through her creamy folds and across to grab my cock. "I'm begging you to fuck me, Chris. Please. We only have an hour, and I'll die if we don't finish."

"Good girl." I fill her with a single thrust and bury myself to the hilt, and because she wants to scream, I grab her hair and yank her head back, cutting off her air and, with it, the sound of her pleasure. "You save those for me." I fuck her without remorse, hitting her plug with my pelvis to ensure she feels both. "You save everything for me for as long as you're in Plainview, you understand?"

She gasps for air, searching, but failing, to fill her lungs.

"Other people are gonna notice you here soon, beautiful. Not everyone is old and senile. We got fighters in this town, and a bunch of 'em are gonna smell you the second they walk through the gym doors tonight."

She cries out, fisting her hands and scrunching papers that probably should've been dealt with months ago. "Shit!"

"They're gonna feel you in the air. They're gonna know you're ripe for fucking, and because you're thirsty when we're in the same room, they're gonna sense your neediness in the air."

"Chris!"

"But you're mine for as long as you're here." I rest one hand on her hip and find my rhythm, riding her sweet pussy the way it was meant to be ridden. "You say no when they look at you." I swing my hand out and smack her delicious ass. "You say no when they ask for your time. Tell me you understand."

"I understand." She crushes her forehead to my desk and groans. "I'll say no."

"Now come for me." I reach around and play with her clit until she explodes, just like I knew she would. She sprays my office floor. My feet. Her own fucking legs, so if she skips the bathroom after this and goes straight to the hospital to collect Franky, they'll *know* what she's been doing. "You're so fucking responsive, Fox." I play with her plug and curl my toes when her squeezing cunt tries to pull me over the ledge. "So fucking responsive. Will you ever fail to come when I call for you?"

"No." Her back bounces with a shudder, her lungs spasming for air. "You command me."

"Chris?" Eliza bangs on my office door, bringing me to a stop and startling Fox into silence. "You in there?"

I pull out of Fox and earn a look of despair. Rejection, glittering in her beautiful eyes. But I turn and plant my ass on my desk, then I drag her onto my lap so we're face to face. Eye to eye.

"Chris?"

"I'm in here." I command Fox's flow, holding her down by her hair, then up again until she finds her rhythm. "I'm busy. What do you want?"

She twists the door handle, startling Fox into stopping again. But I take her lips between my teeth and lave my tongue across the hurt.

"Why is your door locked?"

"Because I'm busy!" I play with the plug, dragging it out just far enough to take her breath away, then sliding it in again until she shudders. Clapping my free hand over her lips, I trap her every sigh and save them just for me. "Code it for me, Eliza. One or four."

"It's just a one," she grumbles. "I was gonna run over the application forms with you, since you just got done doing one with that chick. But if you're busy—"

"I'm dealing with a code four right now. I'll come talk to you later."

"Fine." She releases the door's handle and stomps away.

"Code four?" Fox bites my palm and rides my cock like the vixen she is. "What's a code four?"

"It means someone is dying and needs immediate attention." I slip my tongue between her lips and swallow her, heart and soul. "If I don't come in the next few minutes, it's gonna be a code four. Now eat my cock." I hold her hands and slam her down over my lap. "You're so fucking tight, Fox. You're choking the life out of me."

"You're so thick." She buries her lips by my neck and suckles, just hard enough to make me feel it. Not so hard she'll leave a mark.

Shame.

"Too big," she rasps, breathless and panting. "But it hurts so good."

"I'm gonna need your pussy juice on me every single day from now until June fourteenth. That's when you fly out, right?" I peel the top of her dress down and bite her nipple over the top of her bra. "I can't go a day without you when I know you're so close and so fucking hungry for me."

"Maybe I should tell you no." She drops her head back, moaning and crushing my cock in the confines of her pussy. "I like it when you punish me. It feels delicious."

"Don't test me." I wrap my arm around the small of her back and hold her while she trusts all her weight to me, *knowing* I won't let her fall. She drowns in the pleasure of her plug digging into her ass, her new position nudging it deeper. And when she's lost in her ecstasy and leaning far enough back, I stare down at where we join, her soaked lips wrapped around my cock like we were created just for this. But I'm a cruel motherfucker, a demanding, selfish prick who needs her to be right here with me, not swimming in her imagination, so I slap her clit and catch her when she startles.

"Look at me." I grin in response to her snarl. "You're here with me, Fox. Don't fucking forget it."

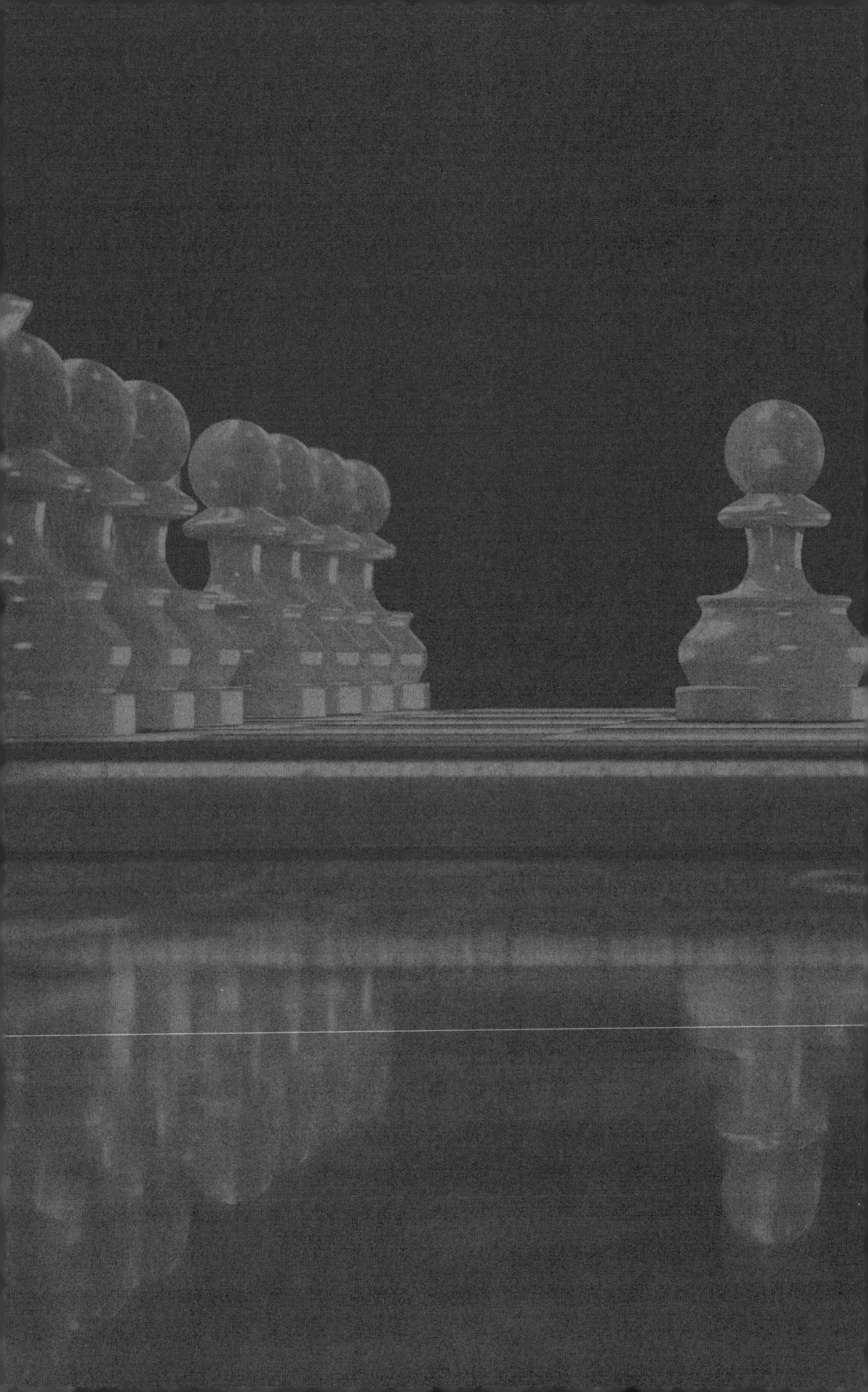

ROUND SEVENTEEN

FOX

My first forty-eight hours in Plainview felt like a lifetime. Like honey dripping through a sieve, and clocks set in slow motion for the sake of taunting those paying attention. But now that the work week has begun, repairs are underway in my apartment bathroom, and better, Alana's no longer in the hospital, it's like time has jumped into fast forward.

"Why did I hear rumors about a bathroom renovation at the bookstore?" Tommy wears his baby girl in a wrap against his broad chest. Like one of those actual crunchy-mama lengths of fabric that hold Hazel's tiny body close to his, her little legs tucked up and her head pressed over his heart.

All so he can eat his dinner with free hands.

He lounges beside Alana at the table on his porch. The lake glistens behind us while the delicious scent of lasagna dances on the air. Franky takes his seat at the head of the table, while I sit opposite a still-tender Alana, and Chris reclines beside me.

Totally cool. Totally chill and not at all obvious that we maybe have a secret.

Tommy cuts a small slice of lasagna and carefully slides it onto his tongue. "I was at the hardware store today and they said how you came by yesterday to choose tiles." His thick brows, damn near exact replicas to Chris', furrow over green eyes.

"Tiles?" Too tired to do much more than eat, Alana brings her gaze across to me. "What for?"

"Oh, the bathroom at the apartment." *Don't tell them you shattered their things while having sex. Definitely don't tell them you're banging Christian Watkins in secret.* "I just wanted to change it up. I hope that's okay."

"I mean…" Alana sighs. I swear, she's half asleep already. "It's not a big deal. But bathrooms are expensive, and you'll only be there for six weeks. I figured the existing tiles were fine."

"You're kinda high maintenance," Tommy chuckles, shaking his head and stabbing a green bean with his fork. "Jesus, Tatum. You renovate hotels while you're there, too?"

"You're making it into a whole thing." I study my dinner like it holds all the world's secrets, which is *way* easier than looking into my friends' eyes and telling a lie. "I like bathrooms to look good, and figured, since I was paying for it, you wouldn't mind."

"You're not paying for it," Tommy cuts in. "I'll pay for it. That's not the issue."

"No, I—"

"It's Alana's asset," he rumbles. "It's her store and her apartment, and eventually, it becomes *ours*, just as the gym becomes *ours*. I'll pay for the damn tiles. But seriously," he bites the bean in half and grins. "It's weird. You're staying there *temporarily*, but you're making permanent changes."

"The tiles were cracking around the taps," Chris inserts. "I saw them when I was fixing the shower head before Fox got to town. Those cracks mean water will get into the walls."

"Yeah." I use my fork to point his way. "Exactly. I was trying to get ahead of a future problem, and seeing as how I'm not sure what else to get you guys for a baby gift, and since I'm using the bathroom, rent-free for six whole weeks, I thought this was a nice thing to do."

"Rent free," Alana rolls her eyes, "but you're working at the bookstore, *also* for free."

"Not for free," Franky drawls. "I saw her eating a cupcake yesterday."

"Dude!"

"And when we counted stock at the end of the day, there was a one-cupcake discrepancy. Which means she didn't write it down."

"What'd we say about snitching?" I reach across and flick his fork slightly off-kilter. "I earned that cupcake, Franklin. I earned the right to sneak a cupcake and not tell anyone about it, too."

Tommy snorts. "We'll dock your non-existent pay at the end of the six weeks. Why'd you order a new shower stall?"

I drop my gaze and go back to studying the secrets of the universe and all that nonsense. "Hmm?"

"Tiles, I can understand. Maybe. Not really. But a whole new shower?"

"Well... Um..."

"Once you remove the existing tiles, you remove the seal," Chris jumps in, saving the day. *Again.* "Can't reinstall the same shower glass once the seal is broken."

"Yup." I hook my thumb in his direction. "That's why."

Alana does a slow blink, drawing bright blue eyes up until I feel them on my skin. "Did you order a new sink?"

"No, there's nothing wrong with the sink."

"So you're putting in new tiles and shower glass," Tommy quips, "but keeping the same ugly sink?" He's too clever—or maybe I'm a terrible liar—so he smirks and fills his mouth with lasagna. "Seems kinda weird that you'd go to the trouble of replacing some things and not others."

"Now, who is high maintenance?" I put my fork on the table and grab my wine glass instead. "You're getting new tiles and a new shower, plus six weeks of free bookstore labor, and all you can focus on is that you *didn't* get a new sink?"

His eyes dance with humor, flickering from me to an overly casual Chris. "Forgive me. I never meant to sound ungrateful. I'm just a curious person."

"I think I'm gonna fall asleep sitting up." Alana sways in her seat, tilting to the side and resting her cheek on Tommy's broad shoulder. "If I choke on my dinner, will someone clear my airways?"

"I've got you, babe." Tommy reaches around and holds her up. "You can head to bed in a sec."

"But Hazel—"

"Is doing just fine." He presses a kiss on Alana's forehead. "She's asleep and won't wake for a few hours yet. When she does, I'll bring her to you so she can eat, then I'll change her diaper and put her down for the night. You hardly even have to wake for any of that."

"But Franky—"

"I'm going to the movies tonight with Aunt Fox." He straightens his fork and glances up with a smile. "We're gonna watch the new Spiderman, since it's almost the weekend, and I only have one more day of school before having two days off."

"You're heading to the movies?" Chris searches the side of my face, his stare warming my flesh like a physical caress. "I didn't know that."

"Guess we didn't tell you." I set my wine down and grin. "Figured you were all about routine and predictability, and seeing as how this is a work night, I assumed you wouldn't be interested."

"I was wondering where the bickering had disappeared to," Tommy chuckles. "Things were a little too quiet. I was starting to worry."

"We're not bickering. We've *never* bickered. Oh, and," I check Alana to make sure she's most of the way out, before bringing my eyes back to Tommy. "We're having a party at the gym in a few weeks. I need you to block out the schedule and leave the building available for that entire Saturday. And probably hire a cleaning crew, since *eau de sweaty balls,* isn't *it.*"

He scowls. "My gym smells like hard work! Not balls."

"Smells like Satan's butthole. Have someone disinfect the place. And send me a list of invitees, so I can coordinate catering." Then, I bring my focus around to Chris. "Did you order the cake yet?"

His eyes flash with guilt. "Yes?"

"Really?" I hold his stare and watch his Adam's apple bob with nervousness. "That's what you're rolling with?"

"Okay, no. But I'll go to the bakery tomorrow and do it. I promise."

"Good." I come back around to Tommy. "I expect at least a hundred bodies in attendance."

"Woman, I don't even *know* a hundred people! My entire graduating class was, like..."

"Nineteen," Chris grumbles. "Nineteen people graduated with us."

"So find eighty-one more. I'm carrying most of this party, inviting people I don't even know. Meanwhile, you've lived here your whole life, and you're telling me you can't find *anyone* who might like free cake and a cute baby to fawn over?"

"Guess I'll find eighty-one more people." Moping, he drops his gaze and stabs his dinner. "I'll stand on the freeway with a sign if I have to."

"Exactly. Because Alana deserves to feel special for once in her damn life. That no one thought to throw a shower before now is a sin."

"What kind of shower did you buy, Aunt Fox?" Franky sips his lemonade, his dimples popping as he side-eyes the rooster strutting across the lawn. It's ugly and old, missing half its feathers, and has a ball-sack hanging off its chin longer than a ninety-year-old's inside a sauna. "Is it gonna be bigger than the one that was already there?"

"Yes. And way nicer, since the old one was ugly and outdated."

"High maintenance," Tommy coughs out. "Good luck to your future husband. He better be a contractor with a Jack-of-all-trades skill set. Or stupidly rich."

"Why not both?" I swirl my wine and bring it to my lips. "I'd prefer not to limit my options, and money is important when discussing future renovations. And husbands," I add playfully, bringing my focus to Franky. "Hurry and eat, buddy. We don't want to be late for the movies."

"And Alana's going to sleep," Chris grumbles. "Guess I'll go home and hang out by myself, then."

"So sad," I quip. "So, so sad."

"Chris!" Franky spills popcorn to the lobby floor, beaming when his favorite brother-slash-uncle—*what did I say about small towns?*—wanders through the cinema's front doors.

Am I surprised he came? Not even a little.

"Hi, Chris! Are you watching the movie, too?"

"Sure am." He comes to a stop just inches from my back, his chest touching my shoulder and his aftershave swirling to the base of my lungs until a smile stretches my lips wide.

Stop it, Fox! Stop it right now.

"I like Spiderman, too, and there was nothing on the TV. Your mom already passed out at home, and Tommy wanted daddy-daughter time with Hazel. You don't mind, do you?"

"Nope." He gazes up at his idol—*I swear, he likes Chris more than he likes Tommy.* "You wanna sit with us, too? There are probably gonna be enough seats, since not many other people are here."

"Sure, thanks." He inches forward, leaning into my peripherals with a smug grin. "You don't mind if I sit with you, do you, Fox?"

"Of course not." I'm not in the business of lying to myself—*others, sure. But myself? I prefer honesty*—which means I was *totally* hoping he'd come. He's a stickler for routine and the comfort of his own home, but damn, I held hope he'd give those up in favor of hanging out with me.

Us.

Me.

Whichever.

"Surprised," I continue, pulling my phone from my back pocket and checking the time. "Since it's... Oh geez, Christian. It's nearly eight o'clock. Movie won't be done till around ten."

"I tend to stay up late."

"But you tend to stay *in*." I turn and pat his arm. "I'm proud of you for skipping *comfortable* tonight, buddy. This is growth."

His nostrils flare and his eyes flicker. He wants so badly to say something about fucking me into submission and tearing the sass from my tongue. But he can't, not while Franky's so near.

And knowing that brings me a sense of power I'll forever take advantage of.

"You should grab your ticket and popcorn." I wrinkle my nose and catch the promising flex of his palm. Already, I feel it on my backside. "We'll meet you in there."

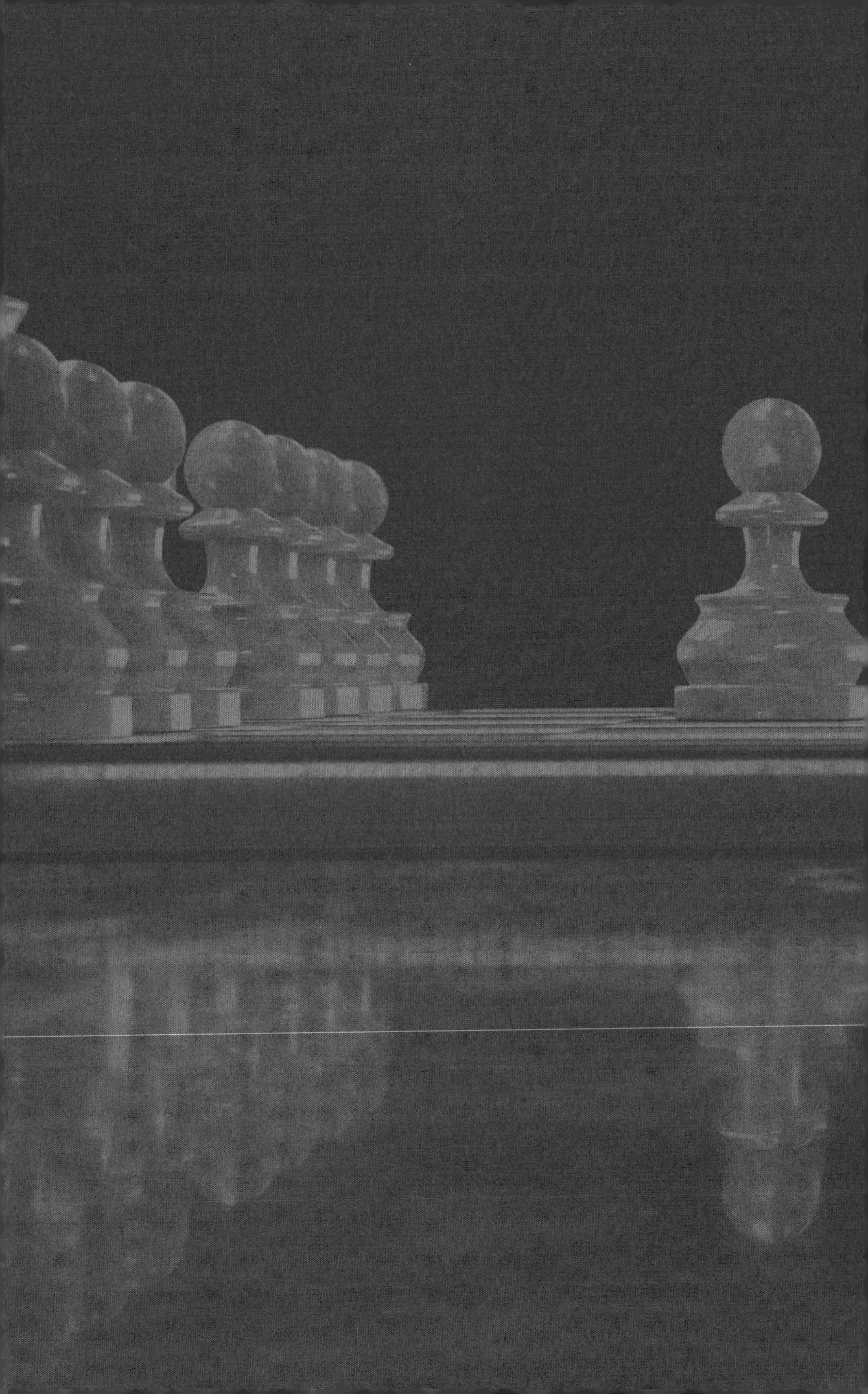

ROUND EIGHTEEN
CHRIS

My cock thickens in my jeans, expertly hidden behind a zipper and boxers. *I knew she'd try to test me tonight.* Wandering toward the ticket booth, I lift just one finger for the attendant, and when my phone vibrates in my back pocket, I reach around and swipe to answer, Tommy's name flashing on the screen.

"Hey?"

"The fuck is going on between you and Fox?"

Shit. Damn. My stomach jumps, and my cock softens. "Hmm?"

"Christian, I'm not blind, and you're my twin brother. I've known you your whole fucking life. So when I'm asking you about something like this, it's because I'm getting some twin-telepathy bullshit. Or," he growls, "ya know, I'm seeing you with my own fucking eyes."

I place a twenty onto the counter in exchange for my ticket and turning away, I stalk toward the building front doors rather than head into the cinema. "I don't know what you're talking about."

"The hell you don't! Alana's basically comatose this week, so she's not noticing shit. But you may as well have pissed on Fox at dinner, 'cos I saw the way you watched her."

"I didn't watch her like anything!"

"You watched her like you were the big bad wolf, dickhead. And she was your Red."

She wanted discretion, and I'm a shitty liar. That was our first mistake. I drag my free hand through my hair and bite down on my groan. "You're seeing things. I was just eating my dinner and enjoying an evening where she was irritating me *less*. I thought you wanted us to get along, anyway?"

"I *do* want you to get along! I *don't* want you to take her to bed and break her heart when it's all done. Because then Alana will be forced to choose sides."

"Wait..." My pulse skitters and my stomach drops, so I step outside the building and onto the sidewalk, where the cool breeze hits my skin. "She would choose? Who the hell do you think she'd choose? Because she was mine way before she was Fox's."

"That's the whole fucking point! We don't want her to have to choose. If you and Fox are doing the dirty, then do it. Have fun. Be safe. But if shit goes bad and hearts are broken, it won't just be yours or Fox's. It'll be Alana's because she loves you both. If she's forced to split her time between the two of you or choose one over the other to invite to her important family events, then I'm gonna snap some fucking necks."

"You sound especially violent on the matter." I draw my tongue across my lips and exhale. "Fox and I are... nothing. We're just friends."

"Friends?"

"Barely! We hardly tolerate each other. She annoys the ever-loving shit out of me, *on purpose*, by the way. And I annoy her, since stable, sensible, normal people with a healthy respect for keeping time and routine is something that bothers her."

"Chris—"

"Nothing is going on between me and Fox. She's in town for six weeks, helping Alana. I fucking told you—*both of you*—that she didn't even have to be here, since I could help with Franky and Caroline would help with the shop. You didn't listen, which is fine. That's on you. But don't come at me with your bullshit just because she and I *weren't* swiping at each other at dinner. Not fighting doesn't automatically translate to hooking up."

"Yeah?" he questions slowly, allowing the silence to settle between us. "Well, I don't believe you."

"Twenty-nine years, and *now* you call me a liar?" I shake my head and feel the insult lash at my heart, though, technically, I *am* a liar. "Hurtful."

"What are you doing right now? I saw you driving out, but you said you were going home to watch TV. Not at the cinema by chance, are you?"

"I am, actually. But!" I add quickly. "I told you from the start I'd be keeping a close eye on them. Franky's my family, Tommy, just like you are. She springs a movie on us at dinnertime? She even springs it on Alana? That's not very nice of her."

"So you're there to supervise?" he drawls. "Really?"

"Yes, really! Who's to say she was *actually* bringing him to the theater? Maybe she was taking him for ice cream and a little chat about moving back to New York?"

He chokes out a laugh. "New York? She's not going to abduct him, stupid!"

"No, but she might try a little manipulation." Do I believe that? No. But did I, back *before*? Yep. "Fox is here as Alana's rep, and I'm here as yours. I see no reason for you to be pissy about that."

He draws a long breath in through his nose, the whistle easily painting a picture in my mind. Then he exhales again and ends it with a grunt. "Are you sleeping with Fox? Are you *considering* sleeping with Fox?"

"No, I—"

"Do you have a plan for the possible eventuality where one or both of you catch feelings but live half a country apart? Or one of you breaks the others' heart but have to co-friend Alana and Franky for the next seventy years?"

"Tommy—"

"Tell me the truth, Christian. Tell me where you're at, so I can slide in and cushion the blow for the people I love. Because, believe it or not, Alana isn't the only person I'm worried about. Your heart might be the most fragile of them all, and I'll go to war to defend you. But if we reach a point where my enemy is Fox Tatum, who just so happens to be my future wife's best friend, then I'm gonna end up on my fucking knees in no-man's-land, begging for a truce and secretly hating Fox for the rest of my life, because she hurt my baby brother."

"I'm not *into* Fox," I grit out. "I'm not interested in her scattered, flaky, fake-ass job having self, nor do I have any interest in pursuing a woman who lives as far away as she does. On June fourteenth, I'm putting her back on a plane heading east. *That's* when I'll breathe easier again. She's a pain in my ass, Tommy. But she's a short-term pain that'll be gone soon. So stop stressing out. Are you done now?"

"Done prying into your personal life?" Finally, he releases a chuckle and moves from whatever chair he's in when Hazel's cute little squeaked exhale proves she's awake. "Yeah, I'm done. I'm sorry for calling you a liar."

"It's alright. I've said some shit about you in the past."

"To my face?"

"Behind your back, too." I spin on my heels to head inside, only to be caught in Fox's eyes, so fucking pretty, so big and vulnerable, and waiting for me, right in the cinema doorway.

"Asshole," he snickers, oblivious to what's right in front of me.

How fucking disrespectful am I to say what I've said and deny the very things he saw with his own eyes.

For acting hurt that he called me a liar.

When I am.

"Uh... Movie's gonna start soon, so I'll talk to you later. Tomorrow, probably." I drag my free hand down to smooth my shirt. "Take care of my niece, and don't forget to make Alana drink water. She'll dehydrate if you don't."

"Thanks," he drawls. "Do I need to remind you she's mine and not yours?"

"Nope. I know where everyone sits on the pecking order. I'm hanging up now." Instead of waiting for his goodbye, I kill the call and slip the phone into my pocket, and glancing left, then right, to make sure we're alone, I gift Fox with a wide smile and meander closer. "Hey. Where's Franky?"

"Inside already." She chews on her lip and takes a step back. "I needed to pee, so he's minding our seats and watching the trailers. I was heading back in when I saw you out here on the phone."

"Oh, yeah..." I'd rather be inside, hidden in the dark, where it's entirely okay to touch where no one can see. Where I could lean in and bury my nose against her neck and no one, not even Franky, would be any the wiser.

Knowing I can't grab her hand out here, I dig mine into my pockets and start through the door. "Tommy needed to talk for a second."

"He okay? Is Alana alright?"

"Everyone is fine." I grab the heavy cinema door and pull it open to reveal a dark room, with a massive screen on one wall and a few dozen all-but-empty seats rolling toward the back wall. Best of all, this cinema isn't like those fancy kinds in the city, with cameras watching every angle and every seat filled.

In fact, besides Franky, there ain't a soul here who could attest to the fact Fox and I wander in together.

"Wanna sit beside me, Fox Tatum?" I slide my fingertips over the small of her back. "Please?"

"Sure." She brushes my hand away and heads up the stairs toward the boy, who hugs his bucket of popcorn against his chest.

But he doesn't eat a single piece.

Not until the movie begins.

"Looks like we have the whole cinema to ourselves." She moves into his row and folds her seat down, giving herself somewhere to sit. "This *never* happens in New York."

"That's 'cos there are more people in New York." His eyes remain plastered to the screen, an ad for some other Marvel universe movie flashing over the lenses of his glasses. "Statistically, it's just not possible to be the only person going to the movies in New York."

"Well, of course." Fox settles in, folding one leg over the other and bringing her seductive eyes my way. She sets her hand on what would be my chair, pushing it down in offering. "Will you sit here, Christian?"

"Can I sit in the next row?" Franky swings his gaze around, excited and jittery. "Since there's no one else here. It doesn't really matter if I sit in the next row, right?"

"It doesn't really matter." Fox snatches a piece of his popcorn, infuriating the boy—rightfully—and grinning when he scowls. Then she gestures forward. "You can sit in any of the seats you want. Your choice. Just make sure you tell me if you need to get up and go to the bathroom. Don't sneak out in the dark."

"Can I take my popcorn?" Slowly, he leans forward on his chair. Not yet committed to his plan. "Do I have to leave it behind? Because I don't want to take all your popcorn, but I want some, too."

"You can take it with you." She rubs her belly in slow, dramatic circles. "I'm still digesting my dinner. Don't eat that too fast, though, okay? You know it'll give you a stomachache if you do."

"Okay!" He bounds to his feet, his chair flipping back now that his weight no longer holds it down, and charging toward the end of the row, he moves down one stair and considers... then another... and considers that row, too. Finally, three rows away, he nods and steps in, counting seats until he finds the very middle one, before plopping to his butt and twisting back to give us a thumbs up. "I'll just be here!" he shouts above the roar of... something. Iron Man, maybe. "I won't move after this."

"Okay." Amused, Fox settles back, smoothing her skirt down to cover her delicious thighs, and when she's comfortable, she grabs her soda and takes a slow sip.

"You didn't even ask me to come to the cinema with you." I adjust my position on the not-very-comfortable chairs, and since we have the privacy to do so, I set my fingers on the hem of her skirt and drag it up just an inch. Not inappropriate. Not even revealing. Just a little something for me to see. "I thought we were getting along, but you make a movie date and don't even think to ask if I have plans?"

"I didn't want to influence your choice." Seductive, deliciously sexy, she studies me in the dark, her long lashes coming down to kiss her cheeks and her plump bottom lip trapped between her teeth. "If I'd asked you to come, you probably would have said yes, even if you didn't want to. Instead, I made sure you were aware of our plans, and now you're here of your own accord."

"What if my feelings got hurt, and I was too proud to come without an invitation?"

"Then we'd have both missed out." She glances down at my hand, smirking as I draw a long, lazy pattern on her thigh. "I heard you say I was flaky and annoying to Tommy." Troubled, she brings her eyes back up again. "I wasn't trying to eavesdrop, and even when I did, I wasn't going to say anything. But this is who I am, Christian. Irritatingly in your face. Do you still consider me an annoying pain in your ass you hardly tolerate?"

"No." I cup her jaw and throw a last look down the rows of chairs to make sure Franky's eyes are where they need to be. Then I come back around and pull her in until our lips touch. "I *do* think you're an annoying pain in my ass with a mouth full of sass and a body I can't get enough of. But I don't *tolerate* you. I hoard every minute I'm given and spend an unhealthy amount of time manufacturing reasons to be near you." I draw her plump bottom lip between my teeth. "Do the shop windows need a clean?"

Curious, and confused, her brows pinch. "No...?"

"But I'm gonna come clean them tomorrow, anyway. Got cobwebs in the corners of the shop, way too high for you to reach? I'm your man."

She trembles under my touch, leaning closer, closer, close enough that even Franky, a ten-year-old kid, would know this isn't how Aunty Fox and Chris interact normally.

"We're casual, and the time we have is limited. But there isn't a single fucking rule that says I can't make up reasons to be near you. Honestly, you're lucky I haven't already walked my ass into your apartment in the middle of the night."

"Really?"

"I've laid awake at my place, wondering if you were lonely. Because fuck, I was." I swoop in and press one last gentle kiss to her lips, then as the final trailer ends, I release her and wait as, predictably, Franky spins and shows us two thumbs up. Settling back in my seat, I smile and wait for him to twist back to the front, then digging my hand into my jeans, I rearrange my cock before placing my free hand on Fox's thigh.

She shudders under my touch. Pent up and anxious, she watches as I walk my fingers over her goosebumped skin and into her panties. Then I touch her core and groan at her explosive exhale.

She unfolds her legs and presents herself for my exploration.

Good fucking girl.

"I hardly sleep, Fox. I lay in my bed for at least eight hours every single night, but I'm lucky if I sleep four of them." I look over and find her lips dropped open into a lovely O, her chest rising and falling, and her hands clutching the armrests like she might float off without them. "That leaves me with hours and hours and hours to consider climbing into my truck and visiting you."

"Maybe you should." She whimpers as I slide just one digit into her wet pussy. "Maybe I lay awake, too. A little sad that we're in two different buildings, two different beds, when we could be in one."

"Is that a formal invitation?" I push in as deep as I can, then out, before adding a second finger. "Can I climb into your bed at night? Even if you're already asleep?"

"Yes." Fuck Spiderman. Fuck Iron Man. Fuck them all. Fox white-knuckles the armrests and tips her head back. "Shit. Yes, Christian. You can visit me at night, even if I'm already asleep."

"Can I fuck you, even if you're already asleep? I could make it so you're not sure if I'm there for real, or if you're just dreaming of me. When I fuck you, you'll come not knowing if I was the one who drew you to your peak, or if it was your very own incubus demon come to visit."

She licks her dry lips and nods.

"Have you ever done that before?" I dip a third finger in and stretch her wider. "Let someone fuck you while you were asleep?"

She shudders around my fingers, gasping and filling my palm with her release.

"I've never been fucked while I was asleep before." She swallows, choking on her inhalation. "I would like you to do that to me."

I use her lubrication and inch my hand further around her ass, and because she so willingly adjusts to make room, I slip a digit into her throbbing hole, a vibrating tremble rocking through my system when she accepts me with needy anticipation.

"I'll come by tonight," I whisper. "After you're asleep. I'll let myself in to your apartment and have your body while you're unconscious. You'll like it, and I'll blow my load knowing how defenseless you are."

"Chris—"

"Come again." I dig my fingers into her pussy. "It turns me on how trusting you are of my intentions. I could do whatever the fuck I want, but you know I'll make it feel good."

"Probably makes me an idiot." She chokes out her attempt at a laugh, but her release takes hold, trapping her in her ecstasy as her stomach clenches and her pussy crushes my fingers. "Shit."

"Makes you perfect." I lean closer and kiss her cheek. "Enjoy the movie, beautiful. And wear your plug to bed. I'll reward you for it."

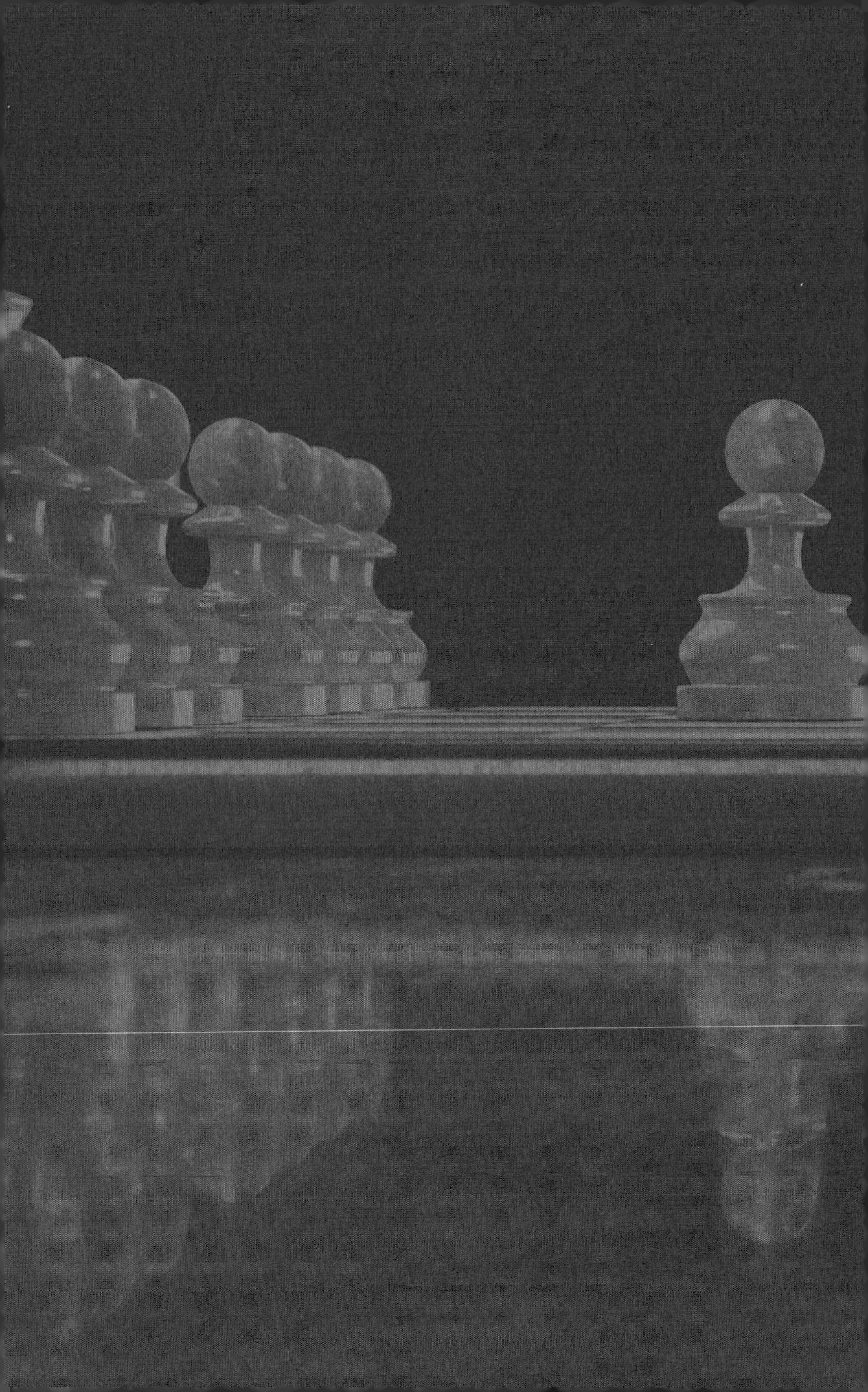

ROUND NINETEEN

CHRIS

Anticipation is like a drug, sizzling through my veins and burning the tips of my fingers. But I'm a desperate man—not only for Fox's body, but for sleep. The kind of sleep I find only after being inside *her*.

I leave my truck parked down the street near the bakery, to buy myself a cover story, and letting myself in to the bookstore, I keep the lights off and my movements silent as I make my way up the stairs, through the door, and around again to ensure I lock up.

I turn, my cock already raging and hard, and catch a beautiful view of Fox asleep under just a sheet, her belly pressed to the mattress, and her long, mahogany hair splayed over her face. Her eyes are closed. Her breathing, regular and relaxed.

And because she's a good girl, eager to please, I allow my eyes to wander down the messy sheet to her body wrapped only in a silk nightie, the end riding up to reveal a delicate lace thong.

She prepared for me, just like she promised she would.

Parched and desperate, I swallow, lubricating my throat. Making a detour to the bathroom, I find the bottle of lube in the vanity drawers, and beside it, the box of condoms I kinda made a scene over and partially stole.

Ish.

I bring both back into the living space and bend to untie my boots while I walk, toeing each one off when I get to the end of the bed. I unsnap my jeans and set my things on the mattress within easy reach, and because the waiting has been my foreplay for hours, I pull my cock from my jeans and bite down as pleasure eagerly claws along my throat.

There will be no waiting tonight.

There will be no slow seduction.

I peel my shirt off and set it on the floor, and pinching the corner of the sheet between my fingers, I draw it down her body to reveal all of her under the light of the streetlamps outside.

"So fucking beautiful." I want to destroy her pussy, slamming home without finesse and devouring what she offers without remorse. But there's another part of me, a surprising part, that wants to climb in and take things slow. To wake her up and look into her eyes while I move over her. Lazy strokes. Gentle touches.

Jesus, is that what lovemaking is?

A part of me wants that, too.

But that's not what I asked for earlier. It's not what I have permission to do. And fuck, but as a man who knows what it is to have his control and autonomy stripped away, I vow to always and only ever do the specific things she consents to.

Even if that means lying to my brother about my feelings toward a certain siren seductress.

I push my jeans down my thighs and kick them to the floor, and setting one knee on the mattress between her open legs, I grab her ankles and carefully, slowly, straighten her out without waking her up.

I press a kiss to the swell of her ass, nibbling on her flesh as goosebumps race along her spine and down to mark her thighs, and because I want so desperately to be inside her, I draw her thong over her hips and down her legs, dropping it to the floor beside my jeans. Already, pre-cum falls from the head of my cock and onto her ass, dribbling over the highest swell and down to settle right where her plug waits for me to play.

I fist my cock, too needy to wait, too anxious to deprive myself, and though I consider squeezing lube onto my length to make the glide smoother, I reach between her legs and find her wet anyway.

Surprised, I put my hand on the bed beside her ribs and lean around to peek at her face, only to find her lips curled into a devious smile. Her eyes are still closed, but her mind wide, wide awake.

"You were supposed to stay asleep."

"Couldn't." She twists beneath me, carefully pulling her legs around and circling my hips with them. Then she uses her strength and tugs me forward. "You try sleeping with a plug in your ass. It's not all that relaxing."

I snort, but my laughter turns to a moan as my cock touches her fiery core. She eats me up with a sigh, squeezing me extra tight, the hard line of her plug grating along the bottom of my dick.

"Shit." She tilts her head back, stretching her neck, and leaving me with the perfect view and a buffet to taste. "Jesus, Chris. I didn't come to Plainview expecting to get laid as often or as well as I have been."

"Happy surprises." I latch on to her neck and suckle right where her pulse thunders, and rocking my hips back, I slide forward again and seat myself all the way to the base. "You have the sweetest pussy I've ever known, Fox. Fuck."

She drapes her arms over my shoulders, her cry of pleasure hitting my ear and crawling somewhere deep and dark and entirely unexplored within my soul.

"You can sleep inside me, if you want." She tangles her fingers in my hair and pulls me back, searching my eyes in the shadows. "Try. See if you can manage more than four hours."

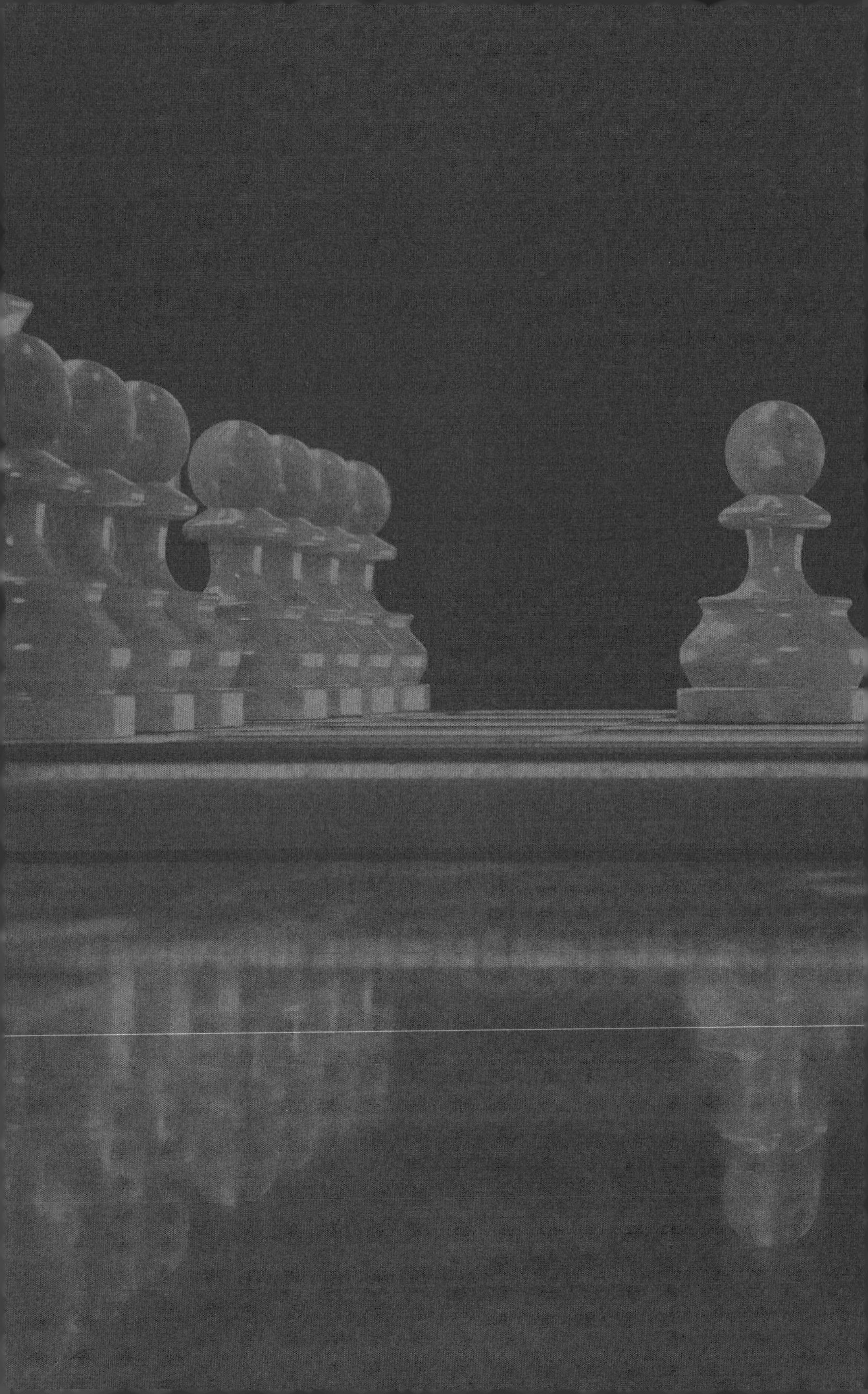

ROUND TWENTY
FOX

I wake at a little before nine the next morning, *long* after my usual seven—New York time—and sit up with a start. Gulping for fresh air, I search the apartment for all the things that feel different.

All the things that feel off.

But then I bring my focus down again, to the man lying flat against my mattress, his belly pressed to the bed and the ends of his hair tangling with his lashes. He sleeps silently, his plump lips pressed into kissable lines and his soft breathing almost as gentle as a lullaby.

Jesus. He's perfect and has no clue.

His leg drapes over mine, his arm lying heavily across my hips. He's naked as the day he was born. His muscular ass on show and his broad back, a delicious canvas to stare at and study… any other day.

But not today.

It's a school day!

Frantic, I twist and snatch up my phone, jumping to my call log so I can call Alana and beg for her forgiveness, but I catch Tommy's name in my text inbox first, his messages—three of them.

> I think you might've forgotten something, New York. Don't stress it. I'll drive Franky today, since I'm heading to the gym after anyway.

> Alana thinks you and I made that deal already, so don't admit you forgot. It'll hurt her feelings, and she's deep in the post-baby hormone surge. She finally had a good sleep, so whatever you do, don't ruin her mood.

And then finally,

> Alana says she's up to exploring outside the house today. Which means she and Hazel are on their way to you. Remember what I said about school drop-off. You're still the perfect best friend who could never step wrong. No need to admit you're human now. Probably shouldn't hit an eight o'clock movie on a school night, though. Franky's tired, too.

"Shit! Shit, shit, shit, shit, shit!" I toss my phone and smack Chris' ass. "Wake up!"

He startles, pushing up to his elbows and looking straight ahead through squinting, unfocused eyes. "What?"

"Get up!" I throw his leg off and roll off the bed, bending and snatching up his jeans and shorts. "Get up, Chris! You have to go."

"The hell is wrong?" He searches the room in a daze, glancing toward the window and crushing his eyes closed. "Time is it?"

"It's nearly nine!"

Finally, his eyes snap open. "What?"

"We slept in. Like, *a lot*!" I sprint to my open suitcase and dig out a pair of underwear, pulling them up my legs and settling the band over my hips. Then I look for a shirt.

Chris slumps back to the bed with a huff. "Can't be nine. I don't sleep that long."

"You did today! And now Alana's on her way here."

He pushes up again, meerkat style, and far more alert this time around. "What?"

"Get dressed!" I drag my shirt over my head and down to cover my torso, and running back to the bed, I grab his boxers and toss them at his chest. "There is literally no story we can tell Alana that would explain this away. Get dressed and leave. Now!"

Finally, he bounds out of bed and stumbles, tripping over his boots. He tears his boxers up one leg, hopping to get the silk up the other. "She's coming here? When?"

"I don't know! Soon. Tommy said—"

"Fox?" Alana knocks on my door, the jingle of her keys like a storm siren screaming across a silent town. "You awake?"

"Oh my God!" I grab his jeans and shirt, balling and slamming them to his chest, then I fist his hair and shove him *down*. "Under the bed," I hiss. "Get under the friggin' bed!"

"Are you insane? Fox, I can't—"

"Now!" I find pockets of strength and slam the monstrous fighter down. Then tossing my blankets over the bed so it looks half decent, I make damn sure the covers drape all the way to the floor and hide the guy almost too long to fit without curling up on himself.

He releases a grunt, smacking his... *something* on the frame. A shoulder, maybe, but when the lock tumbles open on my front door, I spin and sit, straight spine and a fake smile plastered on my face so I'm ready when Alana steps through.

"Hey!" I'm still in my underwear. Just a shirt. No bra. Standing again, I stalk across the apartment and help her with her million things, pulling an overloaded diaper bag off one arm, then scooping Hazel's heavy car seat from her other hand until her tired frame is... well, a little less weighed down. "You look more rested than last night." I turn into the room and set the bag on the floor by my suitcase, and placing Hazel's seat down, I unsnap her restraints, feeding her sweet little arms through the straps and lifting her out. "You fell asleep at the table." I turn and watch with my heart in my throat as she silently, robotically, wanders toward my bed. "Uh... you doing okay, honey?"

She sits right where I sat a moment ago, dropping her posture and exhaling a long, noisy breath. "I slept all night, and I still feel like I could sleep for a year."

"You're recovering from having a baby." I choke on my tongue and lock eyes with Chris', his nose just inches from Alana's foot. "It hasn't even been a week yet, Lan. You're almost over the worst of it."

"I forgot how rough the hormones are." She brings sad, sleepy eyes to mine, the whites shining a light pink, like she's been crying... or perhaps *needs* to cry. "I forgot how cruel it all is, tearing ourselves apart, making our bodies available to a baby to eat from. Then we have the massive hormone dump, and even with the world's sweetest, most attentive partner, I'm still waking every two hours through the night." She pouts. "Prisoners of war are treated more humanely than this."

"Aw." I cough out a soft, amused snicker, and carrying baby Hazel with me, I wander to the coffee machine some wonderful soul had placed in here before I arrived. "You need caffeine, babes. You need a pick-me-up like your life depends on it."

"I need a reminder next time I consider having a baby that, no, I probably shouldn't. No more sex for me. No more sex ever."

I snort, juggling the baby in just one hand while I place a mug under the Keurig spout with the other. "Sex is fun, though. Doesn't always have to end with a baby."

"Sex is really, *really* fun," she sulks, slumping, and, without paying true attention to what the hell she's doing, she grabs my bottle of lube and studies the label as though it's as ordinary as a bottle of soda. Or shampoo. "Sex with Tommy is like... It *used* to be a lot of fun. But now I have stitches that go from my butthole to my vagina, and I'm honestly not sure I'll let that poor man touch me ever again."

In pain, Chris' eyes glitter and strain, his hands clamping over his ears.

My cheeks blaze bright, bright red. I feel the warmth.

"Well..." I cough out a nervous laugh. "I'm sure it'll all work out in the end. Tommy will be patient, and your stitches will eventually go away. Your vagina will go back to its normal shape, and life will go on."

Chris shakes his head. *No, no, no, no, no, no. Please make it stop.*

"You don't need to worry about sex right now, Lan. Your body is not ready, and even if your vagina was fine, you still have a giant, gaping wound inside of you where Hazel was just a week ago. Focus on you and on healing, and everything else will work out." I walk to the fridge and take out a carton of creamer, and since it's good for her breastmilk, I add a little extra to Alana's mug. "Is there a reason you came by today, or did you just need some girl time?"

Tears well up in her eyes and spill onto her cheeks. "Do I *need* a reason? Can't I just want to see my best friend without a gold-etched invitation?"

"Of course, you can come without a reason." I've lived this one-week-postpartum-Alana before, so I stroll back to the bed and sit down beside her, leaning across to place her coffee on the bedside table. "You're welcome in my life any day of the week, sweetpea. You never have to call or ask for permission."

"I just love you so much," she cries. "And last time I did this, we were practically living together. You saved my life, and I love you so much for it. But now I'm basically married to Tommy, and I love him, too. But I miss *you*! I miss you being in my bed sometimes, and I miss staying up late with you, watching a movie, even though I was tired, since I knew Franky would be awake at midnight anyway, so we waited up for that feed together, then we all slept for a few blissful hours."

"You're talking in really long sentences, babe. You understand this is your hormones, right? You're experiencing the baby blues, and that's why you feel this way."

"I feel this way because I miss you!" Sobbing, she wraps her arm over my shoulder and rests her cheek against mine. Then she hisses in pain. *Ouch.* "I wish New York and Plainview were the same place. I wish we lived in the same town again, 'cos I don't want to move away from Tommy, but you don't want to move away from New York. Now my heart is torn in two, and I'm the baby."

"The baby?"

"Solomon's baby!" Her chest heaves from her stuttered breaths, her lungs spasming for air. "Didn't Solomon tear his baby in half?"

"Uh..." I grit my teeth. "I'm not sure, sweetie. I never went to Sunday school."

"I'm pretty sure," she hiccups. "I'm pretty sure that's what the story was about! Neither parent loved the baby more than they hated the other, so they tore it in half. Now you're in New York, and I'm here, and Tommy's here, and I love Chris, too!"

Good. If nothing else, I'm glad he gets to hear her say so during her hormonal rant.

"You don't have to worry about Solomon or the baby, sweetie. Because I'm not tearing you. I'll never beg you to choose me."

"I'm begging you to choose me!" She brings devastated eyes around, trembling jaw and shaking lips. "I want to co-parent my baby girl with you, the same way I co-parented Franky with you. And I'm sorry!"

"You're sorry?"

"I'm sorry because I didn't even consider what taking him away would do to you. *We* co-parented him! Me and you. But I just took him! I didn't even ask your permission. I just said, '*hey, we're moving to Bumfuck Nowhere next Thursday. Deal with it.*'"

Snickering, I reach across and wipe her tears. "I forgive you."

"Or maybe you didn't even care at all. Maybe you were relieved to be rid of us because I was the needy, whiny, annoying trauma girl who dumped her trauma on your head even though you didn't even ask to hear the story, then I trauma dumped my trauma into a trauma book and made you read every single draft, *and then,*" she raises her voice an octave or two, "then! I didn't even sell the stupid book because I was afraid to trauma dump my trauma all over the country. But then I moved to Plainview and *didn't* trauma dump my trauma all over Tommy because I didn't want to hurt his heart. And I didn't want to hurt Chris' heart. And I didn't want either of them to go to jail. But it was all for nothing, 'cos they saw it on the news, anyway. Then they went to Grady's hotel, and I just…" She whimpers, big fat tears dribbling over her cheeks. "I'm pretty sure they hurt him real bad, Fox. Like, really, really bad. But I'm too scared to ask, and Tommy is too much of a gentleman to say so. And for as long as no one says it out loud, they won't go to prison."

I hold my silence, knowing she needs to purge. Brutally aware she has a million feelings bottled up inside her beautiful brain.

"And I know Ollie feels guilty, too," she cries. "Even though he didn't do anything wrong. And sure, he hurt my feelings when he was mean to me about leaving, and for just a second, one teeny tiny little second, in my brain, I thought, '*Well, I wouldn't have left if you never got arrested, you jerkoff!*' But that's a vile, horrible thought, and I didn't mean it. I didn't mean to think that thought, but now I think he thinks those thoughts, and I don't know how to make it all better."

She thinks he thinks she thinks those thoughts. I deserve a medal for keeping up.

"Well?" she snaps in the silence, glancing across with wrinkled, trembling lips. "Aren't you going to say anything?"

I slide my arm over her shoulders and pull her in, pressing a juicy kiss right on the middle of her cheek. "I was letting you get it all out before I interrupted. First," I take the bottle of lube and drop it to the floor, and because I enjoy being a mean girl sometimes, I kick it under the bed, knowing damn well Chris will receive it. "Don't play with my sex things, Lana. It's kinda weird, and I can't take a conversation seriously while you're reading the label of my lube. Second, I miss you, too. I miss staying up late with you and sneaking into your bed sometimes. I miss feeding your baby in the middle of the night and changing a diaper sometimes—not all the time," I amend with a snigger. "Since those things are gross. But being an aunty means I get to pick and choose which ones I change. I miss living in the same place as you and thanking Colin for the coffee he delivered to our weird, not-quite-lesbian codependency. He didn't judge. He just provided."

"I would have been a lesbian with you if I didn't like Tommy's penis so much."

"Relatable," I laugh, shaking my head when I realize identical twins might mean more than I ever really thought it meant. "Men annoy me, Lana. They annoy me *so* much. But I have a thing for the D, too. So I guess that means we're straight and just friends."

She swipes her tears from her cheeks. "Stupid penises."

"I know. The injustice. As for trauma dumping... it's okay. I wanted to hear your story, and when you wrote it into a really *good* book, I wanted to read it. I fell in love with your fictional Tommy within a matter of pages. And I loved his brother, too, because you, the author, loved them both so much. The stunt your agent pulled, announcing the book despite your refusal to make the deal, was extra shitty of her. And Tommy finding out the truth because of the news was cruel. But it all worked out, huh?" I look down at a sleeping Hazel and her thick lips, wrinkled exactly how Alana's wrinkle when she sleeps. "I'm holding your baby right now, Tommy's baby. And she's the prettiest, sweetest, loveliest prize after a lot of pain. And although I know what you went through was horrible, I'm not sure you'd go back and trade her, would you?"

With a trembling jaw, she shakes her head and sniffles. "No."

"And I know for a damn fact you wouldn't trade Franky."

She wipes her boogers and whimpers. "Not for a million re-dos."

"Exactly. So everything that happened, happened. It was your journey. And if Tommy and Chris *maybe* did something bad to Grady, then I say *hell fucking yes.*"

"You do?" Heavy tears dribble from the corners of her eyes. "You support violence, even though your job is literally *happiness*?"

"I support castrating rapists and making them hurt." I search her eyes, remembering *exactly* how I felt when she first told me what had happened to her. "I support treating people the way they treat others. If I'd known Tommy and Chris then like I do now, if I'd known where they were going that day and what they intended to do, I would've hopped into the bed of that truck and taken turns doing something *bad* to Grady, too. They love you, Alana. And you love them. You make an amazing family. Which means you belong right here in Plainview. You belong wherever they are."

"But I belong wherever you are, too. You're my family, Fox, and it hurts every single day when I wake up and you're not here."

"They don't need Chief Happiness Officers out here." I hold her and wait for her eyes to come back to mine. "I don't belong here. Not like you do."

"But—"

"But you named your baby for me, so I'll visit a lot. And you'll visit me. And every time Tommy fights professionally, I'll come to that, since I get exceptional front-row seats."

She coughs out a teary, silly laugh. "I made sure he didn't forget. He's too afraid of me to mess something like that up."

"Good. A little fear never hurt anyone. Also, I have to ask…" I lean closer and study her eyes. "How did you never consider taking both of them to bed at the same time?"

"What?" she explodes. *Oh dear, how scandalous!* "Fox!"

"I'm serious! They're identical. They adore you. They're both kinda obsessive and commanding, and underneath all the muscle and bravado, they're giant babies with a mommy kink, and you, my darling girl, are their mommy."

"Ew!" She smacks my arm and surges off the bed. "You're disgusting."

"You're not crying anymore." I bring Hazel down to lie in the crook of my arm, and because I have a free hand, I stroke the tip of her nose. *She got it from her momma.* "Not even once? Seriously? There wasn't one single time in all those years you saw them together and thought, *wellllllll…?*"

"No!" She storms back to the bed and snatches up her coffee. "You're nasty."

"How is that nasty? You can't possibly think Chris isn't attractive, considering you sit on a face identical to his."

"Fox!"

"Stop screeching and open your mind to the possibilities. You could even do the oopsie with Chris and say you mixed them up."

"You're such a pain." But she giggles. And cries. Mostly, she giggles and sips her coffee. "They look the same on the outside. But inside, Tommy has my heart."

"And Chris? He's just tossed out in the cold because Tommy got to you first?"

She rolls her eyes. "I love Chris like I love Franky. I want to protect him. I want to see him happy. I want to know that he's going to be okay because I've spent twenty years worried like hell that he isn't. He's darker than Tommy." She lowers her coffee, bringing a hand up to wipe beneath her nose. "He was treated worse, I think. When they were kids, I think he was tormented way more than Tommy was. And maybe, physically, it wasn't different. But mentally, because of how he is, I think he was in a worse hell than Tommy. I worry every single day that the darkness will swallow him up before he learns how to live in the light."

The man can't sleep. I wish for the light, too.

"Are you okay now?" I push up to stand, if only to draw her eyes somewhere else and not down to the man who lurks under the bed. "You came to me so you could cry and not terrify Tommy. But are you good now?"

"Yes." She drops her lips into a pout, sad and sorry and all the way pathetic. "Also, I came to ask why the hell you forgot to bring my kid to school today?"

My heart stumbles violently in my chest. "Hmm?"

"Tommy said you and he had agreed, but I know when he's lying, Fox. His nose," she points up at hers, "it does this squidgy, squinty, weird thing. I figured that out when he was only twelve years old. Besides, you're still in your undies, and despite how ridiculously overwhelming my baby hormones are right now, I didn't *not* see that bottle of lube. Which leads me to the conclusion you're a nasty hussy, and you're getting laid. But by who?" She wonders, tapping her chin. She's a regular Watson... or whoever the hell that inspector was. "Do I know him?"

"No, I—"

"I mean, surely I do. Unless you're shipping penis in from out of town, everyone knows everyone in Plainview. And the only reason you've snuck this past me is because of the whole baby and vagina stitches thing."

"Alana—"

"Is it Cliff? I heard the whispers about your bathroom."

"Cliff?" My voice squeaks. Good lord, why does my voice squeak? "The fighter? No. Of course not."

"I heard that Barbara saw him coming up here last week." Hormonal overage *done*, she walks a lap of my living space, stepping ridiculously, sickeningly close to Chris' boots, but too tired to look down and notice them. "I rarely listen to town gossip, but I was in the hospital for three days, and gossip is the *only* thing anyone has to pass the time in there. I heard you and Cliff were cutesy and giggly."

"We were not!"

"But he was here?"

"Yes, he was here. He's helping me with the bathroom renovations. But we weren't giggly. I'm never giggly."

"So someone else, then." Her belly is still round-ish, though not as round as it was this time last week. So when she reaches the window and turns back to face me, smug taunting in her eyes, her belly is the first thing to turn. "I heard you were at the gym a few days ago, too. So it's someone there."

"Good lord, woman. You sound an awful lot like the old biddies you call and complain about! You *heard* this, you *heard* that?"

"I heard a heard and heard." She snickers. "Am I wrong?"

"About me being at the gym? The day I *took your son to the gym*?"

"Oh... hmm..."

I knock the wind from her sails and draw her to a pause. "Okay, so although that rumor is true, it might not mean anything more than taking Franky to the gym."

"Ya think?! Jesus. Have I ever not told you about my sex life?"

"Never. Which is why I'm so curious now. Why hide him, if not because you think I'll be scandalized by whoever he is?"

"Or maybe you're overthinking things and letting your baby hormones take over." *Great! Gaslighting your best friend is a new low for you, Fox.* "I was out late last night at the movies, and I slept in today. It's not a crime. Can you head down and open the shop while I get dressed? I'm running late, and it's unprofessional for a store not to open when they say they'll open."

"You want *me* to open? Really? I'm six days postpartum, and you're already putting me back to work?"

"Oh, bring out the violins!"

"For shame. For shame!"

"Go the hell away. Open the shop. I'll be down in five minutes."

"Fine."

She sets her coffee cup on the counter and wanders forward with her hands outstretched. But I turn and snarl. "Leave the baby. I'm not done snuggling with her yet, and you're irritating me. I deserve her hugs, and you deserve to work."

"Even though I have stitches in my vagina?"

I choke out a delirious laugh, not because of her stitches but because Chris is being forced to hear about them. *Again.* "Even then. Are you sticking around for long?"

"I'll stay until I stop wanting to cry every time you and I are not in the same room. So…" She meanders to the door and picks up her diaper bag. "A couple of hours'll do it. Assuming I'm sitting for most of them so I don't bleed out. Then I'll head over to the gym and watch my man exercise for a little bit. He's all worked up and undersexed. So he's got energy to spare."

"Undersexed," I snort, dropping my chin in a nod. "So glad I know that about him. Maybe I should come by the gym too, watch a couple of frustrated Watkins boys whale on each other."

"Not sure Chris is as frustrated as his brother. *I heard* he went running through the drugstore last week, buying condoms and making a scene." She swings my apartment door open, *allllmost*, but not quite rested up enough to connect a couple of ridiculously obvious dots. "I should talk to him about that. I wonder who he's banging this week?"

"*This week*?" Jealousy is like a sharp barbed knife piercing my stomach. "Does he shuffle lovers regularly?"

She lifts her shoulder in a delicate, teasing shrug. "Pretty sure he shops from out of town these days, seeing as how he's tasted everyone within a fifty-mile radius who isn't married and isn't Barbara's age."

"Ew." I lose my smile and screw my nose in disgust. "He's out here banging grandmas, and you're worried about *my* sex life?"

"Not grandmas," she cackles. "Just... *mas*. Single motherhood is a lonely time, and he's just doing his civic duty, keeping them loose and limber. It's like community service at this point and could probably buy him leniency within the court system if he's ever busted for something bad."

"Go away now." I follow her to the door and close it at her back, then pressing my ear to the wood and making damn sure she moves down the stairs, I turn again with a growl. "Community service, Christian Watkins? Is she serious right now?"

"Stitches in her vagina!?" He pops up on the other side of the bed, tossing his jeans to the mattress and coming around to meet me, toe-to-toe. "You and Cliff?"

"He's fixing my bathroom!"

"Giggly and cute?"

"I'm *never* giggly."

"The condoms were for you!" He sweeps Hazel out of my arms and holds her in a gentle, horrifyingly endearing way. "Why'd you keep the baby if you want to shower, anyway? You would need to get out and tend to her again if she cries."

"Because I knew *you'd* want to hold her, dummy. Because I knew *you'd* be pissy that she was so close, but you didn't get a hug. Because *you* are a community icon, allegedly, and I knew having the baby between us would stop *me* from ripping your face to shreds!" Tearing my shirt off and tossing it into my suitcase, I stalk into the bathroom and flip the taps on. "You shop for ass outside of Plainview, huh? How many hearts have you broken?"

"None." He saunters to the bathroom door, rocking his baby niece with a barely there sway of his hips. "I break no hearts. I merely serve physical needs."

"Not for as long as I'm in town, you don't. You'll serve only *my* physical needs, and if I hear you're serving on the side, I'll pry a skull open with a crowbar."

"Whose skull?" His eyes glitter with torment. "Hers or mine? Because that'll help me make future decisions."

"Yours. Since it's hardly her fault she wants to be serviced by the magical Watkins penis. It should be a regulated substance. Your dick is ad*dick*tive."

He purses his lips and looks me up and down. "Really? You can play on words when you're mad?"

"I'm not mad!" I spin under the spray of the shower, only to slam my elbow and hiss when the pain takes my breath away. "Shit! Dammit."

"You okay?"

"Shut up! If I find out you're sharing your dick with someone else for as long as I'm in this godforsaken town, you'll find out exactly how annoying I can be."

"Fox—"

I rub my elbow and pretend the idea of him with someone else doesn't make my chest ache. "Did you order the cake yet for the party?"

"No, I—"

"Put the baby down, get dressed, and Spiderman your ass out the damn window! Order the cake before I hurt you."

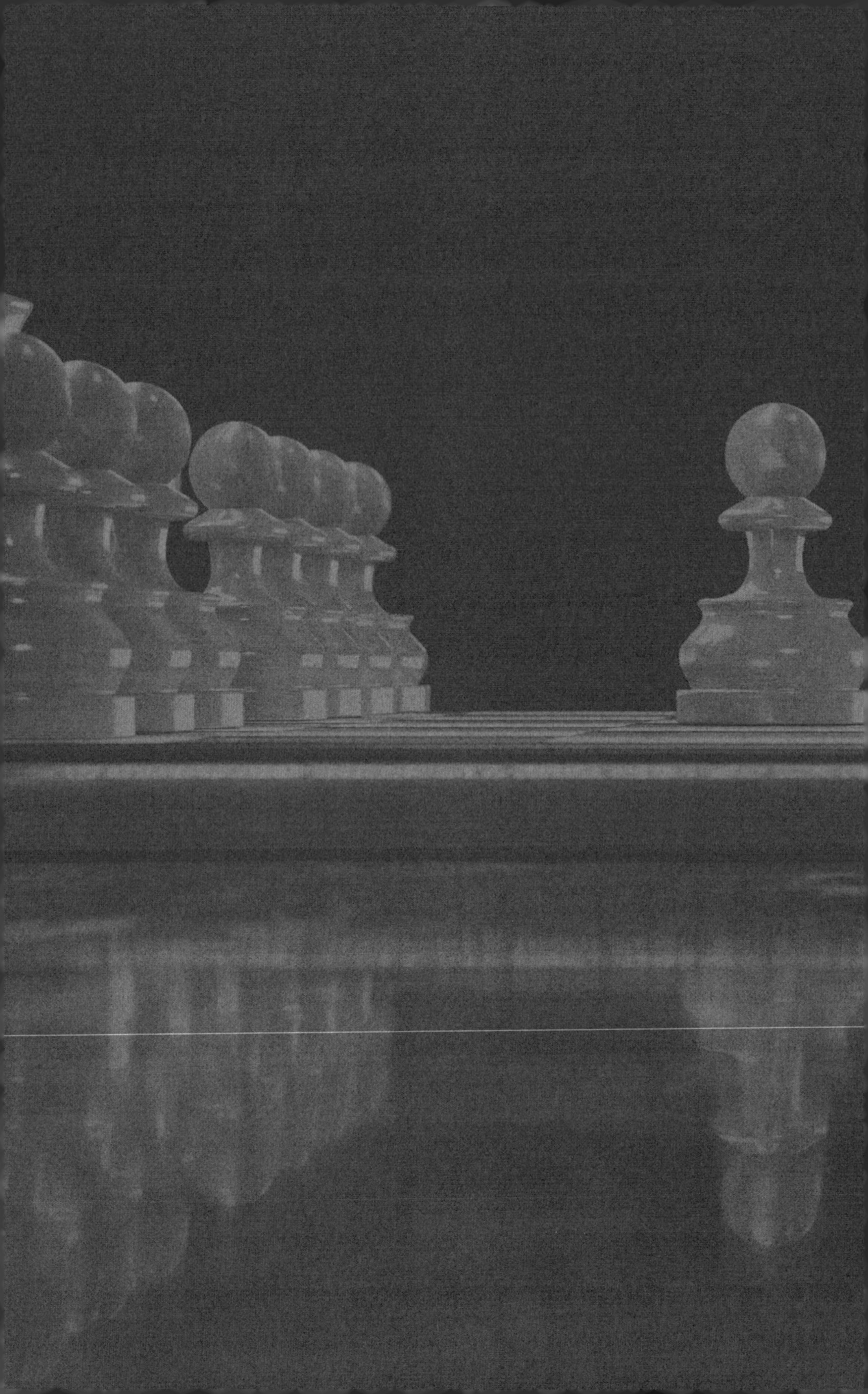

ROUND TWENTY-ONE
FOX

"I heard a rumor about you, Christian." Alana crosses her kitchen, more rested now than she was a few days ago, a little less hormonal the further she gets from Hazel's birthday. Setting a plate of cheesecake beside Chris' waiting hand—*he brandishes a clean, diamond-detailed fork, of course*—she places a second plate in front of Franky and carefully sits down opposite me while Tommy carries three more. "It was a juicy rumor I've been meaning to ask about, but you've been keeping yourself busy, it seems."

"Hm?" He digs in, stabbing the end of his dessert and breaking off a chunk. "What rumor?"

"Yeah?" I smile in thanks when Tommy hands me my slice. "What rumor?"

"You already know," Alana waves me off. And though Tommy places a plate in front of her, Alana leans on her elbows and burns Chris with her stare. "I heard from not *one*, but *two* different sources, that you were running through the drugstore a couple of weeks back. Shouting at people not to talk to you."

"You shouted at people?" I clap a hand over my mouth, trying—and failing—to muffle my laughter. "You shouted, Christian?"

"Why were you running at the drugstore?" Franky asks innocently. "Needed a Band-Aid?"

"Yes. Exactly." Chris intently focuses on his cheesecake. "I needed a Band-Aid."

"I heard you bought... special flavored Band-Aids," Alana snickers. "A whole jumbo box of them."

"Shut up, Alana—"

"Don't tell my mom to shut up!" Franky growls.

"So then I'm led to wonder, who were you sharing these Band-Aids with, Christian? Why so many? Why so loud?"

"Must've stubbed his toe," Franky grumbles. *Slow to forgive: not even his idol and favorite Watkins gets a pass.* "I stubbed my toe the other day 'cos the stupid rooster chased me onto the dock. Jerk."

"Such a jerk," Alana giggles. "Christian? Care to comment on the situation?"

"Sure." He fills his mouth and settles back in his chair, folding his arms. "Whacky is old, and his brain has mostly already rotted. His body will give out soon, which means the situation will resolve itself naturally. Eventually."

Tommy finally sits, snickering. "Smooth. Probably not gonna get you over the line, though."

"Who are you currently dating, Christian?" Alana picks up her fork and slowly shaves just a little cheesecake off the side. "Do we know her? Do you intend to bring her home to meet the family?"

"Yeah, Chris." Tommy flashes a large, taunting grin. "What's her name? What's her star sign?"

"For fuck's sake." He shoves up from his chair, snatching his plate and taking his fork with him. "I demand privacy within my private life."

"Hardly private," Alana giggles. "I heard this rumor from Mrs. Tower."

"Mrs. Tower?" Franky asks. "The mean high school drama teacher?"

"That says it all," Chris scowls. "She's apt to make up stories and add dramatic flair to please her audience."

"Oh, so you're saying categorically and confidently, this event did *not* take place?" She drags her fork on her tongue, smugly suckling cheesecake from the pokers. "Despite my *multiple* sources?"

"I'm saying that my private life is none of your business. It has never been your business, and considering you have a whole human being relying on you right now to survive, I suggest you don't bother yourself by sticking your nose into my business. Save yourself the hassle."

"I'm a woman," she teases. "I can multitask."

"How are your stitches, anyway?" My cheeks ache from the laughter I keep trapped inside, because literally every person in this room—except Chris—has seen, or was shot out of, Alana's vagina. "Healing?"

"Much better." Changing gears, Alana scoops cake onto her fork and brings her eyes to me. "A little itchy, which can get kind of uncomfortable."

Chris groans, his face turning an amusing green tinge. "While we're eating. Really?"

"What's the problem, Christian?" I turn with a saccharine smile. "Childbirth is a beautiful, natural thing. But it doesn't come without its risks. Pushing a watermelon through a hole the size of a passion fruit is likely to end in tearing."

"Fox!"

"Skin tears, little buddy. You would literally know about that." I look to Tommy. "Is that not why they smear Vaseline on a fighter's face?"

His cheeks burn a dangerous, dark red. "Uh… yeah, that's a fact."

"Right! So it's just skin." I bring my focus back to the green Watkins. "You're *uncomfortable* because this particular section of skin is located in and around Alana's vagina."

"Woman!" He points toward Franky. And three feet behind him, a sleeping Hazel, tucked into a transportable crib. "He's a child! Why are you saying that word in front of a child?"

"Vagina? He's not bothered. It's just a word, like arm and anus."

"Oh my God!" He slams his plate to the counter and grabs his hair. "Is this who we are now? Animals in clothes? We can't even have a respectable dinner without saying words like…"

"Arm?"

He snarls.

I bring my eyes back to Alana. "He must've been *fun* during health class in high school, huh? Did he climb under the table and curl into the fetal position?"

"He was mysteriously sick during *several* of those lessons." She places cheesecake onto her tongue. "There were the days Chris and Tommy were away because… well… ya know. Life was tough. But then there were the days Chris was away, and those days suspiciously coincided with specific discussion topics in health class."

"Which would explain why he was running through the drugstore, screaming at people instead of just being a normal, functional human being who wanted to buy… Band-Aids."

"Which brings us right back around," Alana twists in her seat, pinning him with a smile. "Who is she?"

Furious and ready to fight, he burns my forehead with his glare.

"So, Alana knows about the party," Tommy chuckles, saving his brother like he always does. "She heard about it from Barbara, who was talking to Glenn and Doris about it."

"Aww, yeah." From tormenting to content, Alana comes back around with a sweet smile. "You're throwing me a party, Fox! That's so sweet of you."

"Someone has to do it. You live with three Neanderthals, two of whom are seemingly allergic to social gatherings, and the third," I hit Tommy with a look, "I *assume* the initiative just hadn't smacked him in the back of the head yet. Everyone is so busy running a gym and a bookstore and folding Franklin into his new school, and now Hazel is here. Worthy distractions, for sure, but it saddens me no one thought to do this."

"I heard you've been threatening people," she giggles. "If they don't come, they're gonna get hurt."

"False." I slide my fork into the cheesecake and slice a little more off. "I said if they don't come, *and bring a guest or ten in addition*, then they're gonna get hurt. I expect the gym to overflow with bodies, and every single one of them better be telling you how wonderful you are."

"Nothing like the threat of corporal punishment to get folks into the celebratory spirit." Tommy settles back, draping his arm over Alana's shoulders. "Cliff said he invited a bunch of people, too. Just FYI."

"Good. The more, the merrier. So long as he gets me actual numbers a week before the event."

"You'll probably live to regret your choices," Alana taunts. "Cliff knows a *lot* of people. You know how vampires get strength from blood, and introverts suck the fun out of parties they never wanted to go to?"

So, Chris? "Sure. I'm following you."

"Well, Cliff gets strength from meeting people and making friends. He's independently..."

"Not, like, rich," Tommy intercepts. "But the dude is probably selling cocaine on the side or something because there ain't no way he's living the life he does on whatever he makes fixing up homes."

"Oh! Speaking of Cliff." At Hazel's first peep, just a single chirp of sound, Alana rises from her chair and wanders around to the crib to sweep her baby girl up. And because they're so practiced, Alana frees her boob, and Hazel traps it between her gums, all in under a second.

Chris, of course, spins away and slams his hip on the counter, his pained hiss traveling across the kitchen.

"First of all," she comes back around and settles exactly where she started, eating one-handed while Hazel hungrily guzzles her mom's milk.

"He's not a drug dealer. I wanted to put that out there, since you're not from around here, and you might've believed that lie."

"Well shucks, Page." I set my fork on my plate and sit back with a full belly. "So glad you cleared that up."

"Second, his parents owned a bit of land out here when we were kids, and then they sold up a couple of years ago to retire somewhere else. They banked their money and gave Cliff his inheritance early, so he's *kind of* independently wealthy. He'd be smart to maintain a day job, if only to keep his skills growing and his reputation within the town. But he can be chill about it all. Unless he blows it all on strippers and gambling, he should be fine for the rest of his life."

"Uh, well..." A thick crumb pulls my attention, gleaming from the edge of my plate. So I place the pad of my pointer finger over the top and pick it up, placing it on my tongue. "Thanks for the history lesson about a guy I hardly know."

"No, well, that's my third point. You should go out with Cliff!"

Chris turns, quiet and dangerous, and narrows his eyes.

"He's single," she continues. "You're single... ish."

Tommy's eyes widen. "Ish?"

"She's been enjoying male attention in secret," Alana croons. "She's not saying who, and she's definitely not the type to get attached. So that makes her relatively single enough to entertain dinner with Cliff."

Thoughtful, Tommy's eyes flicker. "That so?"

"He's a total sweetheart," Alana continues. "Honestly, one of the most decent guys I've ever met. He'll always speak respectfully, hold a door—"

"Can I be excused?" Franky drags his finger over his now-empty plate, collecting any last-minute dessert. "I want to watch TV. Please?"

"Sure, honey." She smiles and waits for him to stand, and when he's out of the room, she brings glittering eyes back to mine. "He's the hold a door for you in public, pull your hair and smack your ass in private type."

"Alana!" Tommy rounds on his baby momma. "The hell did you just say?"

"What? I'm calling it how it is. He's kind and courteous. He's handy with the tools, helps little old ladies at the grocery store, says *yes ma'am, no ma'am*, can fight, supervises the pedestrian crossing outside the school sometimes, is an extrovert like Fox, and comes with absolutely no scandal, which is a pretty big deal in this town, since literally *everyone* around here has a skeleton or two in their closet."

"What skeletons?" I taunt. "What scandals?"

"Well, my skeleton is the whole teen pregnancy thing. And running away. Then, coming back. Then getting pregnant again." She wrinkles her nose. "That puts me firmly in the *loose whore* category." She hooks a thumb to the side. "Tommy and Chris' biggest mistake was, ya know, being poor." She rolls her eyes. "Yours is that you're an outsider. But Cliff is just…"

"He's just what, Alana Bette?" Tommy glowers. "What is it you love so much?"

"He's broken no hearts," she sighs. "I can't find a single female in this town or the next with anything bad to say about him. He has no random babies or baby mommas. He's a good sport. As in, he fights and he trains, but he doesn't even care to win. If the participation ribbon was a person, it would be Cliff."

"Hmm…" I glance over at Chris and grin. "He sounds pretty amazing."

His eyes burn hot, like lava traveling along the side of its mountain.

"I could talk to him," Alana offers excitedly. "Set it up."

"You make quite the assumption," I counter. "Who's to say he finds me attractive? He might think I'm an uppity Yankee troll, too."

"No, he—"

"You count on his kindness, so his acceptance may be nothing more than good manners."

"He already told me how pretty he thinks you are."

"What?" Chris strides back to the table and sits heavily in his chair. "Cliff thinks Fox is pretty?"

"Uh… yes?" Alana scoffs. "*Everyone* thinks Fox is pretty."

I fan my face. "Shucks, Lana."

"But he said those words?" Chris presses. "He said he's into Fox?"

"Yeah?" I question. "He said *those* words? He's into me?"

"Uh-huh." Alana scoops cheesecake onto her tongue. "He sure did. And since you're my friend and everyone else around here looks at you like you've got some weird New-Yorkian fungus growing out of your eyes…" She stops and shakes her head. "You don't. You're perfect, by the way."

"Thanks." I slide the tip of my finger across the surface of my plate. "I needed to hear that today."

"Since you're my friend, he knew to come to me. He thinks you're pretty and smart. He mentioned how hard you worked to get those tiles out of the bathroom, since you wanted to save him the work and time. He's as tuned in to the local gossip as the rest of us, so despite the fungus thing, he's heard only good things about your management of the shop. He knows you work for some bigwigs up in Manhattan, which implies a certain level of success and brains."

"She's the chief happiness officer!" Chris snarls.

Incredulous, I cock a brow and shoot a look his way. *Really?*

"I'm not saying you lack brains! I'm just saying that's not even a proper job."

"By the end of our conversation, he asked if you were seeing anybody."

"He asked that?" Furious, Chris swings his gaze back to Alana. "He specifically asked?"

"He did." She sets her fork down and pats Hazel's bottom. "He's a gentleman, so he never would have stepped on toes if you were already seeing someone else, and he understands your vulnerability, considering the work he's doing at the apartment. He would never want to express interest, receive a rejection, and then have you feel uncomfortable while he's finishing out the job."

"He sounds exceptionally thoughtful." I roll my lip between my teeth and meet Tommy's dancing eyes. "That's rare these days."

"So, if you're interested, too," Alana continues, "I can let him know. Once he has the green light, he can ask you out for real and not worry about offending you."

"Geez, Fox." Slowly, violently, Chris brings his eyes around and stares at the side of my face. "Sounds like it's all worked out. Will you say yes?"

"I think you should say yes." Tommy sits back with a smug grin, folding his arms and scratching his chin like he thinks that'll hide the tremble of his jaw.

"You think so, huh?" Chris glares at his brother, anger wafting off the man like waves lapping at the beach. "You think it's a good idea to set one of your fighters up with Alana's best friend?"

"Why not? She's a free agent, ain't she?" He brings his gaze to me. "And Cliff travels a lot. So you could probably meet up in New York pretty regularly if you decide you like each other enough."

"It's decided, then." Alana detaches Hazel from her boob without flashing even a speck of nipple, and bringing her up, she lays the baby on her chest and elicits a full-bellied echoing belch. "I'll tell him next time I see him."

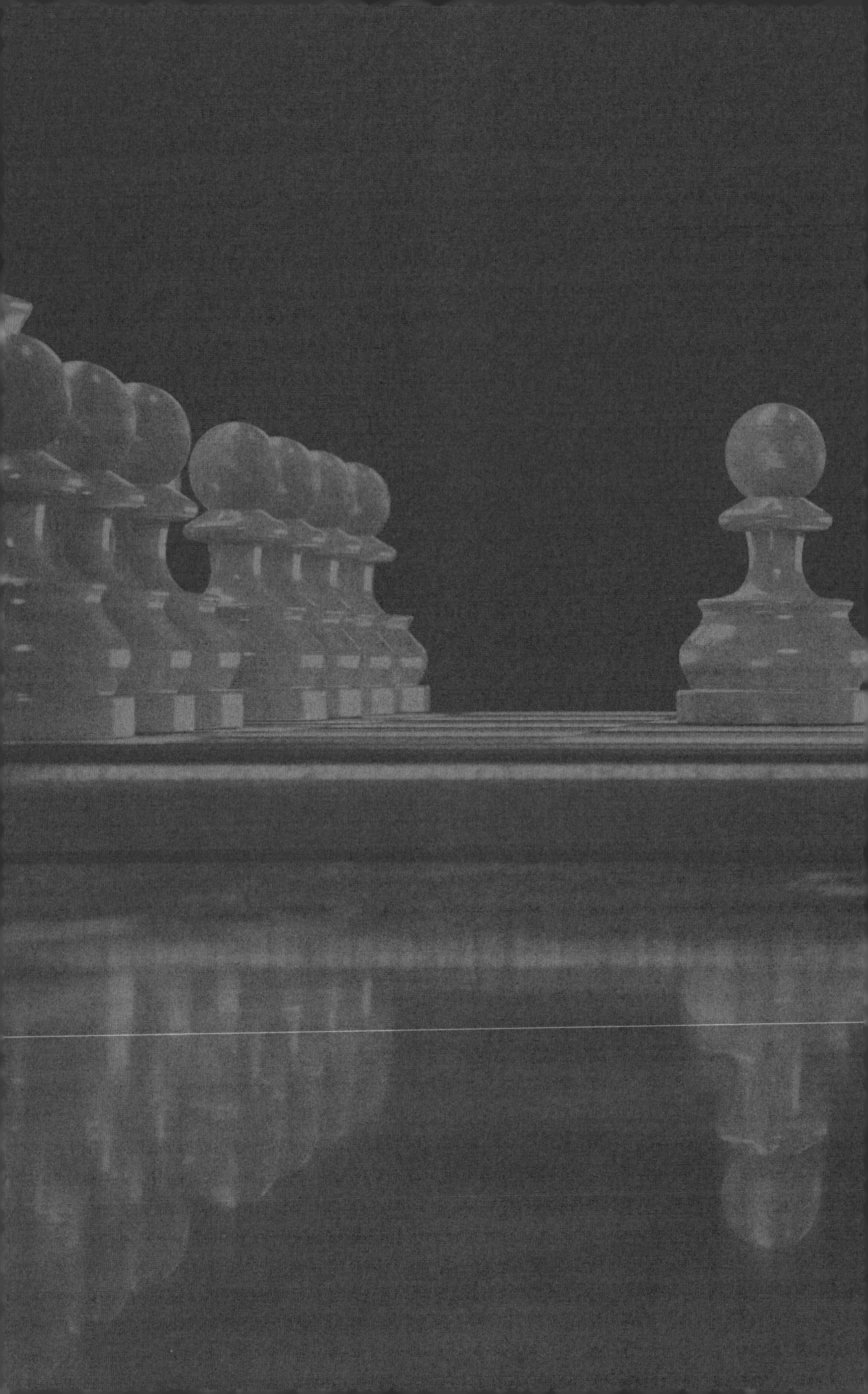

ROUND TWENTY-TWO
CHRIS

It takes another seven days before Cliff returns to the gym. Seven whole fucking days, like he knew he had a target on his back and a day of reckoning, just waiting for him.

But he doesn't know.

He can't know.

Because Fox decided the things we do behind closed doors will *stay* behind closed doors.

"The fuck, Coach?" Cliff stumbles back a half-dozen steps, dazed and spitting blood onto the canvas by my feet. "You on the juice this week, or what?"

"Keep it clean," Tommy grumbles from outside the boxing ring. He stares at the side of my face, waiting for me to look. But dammit, I won't. I refuse. "Keep it legal."

"What'd I do wrong?"

Rage makes me a sloppy fighter. The fear of losing access to Fox makes me a shitty grappler. Yet, I charge forward anyway, arms wide and fury my constant companion, only for him to skid out of my way, so I slam against the ropes.

"Coach! The fuck?"

"He's just working through some stuff," Tommy teases. "You either fight, or you step off the canvas. Because he's not all that reasonable right now."

"Shut the fuck up!" I turn and bounce on the balls of my feet, dragging my hands up to protect my face. And because Cliff is a pussycat, I stalk forward and force him to engage. "Tommy's not coaching at this point. He's spectating. Focus on me, Cliff."

"I am focusin' on you!" He skips left, running from my advance. "But I'm not entirely sure why it feels like I disrespected your momma or something. One: *you* don't even like your mom! And two: I didn't say shit about her."

"It's about Fox Tatum," Tommy sighs.

Her name on his tongue is like fire in my veins. Like an elastic band snapping. I swing my gaze across to him and snarl.

"What?" He throws his hand up. "You're not gonna say it, so I will."

"Fox?" Cliff is a wily fucker; he uses my distraction and lands a left jab against my jaw that has stars bursting in the corners of my vision. "I told her I was heading out of town for a few days. She said it was cool if I finished the bathroom once I got back."

Tommy snickers. "This ain't about the bathroom, dude. This is about so much more."

"What more?" He ducks and runs, escaping my roundhouse kick by the skin of his teeth. "Dude! What more? I didn't do anything!"

"You're interested in her?" My lungs long ago stopped working properly, and my brain... well, shit, I think I left that at Tommy and Alana's kitchen table. But muscle memory, at least, is something I can count on. I rush Cliff against the ropes and throw him to the ground, the floor rumbling under the weight of our combined four hundred pounds, and because I can, I scramble over his back and wrap my arm around his neck.

"This is a stand-up fight!" Tommy growls. "Chris! We're not grappling."

"Fuck we aren't." I crush Cliff's larynx and murmur by his ear. "You like Fox Tatum?"

"I mean..." He taps my arm—which *should* be the end of the fight. But alas... "Yeah. She's cute, right? And she's nice as hell. What's not to like?"

I slam my free fist against the side of his face. *I'm a bastard, I know.* "Wrong answer, son. You like Fox Tatum?"

"Christian!" Tommy rattles the ropes. "He tapped!"

"I *thought* I liked her!" Cliff's voice crackles under the pressure of my arm. "Guess not?"

"You guess?" I hit him again. "You sure about that?"

"I know!" He tries to slide his fingers between my arm and his neck. Anything to break my hold. "Dude!" Panicking, he kicks his legs out. "I know! She's a monster. She's horrible. Didn't you hear?"

"Chris!" Tommy climbs into the ring and presses the bottom of his foot to the side of my face, pinning me to the canvas. "Let him go."

"Let me go!" Cliff snarls. "Fuck!"

"You're *not* interested." I release him and flop to my back, dropping my arms wide and splaying my legs open. All so I can lay here and rot in my own sweat. "Not interested."

"Fuckin' hell, Coach." Cliff rolls to the other side of the ring, heaving for air and massaging the front of his neck. "Was that attempted murder?" He swings desperate eyes up to Tommy. "That was attempted murder!"

"Nah," Tommy growls, "just an idiot, completely incapable of regulating his emotions or speaking like a fucking adult." He stands over me, his lips peeled back in a sneer. "You could catch charges for that shit, you know that?"

"It was a fair fight." I drag my hands through my hair and use the heels of my palms to crush my eyes. "We were sparring."

"It's not a fair fight if your opponent hasn't consented to ground and pound, dickhead. You were supposed to be boxing. Legs are for standing, not for kicking."

"I'm not actually gonna snitch." Cliff spits again, so the splash hitting the canvas becomes my punishment. My brain, attaching itself to that one, filthy noise. "Physically, I'm fine. Kinda got my feelings hurt, though."

I lower my hands and glance across to find him sitting in the corner, his back pressed to the post and his elbow perched on one raised knee.

"You have a problem with me, Coach? I expect you to be man enough to say so to my face. You wanna kill me and call it sport? That's cool, too. But give me a head's up, so I can pull out the razor blades and hurt you, too."

"You've been stewing on this for a fuckin' week." Tommy lowers into a crouch, shaking his head from side to side. "You and Fox are nothing. You say you aren't interested. You act like she's your mortal fucking enemy every time you're in the same room. But at the mere *mention* of Alana setting Cliff and Fox up on a date, you're out here ready to sit behind prison bars?"

"That's what this is about?" Cliff exclaims. "Alana said she was gonna set me and Fox up? Wait." His eyes brighten, and his lips curl into a smug smile. "Fox is interested in me?"

"You mother—"

"Dude!" Tommy grips my shoulder and pins me to the floor. Then he shoots a dangerous glare in Cliff's direction. "Use your brain! I'm trying to save your life here."

"That was my bad. My bad." Laughing, he climbs to his feet, stumbling and swaying, and when he has no other choice, he grabs the ropes and waits for the world to stop spinning. "I've been outta town, Coach, so forgive me for taking a fuckin' second to realize you and Fox are an item."

"We're not an item!"

Tommy drops to his ass. "They're not an item. Allegedly."

"Oh..." Cliff frowns. Then, "Ohhhh! Alright. This is one of those opposite-day things. You and Fox are *not* an item, but when you hear about Fox and me maybe becoming an item, suddenly your brain snaps and homicide becomes your fun new hobby."

"Pretty sure they're together in secret," Tommy scowls. "And they're taking advantage of Alana's exhaustion to hide it from her. But I see it." He brings his glaring stare down to me. "I see you."

"You said it would be a good idea for Alana to set them up!"

"Aw, you did, Boss?" Cliff swaggers closer and offers a fist for bumping. He waits... waits... waits some more. "No?" He puts it away again. "Well, I appreciate your vote of confidence, anyway."

"Either own this mess, or don't," Tommy snaps. "You want her or you don't. You don't even have to tell Alana—in fact," he adds viciously, "I forbid you from telling Alana. But for the love of God, figure this shit out soon so you and Fox know where you stand."

"We stand nowhere! We aren't together."

"So that makes her a free agent, then?" Cliff takes a *long* step back. "Hypothetically."

"Hypothetically," Tommy continues, "*someone's* about to get their heart broken. Because *my* baby brother beds a broad, then hand delivers her with a pat on the rump and a *good luck* when, later, she's getting hitched and invited him to the wedding. You spend time with a woman, and then you move on. You have entire, respectful conversations with her and her new beau when you cross paths on Main Street, easily done because feelings were never involved. But now Fox is in town, and you're ready to destroy a friend when he didn't even ask her out yet!? What the fuck is that?"

"I was in a fight all week, and I didn't even know it?" Cliff whistles. "*Jaysus*, Coach. I swear, I felt my ears burning while I was away. But I never would've guessed *why*."

"You told me you weren't interested." Tommy grabs my face and forces me to meet his eyes. "I asked you point blank, asshole, and you told me you had absolutely no interest. Not only that, but you said how she's a pain in your ass, a high-maintenance broad, and you're basically counting down the minutes till she goes back to New York. You lied to me."

"I am counting down!" I slap his hand away and sit up, resting my elbows on my knees and letting my head dangle between my shoulders. "I'm counting every fucking second, knowing June fourteenth will get here before I'm ready. I'm counting down, knowing that when she leaves, she'll go without so much as a backward glance."

His eyes soften. Worse, his breath comes out with a sigh that tells me everything I need to know.

Sympathy. Sorrow. All the same shit he felt for me for the first eighteen years of our lives.

"You went and fell in love, didn't you?" He shakes his head in my peripherals, figuring out what I already know. *Fuck.* "Whatever arrangement you have, whatever it is she wants, you agreed to keep it on the down low. Now you've tossed your heart in the ring, and your temper rides on every other decision you make because you're terrified that someone else is gonna slide in and take her. Does she not feel the same way?"

"Does she love me, too?" I choke out an aching, almost delirious laugh. "Nah. She's untouchable. She's in it for fun and for something to do in the dark. She's counting down the seconds until she gets on that plane and flies back to New York, too, but for entirely different reasons than I am."

Cliff grunts, resting his chin on his chest in commiseration.

"She enjoys spending time with Alana and Franky and Hazel. And hell, she even seems pretty happy when we're together and no one else is around. But she fucking *hates* this town with a passion. She'll escape the second she can."

"Sounds like you're screwed." Cliff leans against the ropes, stretching his spine until the bones crackle. "You're banging in secret, won't talk about it out loud, *and* on a deadline, since she's leaving soon. But *I'm* the poor motherfucker catching hands because Alana thought she'd like to set some shit on fire today?"

Tommy rolls his eyes. "You're the one out here, all, '*Oh gee, Ms. Page. I sure do think that Fox Tatum is pretty like a dewdrop.*'"

Cliff chuckles. "I've never said dewdrop in my life!"

"'*If it wouldn't be too much trouble, ma'am, maybe you could gauge Ms. Tatum's receptiveness to an offer of courtship. I'd hate to jump the gun and make her feel uncomfortable, so I'll make you, a brand-new mother with better things to do, play middleman for me.*'"

"Courtship?" He straightens his back and lifts his arms to the sky. "Am I a duke from… whenever dukes were around? Because I don't think they said ma'am. They were more of the *m'lady* types. Which," he adds, lowering his arms and tapping a single finger to his chin, "I could probably slide into my vocabulary. M'lady has a certain royal appeal to it, dontcha think?"

"Call her m'lady, and I'll snap your fuckin' neck."

Smug, he brings dancing eyes across in challenge. "Don't see why I can't, seeing as how you ain't stepping up and saying what needs to be said."

I look to Tommy. Pleading. *Homicide isn't so bad.*

He sighs. "Shut up, Cliff." Then to me, "Either say what you need to say, lay your cards on the table, and tell her how you feel. Or get the fuck over her, keep her at arm's length, and when her time is up, you let her go. Neither of those options includes murdering Cliff just because he said what most other dudes in Plainview already thought."

"Yeah," Cliff quips. "Least I had the balls to speak up."

"You're gonna get your brains scrambled if you don't back up." Slowly, Tommy turns his head and pins the guy I've never, before now, hated. "You're feeling kinda arrogant because you think I'll step in the way and save you from my brother. But soon, he's gonna get up, and by then, I can't stop the rage. Say your prayers, Clifford, because you'll want a clean slate when you meet your maker."

"I'm just playing." He sweeps up a plastic water bottle, squirting liquid into his mouth and wandering closer to stand over me. "I'm a lover, Coach, and if your heart went and fell, then maybe it knows what it's doing. Tell her how you feel. Test it out."

"And break the agreement we had?" I scoff. "We're casual. That's all she wants."

"Maybe she fell in love, too! But she's afraid to say so because she doesn't wanna make things weird."

"I mean…" Tommy grits his teeth, lifting a shoulder in surrender. "He's got a point. You're both stubborn mules who feel big when feelings are to be had. But you're proud, too. You're afraid to tell her because you don't want her to reject you. Maybe she feels the same way but knows you're a fucking bear who doesn't like change. Better to be honest, and lose her, than silent… and still lose her."

"Or…" I counter, if only to assuage the ache in my pounding heart. "I shut my fucking mouth, honor the agreement we have, and visit her in New York sometimes. It can be a forever casual thing. But, like, monogamous."

"Monogamous for you!" Cliff guffaws. "Meanwhile, she's dating in New York, oblivious to the fact you give a shit. You can't expect her to be loyal to this long-distance thing if she doesn't even know she's in it."

"This is why I fucking asked you, Christian." Tommy drags his fingers through his hair, tugging and groaning. "*This!* Because now you're gonna get your heart broken, and that heartache will turn to hate. Fox will have no clue *why* you hate her, just that it hurts. She'll move on once she's back in New York, since you give her no reason not to. Alana's gonna notice the tension, and eventually, she won't even be able to have you both in the same room. All because *you* went and did something you said you weren't doing, and now you're too scared to stand up and own it."

"Meanwhile, Fox is still, *technically*, a free agent," Cliff teases. "And Alana thinks we should go out on a date."

"I'm gonna kill you." I press my hands to the canvas in preparation to shove to my feet and destroy the dude I considered a friend before all this. "Forget *attempted*. I'll get it done."

He flashes a peace symbol and backs up, chugging water that spills onto his chin. "At least I've never gotten myself into a situationship I was too scared to claim. If I like someone, she knows it. If I want someone, I tell them. Miscommunication is cowardice."

"The fuck you want me to do?" I bound to my feet and follow him all the way to the ropes. But I don't hit him. I turn and pace instead. "She lives in New York, and I live here. Relationships take time to build, not six weeks of sneaking around. So even if we *could* agree we kinda want to explore something more, she lives there, and I live here."

"If she wants more," slowly, Tommy straightens out, "then she might consider staying a little longer. If she has reason, it's not out of the realm of possibility that she might move here."

I snort. "She *hates* Plainview. The only reason she's here is for Alana and Franky. Her life is in New York."

"Have you considered... oh, I don't know," Cliff taunts. "Maybe you could go to New York?"

"Me?" I skid to a stop and stare down at the sweat-spotted canvas. "The hell would I do in New York? Without Tommy and Alana and the kids?" I bring my eyes across to my brother. "I can't be where you and the family aren't."

"You're choosing *my* family, the one I made with Lana, over your family... the one you *could* create with Fox."

"I only have one family! I can't fucking function without you in my life, Tommy. I can't be where you and Alana and the kids aren't. What the fuck do you think I'll do over there? Sit in her apartment all day and wait for her to get home from work? While she's living her life, exactly how it's always been, going off to the amazing job she loves—*which is another reason she won't move here, by the way!*—and I'll just wait for her to get back each evening?"

"You could get a job, too," Cliff inserts. "Like a regular, functioning member of society."

"*This* is my job." I gesture outside the boxing ring, toward the bags hanging from the ceiling, and the curious side-eye Eliza shoots from the doorway. "This is my gym. This is what my brother and I built together. Those students." I point at Cliff. "These fighters. I'm not cut out for the kind of change you expect of me, man. I'm not built to pack up and cross the country, to fit into a society I have no clue how to navigate, where I make my entire existence all about waiting. *Waiting* for her to come home from her fancy Fortune Fifty career. *Waiting* for her to travel back here again to see Alana and the kids, just so I can come, too, and not feel like I was the one pressuring her to do it. *Waiting* for the work week to pass, so we can have two days together without the rest of the world intruding." I cast desperate eyes to Tommy. "I already did my waiting. For eighteen fucking years, I sat inside that house, getting the shit kicked out of me, or worse, watching them kick the shit out of you. Starving. Scared. Hoping neither of us died before we were old enough to escape. Then, waiting for Alana, when she hopped a bus and abandoned us. I waited, Tommy, a weekend, and then a week. Then a month. I thought, surely she would come back soon. I waited a year. And then five. And I waited for *you*. Waited for you to come back to me, because even if you were here, physically, your mind wasn't. Now everything is the way it's supposed to be; you're happy, and Franky is one of us. Hazel is here and safe. Alana's wearing a diamond on her finger, and she's made promises to be your family. Which means she'll be mine, too."

"Chris—"

"Everything is how we dreamed it would be. Finally! But *now* you tell me to leave? To sit in a different house? To wait for something good to happen?"

Aching, he drops his shoulders on an exhale.

"Or I let her go and wait... wait to see if she'll come back? Wait to see, *when* she comes back to visit Alana and the kids, if she could still be mine? Wait to find out if she's moved on. Wearing someone else's diamond on her finger."

"Jesus, Chris." He stalks forward. "You're making a mess of it."

"It was supposed to be casual!" I turn to the ropes and yank them wide, climbing through the gap and onto the floor outside. "It *is* casual. That's what we agreed on. That's what *she* asked for."

He walks to the edge of the ring and leans, his hands dangling forward and his shoulders bowed in defeat. "You're catastrophizing. Change is scary, I know. It's uncomfortable."

Uncomfortable. Such a simple term, yet completely paralyzing.

"You still have a couple of weeks left with her. So why not just..." He shrugs. "Ya know? Enjoy it. Gauge her interest. You don't have to go all in, screaming about love. But you could ask her questions and see where her head's at. It might come to nothing. Or it might give you closure. But either is better than what you're doing to yourself right now."

Closure. A gift not all are fortunate enough to receive.

"Yeah." I lick my lips. "Sure."

"I know how you hurt," he murmurs. "I know how your brain torments you. I *am* you, Chris. But you carry more pain than I ever have. If this thing with Fox is supposed to be short-lived and fun, then have fun. Enjoy it for what it is. If it's supposed to be long-term, then I have faith you'll figure it out."

I scoff.

"But what it's *not* meant to be, what it was *never* meant to be, is painful. Don't hurt each other while you're figuring this out."

"Right." I exhale a long, noisy, chest-shrinking breath. "Good talk. Don't tell Alana, okay? That's one thing Fox and I are on the same page about."

He laughs. "No fuckin' shit I won't tell Alana. I'd rather not be the reason she cries herself to sleep tonight. And probably don't go near Cliff for the next couple of weeks, okay? He's not your enemy, but you're not in the right headspace to differentiate those details at the moment."

"Hey," Cliff exclaims. "I didn't even do anything!"

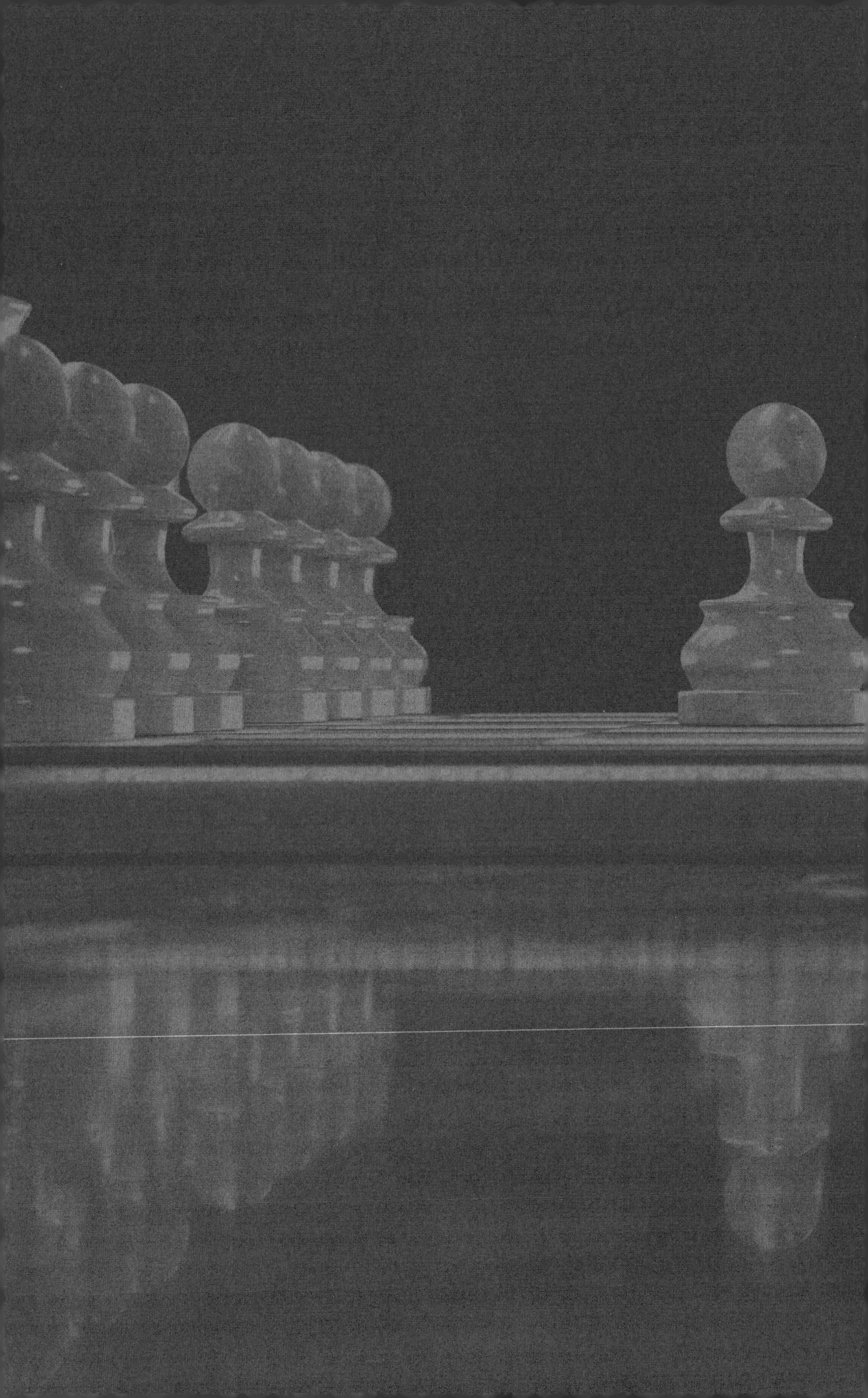

ROUND TWENTY-THREE
FOX

I work the register at Alana's bookstore and hear the jingle of the bell above the door. I paste on my polite '*hello, old person, welcome to our establishment*' smile, and consider removing the free cookie platter from above the pastry fridge—not, like, *all* the cookies.

Just most of them, to minimize loitering time.

But glancing across, I'm met with a face far friendlier than any of the others I was expecting.

Raya bounces through the door, sans-apron, and beams when our eyes meet. She wears a dozen neon butterfly clips in her hair, the kind the eighties and nineties babies rocked for a solid decade and a half, and shiny black boots with three-inch soles and silver buckles along the side.

She's a statement wherever she goes. Fashionable and unapologetically her, even if those who surround her don't share the same ideas.

"Well, hey there." I close the register and settle in for a visit, resting my hip against the counter and folding my arms. "I was wondering if you'd ever come visit me."

"I see you every second morning!"

"Yeah, but at the bakery." I slow my words, teasing the girl who could probably out-brain me any day of the week. "I wasn't even sure that you had hips before, since they're always hidden behind an apron."

Blushing, she brushes her hands over the front of her shirt and down to her belt. "Yeah. I'm surprised my parents even let me leave the house, to be honest. Showing an inch of my belly is totally uncool."

"You look great. Classy and badassy."

"Chris came in and ordered that cake."

"Oh. I know." I snicker. "He told me so. In fact, he gave me the receipt to prove it. I think he was scared I'd hurt him if he didn't. Are you coming to the party?"

"For sure." She sets her hands on the counter, dozens of metal bangles jingling together. "I think the First Family is coming at this point. You've put the whole town on notice: *turn up or die*."

"Fear can be a great motivational tool sometimes. Never underestimate the power of a woman with a little notebook and a borrowed pen." From smiles to a frown, my mood sours. "I still can't find mine. It's sending me insane."

"Can't find your what? Your pen?"

"I swear it was in my bag on the plane. I don't remember seeing it since then."

"Er… okay. Was it a special pen? A gift or something?"

"No. It was just a regular pen." I pick up the pen I've been using all day. "Exactly like this one. They come in twenty-packs. Five bucks a pack."

"So just grab another from the pack," she snickers. "It's just a pen."

I slam my hand back to the counter and faux-snarl. "Listen, girly. Don't come to my place of work and judge me for my unhealthy obsession with a truly unremarkable pen. You don't see me standing in line at the bakery calling you out on things."

"You mean like how you asked—as in, shouted—yesterday morning, in front of a dozen other customers, if I'd pulled the Fashion Institute application forms off the school website yet?"

"What?" I fold one arm across my belly and draw the opposite hand up to my lip. "I was just helping a girlfriend out, is all. That's a good school, so you gotta be prepared. Get ahead of the pack. The *last* thing you wanna do is become complacent and stay in a small town you don't like, working a job you don't want, simply because it's easy. Get out." I gesture toward the door. "See the world."

"See New York," she snorts. "I won't become complacent, I promise. Nothing will keep me here."

"Good. I'm proud of you." My stomach grumbles, the four o'clock sugar cravings hitting right on schedule, so I drop my hands and stride to the pastry fridge. Snagging the plate of cookies, I bring them back and place them on the counter between us. "What's the goss, anyway? What's happening over at Plainview High?"

She selects a cookie and brings dancing eyes up to mine. "You sound like a regular local already."

"Yeah, but the locals gossip about dumb things."

"As opposed to... high school drama?"

"Exactly! Way more exciting. So who is dating who? Who's pregnant? Prom's coming up, right? Got a date yet?"

She rolls her eyes. "Not *my* prom. And none of the senior guys are likely to ask me. My friend Ericka has a new boyfriend, though." Eyes alight, she leans closer to tell a secret. "He goes to school in the next town over, since anyone with class wouldn't dare date a Plainview boy."

"Obviously." I flutter my lashes and nibble on the edge of my cookie. "Is he nice to her? Is he a decent person?"

"Yeah, I really think so. A lot of the girls my age are thirsting for the bad boy thing right now. You know, the guys who skip school and smoke and talk back to the teachers to feel tough?"

"I was never into those types. Rebellion for the sake of rebellion seems like a waste of effort."

"Exactly! Fight for what you believe in and all that, but being a douchebag just to sound cool is dumb. This guy, though, Everett? He seems alright. He makes my friend happy."

"And what about you?" The shop doorbell rings again, drawing my lazy attention. That is, until my eyes lock on to the devastatingly handsome Christian Watkins. Then my laziness dissipates, and in its place is an odd fluttering in my belly and my hand coming up and brushing my hair back.

Dammit. I want to feel pretty when he walks into a room.

"What about me? Am I dating someone?" Raya doesn't notice our newcomer. Or maybe she just doesn't care. "Everett has a friend, Cal, and he's pretty nice. He comes to Plainview whenever Everett does, and since Everett's busy making starry eyes at Ericka, that usually leaves time for me and Cal to hang out. He's interested, I guess."

Chris meanders toward the pastry fridge, his thick legs wrapped in jeans I swear were made just for him, his hands resting on his hips, and his broad chest showcased in a black shirt, the same shape and fit as basically every other shirt he owns.

He looks freshly showered with damp hair and a glinting smile, but when Raya selects another cookie, I drag my attention away from him and back to her.

"I'm not sure I wanna get into something with him, though, since he doesn't live in Plainview, and maybe Ericka and Everett won't work out."

"You don't think you can be with him, even if they're not?"

She shrugs. "Just not sure I want to invest in something I'm only *meh* about, since I'll be heading to New York in a year and a bit, anyway. If we don't work out, what was the point, ya know? And if we do, it'll make leaving even harder."

"I mean…" *Damn.* She poses an excellent question, so I take a bite of my cookie and ponder. "The point was the experience, I suppose. Even if you don't work out. Being treated well by a nice guy is something you should know, even if it's only short-term. If you break up, you've got that under your belt, something to dissect and learn from as you grow older. Once you hit New York, your world will get a hell of a lot bigger, which means the long list of viable male options will explode. Dating this dude could be a safer, more controlled situation where you're still at home, still surrounded by what you know, and since he's that other guy's friend, it kinda provides credibility. Dating in New York won't come with a lot of the safety nets you currently have in place."

"Well…" She stares over the top of her cookie, her lovely blue eyes glittering with amusement. "Maybe when I get there, I can look you up. We can hang out sometimes, and *if* I meet some dude, I can run him by you. *You* can be my safety net."

"Oh, great!" I choke out a nervous laugh. "No pressure at all! That's a helluva responsibility to lob on a woman who hasn't even got her own life under control."

"Ladies." Unable to help himself, Chris sidles up on Raya's left and smirks when her eyes grow wide and her heart skitters, visible in her throat. *Okay, so maybe she does care that he's here.* Arrogant, he slides his eyes across and stops on me. "Ms. Tatum."

I pick up the cookie plate and offer. "Christian. How's it going?"

"It's going." He peruses his options—though every single cookie is the same—then pinching one between his fingers, he winks for the staring girl. "You make these, Raya?"

"Uh… um…" She swallows, nodding a little too doggy-on-the-dashboard style. "I-I did. I made them."

He takes a bite and chews long enough to test each flavor on his tongue. It's slow and drawn out, unintentionally torturous for the girl who has a crush on a full-grown man.

My full-grown man, dammit.

"Delicious." He grins. "You did good."

She drops her gaze, hiding her blazing cheeks, and folds her fingers together. Good lord, the poor girl is a mess. "Thank you."

"I was actually coming to see you, Fox." He's oblivious to his teenage admirer. Blind to her fiery blush and shallow breathing. Instead, he searches my face with a long, caressing sweep of his eyes. "Alana wanted us to discuss bookstore plans this afternoon." *Lie, lie, lie!* "She and Tommy and the kids are going out, but she wanted to make sure I didn't forget about this."

"Yeah?" I toss the last of my cookie onto my tongue. "What kind of stuff, *specifically*?"

From adoring to irritated, he grunts. "Just... *stuff*. You're busy right now, but I'll come back and—"

"Oh, nah. I'm done." Like her three-inch soles turn to springs, Raya bounces away from the counter. "I have homework anyway. But I'll see you in the morning, okay, Fox? At the bakery."

"Sure." I finger-wave and watch her go. Then, I bring my attention back to Chris. "You're terrible at on-the-spot lying."

"Yeah, that makes *me* the bad guy," he growls low on his breath. "How horrible of me not to be a fluent bullshit artist." He leans closer, snarling, "Alana and Tommy actually *do* have plans. So I wanna come over and—"

"*Bang*? Really? I have it on good authority Clifford Troopman intends to ask me out soon." I glance down and study my nails. "Could you not even *try* to romance me? Is chivalry dead?"

"Come over and pick you up," he continues, seething. "I was going to ask you over for dinner."

"Oh?" I bring my eyes up again. "Dinner?"

"A date. At my house. I planned to cook for you, since we haven't done that yet. But if you'd prefer to keep your schedule open for Cliff, then I suppose I'll just back the fuck up and not bother."

"You wanted to cook for me?" *Good Lord. Why does my heart cartwheel?* "Really?"

"Not if you have plans with Troopman. I'd hate to get in the way of true love and all that shit."

I roll my eyes. "You get so freakin' cranky. Geez. You were at that dinner with Alana. The Cliff joke is funny."

His eyes flicker with something akin to desperation. Or perhaps, desire. For violence, that is. "It's not funny to me. Can I pick you up? Leave your car here and not in my driveway. I'll bring you back later, and no one will know we even hung out."

"Dinner hidden away at your house. Where no one will see us." *Don't even think about being weird about it, doofus!* This is the deal we made. "That makes sense. It would be impossible for me to park in your driveway and not expect Alana to notice."

"And the *last* thing we want is for Alana to notice." He softens his expression, curling his lips into a gentle smile. "You close the shop at five. Can I pick you up at six? It feels like we've hardly hung out this week."

"We haven't." I snag the pen—my inferior imposter pen—and rest the capped end between my teeth. "You've been at the gym a lot. And I've been with Alana and the kids. Party planning is taking up a lot of time."

"But I've been in your bed most nights." He licks his lips and studies my eyes. "I've made sure to stop by almost every single day."

"Drive by pussy." I lower the pen and try not to feel quite so... *cheap*. "Your hard work is appreciated, and your dedication is admirable."

He smirks. "Six o'clock? I've got Cliff running my classes tonight, so I'm free from now until tomorrow morning."

I narrow my eyes. "Tell me you didn't roster that poor man on just to make him unavailable for our date."

"Shouldn't matter to you." He takes a step back, his voice low and his fingers tightly wrapped around a cookie. "You have no reason to be thinking about him or the things he does at night, Ms. Tatum. Your schedule is full, and I seem to recall you mentioning—*demanding*, even— that for as long as you're in town, my focus remains exclusively yours." He takes a bite and grins. "Tit for tat, Fox. Tit for tat. Wear your hair up."

I reach back and touch my hair, the long locks hanging loose and the ends dangling over my shoulder. "That's an interesting request."

"Catch you when I catch you." He meanders past the sofa square of old women trying desperately to listen to a conversation they weren't invited into. But when he tips his chin in farewell, they scramble. A henhouse filled with nine chickens and one hungry fox. Whipping unread books open and sipping empty cups of tea, they fix their hair and pretend they're not nosy old bitches begging for a scrap of gossip.

Imagine being so bored and brainless.

Kill me if I ever become like them.

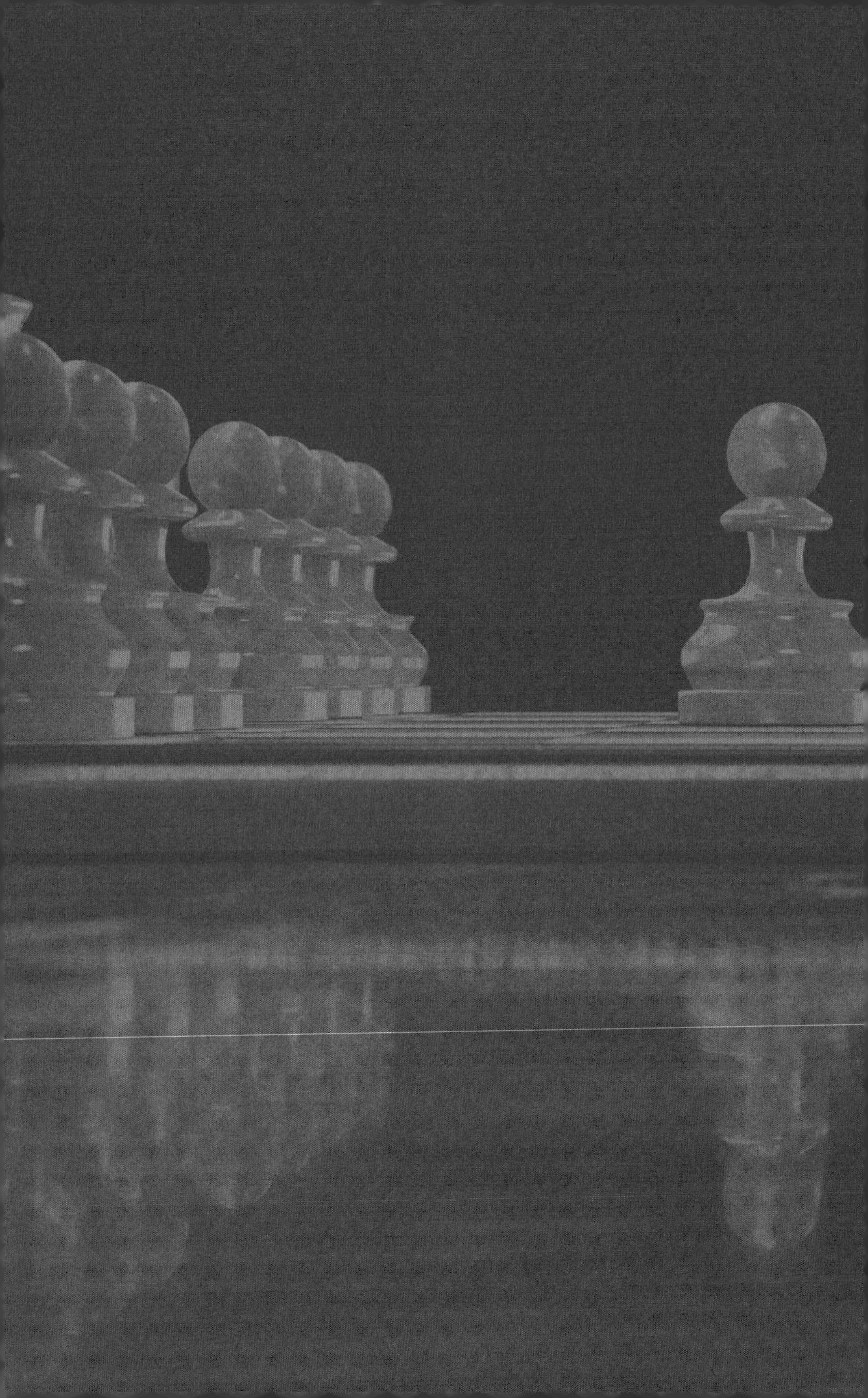

ROUND TWENTY-FOUR
CHRIS

She was joking when she requested romance. But hell, if I don't intend to deliver.

"I'm not saying no to hair pulling, and I don't mind neck-breaking maneuvers. I'm just asking you to warn me before you try a new direction. I'm nearly thirty years old, Christian. I'm getting on in age, and strapping an ice-pack to my back to sleep, while practical, is hardly sexy."

"Just shut up already." I lead her through my front door, one hand pressed over her eyes to keep her blind, my arm draped across her back so she feels secure in the dark. And because I know Tommy took Alana and the kids out—his gift to me—I walk her all the way through my kitchen, the rich scent of dinner making her nose twitch, then outside again to the back porch.

Here's hoping this is a date night she'll always remember.

Maybe we'll get longer than our six weeks. And fuck, maybe we won't. But whatever happens, I intend to make sure she remembers me for *this*. For the happiness we can feel and the romance I could provide, if only she wanted to give me a chance.

Not for being *neurotic, uptight, and a little rough in the bedroom*.

Nerves kick against my heart, a whiplash that almost leaves me breathless. But fairy lights hang from the ceiling, more lights than all the Plainview shops stocked, *combined*, so I drove to the next town over and bought theirs, too. The lake creates a backdrop of beauty, a canvas I know she enjoys—dammit, I know she stares when she thinks no one else is looking

—and I... well, I'll try my best not to be neurotic and uptight and weird tonight.

"Chris...?" Hesitant, she clings tighter to my side. "If Stephen King wrote our story, this is the part where lake monsters would come out and hack me to death. Did I ever tell you surprises aren't my favorite thing?"

"Really? Ms. Spontaneity and Sass *doesn't* like surprises?" I peel my hand away and take a step back, allowing her a moment to study what I've created for us. The flowers on the table and the plates, stacked like they do at fancy restaurants in New York City. The silverware—diamond-decorated, of course—and candles that make the crystal glasses glitter.

She gasps and looks up at the porch ceiling, absorbing the beauty of an artificially starry sky, then out at the *real* sky, the constellations flickering to life now that the sun races toward the horizon.

"Holy shit. Chris." Spinning, she hits me with beautiful eyes that hint toward emotional. *So maybe she's not entirely untouchable. Just... guarded.* "I thought *date* was a euphemism for St. Andrew's Cross."

I take my phone from my back pocket and tee up my playlist. Then, tapping the screen until music pipes through well-hidden speakers, I set the device down again and take her hand in mine.

I tug her closer, catching her against my chest and swallowing her sweet gasp of surprise.

"Not *everything* is about sex, silly. I said dinner, I meant dinner."

"Sex later, then?" She wraps her arms over my shoulders, falling into rhythm with the music as easily as sliding into a warm bath, her delectable thighs sandwiching mine and her plump lips curling into a smile. "Romance me first, then blow my mind."

"Maybe we shouldn't have sex tonight at all."

Jesus. Who am I?

I track my hands over her back, memorizing her every line. Her shape. Her hips and the deep valley of her spine, artistically exposed under the cut of her dress and the missing panel of fabric that turns a *pretty* outfit into something utterly breathtaking. "Romance only," I rumble. "Then more romance, to prove I'm no one-trick-pony."

"Hmm..." She presses her cheek to my chest, twining her fingers at the back of my neck and scratching her nails through my hair. She creates a sensation that is both electrifying and ridiculously comforting at the same time. "You have my attention. Though I won't lie, your tricks so far have been entirely satisfactory. If something is not broken, I hesitate to fix it." Grinning, she tilts back and searches my eyes. "I'm pleasantly surprised by all this, Christian. I honestly thought you were setting me up for something a little less... dreamy."

"We're on day twenty-eight of forty-two." She's so close, her lips so plump, tempting and delicious. So I do what any sane man would do, lean in and get a taste. "You came to Plainview with a bad attitude and a mean tongue," I tease. "But we're four weeks in now. Has the small-town charm changed your mind yet?"

"Is that what that's called? *Charm*?" Laughing, she remains oblivious to the way my heart pounds. To the fact, her answers have the power to shatter my soul. "I don't know that I consider mean gossips 'charming'. Or unkind side-eyes, literally because these people and *my people* fought on different sides of the civil war, 'charming'. Or the weird little raised stones in the sidewalk, that *never* fail to trip me, charming."

"So Plainview is still a *never gonna happen* for you?" I slide a lock of hair behind her ear and stare down into perfect brown eyes. "Not even for Alana and the kids?"

"To live here?" Her brows pinch, curiosity flittering throughout her gaze. But then her stomach rumbles, noisy enough to hit my ears, even above the soft melody of something country playing through the speakers.

Her cheeks burn a sweet red, like being hungry is something to be embarrassed about, so I take her hands in mine, and walking her to the table I set, I drag her chair out, careful not to mess up the ribbon I tied by hand—and felt stupid doing it—nor the cushions I bought today—after sitting on a dozen in search of the perfect ones.

I had no fucking clue there were so many options.

"Wait here a second." I snatch up a stark white cloth napkin and drape it over her lap. Then, kissing her temple, I turn on my heels and stride through my kitchen.

Let's go, Christian!
Lock this shit down before we hit day forty-two and time runs out.

Yanking the oven open and digging my hands into mitts, I take two warm plates from the rack and kick the door shut with the back of my boot, then I head out to the porch again. "I made chicken cacciatore." I set her plate down between her silverware. "You like that, right?"

"With olives?" She studies the dish and smiles. Though I swear, this smile isn't like the smile from before. "It smells delicious."

"You don't like olives?" I put my plate down and toss the oven mitts, the dull thud of thick material hitting the wall and falling to the floor playing somewhere in the back of my mind. "If you don't like olives, I can make something else—"

"Relax. I like olives." She takes her fork between her fingers and pokes at the chicken, inhaling a long, appreciative breath, before glancing up at me from under thick lashes and exhaling again. "Thank you. You made this yourself?"

"I did." What was smooth before, becomes stilted now. My hands on her back, shaking as I bring my chair in. My thighs, previously strong, weak now as I grab my napkin and drape it over my legs. *God, why am I nervous?* "It's one of my go-to recipes. So, no to small towns?"

Jesus Christian. Can't you just fucking drop it? I hate this shit hole!

Or at least, those are the words my brain insists I hear.

Instead, she selects a chunk of carrot with her fork and brings it up to smiling lips. "I guess I think of this a bit like an organ transplant. Which makes me the replacement lungs or heart or whatever. I'm not sure this body—*Plainview*—will ever willingly accept such a foreign transplant. Especially not when the little old tea-and-gossip ladies so *badly* want to reject me."

"You put a lot of stock in what other people think of you." I pick up my knife and fork and slice into my chicken. "For someone openly and unashamedly confident, it surprises me you'd care so much what the tea-and-gossip ladies think."

She scoffs. "You'd be surprised by the things that go through my mind when I catch them whispering about me." She nibbles on the carrot. "It's not all about them, of course. And ultimately, their opinions about me hardly matter. Though, the volume with which they speak can't be ignored. Their animosity toward someone for..." She pauses and grins. "Literally existing is pretty gross. Then there's the fact Plainview's largest grocery store closes at nine p.m., and Bealls is the only clothing store for a fifty-mile radius."

"You don't like Bealls?"

"I don't *not* like it, but variety is important, too. I like not wearing the same thing as everyone else. I like wandering a department store with nothing in mind, exploring their offerings until something jumps out and inspires me."

Fuck me. Why does sweat trickle along my spine?

"I like meeting new people, and I like that those people don't all look exactly the same, with the same skin color and the same life experiences and prejudices and stories to tell."

"Well… if you lived here and traveled with Alana and Tommy for his fights, you'd get all those things still."

You're reaching, dickhead.

Amused, her glistening lips curl up. "I like not always knowing what to cook for dinner, so I can walk outside my apartment building and headfirst into a dozen different restaurants with a dozen different smells. I follow whatever inspires me and eat something new each night. This..." She looks down at her dinner. "This is one of the most aromatic meals I've smelled since being in Plainview, which is both wonderful and horrifying at the same time."

"Horrifying?" She still hasn't picked up an olive. In fact, she hasn't eaten *anything* except a corner of a carrot. "You don't like olives, do you? You can tell me. I won't be mad about it."

"I like olives," she snickers, poking at them. *Just like one would when avoiding eating something they don't like.* "I'm not horrified by the meal you've prepared, Christian. I'm horrified that nowhere else in town offers anything like it, so if I were to live here, I'd have to rely on irritating you into cooking for me."

She so easily scars my heart, slashing at it with a newly sharpened knife.

Worse, she's clueless to the fact it's her hand that wields the blade.

"I wouldn't mind cooking for you." I set my silverware down. I can't fit a single bite when my stomach is so full of dread. "Anytime you wanted it."

"You're just saying that because we're getting along right now." She flashes a bright, beautiful, *oblivious* smile. "But eventually, the magic of sex will wear off, and when it does, we'll go right back to who we are beneath the orgasms; annoying and petty." She slices into her chicken and brings a chunk up to her lips. "What about you?"

"What about me what?" Still no olives. And fuck, the entire dish tastes of olives. *I ruined everything*! "What do you wanna know?"

"Would you ever move *away* from Plainview?"

My heart flips at the very thought. "Doubt it."

So fucking quick to answer. So sure. I destroy us before I even give us a chance to breathe.

"Oh?" She opens her mouth and places the olive-flavored trash on her tongue. "You wouldn't even consider it?"

"And go where? My entire life is wrapped up in the gym. Tommy and Alana and the kids. My house." I settle back and gesture toward the starry ceiling. "I've only ever known Plainview. Not sure I'd even know *how* to live somewhere else."

"New York is an amazing city." She chews, careful not to show the food in her mouth. "It's so large and magical. The people can be really nice, and butting up against such diversity is like living multiple lives all at once. I wouldn't be the same Fox you know if I never experienced the things I have."

Pausing, she takes a moment somewhere in the depths of her mind she chooses not to share with me.

Fuck. Why won't she share it with me?

Shaking her thoughts away, she brings her eyes back up and smirks. "Who knows, maybe you wouldn't be the way you are if you'd been raised somewhere other than here."

"The way I am?" Thirsty, I snatch the bottle of wine I set out earlier, crack the seal, and pour it into her glass. But the thought of fruity alcohol makes my stomach turn, so I set it down again and choose water instead. "You don't think I should be who I am?"

"No, I mean... look at Franky, right?" She trades her fork for wine, bringing the glass to her smiling lips. *God, it's the olives. She hates them.* "You and Franky have a lot in common. But the fact he spent his first ten years in New York means he has a different perspective on the world than you do. He still has his quirks, his favorite fork—" Teasing, she casts her eyes to the diamond patterns set out on each side of our plates, "—he still prefers his own company over large gatherings, and he's quick to call someone out if he thinks they're being unfair or not entirely truthful. But he also appreciates and celebrates people who are *different* than he is."

Fuck my dinner, I sip my water and settle back in my chair. "Different?"

"Well, he, himself, is different from his peers. And he's drawn to you—even over Tommy, despite his relationship with Alana—because he recognizes how you're different from yours. Raised in a city where no one is the same, he spent his most formative years being accepted for exactly who he is, and he accepted others for their differences without question. His friend group included children with varying shades of skin. Girls. Kids with glasses or braces or a walking frame. One of his closest friends was a little girl with cerebral palsy, and not once in all the time I can recall did he wonder if she was *less than*, or if she should be mocked. And yet..." She sets her wine glass down and meets my eyes. "*I'm* stared at in Plainview like I came from Barnham's circus of freaks. On the outside, I look exactly like most others around here: I have the 'right' skin color, the 'right' weight range. I don't walk differently, and nothing odd grows from my face. At first glance, I *fit*. But the fact is, I wasn't born or raised here. *My people* don't come from here. And God forbid I *not* be sorry for it."

She picks up her fork, scoffing. "If I was a less secure woman, I probably would've cried myself to sleep on the first night and started counting down the seconds until I can escape again."

"You're not counting down to escape?" A sliver of hope. A tiny speck of potential sparks somewhere in the back of my heart. "Despite them, you're happy to be here?"

"Sure. Their opinions don't *actually* matter to me. Not when I know I'm here for Alana and Franky and the baby. My reward is seeing my family, helping them with the store while they need that help. I don't care for the opinions of people I don't care about, and knowing I'll leave again soon helps me keep my shoulders back and my chin up. Visiting Plainview is fine. *Living* in Plainview would likely end with me behind bars. Something about aggravated assault and public nuisance."

And there goes my hope, dashed as quickly as it came.

I draw a long breath, silencing my inhale so she doesn't see how easily destroyed I am. Then I paste on a fake smile, because I'll be damned if I ruin our night.

More than that, I refuse to ruin our last two weeks together.

"If I visited New York sometimes, would you take me out to dinner and show me your bedroom for dessert?"

She coughs out a soft, amused laugh. "Probably. I did mention the magic of sex, didn't I?"

"You did." I bring my water up to my lips. "What if you're dating someone else by then?" *Shut the fuck up, Chris! She asked for casual. She asked for six weeks and secrecy.* "How do you explain to your future boyfriend that you need the weekend off because this other dude from Plainview was dropping by?"

"A weekend off?" she snorts. "A hall pass, where loyalty is placed on pause? Hmm..." her lips twitch with humor. "Not sure that'll work out."

"Afraid he'll get mad?"

"If I were afraid of him, then he would no longer be my boyfriend, would he?" She brings beautiful brown eyes up to mine. "I prefer relationships built on trust and respect. Male or female, work or any other. If there's no trust, and if there's no respect, then I move right along. Life is too short for anything else."

"Also, pettiness and bickering."

Confused, she frowns.

So I add, "Us. We're built on pettiness and bickering, no? That's how it appears from where I'm sitting."

Finally, she cracks and snickers, settling back into her chair. "I respect you, Christian. And I trust you. I respect the hell out of you."

"Even though you think I could be different, if only I'd been raised somewhere else?"

"I didn't say you *should* be different or that I want you to be different. Though we both know you cling to certain comforts and you do so because of how you were raised. If you had different parents or a different town, it's possible you'd be less rigid in the way you react to change."

"You want me to be less rigid?"

"I want you to be happy." Her perfect bow lips curl into a sincere smile. No taunting anymore. No teasing. "I know you think I get off on irritating you, but I see you when you're wound tight, Christian. I see how you grip on to same-ness like your life depends on it. And I know, to you and your nervous system, it feels like your life *does* depend on it. Everything hurts and everyone is loud, and all you want in those moments is for silence and things to slow the hell down. To you, same-ness matters. My wish isn't for you to change. It's for you to experience change and it *not* feel like splinters under your skin."

How does she know about the splinters? How can she possibly know how loud the world is?

"But back to your original question." She sits forward again and picks up her fork. "If I'm already dating someone else, then I'm not sure we can continue the magic penis thing, since… well…" She spears a chunk of carrot and places it on her tongue. "Loyalty and trust matter to me. How can I continue a casual affair with you—sans-condoms, even—if I'm dating someone else? Worse, when I'm hearing stories of *your* courageous community service?"

"She was kidding, by the way." *Dammit, Alana!* "I don't *service* people."

"I'm terrified to know the specifics, since they'll certainly ruin a perfectly pretty date." She swallows and slices into her chicken. "When I ask if you'll ever move away from Plainview, I don't do so because I think you should be someone you're not. I just wish you knew the world outside of this town is kinda beautiful and large and wondrous."

"I'm sure it is, but—"

"But if it hurts to even discuss it, then…" She gestures in my direction with the end of her fork. "I respect that. I won't push it."

And so we arrive at our impasse. She won't come here, and I won't go there. And fuck, but she already has this hypothetical boyfriend and loyalty placed at his hypothetical feet.

"You seem kinda stressed tonight." She drags her napkin up and wipes around her lips, careful not to smudge her lipstick. Then setting it on the table beside her plate, she stands.

It's a slow seduction. A gentle smoothing of her dress and a glide of her hands over her hips, down to her thighs. She wears heels tonight, not sexy little sneakers, and rewards me with a view of her legs that'll stay with me for life.

Sauntering around the table and stopping only when my shoulder touches her ribs, she looks down into my eyes and grins her approval when I inch my chair back to make room.

Pleased, she lowers onto my lap and trails her fingertips over my jaw. "You're always a little stressed. Your stress makes me worry about you. But tonight, you've surprised me."

I search her eyes, studying the pair and praying for a simple answer that'll make us both happy. I want to keep her, but I don't want to destroy her soul or tie her to a town that'll send her crazy.

"You mention a date." She leans closer and presses a feather-soft kiss to the edge of my jaw. "I assumed it was code for sex. You brought me to dinner under the stars, *under the stars,* by the lake, instead. You cooked a delicious meal, but you sat across from me with white knuckles and worry in your eyes, making it impossible for me to relax. I'm kinda terrified you're about to drop bad news on my lap."

"I have no bad news for you." I lay my palm over her pounding chest, her heart thundering against the tips of my fingers. And when I can't hold out for a moment longer, I extend my neck and take her lips with mine. "I promise. We're eating a meal, just like we've done a few times already. I live by the lake, and I know you kinda like it out here, so I wanted to give you that instead of the bland four walls of the apartment."

"Sweet of you." She side-saddles my lap, crossing one leg over the other so her ass sits squarely on my cock. And because I'm a toxic motherfucker, I still manage to summon a hard dick, even with a broken heart. "It's really pretty out here. You're very fortunate to call this view *yours.*"

"My view?" *You are my view, and I'm terrified I'm fourteen days away from losing it.* "Very pretty." I nibble on her bottom lip and gently pull it between my teeth. "What are you most looking forward to when you get back to New York?"

"Oh, geez." She pulls back, her eyes burning brighter at the mere mention of the home she loves. It's not a conscious thing she does. Not a taunting response or something she has to think about. *New York makes her happy.* "I'm excited to see my apartment again. To see if my hamster, Harold, has survived without me."

"What?"

"Six weeks is a long time without food or water, but he's pretty self-sufficient, ya know?"

"Fox! Your hamster is dead."

"I'm kidding." She walks her fingers over the top of my ear, tucking the longer strands of hair back. "I don't have a hamster. Whacky is the closest thing I have to a pet, and he's a total asshole."

I glance to the lawn and watch that ugly fucking chicken limp across the grass, pecking every few steps in search of a juicy grub. "Such an asshole."

"I travel too often to have a pet." She brings my face back around, smiling when our eyes meet. "And paying someone to come over twice a day to check in on a neglected, lonely little thing is not my idea of a life well spent. Animals deserve owners who spend time with them."

"Not Whacky, though. He deserves an oven and a little seasoning."

Her eyes dance with laughter, even if the sound remains trapped in her chest. "I'm looking forward to sleeping in my bed again. Although," she inches back. "I've considered stealing the sheets you bought for the bookstore apartment."

"You want to steal them?"

"They're so soft," she sighs. "It's not even about the price. I have expensive sheets. I don't mind spending the money. But it's like you sourced *these* sheets from the fanciest silkworm on the planet, and if you don't tell me his name, I might cry."

"Why would I do that, all so your next boyfriend can enjoy them?" *Jesus, Chris. Shut the fuck up.* "No chance."

She snickers. "So I'll steal the ones at the bookstore, and I'll come back just often enough to loot your home and take more."

Sheets are the price of ensuring she returns to Plainview? Sold.

"I'm looking forward to returning to work. My boss, Booker, hinted at something exciting coming up. He said we'd get dinner and discuss it once I'm back."

"Oh yeah?" Fuck Booker! Fuck his dinner. Fuck what I know is leading to, '*Six weeks apart proved I can't breathe without you. Marry me and never leave again.*'

Or maybe that's just me, spinning into absolute fuckery.

"What do you think he wants to discuss?"

"I think... maybe..." She chews on the inside of her lip. "I don't know if I want to jinx it." But she giggles and slides her thumb across my too-tense jaw. "It's possible I'll shift over to marketing soon."

"I thought you loved your position as chief clown car organizer?"

Unimpressed, a thick line digs between her brows. But she's cute as fuck, and bickering is at the bedrock of who we are.

"You're the one who has been praising that job since you got here. Now you're telling me you're excited at the prospect of changing it?"

"I *do* love my job. A lot. But I also love marketing, and he knows that. So I wonder if he's readying to give me experience in both."

"Double the workload, one salary. Sounds like corporate New York to me."

Frustrated, she flicks my earlobe. "Double the experience, the same forty-hour work week, smarty pants. It'll mean juggling both of the things I love and expanding my resume. Meeting new people and stretching my brain in an exciting new direction, all while losing none of the benefits I already enjoy."

I splay my hand over her chest, studying her collarbones with my fingertips and enjoying the constant thrum of her heart. "I was kidding. It's obvious you have a knack for making people happy, considering I was out here buying chair cushions and stringing up fairy lights."

"It made you happy to do those things?"

"The idea that they'd make you happy made me happy. Being around you makes me happy, even when you take my fork or screw up a game of chess on purpose. Your soul is happy, I think. And because your soul is happy, being near you means I get to feel that happy, too."

Her brows crinkle, furrowing over emotional eyes. "Damn, Christian." She sniffles. "That might've been the kindest thing anyone has ever said to me."

"Well, you know me. I have a reputation for poetry."

"Sure." She laughs. "I've heard that about you. And because you were so generous with your poetic words, I figure I'd like to show you my appreciation." She peeks down at my shirt, undoing the top button with an easy flick of her fingers. "I enjoy talking about New York. And I love the idea of my professional dreams coming true. But we're on a deadline, don't you think?"

Another button.

"From six weeks down to two. A beautiful evening in your home, though we can't ignore the very real risk that Alana could see us out here on the porch."

Another button.

"Maybe we should go inside," she murmurs seductively. "Play a game of chess."

Stunned, I place my hand over hers and stop her progress. "I'm not saying no, but I have to admit, not once in my entire life have I considered chess a prelude to mind-bending sex."

Grinning, she pushes off my lap and drags me up by my shirt. "I guess you haven't been playing chess with the right people, then." She moves onto her toes, buying herself just another inch, before tugging me down and rewarding me with her tongue sliding against mine. "Strip chess, perhaps? I take one of your pieces, you lose an item of clothing."

"Sounds like I'm gonna be sitting in there, fully dressed, while you're naked and panting."

"Arrogant." She lowers to flat feet and turns on her heels. And like the obedient mutt I am, I follow. "Though we can't dismiss how hot that would be. You, fully dressed and winning. Me, naked and vulnerable." She leans over the table and gently kills the candle flames with an exhaled breath, then straightening again, she releases my shirt, but takes my hand and places it on her hip. "Maybe I'll lose on purpose *because* I want that outcome."

"I hear you trying to be sexy right now." I follow her all the way to the door, but before she can swing it open and pass through, I spin her around and pin her to the frame. "But I need you to know that playing it wrong is *not* sexy at all. It'll annoy the shit out of me."

She barks out a loud laugh, her cheeks turning a beautiful pink. Pushing me back, she turns and pulls the door open. And because I can't bear the thought of letting her go, I rush through after her, draping my arm over her shoulders and steering her left when her body angles right.

"This way, silly."

"Well, of course you have an actual chess board room and not, say, a little travel set you could bring to the bedroom."

"I have one of those, too. But since we're in *my* home and this was *my* date night idea, I say we go this way." I lead her through my living room, as bland as it is, with a long black leather couch and a TV hung on the wall, then I walk her into the hall and past the spare bedroom. Then another. I have a half dozen of them, useless to me, so I keep the doors closed.

Stopping at the room right beside mine, I nudge the door open, flip the lights on, and lead her into my office. And because I know it's kinda special in here, I stand back and enjoy her intake of air. Her gasp of surprise and the hand she places over her heart.

"Holy hell, Chris." She casts her eyes to the bookshelves on the right. Then to the left, where massive bay windows overlook the lake and boast one-way glass. *We can see out. No one gets to peek in.* "Who needs a red room of pain when I could be Belle and have a whole ass library?" She wanders past my desk, a rich mahogany that matches the color of her hair exactly, then around a chess set, large enough to require its own table. Its own chairs and section of the room. She doesn't stop until she reaches my floor to ceiling shelves, and parked at the far left, a rolling ladder she runs her fingertips along. "You have Captain Underpants books in here." Beaming, she glances over her shoulder. "And Diary of a Wimpy Kid."

"I rarely throw things away just because I'm finished with them. I like to read, and those were some of my earliest, happiest literary memories."

"Which is a perfectly good reason to hold on to them." She goes back to perusing my collection, dragging the ladder along with her, like she's afraid it'll go away if she releases it. "The Fantastic Five. Percy Jackson. The Chronicles of Narnia. You were a well-read young man."

"One would assume." I chuckle. "The fact is, I couldn't afford any of those in my youth, which means I bought them once I became an adult." *Make your trauma the butt of a joke. It's how we deal with these things.* "I sometimes borrowed from the library when I was a kid, but if my parents found them, they usually destroyed them. Eventually, the library stopped lending them to me."

No longer smiling, she turns with a frown. "That was cruel of them."

They were cruel people.

Alana knows that more than any of us.

"Tommy used to borrow them for me too," I murmur. "Until the same thing kept happening. And then Alana." I scratch my neck. "Small towns. They knew who I was related to, and who my friends were. So they made sure to ban anyone who supplied me."

"And so the literary escape dried up." She releases the ladder and wanders closer. Her perfume precedes her, and when she stops with her hands on my chest, the scent of her shampoo fills my nostrils. "It makes me happy that, as an adult, you've surrounded yourself with the things that bring you joy. You lacked control over your own life back when you were younger. Now, you have it back."

"You think my desire for control is annoying."

She tilts her head to the side, searching my eyes. "I think your desire for control is not something I get to comment on, because I wasn't that little boy living in hell. I wasn't even Alana, watching from the edges. I think I don't always relate to the same things you do, and I don't always understand you. But it's not for me to judge, and it's sure as hell not for me to tease you for it."

I broke her.

Her taunting smart-assery is half the fucking reason I fell in love with her. But my obsession with holding on to the past, to maintaining control, has stolen that from her just as callously as the books stolen from me.

"I don't want you to stop being who you are." I cup her face and draw her to the tips of her toes. "Being annoyed by you is half the fun, Fox. Fighting with you makes my heart skip a beat. Just…"

"Just, what?"

"Just leave my forks alone. They really matter to me."

She laughs, throwing her arms over my shoulders and trembling when I take most of her weight.

"You want to be white or black on the chessboard?"

"Hmm…" She peers across and considers the pieces that are always set up. The board that is never dusty. "Which one do you want to be?"

"White. White goes first."

"Well, alright then." Leaning back until she's on her feet, she unravels her arms and turns, seductively peeking over her shoulder and tugging the hair away from her neck. "Could you help me with my zipper before we start? I figure, even if I actually *try*, I'm bound to lose a few pieces."

"Confidence is important in battle." I pinch the tiny zipper between my fingers and peel the metal down, careful not to catch her skin. "You're very good at seduction, by the way. Letting a man unzip you is a boss move."

She snorts, sliding out of my grasp and meandering toward the chessboard. And because she's a pain in my ass, she grabs a white pawn and moves it forward.

Because I said I wanted it.

"Boss move number two. Get a pen, Watkins. You're about to be schooled."

"Jesus." I reach into my pants and rearrange my cock, and following her to the board, I counter her move with a similar one of my own. Pawn, one square forward. "I'm not sure how I feel about associating sex and chess. I'd hate to rock a boner every time I play in the future." Releasing my piece, I bring my eyes up and lock on to hers. "I usually play against other guys. You're making me uncomfortable, Tatum."

"Pretty sure we've discussed discomfort ad nauseam. I push you into situations you don't like, you whine about it and, eventually, fuck me. I tell you I *won't* do things to annoy you anymore, you whine and, eventually…" She grabs another of her pawns and charges forward, two squares. "You fuck me. Will I ever satisfy you?"

Without giving it much thought, I grab a different pawn and move it forward two squares. "You satisfy me often. More often when my cock is in your mouth."

Playful, she tours the room, swaying hips and seductive side-eyes. She strokes the spines of my books, the way she strokes my spine when we sleep in the same bed, and when she deigns to rejoin the game, she takes her already forward pawn and places it beside mine.

Tap goes the timer.

"I could've taken your pawn just now. I'm going easy on you."

"Mmhm." I grab my bishop and cut it halfway across the board, stopping beside her pawn so she's sandwiched between my pieces. "Do you have a grand game strategy, Fox? Or are you moving pieces and biding your time?"

"Biding my time for what?" She selects a pawn and drives it forward, quick as a flash and with seemingly no brain power expanded. But then she comes around the board, circling my body and stopping behind me.

I remain stock still, shuddering breath, as she presses her chest to my back and her hands on my stomach.

"I feel no need to bide my time when I could simply take my panties off and sit, open-legged, on your desk." She trails her palms down my stomach, dipping her fingers into the waistband of my pants. "I can think of far easier ways to secure your undivided attention and use as much, or as little, time as I desire."

I select an unmoved black pawn and slide it forward, blocking her advance and stopping myself—barely—from hitting a non-existent timer. *Jesus, I'm such a fucking weirdo.* "Your turn."

"Hmm." She pulls her hands from my pants and meanders around the table, slowing to study a globe displayed against the wall, its wooden framing and intricately carved lines put there by a skilled artist. It holds her captive for a moment, distracting her from her seductive dance, and when she can't help herself, she places a gentle finger on the sphere and turns it until a long, delicious smile stretches her lips. "I haven't been to the Galápagos Islands. Did you know they have a beautiful white-petaled flower there, with vibrant purple centers?" Dropping her hand, she turns and approaches the chessboard, and selecting her knight, she brings it into battle, placing it behind one of her already engaged pawns. "They're called the purple passionflower." She peeks up at me from under long lashes. "Very pretty."

I select my knight and bring it forward, busying the middle of the board now that we've taken a half dozen turns each. "The Galápagos are the only islands in the northern hemisphere with penguins. Did you know that?"

She beams, an expression that may become my most haunting memory once she's gone. "I *did* know that. And that giant tortoises are native to the area. And that iguanas swim in the water, too." Glancing down, she pauses for the first time since we started, considering her next move, before she selects an untouched pawn and brings it forward. "Any time is a good time to visit the Galápagos. The weather is always perfect."

"Maybe you should go there." I select my unmoved knight and bring it into play. "Maybe I should go, too. Totally nonchalant and coincidentally." *Don't laugh at me. Don't laugh at me. Please, Fox, don't laugh at me.* "If we just so happen to be there at the same time, we could hang out. Read a book in the sun."

"Fuck in the shade?" She mirrors my move, pushing her knight forward and hitting me with a look that warms me all the way to my toes. "How do you handle vacation, Christian? There are no routines. No places of familiarity. We can drink before lunch, and have dinner at four in the afternoon. Or ten at night." She slides her tongue along her front teeth. "Are you relaxed on vacation, because vacations are inherently stress free? Or are you on edge, because all routine is lost?"

"I don't know if you're poking at me or asking a genuine question." I pick up my bishop and retreat diagonally, just one square. "But the honest answer is, on day one of vacation, I get kinda tired. Like my brain is working a million miles faster than normal to keep up with all the changes. It makes me sleepy, which makes me irritable, since vacation is supposed to be about having fun. By days two and three, the brain fog usually clears and shit starts to feel good. That's when the world becomes chill as hell."

"That was…" She licks her lips and ponders her next move, selecting a pawn and shoving it into battle. "Refreshingly honest and surprisingly sensical."

"And irritatingly rigid?" I'm annoying myself, turning what was supposed to be sexy and flirty into a bad therapy session. I grab my knight and move it forward. "Don't worry, I won't crash your vacation."

"Oh…" Visibly sad, her smile transforms into a pout. "I was about to say day one is for laying in bed, anyway. There are other ways to fuck, ya know? Slower, gentler, the not so frenzied version where a person still gets to come, but it's not a competition of one-upping each other."

She pinches her untouched bishop between her fingers and drags it diagonally just one square. "I was getting kinda psyched for the tortoises and flowers and lazy days spent in bed. But I was imagining all that *with you*. Can't fuck myself. Well…" She snickers, coming around the table and taking my hand in hers. She isolates my fingers, pulling them apart before placing just one, my pointer, on her tongue. "I can. In fact, I'm pretty good at it. But I'd choose your fingers over mine any day, no matter which island we were on."

"Fuck." My lungs spasm and my chest rocks with them. My cock grows behind the zipper of my jeans, crushed against the unforgiving material and desperately searching for freedom.

Without caring too much, I grab my bishop and send it three-quarters of the way across the board, settling it in enemy territory, sandwiched between her knight and an untouched pawn. "For the first time in my life, I'm considering knocking the whole table over just so I can undress you."

She grins, staring up at me from beneath long lashes, and when she knows she has me, she suckles on my finger and scratches her teeth along the digit to taunt me. "Not allowed to cheat." She grabs her bishop and sets it almost toe to toe with mine. Not quite. But close. "The anticipation is half our foreplay. I figured you, of all people, would appreciate that."

"Me, of all people?" I take my queen and slide her to the left, switching her out with my rook to give her a little extra protection. "Because I like chess?"

"Because you're a patient man who plays chess for fun, and you waited all your life to buy books for the boy who never got to enjoy them when he was young. Also, I didn't know we could do that move." She breaks character, her eyes dancing with humor. "The queen whoop-de-do thing you just did. And it occurs to me now, you could do whatever the hell you want, move whatever piece you please. You could tell me it's legal, and I wouldn't be able to say you're wrong."

"So I guess you're gonna have to trust me." I take her chin in my hand and draw her around. "Your move."

Smirking, she leans closer and rests her chest against mine—it's a hug, no seduction—and with her left hand, she mirrors my move. "If it's legal for you, it's legal for me. Queen whoop-de-do has spoken."

"Your arbitrary naming of a move that already has a name would bother the more rigid, pre-Fox-Tatum version of me." I select a pawn and push it forward. "But I'm a better man now. I've grown and matured."

She studies the board and moves a pawn. "I'm proud of you, little buddy." Bringing her eyes back to mine, she taps my chin with the tip of her finger. "So proud."

"So fucking patronizing." But I chuckle anyway, slipping my free hand into the back of her dress so I get to feel her skin on mine. "Getting kinda impatient that no one has lost a piece yet. You're still dressed."

"Maybe you're not as good as you thought you were." Just like chess, she mirrors my move, digging her hand under my shirt and flattening her palm against my back. "Your turn, handsome. I'd hate to fall asleep before you touch my vagina."

"We could reconvene this game tomorrow, and I could touch your vagina now." I inch my hand downwards, over the curve of her ass until I can ascertain if she came prepared tonight.

Plug or no plug.

"No." She traps her bottom lip between her teeth. "Figured you'd have me so turned on with the Saint Andrew's cross thing, we needn't bother with prep."

"Your assumption that I had a giant fucking cross in my house is..." I grab my bishop and bring it back, out of danger of her well-placed pawn. "Interesting. Where did you suppose I hid it?"

Smug as a pig in mud, she grabs her pawn and slams mine out of the way, callously knocking it off the board and setting hers down in its new place.

"Oopsie. Guess I drew first blood." Her lips tremble with a smile, then she tilts back and offers her hand, palm-side up. "Maybe it'll be you laid out on the desk, naked, while I survey my prize. Shirt, please."

My heart thunders and my cock thickens, but I peel my shirt over my head and let it fall to the floor. "Well played, Ms. Tatum. But don't get too cocky. Kingdoms usually fall when their leaders least expect it."

She gently scrapes her nails over my chest, over my hardened nipples. "It's your turn. Pay attention to the game, not to what I'm doing."

Fuckkkkkk.

I force my eyes to the board, but she takes my nipple between her teeth and destroys my concentration. My body vibrates and my lungs collapse just long enough to turn my knees weak. So I select a pawn and make my move. "Time." I wrap my arm around her back and pull her in so she feels my cock. So she knows just how much fucking pain I'm in, and how desperately I'd trade chess for her, for the rest of my life. "Can I forfeit now?"

"Nuh-uh." She switches nipples, laving her tongue over my flesh until goosebumps follow. Then she swaps my bishop with a pawn, knocking another piece off the board. But instead of sitting it beside my first captured piece, she stares down at my cock and places it snug between the front of my hipbone and the band of my shorts. "Gosh, Watkins. I was *so* sure this game would make me look foolish. But here we are. Pants, please."

"You're arrogant when you're winning." I unsnap my jeans and tear the zipper down, hardly upset by the fact I get to free my cock from its steel confines. Toeing my shoes off and working the denim along my legs, I peel shoes, socks, and jeans down all at the same time.

In just two captures, she has me in my underwear.

"Not entirely sure you should dictate which items of clothing I lose. The fairer loss just now would've been a shoe. *One* shoe."

"Eh." She trails her fingertips over my stomach, tracing the lines of my abs and licking her lips. Because fuck it, she's hurting for me, too. "I'm not nearly as patient as you are. I don't even pretend to be. I'm just playing, because your brain turns me on as much as your body does. Strip chess means I get both." She tilts her head toward the board. "Your turn."

Do I even have a brain to use right now? Am I capable of making sensible choices?

Evidently not, because I pick up my queen and sling her forward to capture a pawn.

Hardly an equitable trade.

"Your dress, please."

She laughs, dropping her head back and treating me with a view of her delicate throat and the pounding pulse knocking at her flesh. "Sheesh. Cutting straight to the point, Watkins. You could have asked for a shoe."

"I have no intention of allowing you to stay in that dress a single second longer than necessary." And because I'm a gentleman and all that, I tug the fabric down, lowering to my knees until the bishop in my waistband stabs my stomach and the scent of her arousal hits me in my fucking soul.

I help her step out of her dress, stroking the back of her thigh, and when my nose and her pussy are on the same level, I dive in and bury it between her legs.

I just want to smell.

I just want to feel her warmth.

She cries out, fisting my hair and dropping an inch when her knees fail. But I keep her on her feet. On her heels, which is a million times better. Holding her up, I run the tip of my nose over her clit, purely to make her jump.

"Chris—"

"I'm taking my winnings soon." I don't taste. I don't cheat. Instead, I straighten out and set my hands on her hips, dipping the tips of my fingers in the waistband of her panties. "Fuck, babe. Are you for sale?"

Her eyes narrow to slits.

"I'd pay you to walk around my home like this. Lace underwear. Sexy heels. All mine, where no one on the outside even knows you're here."

"I won't exchange money for pleasure." She pushes onto her toes and nibbles on my lips. "But I'll accept your soul. I don't think it's too much to ask."

"You already have it." I slide my tongue against hers. Suckling. Tasting.

And losing my battle against casual, I pull her impossibly close. "If my soul was the price, then the deal has already been made. You belong to me. I belong to you." I press my forehead against hers, staring down at her slender body and the way her chest lifts and falls. Fast and heavy. Warm and reddening.

I sure as fuck can't look into her eyes.

"It's your turn." I clear my throat and turn to the board. Anything to avoid confronting whatever expression she wears. Mocking? Disgust? Gentle taunting, or worse, a reminder she won't be mine, *can't* be mine, because she's happiest in New York. And I… I can't exist anywhere but here in Plainview.

She releases a shuddering breath, and without much thought, she moves her castle into an empty square.

I could take her pawn. I could take her castle. But then again, she could have taken mine, too.

So I select my knight and move it into an empty square.

Are we afraid to push on while my ridiculous declaration hangs heavy in the air? Did I ruin the mood?

Probably. I'm pretty fucking good with that shit.

Quick as a flash, she sends her castle across and captures my pawn, and before she can ask for my shorts, I counter by taking her castle.

It's a fast one-two, over quicker than either of us can blink. But she smiles, at least. I see her in my peripherals, farewelling her castle.

"That was smooth." She grabs her rook and sets it beside mine, so I take my knight and place it on her side of the board, joining the ranks of two of her pawns. "Do you plan your moves while I'm still thinking about mine? Because you're pretty fast at this."

"I've had a lot of practice."

"Which is surprising, considering I took the first two casualties."

"War isn't about those who fall first." I wait for her to move a pawn, and then I take her knight. "It's about who's standing at the end. You're all about flash, Fox. You want to be fancy and loud. I'm more subtle in my approach, so when I slice your king's throat, you won't even know I was holding my knife."

"Now who's getting cocky?" She jumps forward with her queen and captures my bishop. Bringing the pointy end toward her mouth, she gently, without denting the delicate wood, rests her teeth around the tip. "Gotcha good on that one."

"Pretty sure you owe me your panties." I use my pawn—insult on top of injury—and knock her queen to her death, and taking my captured bishop from between her fingers, I set both beside the board. "You've taken heavy casualties, Ms. Tatum. What will you do now?"

She studies the game, counting her soldiers—plus her missing queen—then swallowing, she lowers to her knees, pulling the waistband of my shorts down and freeing my cock until my captured bishop clatters to the floor.

"I *am* the queen," she murmurs, sultry and delicious. "And I still have moves available to me."

I choke out a laugh, impressed by her wily game-playing. But then she traps my cock between her lips, dragging my breath out on a gasp and drawing a gritty groan from the depths of my lungs. With a swipe of her tongue and a skilled circle of her lips, she almost undoes me. "Fuck!" I grab the back of her hair and jut my hips forward, slamming my length into the back of her throat. "This is not how we play chess, dammit."

"Sometimes a war must be won on our back, and not our feet." She drags her tongue along the bottom of my shaft, circling my cock with her fingers until her tight grip almost brings me to my knees. Suckling on just the tip, and staring up at me from beneath long lashes, she reaches between her legs and inches two fingers inside her panties. "Shit."

"You lost your queen, so now you must suck my cock." I rock forward and fill her throat. "You don't get to pleasure yourself, too. That's not how punishment works."

Tears wet her lashes, smudging her makeup. But when I retreat to the very tip, preparing to slide forward again, she places her hand on my hip and stops my momentum, drawing a shaky, shuddering breath into her lungs instead.

She looks up at me with eyes that verge on innocent.

Vulnerable.

Sad, even.

"Are you okay?" Worry is like hot sauce in my veins. Concern, like an anvil on my heart. I wrap my hand around her biceps and tug her to her feet, and when she sways, I hold her against my chest. "Did I hurt you?"

"You said I can't pleasure myself." From soft to sorceress, she reveals a wicked smile and slips her fingers between her legs. "I say, stop me."

"Fuck." I jerk her into my arms and crash my lips to hers. Capturing her squeal of delight, I walk to my desk and set her down again, peeling her underwear along her legs until I'm presented with her glistening pussy, creamy with desire and throbbing with want.

With need.

"Longest game of my fucking life." I fist my cock and pray I don't embarrass myself. Fuck knows, I'm ready for her. "You're pretty good at it, though. Just so you know." I tug her to the very edge of my desk, knocking things from the surface so pens roll to the floor and book stacks collapse.

Normally, that shit would bother me. But not tonight. Not for as long as she's here and her heart could be mine if only I said the right things. Did the right things.

I wish it were as easy as playing chess.

I line up at her fiery opening, teasing her entrance, taunting us both, and when her eyes come to mine, I race forward and fill her to bursting. Without asking. Without warning. Without giving her time to adjust. Her pleasure turns to pain and her cry of delight verges on agony, but then I ride her, sliding in until her natural lubrication makes the glide smooth, then out again until her cry turns to caress.

"Jesus. Chris—"

"Be with me like you're scared it's our last time." I drape her legs over my shoulders and stare into her wide, panicked eyes, and hugging her thighs to my chest, I fuck her.

Like it's our last time.

Like I might die if we don't have this.

June fourteenth is a guillotine hanging over my head, and death comes too quickly. Too gleefully.

"Fuck," I massage her clit with the pad of my thumb. "Sweetest pussy I'll ever know."

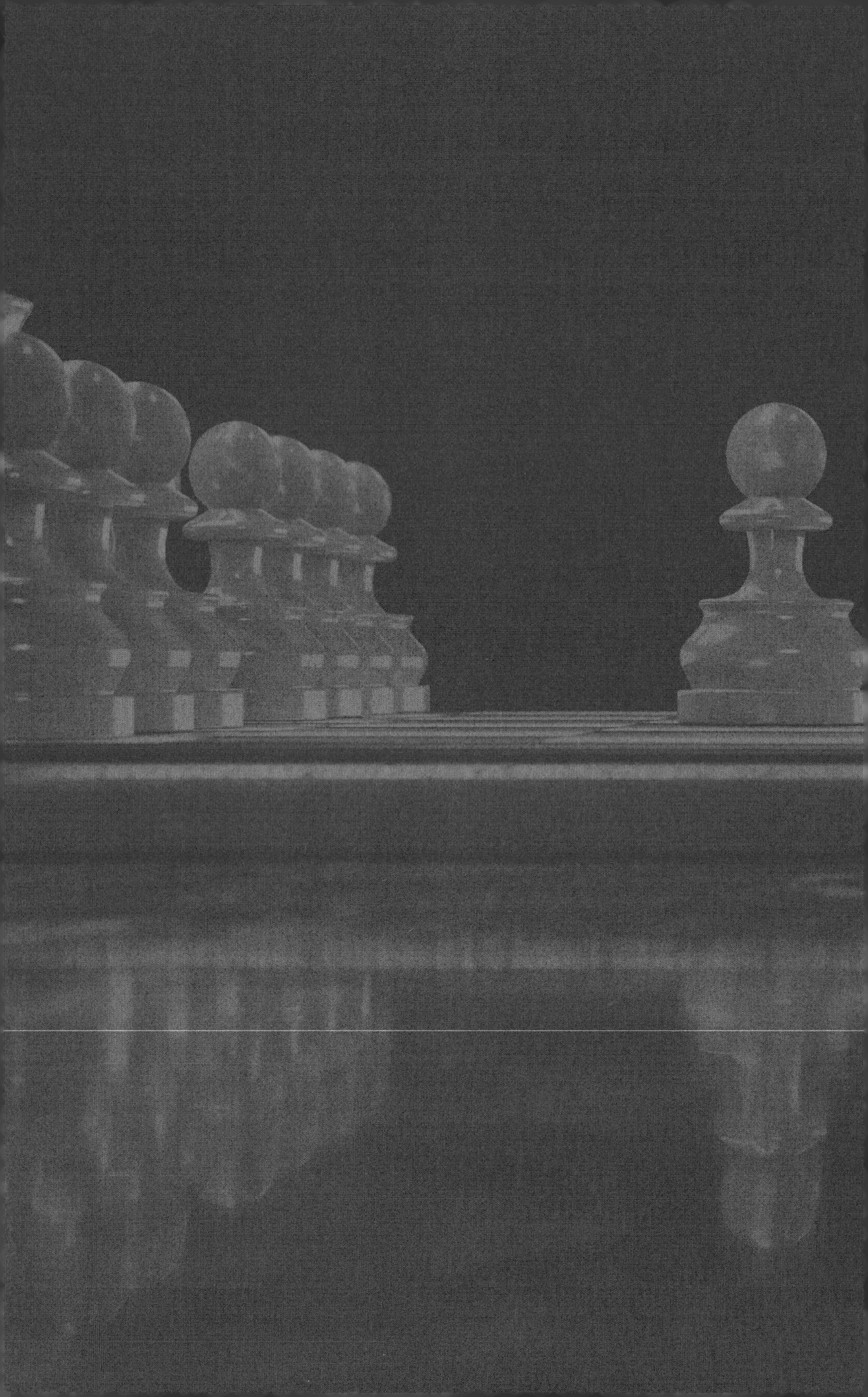

ROUND TWENTY-FIVE
FOX

"The cake's confirmed and set to be delivered by the bakery. Seating's being organized by the guys." I work down my checklist, walking with Alana now that she's part of the planning process. "Catering's done, music's ready, and the guest list is pretty freakin' plump." I come to a stop in the gym's doorway, in the section between the front desk and the room that holds a regulation-sized boxing ring.

Lucky for us, Tommy and Chris are sparring, and even if I pretended to be an evolved human being turned off by the sight of blood, the long line trailing from Chris' lip is, admittedly, enormously sexy.

I'm no better than a neanderthal.

Whatever.

"They make quite the sight, don't they?" I lean against the doorframe, folding my arms and tucking my little notebook and pen against my side. "I could've sworn, when I got off the plane, they were identical. You could put them side by side and demand I tell you who was who. It would've been impossible."

Alana cradles Hazel against her chest, one hand beneath her butt and the other behind her head. Already, the sweet girl is gaining weight and growing at a ridiculous speed. "What do you see now?" she wonders. "Not the same?"

"No." I drag my lip between my teeth and command my heart to calm the hell down. *You're close to the end, Fox. Don't make a dick of yourself now.* "I see two completely different men. They walk different. Talk different.

They smile different. Their eyes are exactly the same, but..." I glance across and meet her gaze. "They're different."

Impressed, she drops her chin in a gentle nod. "I've only ever known them that way. I don't recall a single moment in my life where I looked at them and saw two of the same." Her lips curl higher as she looks their way again. "You wanna talk to me about whatever the hell is going on between you and Chris yet?"

Stunned, my eyes flare wide and my heart skitters to a stop. And when I'm not sure I'll keep my lunch inside my stomach, I snatch her hand and pull her along the hall.

"Hang on!" She laughs, walk-running and readjusting her grip on the baby. When I zoom straight past Tommy's office door, she yanks me back and slings me through, slamming it shut again until the crash startles Hazel.

Frenzied, panicked—sick to my stomach—I toss my notebook and walk laps of the minimal, non-messy portion of floor space. "Who told you?"

"Who told me what?" She presses her back to the door and slides down, sitting on her butt and cradling the baby against her chest. "That you look at each other while we're eating dinner, and my vagina gets a little tingly because of it?"

"Alana!"

"That you argue less and smile more? That *he's* been seeing someone, and *you've* been seeing someone, but neither of you are naming names, and not a single member of the grapevine gossip mill has any clue?"

"Oh, God." I run my fingers through my hair. "Shit."

"That Cliff suddenly needs a security detail, but only *after* I suggested he and you date?"

"What?"

"Or that I just *feel* it?" She stares at the side of my face, warming my flesh and grinning because she knows it. "I *feel* his happiness, Fox, and I *feel* yours. I can't be in the same room as the two of you without getting caught up in your nasty web of lust and secrets and sneakiness when you think I'm too busy to pay attention."

"I'm sorry." I spin and rush across the room, dropping into a crouch and desperately searching her eyes. "I swear, I came to Plainview with the purest of intentions. I was here for you. *To help you.* Not me."

"Why are you sorry?" She frowns. "You didn't steal my man, and no matter how possessive I am of him, my possession only extends as far as a sister's would. His love life is entirely his own."

"I'm sorry because I didn't tell you! Because I kept it a secret. Because I was sneaking around, which is basically the same as lying. And we don't lie." I take her hand in mine, my thighs burning, but I don't dare stand again.

This is my penance.

This is my moment of reckoning.

The one I was terrified of.

"It was never, ever, *ever* meant to be a lie, Alana. It was just... fun. And hot. And really, really crazy."

"I'm sure it was," she snickers.

"And then it just happened. This thing I thought would happen only once. But before we were done the first time, I knew I'd want more. God," I moan. "I knew you'd freak out if you found out."

"Why the hell would I freak out? When have I ever given you the impression I would be upset about this?"

"You mean the six hundred million times you've talked about how protective you are of him? Or the seventy million times you explained to me, in *fine* detail, how no bitch would ever be good enough, and if you ever found yourself in a position where names had been named and his feelings were hurt, you'd take a baseball bat and rearrange her slutty brains?"

"Well..." She softens her scowl to something kinder. "Okay, so I probably said those things. But you're no random bitch, Fox. You're *my* bitch." She gives my hand a tug and pulls me around to sit on the floor beside her. And when I think I might cry, she hands the baby across and seals my fate.

Tears itch the backs of my eyes.

"You're a top-tier, high-quality bitch," she croons. "You're my very best friend in the whole world. So if Chris catches feelings for someone and that someone is you, I'm not grabbing my baseball bat. Except," she adds, turning her head and studying the side of my face, "to threaten *his* brains. Because once you're involved, my protection transfers." She strokes my arm. "From him to you."

I *blink, blink, blink* the hot, salty tears from my vision. "Really?"

"Yes! He knows I have his back, Fox. He knows I'd mess a bitch up for stepping wrong, but you're just..." She places her hand on my shoulder, squeezing just tight enough to make it feel like a hug. "You're honestly the prettiest, smartest, kindest, most amazing person I have *ever* met, but you *still* have this annoying voice in the back of your brain that cuts you down. It's like you think your dad cutting out on you was somehow your fault. Or that your mom leaving was the natural next step, and like that was on you, too."

And there they go, my tears slipping from the corners of my eyes. "I probably shouldn't have told you those things. I never tell anybody."

"I'm glad you did. Because even if I think you're the greatest freakin' catch on both sides of the civil war, I don't disregard the doubt you carry every single day. I don't ignore that voice that *insists* on hurting you. Even if I think it's unwarranted. Even if I think you're crazy and I would kill for your legs… and your ass…"

I choke out a soft laugh.

"And your tits, too. Since they're way perkier than mine."

"You've had two kids. Mine are still untouched… mostly."

"Ew! That's my brother you're talking about!" She slides her hand down and wraps her fingers around my wrist. "None of what *I* think erases the damage those assholes did to you. So despite how beautiful and worthy and special you are, I'm not blind to the pain and doubts weighing you down. If you're asking me who I think Chris deserves, and who I think you deserve, then I promise, I'm tossing you together every single time. You're my favorite people, Fox. You *have* to know I've kinda wished for this outcome."

I drop my head back and release a tired groan. "I was so worried you'd lose your shit."

"Then you don't know me, *bitch*." She leans closer and rests her cheek on my shoulder. "Can I be the maid of honor at your wedding?"

"Oh, God!" I scoff so loud, the sound scrapes along my throat and leaves behind a scratchy ache. "There will be *no* wedding."

"Why not? Did you forget that thing I said about feeling your happiness when you're together?"

"Did you forget that bit where we agreed *not* to tell you? Where we agreed not to tell *anyone*. And he was *so* on board. I asked a week or two ago if we could go out to dinner. In public. He snuck me into his house instead. I suggested we go for a walk down Main Street. We could buy ice cream and just stroll. He countered with going to bed instead." I shake my head. "He's not interested in more, Alana. And he's definitely not interested in letting anyone else see us."

"Because you asked him not to!" She squeezes my arm and waits for my eyes to come down. "I'm gonna hold your hand when I tell you this; *you* asked *him* for secrecy. That's what he's giving you."

"I asked for dinner at a restaurant. He didn't bite."

"Because it contradicts your initial request! He responds to direct communication, Fox. Not hints. Not subtlety. If you wanted dinner out, you needed to say '*Chris, snookums, I'm ready to go public now. I'm not afraid of Alana hurting me, so let's walk Main Street and hold hands. Then we're gonna go bang on Alana's bed.'"*

I search her eyes and show her a taunting smile.

Anything to see her lips crinkle.

"You did it on my bed?!" she explodes. "Dammit, Fox! He's practically my brother! How could you?"

"I'm kidding! Ouch." I catch her hands and hold on tight. "I've never disrespected your bed like that. I promise."

Say it, Fox. Finish it. Pay the piper.

"Um... Your couch, though..."

"Dude!"

"It wasn't my fault! He was sitting there, and I had your... Oh..." I grit my teeth. "I had your cute sleep shorts on, which have perfect sneaky penis gaps."

"Fox!"

"I wanna say I'm sorry. Truly, I do. But I have bigger things to worry about right now than the cum stain on your couch cushion."

"I'm reconsidering the baseball bat brains thing," she growls. But despite the rage in her voice, she wraps my arm in hers and snuggles in with the gentlest touch. "Why are you worried about telling him how you feel?"

"How *do* I feel?" I challenge. "What is it you think I feel?"

"Love?" She exhales a long, sleepy sigh that sounds almost the same as Hazel's. "If you didn't love him, you'd enjoy your casual thing and not stress out. I was telling myself that you were sad because you're leaving us at the end of next week." Swallowing, she pulls back and studies the side of my face. "But I know now, it has nothing to do with me at all. You went ahead and did that thing you swore you'd never do, huh?"

"There's no need to be so smug about it."

"For ten long years, you held me while I cried for Tommy, and all along, you said how your way was superior. *Never fall in love, Lana. No risk, no failure.* Now here you are, in love, and you understand what I knew all along."

"That I'm dumb?"

She snorts. "That it hurts like hell. That the highs feel really, really freakin' good, and the lows feel worse than anything you've ever felt before."

"Feels worse than that time I was called into the principal's office in eighth grade," I rasp. "Where the school counselor was waiting for me, and child protective services, too. I was too old to be cute and loved by some other family, but too young to live on my own. My mom wasn't coming back. So I was tossed into a system that had no room for me, counting down until I was old enough to get on with my life on my own."

"Instead, you aged out and ran face-first into this Podunk kid who just got off a Greyhound bus. I had this weird, marbles-in-my-mouth accent you liked to make fun of, and a baby growing in my belly. You helped me, Fox. You saved my life."

"Wasn't gonna stand by and watch another girl get screwed over a society that refused to support her," I grumble. "And wasn't gonna see another child tossed into a flawed system."

"You were my co-parent more than Colin ever was. He gave us a home and a health insurance policy. But you gave us love. You gave us acceptance. And considering your parents failed you on both fronts, the fact you *could*, proves how amazing you truly are."

"It's all quite pathetic, huh?" I slide my hand over the baby's back, smoothing down the pants ruffles and patting her bottom. "My origin story is so ridiculously cliché, I'm embarrassed to even say it out loud. People probably think I'm making it up."

She snuggles into my arm, exhaling until I feel her breath on my skin.

"Don't tell anyone, okay?" I reach up and swipe a single treacherous tear from my cheek. "I don't like it when people know."

"It's nothing to be ashamed of. Jesus, you're in good company. You, me, Tommy, and Chris... we make up a pretty trash-tastic foursome of trauma clichés. We could turn it into a drinking game. Take a shot if your parent ever made you feel like shit on the bottom of their shoe."

"We'd get drunk pretty fast. And I don't like vomiting after alcohol. It burns."

She nibbles on her lip, chewing contemplatively. "I think you should tell him how you feel. Omit the bit about your parents if you must, but he deserves to finish this with his eyes wide open."

"Why, though? He won't come to New York, and Plainview nearly broke my nose yesterday. They really should put stickers on clean glass doors."

"Have you even asked him?" She trudges straight over my feeble attempt at a joke. "You don't get to decide what he'll do—"

"I did, actually. I asked him." I bring my finger up and stroke Hazel's chubby cheek. "He said no."

"He didn't have all the information! He would've taken that as a hypothetical question, Fox. Not *'I'm in love with you, and I'm begging you to choose me.'* You're not being fair."

"That's where you're wrong. I *am* being fair." I slide my finger over the bridge of Hazel's nose. "What's not fair is to ask the same question a second time, knowing his answer already, but adding on a layer of emotional manipulation."

"Fox—"

"Just let it go. Please. I won't beg him to choose me. I refuse." *I stopped begging to be loved when I was fourteen years old.* "Besides, he's happy here, and he only just got you and the kids back. He's not ready to walk away, no matter who is waiting for him in another—arguably better—state."

She sniffles, breathing out an almost silent laugh. "And you won't come here?"

"I can't be happy in a town I'm not wanted in."

"But *I* want you here! Franky wants you here. Tommy wants you here. And I'd bet my left tit, without a single shred of hesitation, that Chris wants you here. Give him a chance to know what's at stake before you cut and run."

"I'm a bad organ transplant, Lana. And this town is the body rejecting me." I pull back, but only to twist and look down into her eyes. "It's been nice, though."

"Being here?"

I shake my head. "Falling in love. If I was gonna get stupid and pull a stunt like this, then I'm glad it was with him."

"He's pretty amazing, right?" She blinks welling tears from her eyes, swatting a droplet that rolls down her cheek. "There's something magical about these Watkins boys. From absolute horror and cruelty came such incredible men. I'm astonished every single day by how truly decent they are."

"Will you take an extra swing at the next bitch who stomps through town and catches his eye? For me?"

"Baseball bat?"

"Swing high," I sigh. "Put your shoulders into it. Just *thinking* about him and this bitch back here in Bumfuckville makes me want to puke."

"If he meets someone and falls in love and they marry, I'll have to be her friend. You understand that, right?"

Snarling, I pull away and glare down into her eyes.

"I won't have a choice. They're twins. Those boys are two halves of one incredible soul. If he marries and brings her into our world, I'm gonna have to like her. She'll be my kids' aunty."

"Why are you telling me this? Why are you hurting me?"

"Because you need to understand what you're walking away from before it's too late! If I have to be some bitch's best friend and sister-in-law,

I'd rather that bitch was *you*. But if you walk away without even trying, then I guess you're not really invested, anyway. Think wisely," she warns. "Think hard. Because no one is leaving you this time. You're leaving them."

"And you're being a jerk! You sit arrogantly upon the pedestal of your amazing relationship, but you're yet to set a wedding date so you can marry the man you've been in love with since you were nine years old. I'm happy for you, Lana. Truly. But *my* life is in New York. He doesn't want to move there. He doesn't want to leave the job he loves, or the only family he knows. Small-town living brings him comfort, and the beautiful house he always dreamed of owning would become just another sacrifice in a string of sacrifices. All for nothing."

"For you," she presses. "Not for nothing."

"No." I drop my gaze and study the baby. "We're too new, and he's too comfortable. What we have right now is nice, but we'll break it if we try to force something we know won't work."

"You're a pussy." She sets her hands on the floor and pushes to her feet. "Never thought I'd see the day where *my* best friend, the bravest, smartest, most confident person I've ever met, would be such a coward. And because of a boy?" Taunting laughter echoes across the room as she spins back and scoops her baby out of my arms. "He would fight for you, Fox. He would tear down every single barrier and destroy every person who stood between you."

She settles Hazel against her chest, patting her bottom to soothe her back to sleep. But she stands over me, her eyes swelling with pity. Disappointment. Sadness. "You're not even giving him a chance. And *that's* why you demanded secrecy. You knew I'd kick your ass for breaking his heart, and you knew you'd break his heart because you're too much of a coward to accept love. Your parents convinced you that you were unworthy, the fucking pricks." She turns on her heels and snatches up my notebook and pen. "Let's go. I'm done with this conversation, and we have a party to plan. I can't believe I walked away from watching the guys spar, all to hear about how much of a pussy you are."

I scramble to my feet and jump out of the way of the door, and following her into the hall, I grab her arm as panic lances through my veins. "You're not gonna say anything, are you? Alana? You won't tell Tommy either, right?"

"And ruin perfect small-town gossip fodder?" she scoffs. "No, I won't tell them. Honestly, I'd be embarrassed. All this time, I've annoyed them with how much I talk about you. *Fox is my best friend. Fox is so brave and amazing. Fox is so confident. I wish I could be more like Fox.*" She glances over her shoulder, pithy and snide. "For ten years, you've been this pillar of strength I aspired to. So strong and sure and pretty and perfect." She shakes her head and continues along the hall. "All for a boy! Now *that's* cliché."

"You're being mean because you want me to snap back." I scowl at the floor and follow her all the way to the doorway we started in, but when I come to a stop and bring my gaze up, I find both Watkins men still in the ring, their fight over and their chests expanded, swollen with adrenaline.

Most importantly, their eyes are on us.

The music playing through the speakers is far too loud for them to have heard a single word of our conversation. But they stare. Twin glares. Matching fat lips and a nasty knuckle-shaped bruise right over the top of Chris' chest.

It's ironic, really.

Alana shuffles closer, fake smiling to placate the guys. But I feel the heat of her burn, anyway. "You deserve better than what your parents did to you. You deserve better than the voice inside your head."

"Stop it."

"Not telling him will be the biggest mistake you ever make."

"I said stop it," I growl.

"You two look like you're up to no good," Tommy calls across the room, those marbles Alana speaks of, garbling his words and adding a country twang behind the rubber guard shielding his teeth. "Should we be worried?"

"Just going over party details," she lies. She lifts her chin in his direction. "Start sparring again. I wasn't done watching the show."

He smirks, growing broader under her admiring gaze. "I can't afford to look this good, babe. You're still healing."

"I'm done." Chris turns from the ropes and drags the guard out of his mouth. And because he doesn't know Alana knows, he thinks I'm the only one who sees his sly side glance. "I'm hitting the showers and going home."

Which is code for: come to my bed, Fox. In secret. I wanna fuck.

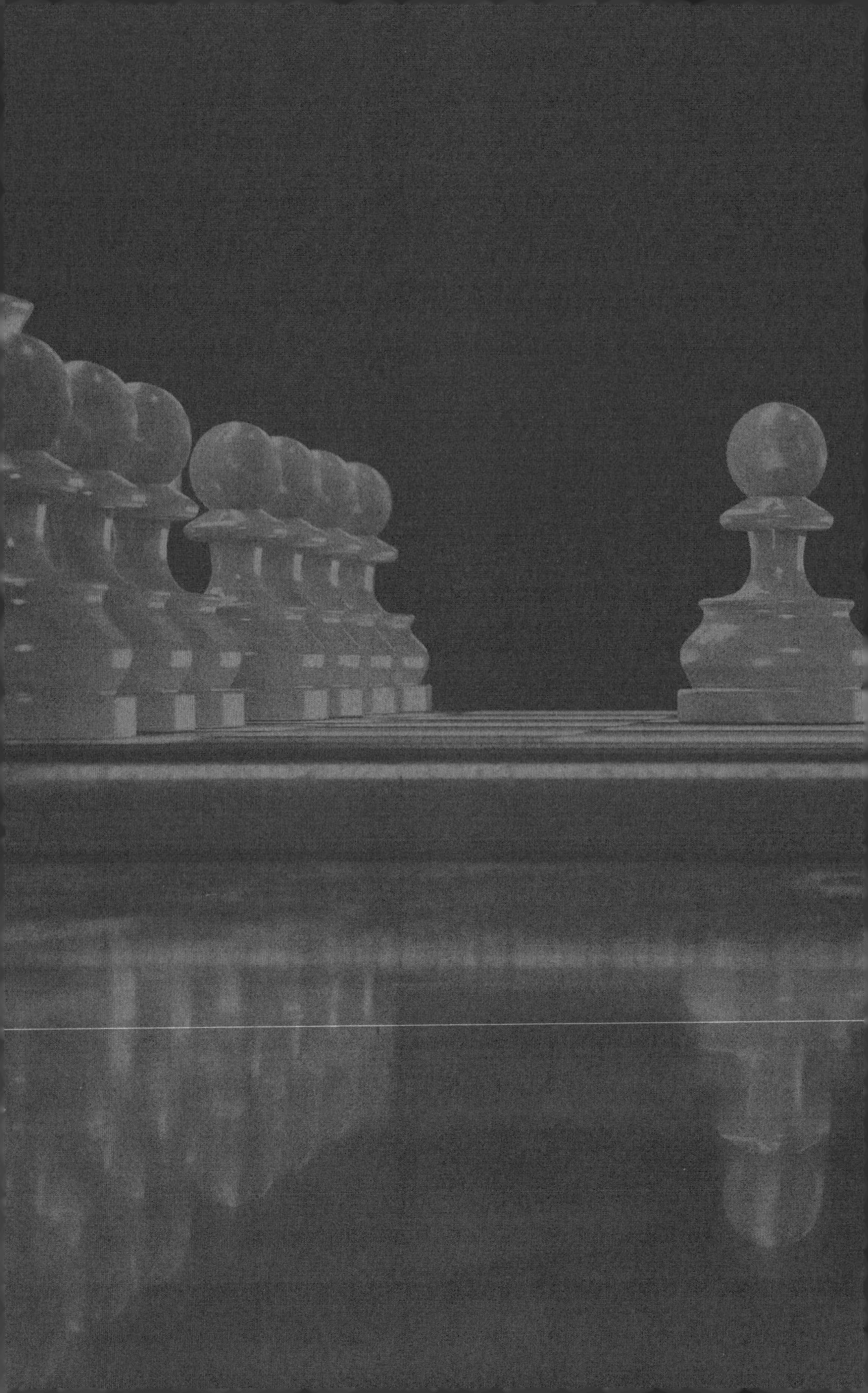

ROUND TWENTY-SIX
CHRIS

I'm not panicking.

No one is panicking.

There's nothing to panic about!

Because it's only day thirty-four of forty-two, which means I still have a week before Fox flies back to New York.

Seven days and seven nights, not including tonight. Seven sleeps. Seven chances to tell her I want to keep her... and pray she doesn't laugh in my face.

"It feels kind of strange dressing up for a fancy party at the gym." Fox fusses in the brand-new-ish bathroom above the bookstore, dropping something into the sink so it lands with a clatter, and following that with the sound of a metallic ting; bobby-pins, hitting the ceramic bowl. "I'm not even trying to live up to my New York hoity toity reputation. I just... it's kinda weird, don't you think?"

"No. I don't think." I wait in her kitchen and glance down at my suit. A whole ass suit, with a tie that squeezes my neck and shiny black shoes that annoy my feet. Comb lines mark my hair, and for the first time in a long time, I've shaved my jaw free of stubble. "We pulled up the mats last night and put down a dance floor." And lights. And a million rows of chairs. And lace chair bows. And flowers. *So many fucking flowers.* "Tommy wanted to do it up nice for Alana, so instead of running classes, the students pitched in and helped us. Whittled a ten-hour job down to two."

"Really?" She sets something heavy on the vanity, then the click-click-

click of her heels announces her steps. So I stand taller. I straighten my coat and broaden my shoulders.

Though there aren't enough nerves in the world to prepare me for the way I swallow my tongue, because she steps out of the bathroom in a gown of red and black, with a boned torso and wispy skirts that come with a definite almost see-though factor. She wears black heels and long, *long* fucking legs that disappear somewhere amongst the flowing fabric.

She twines her fingers together, fussing and blushing. Which is entirely fucking odd, considering how beautiful she is.

"You're staring." She clears her throat and lowers her gaze. "No good?"

"What?" I choke on air and a metric dose of that panic I swear I don't feel, but I take a step forward, then two and three more until I grab her hands and lift, forcing her to spin for me. "Fuck," I breathe. "You look amazing."

"Is it too much?" She comes back around and searches my eyes, nibbling glistening red lips that match her dress exactly. "Not enough? Is everyone else going to wear, like… Sunday best, so then I'll look like an idiot begging for attention?"

"I'm wearing a suit, aren't I?" I tug her closer and draw her hand up, pressing my lips to her throbbing wrist. "Tommy's wearing a suit. Alana's wearing a gown. I'm pretty sure you look exactly right. And if not, you still match me and Tommy and Alana. So we can all look stupid together."

"Solidarity," she nervously snickers, sliding a lock of hair behind her ear. "You look nice. I'm not saying the half-naked, sweating-and-bleeding-in-the-gym look isn't working for me, since it's entirely delicious and currently makes up eighty-five percent of my touch-myself memory bank, but—"

"Wait." I frown. "*Only* eighty-five percent?"

"Josh Hartnett, circa Pearl Harbor," she smirks. "Ben Affleck, same time. Leonardo DiCaprio, Titanic. David Boreanaz, Buffy—"

"Okay, shut up now." I want so badly to clap my palm over her mouth and force her to silence. But her lipstick is so perfect. Her work, appreciated. "I don't need a play-by-play."

"All those other guys have to share their fifteen percent. Five percent now, actually." She brushes the tips of her fingers over my tie. "Suited-Christian-Watkins just gobbled up a bunch of real estate. You mentioned a dance floor, right? Would I be needy and weird if I was hoping you'd ask me to dance?"

In front of other people?

"No?" Smiling, she glances down again. "Alana said there'll be a surprise today. Did you hear that?"

"I heard it from Tommy."

She gently pulls her hand from mine, circling the bed and grabbing a small black purse. She tosses her phone inside. Keys. Then striding past me, her perfume filling my lungs and knocking me back a step, she moves into the bathroom and re-emerges a moment later with a tube of red lipstick. "Did he say what the surprise is?"

I shake my head instead of saying the one word I don't want to hear tonight. So she tucks the lipstick away with the rest of her things and drops her hands. "I guess we should go then, huh? It's important we're there before everyone else, since we're part of the party planning committee."

"We are?" I drape my arm over her shoulders and pull her against my side, because this is my last chance to hold her close for the rest of today. My last opportunity to be with her before the real world encroaches and Alana's eyes notice too much.

I walk her all the way to the door, but when she grabs the handle and attempts to pull it open, I set my foot in the way and bring her around again, pushing her back against the wall.

I just need another minute.

Maybe two.

Unbothered by whatever emotion flashes through my eyes, she reaches up and strokes my chin with the pad of her thumb. "I appreciate your hard work planning this day. We got off to a rough start, but..."

"I don't recall volunteering for a committee."

"I know." She plays with my tie, patting it down gently. "But you ordered that cake like a boss. I'm proud of you."

"I helped lay the floor, too. And changed the playlist from '*kick their ass*' metal to something a little prettier."

"Your talents will never cease to amaze me." She walks her fingers over my collar and up to the back of my neck, then pulling me in, she hums her pleasure as I follow her unspoken order and lean in for a kiss. "I wouldn't have believed you if you'd told me five weeks ago that we'd be here. Doing this."

"In your apartment making out?"

Her beautiful eyes flicker with humor. "In my apartment. Together. Me in a pretty dress, and you in an exceptionally dapper suit. Whispering sweet words and kinda meaning them. I'm also dreading going out there." She drags her lip between her teeth. "Into the real world. Which is weird, since I'm the one who usually needs larger spaces and packed rooms."

I wrinkle my nose in exaggerated disdain. "Can't relate."

"And then, once this is done…" Her eyes dim just a little, from sweet delight to something sadder. "Once today is over, we're on the countdown to my flight."

"Can you extend your leave and stay a little longer?"

She exhales a soft, smiling breath. "My flight is already booked, and my boss is expecting me back in the office a week from Monday."

"So soon." I hate that it hurts. I hate that she hates Plainview so much. Fuck, I hate that I can't find a way out of this without breaking one of us. "We're gonna hang out the whole time, right? From now until you're on that plane."

"I have a week." She drags her thumbnail beneath my lips, cleaning away her lipstick. "I intend to spend every single minute of it with you. And with Alana and the kids. I refuse to waste any of it."

"Sleep at my house every night?" I kiss her again. *Fuck the lipstick.* "Or I'll sleep here. I don't even care if we sleep at the gym or in the back of my truck. But I care that I'm wherever you are."

"You gotta bank those hours," she teases. "Not to sound arrogant or anything, but I noticed your ability to sleep a full eight hours when we share a bed."

Don't I fucking know it.

"I wonder if the curse is broken," she ponders. "Maybe you'll be able to sleep now, even after I'm gone."

Doubt it. The curse is mine to carry from now until I'm dead. Or until I find a Fox I get to keep.

"Listen…" Why does my heart pound so damn hard? Why does telling her the truth feel like I'm about to ruin a perfectly good day? *Because guys like me don't get to keep women like her.* And yet, I can't let go of my hope completely. To do so would be akin to drowning… and letting it happen. "Later, when the party stuff is winding down…"

She searches my eyes. Curious. Sweet. "Mmm?"

"I wanted to talk to you about something. It's kind of important."

"Oh…kay." Her brows furrow with concern. "You wanna talk about it right now?"

"Nah." I empty my lungs, my exhale pushing strands of her hair back. "This is Alana's day. And Hazel's."

"And Franky's, too."

I chuckle. "Bet he *hates* it. Wearing an uncomfortable outfit, and shoes that are kinda tight and stiff. The tie will irritate his neck, and his hair will feel weird, because Alana probably smooshed gel in it to keep it neat."

Amused, she touches the top of my hair; *gelled*. "I promise, Alana's aware of the sacrifices Franky's making today. She'll know how hard he's working, and how desperately he wants to escape to where no one can see him." She steps onto her toes and presses a gentle kiss to the very corner of my lips. "People who love people, know and appreciate their efforts." Lowering again, she drops her hand and twines our fingers together. "Ready to go?"

"Yep." I pull her away from the wall and clear enough space to open the door, then leading her onto the stairs, I keep her hand in mine all the way to the bottom. All the way across the shop. To the door. And then across the threshold.

But as soon as we step outside and onto the public sidewalk, she tugs her hand free, smiling to soften the blow of her rejection, then she tucks her purse under her arm and holds her dress off the ground instead. "Time to go. You're in charge of whispering everyone's names in my ear, too. There's no way in hell I'll know who they are."

"Bold of you to assume I know them." I lead her around my truck and hold the door for her to climb in, then I close it again and jog to my side. "I've probably even met most of them. But assuming I listened when they told me their name is presumptuous of you."

She giggles, setting her purse on the chair under her thigh as she pulls her seatbelt on. "We'll figure it out. I have faith in us."

"Holy shit! That's Bobby freakin' Kincaid!" Fox bounces on my left, trembling with feral fangirl energy as the former world fucking champion, a legend amongst the fight world, approaches the front door of the gym with a bombshell blonde on his arm. "You don't even have to tell me his name," she whisper-hisses. "He was on the front cover of *every* magazine on *every* newsstand I walked past for *years*. Hi. Hello." She extends her hand, squeaking when he shakes it. "Welcome to the Love & War gym."

"Thanks for having us." The dude is only in his forties. Top end, but still. He hung up his gloves a while ago, which means he no longer competes for the belt, but his gym is as alive and pumping as ours. His workout regime, as consistent and brutal as ever.

He's considered old in the fight world. But in the *real* world, where we are right now, he's fit, jacked, and not to be trifled with.

He releases Fox's hand and draws his wife forward. Word on the street is, even after all these years, a handful of kids, and a grandkid or two on the way, he's *still* obsessed with her. "We were honored to receive an invitation," he murmurs. "Surprised," he adds with a playful smirk. "But pleased."

"We're honored you accepted." Fox fangirls for Kit Kincaid, too. Bobby isn't the only fighter in his marital bed. "I won't lie. When Cliff told me who he'd invited, I might've wet my pants a little."

"Cliff?" Confused, Bobby glances around. "Who the hell is Cliff?"

"Troopy!" Evelyn Kincaid is blonde, loud, boasts massive bouncing curls, and wears a beautiful gown wrapped around yet another fighter's body. She strides forward to stop beside Bobby—her uncle—and beams when Cliff spins inside the gym. He heard her. *She's loud*. "Well, hey there, cowboy! I *know* you're not making us line up outside like commoners. This is a wedding. Not a tournament."

Stunned, I meet Fox's eyes. "A wedding?"

"Ms. Kincaid!" Cliff sprints the length of the gym, blowing past me and Fox, and Bobby and Kit, too. Ignoring us all, *and ignoring her husband, too*, he whips Evie in for a squeezing hug that brings her feet off the ground and her wild curls springing with the momentum. "Holy cow! You scrub up nice."

He sets her back on her feet but grips her hips and takes a good *long* look. While, beside her, Ben Conner—the reigning world champ before Tommy slid in and swiped the belt—watches the pair with a twitching left eye.

I can fucking relate.

"You healed up good since December." Cliff vibrates with the kind of happiness only extroverts possess. "We *all* heard that break in real-time."

"It's all fun." She studies her wrist, rolling her hand to prove the limb is back and fully functional. Then, with a grin and a sly peek my way, she brings her focus up again and hooks a thumb left. Right. Wherever. "So, in the spirit of honesty and all that shit, you should know we've been speculating since the invitations arrived in the mail."

Cliff's brows sling high on his forehead. "Speculating about what?"

"About Tommy and Ben. We know they were supposed to fight a couple of years back. We know things got kinda tense when Ben stepped down." Smirking, she inches just a little closer to Cliff. "Is this an evil plot to get them into the cage? Will it happen today?"

"Eve!" Ben yanks her back. "Stop it."

"Because he's been training," she teases. "He *says* he's chill about all this, but he put in the extra hours, just in case. He didn't wanna look soft if Tommy was looking to make a scene."

"Fuck's sake." Ben wraps his arm around Evelyn's face, clapping his hand over her lips and crushing her into his side. "She's going to behave, I promise." He looks at me, finally, and offers his free hand. "I'm assuming you're not Tommy. And if you are, ignore that thing she said about extra training."

"Chris." I take his hand in mine and shake. "Good to see you again, Conner. Thanks for making the drive."

"Honored to be here." He releases me and looks to Fox. "Nice to formally meet you, Ms. Tatum. We talked via email for a minute there."

"Had to make sure you weren't a scammer," she snickers. "I could only assume the-hairy-sasquatch-at-TheRollinOnGym-dot-com was a spoof email address."

"Yes," he rumbles, glaring down at his smug wife. "One normally would assume so. You ready for all the noise?" He hooks a thumb over his shoulder. "You invited a lot of us, and once Evie began *speculating* about a fight, the assholes I hardly tolerate decided they were coming, too."

"There will be no fight," Fox laughs. "I mean... unless you and Tommy want there to be. Though, if that's the case, we could've promoted it properly and made a helluva lot of money." She lifts her purse, giving it a gentle shake, "If you decide to step into the cage, give me a thirty-second warning so I can film it."

Evie drags Ben's hand from her face, but she curls into his side anyway —he belongs to her—and when a new couple arrives with a cute little kid in tow, Evie takes the boy's hand in hers and softens. From loud and brash, to sweet and gentle. "Chris and Fox, meet my mom and daddy and the best baby sasquatch that ever sasquatched." Despite her dress and heels, she bends and sweeps the boy into her arms, setting him on her hip and a noisy kiss on his chubby cheek. "This is Westley. He's the future of fighting."

"Jesus." Ben shakes his head, but damn if he's not arrogant under the eye-roll. "Humility has been chasing you, Eve. But you're always a little too fast." He scoops his arm around hers and angles toward the door. "We should find our seats."

"You should go meet Franklin," Fox volunteers. "He's *not* the future of fighting, but he's sweeter than pie and my favorite little man on the planet. I bet he'd love to make a friend today."

With nods and smiles, they head inside and make room for the next couple to inch closer. But I was given a job, so I lean in and whisper, "Aiden and Tina Kincaid. Bobby's brother and sister-in-law."

"Aiden." She extends her hand and speaks his name like she knew it all along. "So glad you could make it. We really appreciate you taking the time to visit this tiny little town that hardly even exists."

"Tiny little towns that hardly exist come with their own appeal." Tina steps forward in a gown of gold and lace. A slit that goes to her knees, and heels that glitter under the afternoon sun. "Thank you for inviting us, Ms. Tatum. And just to clarify... will there be a fight today?"

Aiden, like Ben, side-eyes his wife.

"I'm not saying I've put money on a fight," she explains. "I'm saying it would benefit my future financial endeavors if you could confirm one way or the other."

Fox beams, entirely at home playing hostess. So I let her do her thing—sparkle within her element—and I do mine.

Stand. In silence.

"I had no idea this was even a conversation," she giggles. "I didn't realize there was beef between Tommy and Ben."

"Not beef," Aiden explains. "Merely, unfinished business. Tommy and Ben had been circling each other a few years back. Prepping for what was coming. The fight had finally been announced, but then..."

"Ben pulled out of the traditional circuit in favor of Evie's tournament." Tina's lips twitch with amusement. "That boy knew where to place his loyalties."

"Maybe later, when everyone has had a few drinks," Fox quips. "Give them gloves and see what happens."

"That's how people get hurt." I wrap my hand around her trim hips and pull her just a little closer. "Stop it."

Smug, Tina looks from Fox to me, wiggling her finger back and forth. "This is cute. I like this dynamic. Most people assume couples like you will never work out, like challenging your partner and bickering is a bad thing. But I promise, I've witnessed some of the unlikeliest pairings create the most magical love story."

"Love story? Oh!" Fox bounces out of my grip, nervously smoothing the side of her dress. "No. We're just friends."

Tina's eyes swing to mine and narrow, holding like she knows the panic pounding in the back of my skull. The ache. The fucking devastation as *just friends* echoes in my brain. She tilts her head to the side, then looks to Fox and dips her chin. "So sorry. I misread the situation."

Me too, Mrs. Kincaid. Me too.

"It's fine." Jittery, Fox grabs the woman's wrist and starts through the doors. "You'll stay here and welcome guests, won't you, Chris? I'm gonna help Mr. and Mrs. Kincaid find their seats."

Anything to get away. Anything to escape.

"Sure." I dig my hands into my pockets, if only to keep them from my aching heart, and drop my gaze. But fuck, I can't ignore Cliff's pointed stare burning the side of my face. "Shut up."

"This is the final round, Coach. Either you win, or you go home empty-handed." He pastes on a fake smile, shakes hands, and directs guests through the front doors. Then he brings his ire back to me. "If you let her go without telling her how you feel, then I'm never gonna respect you again."

I swing a glare up at the guy I thought was my friend.

"I *could* have gone out with her," he growls. "I know I'd have had a helluva time. And I would've made sure she did, too. Some of us are out here willing to tell people when they matter. We know what's on the line, and we're not willing to lose them because we're scared. But then there's you," he sneers. "Pussyfooting around and wasting everyone's time." He shakes his head. "I can't respect that."

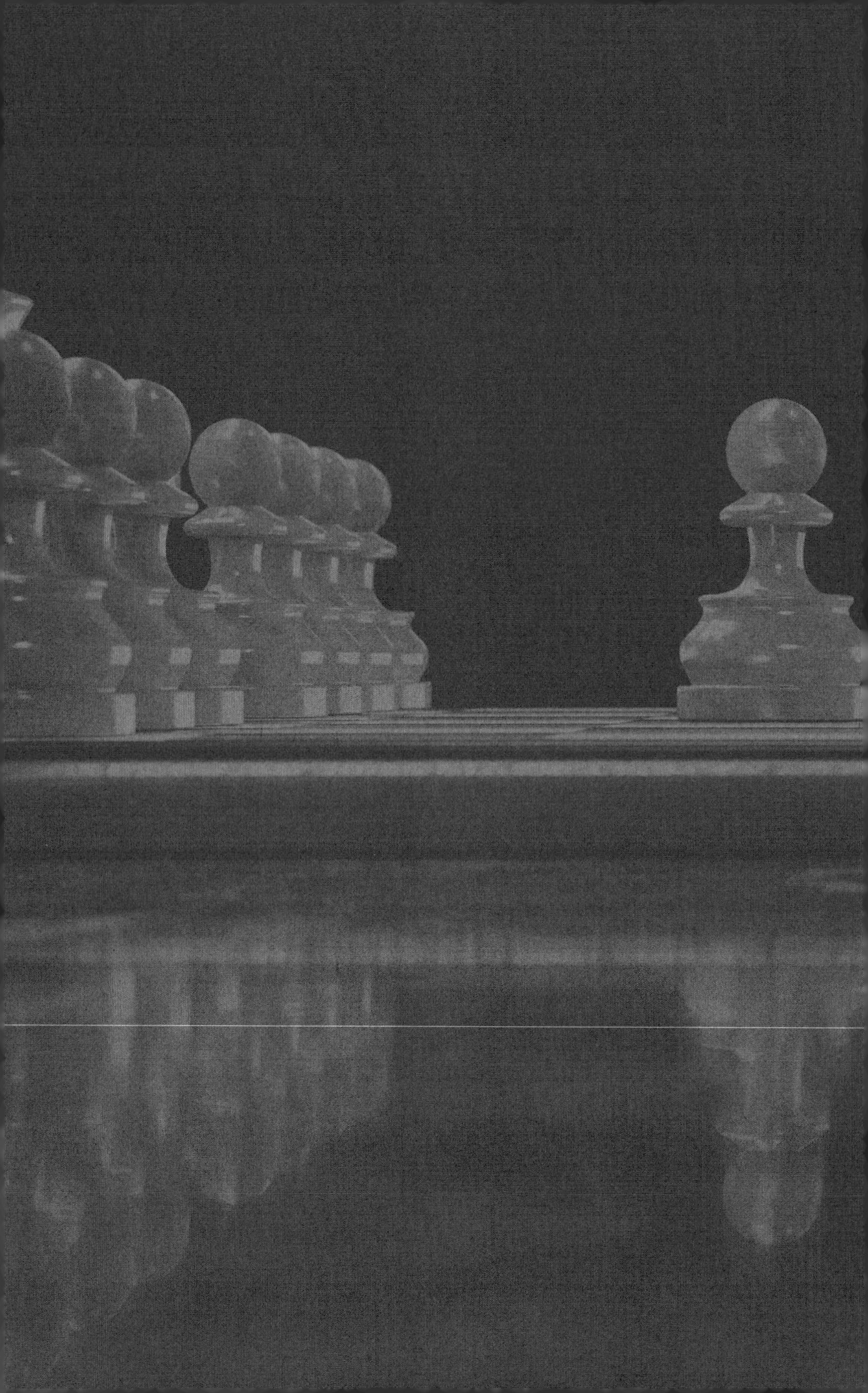

ROUND TWENTY-SEVEN
FOX

My heart thunders, and my lungs, well, they chose today to be the day they stop working properly. On the verge of what I think is a panic attack—a feeling I haven't experienced since that one time in eighth grade—I stalk into Tommy's office and slam the door. I press my back to the thick wood and blink through the tears in my eyes until I'm met with Alana's penetrating gaze.

She walks slow, calm laps of the office with Hazel latched to her nipple, a scene of serenity in a beautiful white gown and flawless makeup.

And I'm... a mess.

"You look beautiful." I ignore the darkness inching across my vision. The sweat on my palms. Hell, I ignore the very real possibility that I might puke before this day is over.

Because being a good friend means tabling my problems instead of slinging them to the forefront of someone else's special day.

"That dress looks fantastic on you, Lana." A three-foot train follows her every step. A trailing, glittering veil hangs from her hair. Her blue eyes, brighter than the ocean on a warm spring day, glisten with emotion.

She's perfect.

I swipe my cheeks and pretend my shuddering exhale is a reaction to her beauty—not my broken heart—and drawing a long, heaving breath, I push away from the door and toss my purse to Tommy's desk. Instead, I scoop up a cloth and turn to the pair, knowing Hazel will need to be burped in a moment, and wedding dresses are notorious for highlighting even the tiniest stains.

"This has been the most fun, impromptu post-baby baby-shower-turned-birthday-party-turned-wedding I've ever helped plan." I lay the cloth over my shoulder, dragging my hair out from beneath the fabric, and when Alana detaches the baby, I take her and prove we're still a well-oiled co-parenting machine.

What we have was forged in the fire ten years ago. Our friendship, a balm that soothes my heart. Our love, a caress that heals the lashes on my soul.

"It's kinda crazy how it all worked out, huh?" I massage Hazel's back, pleased when bubbles roll along her throat. "Weddings can be complete nightmares to plan, but starting it out as a party and changing the dress code near the very end is basically genius."

She fixes her dress, tucking her boob away and laying the strap of her gown on her shoulder. Then she brings big, bright eyes up to mine and exhales. "I'm getting married today."

Finally, something to smile about. "I know!"

"I've dreamed of this since I was a kid. I wrote *Mrs. Alana Watkins* in every single notebook I've ever owned. I was practicing my new name before we'd even kissed for the first time."

"And now it's here." I reach out and take her hand in mine, squeezing. "Is it everything you hoped it would be?"

"Mostly." She inches closer, setting her hand on my hip and swaying with me and Hazel. "I'm here. And Tommy is here."

"That's a pretty good start."

"Franky's here. And welcome. And happy." She sighs. "My daughter's here, safe and well. My best friend is my maid of honor."

Smug, I allow my lips to curl higher. "Yes, I am."

"And Chris will make the perfect best man…" She snorts. "When Tommy tells him about it."

"You think he'll freak when he finds out he's gotta stand with Tommy? There are a lot of people out there, Lana. Lots of eyes."

"He'll cope. He always does when it matters." She breathes a soft, contented sigh. "I'm getting everything I ever wanted today."

"I'm really happy for yo—"

"So tell me, Fox." She pulls back, angrily smacking me with a glare that burns me all the way to my toes. "Why do I feel sad, knowing that you're sad?"

"I'm not sad!"

"You're a big fat lying liar! You're breaking your own heart, and seriously, it's starting to annoy me. I can *feel* your misery. I can *feel* you with one foot already out of town."

"Which is why I didn't want you to know about us in the first place!" I ride my arrogance as though it were a proud horse galloping toward battle when, truly, my stallion is nothing more than a toy placed outside of shopping centers. A dollar gets you a minute of ride time. "I wanted to get laid, and I set the rules from day one: keep this shit away from *you*."

"So you can blame *me* for your misery? So you can go back to New York and be all alone, and you can tell yourself it's not because you're a coward but because you're noble and selfless and doing *me* a favor?"

"No, I—"

"You asked me not to say anything. And dammit, Fox, I haven't. Not to Tommy, and not to Chris. I'm walking into my wedding day with a giant secret hidden from the man I intend to marry, a secret that affects him, too! But I'm doing that for you. I came into this week banking on the fact you'd eventually crumble. That I could shame you into action."

"Really?" I try to laugh. Jesus, I desperately search for humor amongst my heartache. "Shame me into making a different choice?"

"You mean how I was *terrified* to come back to Plainview, completely and utterly frozen with fear at the thought of facing Tommy again, but you called me out for being a sissy and spurred my ass into action?"

"Yeah, well..." *That'll teach me.* "Joke's on me. I wanted you to be brave, but the consequences meant you'd leave me behind. Worst best decision I ever made."

"And now I'm trying to convince *you* to be brave. Take the leap, you coward! Stop letting fear dictate your happiness. Stop letting your past be the wall that separates you from your future."

"Stop talking all poetic and stuff," I snap right back. "It's beautiful and infuriating and damn near inspiring enough to make me forget this town hates me."

"The town is just a town, Fox! It's just a place. Eventually, all the annoying people will die off, and then us—our generation of really cool, trauma-bonded people—will be the new annoying class, and our kids will complain about us."

"You paint such a pretty picture." I wipe my nose on Hazel's cloth. If I ruin my makeup before the vows, I'm going to be *so* mad. "We could rule this place, inviting people who are *different* for cookouts until eventually, everyone breeds, and we create our own diverse community."

"If that's what you need, then I'll cook. Every single time. If you need a plane and a weekend house in New York, then that's what we'll get you. If you need to renovate the entire apartment above the bookstore, then I'll do that for you. Whatever you need, Fox, I'll make it happen."

"All to keep me here in your town?"

"All to ensure you're *happy*," she presses, her eyes glittering with pain. "That's all I've ever wanted. Wherever you are, whatever you're doing, I just need to know you're happy. But this…" She gestures toward me. "This sadness I see every time I look at you, that's gonna ruin my wedding day for sure."

I snort. Because if I don't, I might sit in the corner and cry.

"Your gift to me could be laying a giant, juicy kiss on Chris' lips right where everyone else could see."

"Oh, God. It's like you don't know him at all. He would *hate* that."

"He would hate the attention. He would *love* the claim. Jesus, he would lose his mind at the clear, direct communication, since your *we should get dinner in public someday* is not the same as *I love you, and I want to be with you*."

Shit. Fuck. Dammit.

Just friends.

I grit my teeth, breathless as my heart somersaults in my chest. "How do you suppose he'd receive *we're just friends?* Because I might've just said that when someone," I hook a thumb over my shoulder, "out there, said we looked cute together."

"*Just friends?*" Groaning, she drops her head back. "You said that right to his face?"

I'm a shitty, sorry, horrible person. "Yes?"

"That's great!" she snarls, startling Hazel and shoving away from me. "Totally great. *We should have sex, but don't tell anyone. We should remain a secret, but I also want to get dinner with you* not in secret. *I love you, but I'll tell people we're just friends.* What the hell is wrong with you, Fox? Why do you insist on sabotaging your happiness?"

"I—"

"Don't even answer that question!" She throws her hand up to stop me. "I know *why*! I know *you*. I also know I'd like to go back twenty years and kick some asses because your parents destroyed a woman who was born to be great. You're beautiful and smart, Fox! You're successful and witty and so freakin' selfless, it makes me want to slam my head against a wall. You're everything other people wish they could be."

"You're exaggerating." *Tell me more. I'm begging you.*

"We see you walking by and think, '*holy shit, she's really got it all.*'

Looks. Legs. Ass. Hair. She's from New York, and she loves her job. You actually *look* like you won at life, Fox. But inside your dumb head, you're telling yourself you don't fit in. You're hammering home a reminder that everyone eventually leaves, so why get close in the first place?"

"You left." *Shut up. Shut up. Shut the hell up*! "You know *all* of me, and you still left."

"I left for my mom! I left for Franky. And Tommy. And Chris! I left because you told me to, and then you made me promise that even if you begged for me to stay, I would still go. I left to save my life, Fox, and I left with your blessing."

"I know. You're right. I'm sor—"

"I left, *knowing* it would break both of our hearts. But *you* promised that if things were bad and you needed us, you'd tell me. So that brings us right back around to you being a lying liar."

"You need to ignore me." I spin, if only so I don't have to look into her eyes, and wander the office, patting Hazel's back and dipping with every second step to soothe a baby who doesn't really need to be soothed. "I'm a mental case, Alana. We *know* that! Jesus, there wasn't a single moment in time that we thought differently. Today is your wedding day, and your guests are waiting outside. So let's just…" I shake my head and turn back. "Let's put this away for now so we can enjoy what today truly means."

"Today means love," she spits out. "Today means promising myself to another person, even if it scares me. It's about expanding my family, even if, a year ago, I never would've guessed it was possible." She stalks forward and points a dangerous finger in my face. "Today is about being brave and allowing someone else to hold my heart, and when we say our vows, it's about trusting that other person to keep it safe."

"And I'm so happy you get this." I knuckle a tear from beneath my eye. "Truly, I really am. You deserve all of this, Lana. I'm honored I get to be a part of it. Even if I'm a totally annoying mental case who needs an intervention and a redo on those formative years."

She lowers her hand, scrunching her nose and lips like an angry little pit bull. *Angry*. She's so, so angry. "I'm going out there in a minute, and I'm doing all the vows stuff. Because I love Thomas Watkins."

"Good." I swallow, forcing an icky lump of nerves down my throat. "I'll join you."

"But before we go, I wanna ask you a question, and I want you to answer like he's not listening. Don't worry," she drawls. "He's not. This is just me and you. Just like it was me and you when I told you about Grady. Same as it was me and you when you told me about your parents."

"You've done a wonderful job keeping all of that secret," I rasp. "I appreciate your silence."

"Shut up. You don't get to be witty right now." She takes another step closer, staring deep into my eyes. "Do you love Christian? With your heart. The kind of love I have for Tommy. Do you see yourself continuing to love him, so if the world was less sucky, and you both lived in the same place, and none of those roadblocks existed between you, would your love for him remain, even though he can be kind of annoying and quirky sometimes?"

"Yes." Fuck it. He's not listening. "Yes, I love Christian Watkins with my heart. And if the world sucked less, I could see myself spending the next few decades loving him, not in spite of the annoying, quirky things he does. But *because* of them. I love that he has a special fork, and I love that he fights for it. I love that he buys really expensive linen, not because he's fancy, but because they're less itchy on his skin. I love—" I pause. Frown. "No, I *hate* that he can't sleep at night. But I love that when he sleeps with me, he gets a full eight hours and never wants to get up. I love that he owns a dozen of the same shirts and hangs them in his closet and rotates through them every single day, because they're comfortable and he knows what he likes. I love that he teaches kids how to fight, and he's so gentle about it. But he also trains Tommy and other adults, and he's *not* gentle with them. I love that he plays chess for fun and considers a quiet evening reading a book a night well spent. Most of all, I love that he tolerates me, annoying tendencies and all. *I'm* itchy sheets, Alana. I'm the wrong fork. I'm noisy and messy and weird. *I'm* the problem, but dammit, he sleeps better when I'm around, and he smiles more when we're alone."

"That's called love, you dummy." Softening, she steps closer and takes her baby, robbing me of the sweet, warm lump sleeping on my chest. "If you think you're itchy sheets and the wrong fork, but he still chooses you, then you're not itchy sheets at all. You're exactly right for him. And he's exactly right for you. But you're both so friggin' terrified of being rejected that neither of you will be brave enough to stand up and say what needs to be said. You're being dumb!"

"You're being mean."

"Tell. Him. How. You. Feel!" She smacks my arm, one for each word she throws out. "If I remember my wedding day *not* by the vows I made, or the man I make them to, and instead, because my maid of honor pissed me off, I swear to God, I'll dedicate my anniversary to talking shit about you. Every single year, Tommy and I will clink a glass of champagne and roast the shit out of you."

Scowling, I drop my lips and chin forward. "That's unkind. And not a healthy way to celebrate your relationship."

"How would you know!? You're the poster child for unhealthy relationships. Hell, you made friends with a homeless, broke, pregnant hillbilly. Forgive me for *not* taking your advice on the matter."

"You're on a roll, huh?" Sulking, I rub my arm and pray her red handprints will fade before the photographer starts. "You're getting all fired up on hatred when you're supposed to be loved up and dreamy-eyed."

"Tell him how you feel! Now let's go. I have a wedding to attend." She stalks to the office door and yanks it open, startling Eliza on the other side whose hand is up, ready to knock.

"Uh..." She looks from Alana to me. Then, back to Alana. "It's time."

"I'm on my way. Here!" She thrusts Hazel into her arms, then turning back, she snatches my hand. "Please hold my baby. Fox can't because she's got some shit to do."

"There are no baseball bats inside this gym, are there?" I stumble forward and cling to the doorframe, Alana's ferocious grip dragging me through. "Right? What other weapons should we know about?"

"My fist," Alana snaps. "I've been taking lessons my whole damn life, so watch your pretty lips before I fatten them."

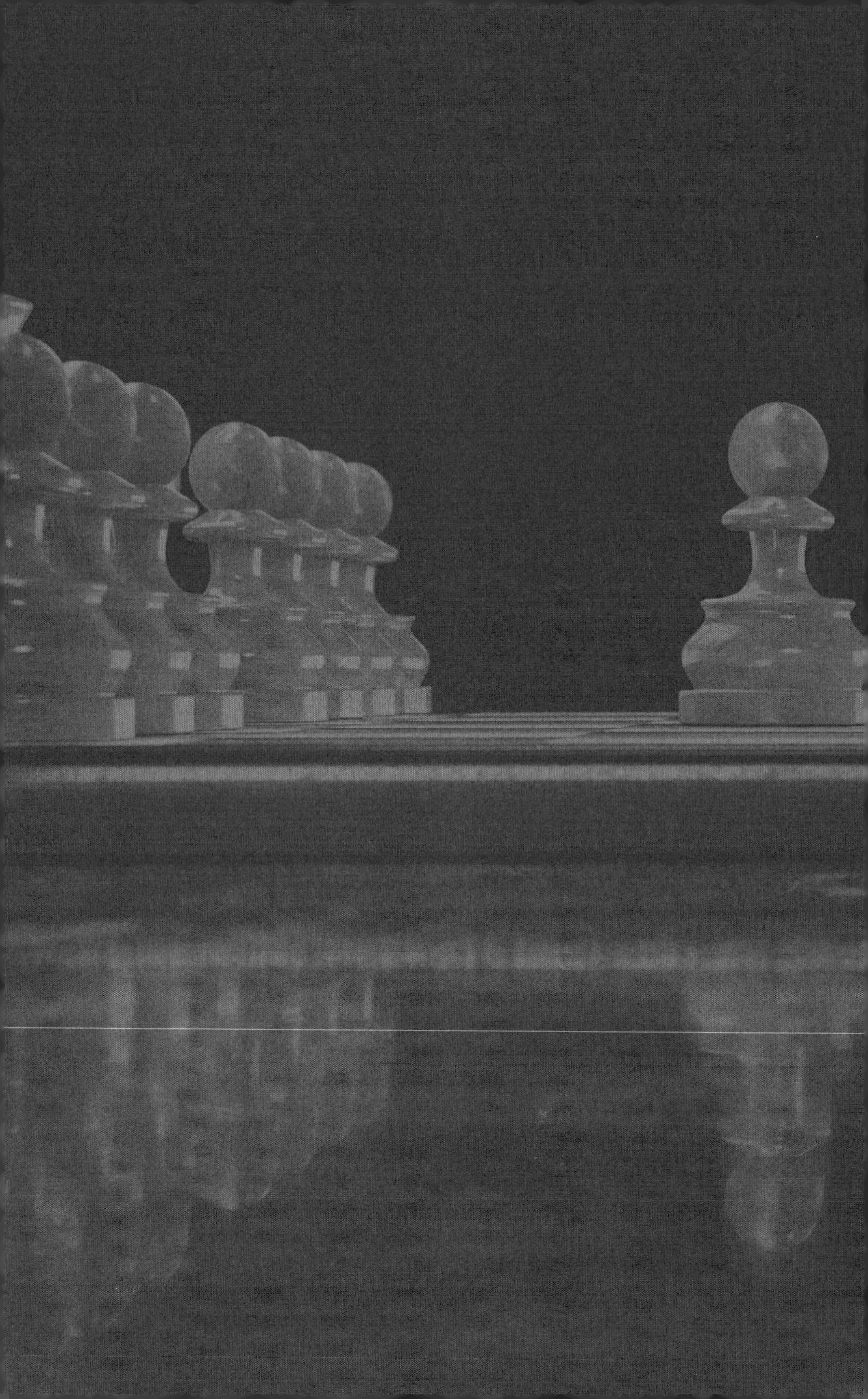

ROUND TWENTY-EIGHT
CHRIS

It's not so bad, really. Standing in front of a couple hundred people, everyone's eyes turned toward us while Alana and Tommy surprised their guests with a wedding instead of... whatever the hell this party was first intended to be.

Sure, people looked at us. And yeah, guys *looked* at Fox.

How could they not, when she's so fucking pretty and so shamelessly stood out in red?

None of this is as horrible as I would've expected it to feel had I had six months to overthink the idea of being my brother's best man.

Six months of suit fittings and practice dinners, wedding talk, and speeches—*fuck, I haven't considered my speech yet*. Six months of *what if it rains*? And *maybe I could convince Ollie to stand up for me instead*.

Honestly, nothing could feel as gut-wrenching as being in the same room as the woman I love... while she considers us *just friends*.

"Beer?" Tommy crosses from the makeshift bar with two glass bottles in his hands and his tie already hanging loose around his neck. Music plays, and guests chatter. The space we normally teach kids in, is now a dance floor. People we see every single day laugh and sway. Others, we see once a year... or almost never, join in like they've been a part of our world all along.

And then there's Fox in the middle of it all, gleefully dancing with the little boy who does *not* want to dance at all.

If that's not the perfect representation of me and her, then I don't know what is.

Tommy taps my shoulder with the bottle, plopping into the chair on my left. "Not sure where you're at with all that, but your staring is kinda obvious. I think even Alana is noticing now."

"Hmm?" I accept the beer, and because he's looking somewhere else, I follow his gaze to a not-so-happy Alana, who glares right back. "Why's she mad at me?"

"Like I said." He twists the cap off his beer and slides it into his pocket. "She hasn't said shit to me, but I reckon she knows. Did you do something to hurt her?"

"Alana?"

"No, Fox. People have been hurting Alana her whole life. She's used to it. If she's shooting those kind of daggers at you, it's because you did something to Fox."

"But I didn't." I twist my beer open and take a fast swig of the cold liquid. "Fox and I are fine." *Just friends.* But fine. "We drove here together earlier. We welcomed guests and helped them find their seats. We're a total team. There's no drama."

"So maybe you did something else to piss her off." Sipping, he settles back in his chair and chuckles. "She's five weeks postpartum. Maybe her hormones are helping her remember all the shit you did when we were younger."

"You think so?" I drag my eyes away and study the side of my brother's face. "I've already got enough problems, Tommy. I have no room for smoke from fifteen years ago."

He shrugs, extending his legs and crossing them at the ankles. "Dunno. I guess we gotta wait till she tells us what's up. You come to any conclusions about the Fox situation yet? She's leaving soon."

"Eight days." Eight sleeps, including tonight. Eight mornings where, if I'm lucky, I might trick her into giving us a little more time. *Wishful thinking, dickhead.* I drag my thumbnail along the beer label, tearing the moist paper in slow, straight lines. "We're just... We're okay. We're gonna have the week together, and I'm gonna pretend it's not like counting down to my own execution."

"I'd laugh at the analogy, except I know exactly what you mean. It felt like I'd died when Alana left, too. Though..." He glances across. "I didn't know my death was coming. I had no chance to prepare and no opportunity to appeal my sentence. You know yours is coming, so why the fuck aren't you fighting to change it?"

"Because she won't stay, and I can't go." That's the crux of it all. Such a small, simple roadblock, but it may as well be entire galaxies keeping us apart. "We might vacation in the Galápagos, though." I bring my beer up and drink a whole bunch more. "That could be nice."

"The Galápagos?"

"Mmm. Beautiful islands. Pretty flowers. Old turtles. But if it makes you feel any better, I'm *this* close," I hold my hand up between us, pinching my thumb and finger almost completely together, "to packing a bag and moving to New York anyway."

Stunned, he shoves forward on his seat and stares at the side of my face. "What?"

I say nothing. I watch Fox dance instead. Her perfect body, wrapped in a stunning dress. Her hair, bouncing, and her eyes, glittering. She's unhappy in this town. But fuck, she's happy when she's with her family. Franky. Alana.

Maybe even me...

"Christian?" He grabs my shoulder. "The fuck did you just say?"

"I have enough savings to last me a while. Could even sell the house, which'd get me something smaller in the city. It would suck a little, to trade the house and land we always wanted for a shoebox apartment. But that, and my savings, would make it so I don't have to worry about homelessness or anything."

He yanks me around and hits me with the intensity of his stare. "You're leaving?"

"I don't think I have any other choice. I might destroy us while I'm doing it, since I'll be sitting at this hypothetical apartment all day long, waiting for her to come home and spend a few hours with me. So my mental health will probably turn shit, and then I'll take it out on her, picking fights and making what was happy, miserable. But I can't stomach the idea of letting her leave without me." I search his eyes—terrified, though he tries to hide it—and pretend his fear isn't mine, too. "Half of me thinks I'm crazy 'cos this was a temporary thing, and no one should make life choices based on six weeks of bickering. The other half of me thinks if I let her go, I'll die anyway."

He releases my shoulder and rests his elbows on his knees, leaning over his legs and exhaling a heavy breath. "You let me go to New York that time. You didn't fight me when I followed Alana, even though we both knew I might not come back. Now it's my turn to watch you go."

"You were the one who suggested it."

He chokes out a frantic, un-funny chuckle. "Yeah! And now I'm starting to sweat. Fuck."

"It's the right thing to do, right?" My heart pounds and my stomach swirls. I feel sick at the thought of going and sick at the thought of staying. "We're not kids anymore, Tommy. We're not broke. So, you leaving ten years ago is not the same as me leaving now. We can fly across and see each other. And Fox will visit Alana and the kids, too. This isn't as permanent as it sounds. But I need you to tell me this is the right thing to do."

"You want me to tell you to go?" He drags his fingers through his hair, frustrated and scratching. "Jesus, Chris. There's what I think you should do, *for you*. And there's what I want you to do, *for me*. And then there's something in the middle, something really fucking terrifying. Because I worry you'll spend all that time waiting for her to finish work. Waiting for her to get home. Waiting for her to come to bed." He shakes his head. "I'm worried about the damage you'll do to your soul. Scared I won't be there to protect you."

"It's not your job to protect me anymore." I reach across and drop my hand on the back of his head. It's a hug. Sort of. An embrace, but without making it weird. "You've spent your whole life taking my beatings. Stepping between me and Grady because you thought that was your purpose."

"Chris—"

"I've spent *my* whole life watching you and Alana fall in love. Watching you *be* in love. I got to see it up close and personal, and I thought to myself a million times that if I ever got to love like *that*, there's nothing I wouldn't do to make it work."

With a grunt, he tilts his head forward and studies the ground. "Right."

"I fell in love like that." I press my hand over my heart. "I fell in love with someone I can't live without. So if you give me your blessing..." I draw a shaking breath. "If you tell me it's okay, then I'm gonna go with her. I don't know what'll happen in the future or if we'll even work out, but I *do* know that watching her fly away will kill me before I get a chance to see."

"Then I guess you have my blessing." He claps my shoulder, squeezing. "I've taken *us* for granted for a really long time. Always assuming you'd be wherever I was. But I won't ask you to stay where your Alana isn't."

I nod my thanks, because words won't come.

"If it was me, and I knew Alana was leaving, I'd already be sitting on the plane, waiting for her to find her seat beside mine."

I grab him and pull him in for a hug. It's awkward and on the side. But it's touch, and we both need it. At least, I sure as fuck do. "This whole thing's gonna be embarrassing as hell if she says she doesn't want me to come."

"Humiliating," he chuckles. "And a little soul-destroying. But if it's any consolation, Alana's pissy mood is a good sign there's something here. She sees it. I see it. This is love, and it's not just in your head. As long as it's real, it's worth fighting for, right?"

"Something about love and war." I straighten out and scrub my hands over my face. "It doesn't have to be easy. But it'll be worth it."

"It was for me." He takes my beer and flashes a gentle, barely there smile. "I wouldn't change any of it, even if the time I *didn't* have her damn near killed me."

"Here's hoping I don't have to wait ten years for this." I push up to my feet and fix my shirt. Fuck knows the material is itchy as hell. Then I run my fingers through my hair and catch Fox's curious gaze from halfway across the room.

She sees me. I see her.

She dances with Franky, but dammit, she's keeping an eye on me, too.

"You might need to go to Alana," I murmur. "Because I'm about to make a scene, and if you read your wife wrong and she *doesn't* know about us, then I reckon things are gonna get noisy."

"Holding her back and kissing away her fury. One of my favorite things to do." Chuckling, he stands and moves around to face me, his back presented to the rest of the room and his hands coming down to fix my collar. "I'm gonna support whatever choice you make, okay? Wherever you go, whatever you do. If you leave me, I promise to only complain about it to my wife. Never to your face."

I snort. "Thanks." Stepping around him and onto the temporary dance floor, I try not to focus on the nerves burning in my veins. The nausea in my stomach. I ignore the moisture trickling along my spine, and good fucking lord, I pretend I don't see Alana's careful prowl as she, too, approaches her best friend.

She's about to fuck me up, if I fuck this up.

My palms turn sweaty, and eyes follow my progress through the dancing crowd. Elbows bump my arms, and couples make out.

Jesus. They're all watching.

I lick my lips, swallowing the spit that tastes an awful lot like *gonna puke*, then coming up on Fox's right, I tap Franky's shoulder and wait for his eyes. "Hey, kiddo. I was wondering if I could dance with Fox?"

I see her in my peripherals. Her brows shooting high, and her cheeks warming with a sweet blush.

"Your mom's right here," I murmur, tilting my head toward a furious Alana. "So maybe you could dance with her for a bit while I dance with Fox?"

He tugs his hands from Fox's and spins to escape. But Alana is fast, pulling him in and forcing him to sway.

He drops his head back and groans, loud and unapologetic.

"I didn't think you liked to dance in public?" Fox steps closer, wrapping her arms over my shoulders in an entirely *non*-platonic way. Pressing her belly to mine, she creates this magic where the music gets a little quieter, and my staring crowd becomes a little less obvious.

Her smile, though... fuck, her smile fills my vision from corner to corner.

"People can see you, Christian." Her eyes glitter with menace, though her fingers trail through the hair at the back of my head, which makes everything else tolerable. "People might be judging you."

"It's so odd you'd say that when you're literally the only person I see right now." I don't kiss her, though I kinda want to. And I don't lay my forehead on hers, though I want that, too. "You look really fuckin' pretty today. Did I tell you?"

"In the last hour?" She tilts her head. "No."

"I'd say you look prettier than the bride, but the bride can hear me right now, and it's not polite to say so on such important days."

"Uh..." No longer playful, her body tenses, and her eyes grow harder, frantic, as she leans closer. "The bride can, in fact, hear you. Shush."

"Because you don't want her to know about us?" *Set it on fire, Chris. Do it. Be brave.* "I know we agreed not to tell her. We had our reasons, and I'm not sorry for them. But things have changed now. A *lot* has changed. Because I've fallen—"

"Fox?"

Like ice water on a sleeping kid, she jerks away with a viciousness that leaves my heart aching, turning on her heels and clapping her hands to her mouth. Then she gasps, locking eyes with a dude I don't know. Broad shoulders, dark hair, and a stare that looks her up and down like he fucking wants her.

"Booker?" She screams, throwing herself into his arms and wrapping him in a hug that makes me want to puke.

He catches her, lifting her half an inch off the floor, only to chuckle when she slams a noisy kiss to his cheek.

Fuck me... I'll just watch. I guess.

"Holy cow, Booker!" Jittery and excited, she stands on her own two feet. But she doesn't let him go. Even when he tries, she holds on to his suit sleeves with the kind of desperation I feel in my heart. "You're supposed to be in Rome! What are you doing here?"

Alana's eyes swing to mine. Probing. Glaring. She widens them, then flicks her wrist like, '*Get in there, stupid. Do something!*'

Frustrated, she slides into their hug and interrupts the reunion from hell. *Because I'm a pussy.* "Booker! Hi."

"Alana." He holds on and crushes her against his chest. "Happy wedding day. I received an invitation, and then I couldn't make it. Now I'm here, and I feel awful for not communicating that in advance."

"You're always welcome." She inches back, and because Tommy's fast on his feet—faster than me—she grabs his hands and drags him into our gathering. "Booker Hemingway, this is my husband. Thomas Watkins."

"Tommy." Tommy shakes his hand and squeezes a little longer, a little harder than necessary. "I've heard about you, Booker. Glad you could make it."

"So sorry for dropping in unannounced."

"It's not a problem." He releases him, then hooks a thumb my way. Because I'm a fucking pussy. Passive. Silent. Completely and utterly cucked by this man who interrupts the single most important sentence of my life.

"My brother, Chris. Chris," he grits out, "this is Booker Hemingway. Fox's boss."

"Fox's friend, first and foremost." Fox practically vibrates, giddy and grinning while I shake the man's hand. "Holy shit, Booker! It's like seeing sunshine for the first time in five weeks. What happened to Rome? You said you couldn't be here."

"Did you leave a gift at the front door?" Franky pushes his way into our group and slides his glasses up his nose. "It's customary to leave a gift when you attend a wedding."

"Franklin!" Alana claps her hand over his mouth. "Ignore him."

"I didn't bring a gift," Booker confesses. "I'm sorry. I was actually…" He brings his eyes back to Fox. "I've been trying to call you for a couple of hours."

"You have?" She pats her hip. Her backside. Right where her phone would be if she wasn't wearing a gown. "Crap! I left my purse in Tommy's office. Why?" From delight to dread, her smile falls away. "What's wrong? You said you couldn't be here, and now you are. Who is—"

"Everyone is fine." He wraps her wrist in his hand. So gentle. So fucking intimate. *Don't touch her!* "I didn't mean to give you a fright. I was actually calling you with *good* news. I left Rome last night, and the timing just kinda worked out. So I flew here, instead of home, because I wanted to tell you myself."

"Tell me what?" She questions. "What news?"

Alana's eyes narrow to dangerous, challenging slits. "What was *so* urgent you flew in from Rome for it?"

"Well, I was flying, regardless," he chuckles. "The destination, though, changed while I was at the airport. Then, like I said, I tried to call. I knew the wedding was today, and I knew you girls are close. So I figured this was one of those serendipitous moments where everyone can be together while I tell you."

"I'm so sorry, Booker." Alana grabs his wrist and curls his hand back in threat. "I don't mean to rush you, but I've had a hell of a month, and I haven't slept more than three consecutive hours in quite a while. If you don't share your good news *immediately*, I might snap your arm."

"The board met yesterday." Quick as a flash, his eyes swing back to Fox. "They decided they'd like you to come to them."

"To Rome? For next year's meeting?"

"For the next *five* years." He beams, like his words aren't a knife at my throat. "They want you to *move* to Rome and help set them up the way you have us."

"What?" Tommy's eyes whip across to mine, then back to the dude. "You want her to move to Rome? *Georgia,* right?"

"Italy," he laughs, brushing a hand over his lips and meeting Fox's eyes. "I had a pretty good feeling they'd jump when I told them you were interested. I didn't wanna get your hopes up, in case it fell through. But they're all in, Fox, which means that dinner I wanted to get once you returned to New York is kinda being pushed up."

"But..." Her voice crackles, rasping and breathy. And though she brings her eyes across to me, they're not nearly as bright as I remember them. Shaking her head, she looks back at her boss. "That's not what I thought you were going to say."

"You've been talking about Rome for *years*. You begged for this."

"I know, I just..." She swallows, her throat bobbing with the movement. "Wow. I thought you were transferring me to marketing. Not to Italy."

"Both, actually." He touches her shoulder, giving it a gentle squeeze. "Amedeo wants you in Rome, and he knows you want marketing. So I pitched the whole deal. They see what you've done for us in New York. They were skeptics, but they saw the proof. So now they want to borrow you."

"F-for five years?" she tremors, visibly shaking and tucking hair behind her ear. "You want me to move to Rome for five years?"

"It comes with an *extremely* sexy salary package that includes accommodation. So you could sublet your New York apartment if you wanna keep it, or you could let it go and stay in Italy."

"Stay in Italy," she gulps. "Jesus."

"Or go to London and do the same again." He practically dances, oblivious to Tommy's glare. And Alana's.

Franky's.

Fuck, what does my face look like?

Trembling, Fox peeks my way and searches my eyes. So I paste on my most convincing smile.

Kill me. Bury me. "You pitched this idea?" Put me out of my fucking misery. "Holy shit, Fox. *You* pitched this, and now he's delivering the good news. That's exciting."

"He gets it!" Booker hooks a thumb in my direction, and because he's clearly accustomed to touching her, he grabs Fox's hand and sandwiches it between his. "You got everything you wanted. *All* of the terms you stipulated. That's why I came here instead of waiting for you to get back in a week."

She studies me, her lips dropped open, and her pulse thundering in her throat.

So I hold on to my smile.

She asked for this!

I'll be damned if I'm the reason she second-guesses her instincts.

"Fox? Honey?" Booker gives her hand a gentle shake. "Are you listening? It's all a bit exciting, I know."

"Uh..." She blinks and turns back to him. "Yeah. It's a lot."

"We need you in New York on Monday to sign the contracts, and Rome by Wednesday before Amedeo flies out to London for a few weeks."

"Monday?" I snap. *That's only two sleeps. Two! Not eight.*

"As in, the day after tomorrow?" Alana questions. "A whole week earlier than planned?"

"Yeah." Booker grits his teeth. "I know. We don't mean to rush you, but Amedeo will be in New York for just a day, and then he's heading to London as soon as you're settled in Rome. To make this a smooth transition, the timeline is tight."

"But she's on vacation right now," Tommy growls. "You approved her for *six* weeks off. Not five. It's not appropriate to discuss business while she's on vacation."

"Why..." Finally catching on, Booker frowns. "Why are we acting like this isn't the single greatest news we've heard this year?" He brings his eyes back down to Fox's. "Honey. This was *your* pitch."

"She's just in shock, that's all." I take a step forward and gently lay my hand on the small of her back. Massaging. Soothing, maybe. "If this was her pitch, then it's good news. She just needs a minute."

"Chris..." Alana admonishes. "This is a lot to think about."

"It *has* been thought about." Kill me. Stab me in the heart and let me bleed out. "It was thought out when she pitched it."

"You think this is a good idea?" Fox gives Booker her back and stares up into my eyes. Hers well with emotion. They glitter with something approaching tears. And when she opens her mouth to speak, her jaw trembles. "Christian. You, uh..." She clears her throat. "You think I should go?"

"Yeah." It's what's best for her. It's what she wanted. The proof is on the fucking wall. *She* pitched this. Six weeks in bed with me shouldn't change the plans she had for her life. "I think you're a traveler at heart, and the idea of living in Rome for a little while would make you very happy."

"Rome is a long, *long* way away, Christian." Tommy burns me with his glare. "It's a whole other country, with visa requirements that mean people can't just vacation there for five years. There's red tape and permissions and sponsors and all that shit."

As in... I can't go.

For a weekend here and there, sure. For a month, even. Absolutely. But not for five years.

"I know." I hold Fox's gaze and show her my most convincing smile. "This was your dream. It was your pitch. Don't let future-Fox pay the price for the choices this-Fox makes, all for the sake of a week in Bumfuckville."

Alana shakes her head, firming her lips and glowering. All in Fox's blind spot.

"I thought I was bringing good news." Booker nervously laughs. "I swear, I thought it would be *extra* excitement added to an already exciting day. But if I've made a mistake, I sincerely apologize—"

"No. It's good news." Closing her eyes, Fox robs me of what I want to see most of all. Then she turns to her boss and opens them again. "This is amazing news. I'm just surprised. This wedding was kind of a surprise, too, so I'm having one of those days, ya know?"

"So you *want* to go?" Alana grabs Fox's chin, drawing her around. "You *want* to move to Rome? All by yourself."

"Sure." She pulls Alana's hand away, but she places it on her cheek. A caress, instead of an attack. "It was my idea, right? It's what I was working towards."

"Great!" Booker exhales a heavy breath, folding at the hips like he's just come from a five-mile run. "Jesus. You scared me! I thought something had changed."

"Something *has* changed," Alana grumbles, tugging her closer. "She's leaving the day after tomorrow. I thought I had a week left with her. Now I have two days. See ya, Booker." And with that, she drags her away, past Tommy and around Franky, and though Fox's eyes swing helplessly to mine, she remains captive to Alana's fierce grip.

"Oh... well..." Booker releases a nervous snigger. "Alright. Well, I guess I'll see her at the office on Monday, then."

"Fuck!" I turn on my heels and stalk in the opposite direction. To drown myself in the lake, if I'm lucky. "Fuck!"

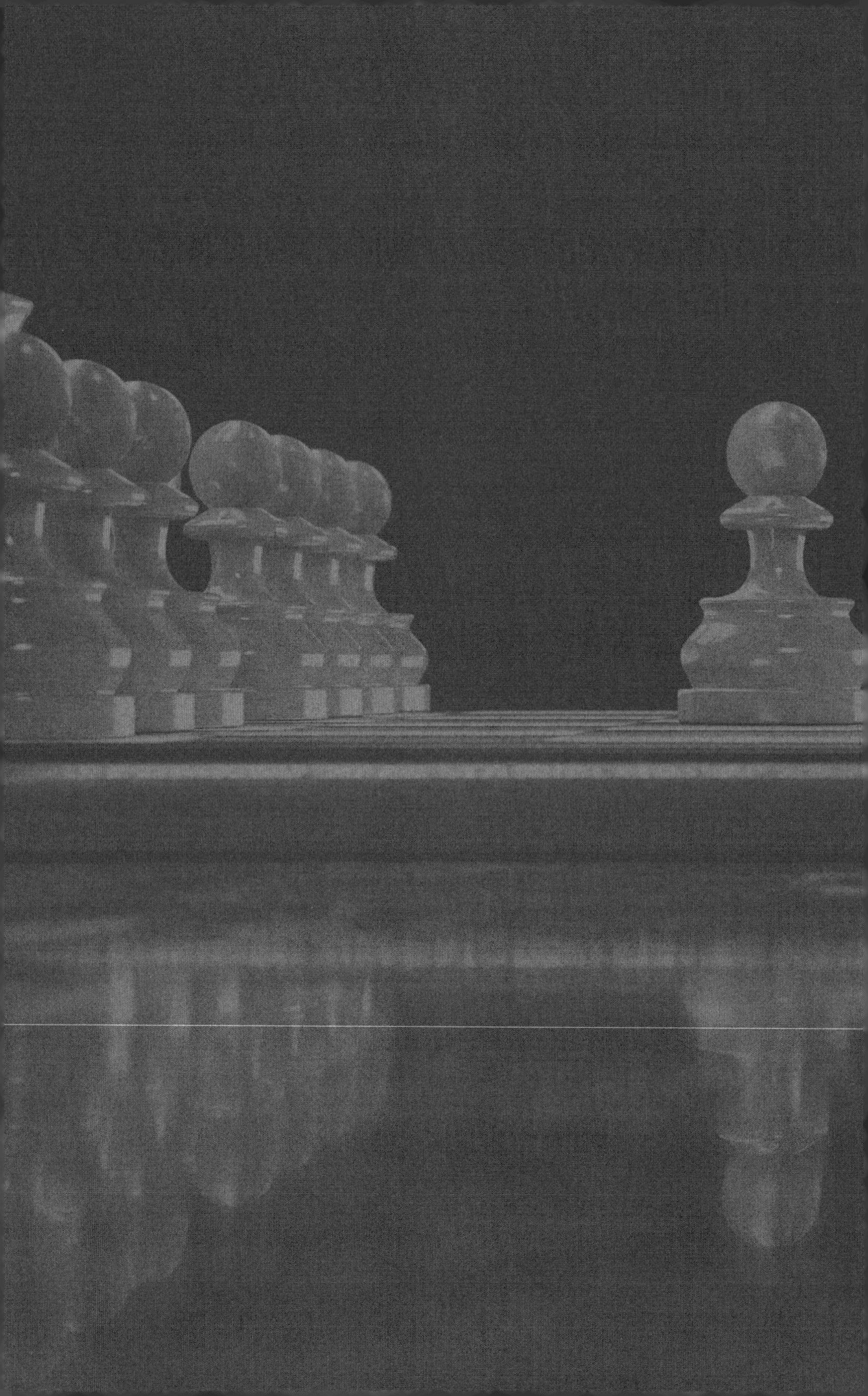

ROUND TWENTY-NINE
FOX

I was supposed to have another week in Chris' bed.

Turns out, I'd already slept for the last time cradled in his arms, and I didn't even know it.

I'd dozed with my cheek on his chest, and I had no clue it would be the last.

I was oblivious to the fact that the last time we stood in the bookstore apartment—me in a pretty dress and him in a handsome suit—would be the last time we'd be there *together*.

I had no clue the last meal we shared on his porch would be our *last*. And damn it, I didn't know the last time—the *first* time—he would ask me to dance in public, would be the *only*.

I hate the things we were robbed of, and I hate even more that he's as toxically wounded as I am because instead of looking into my eyes and spending my final eighteen hours in Plainview *with* me, he chose avoidance. He stayed inside his house with his drapes closed, and his doors locked, and when Alana invited him to her home for Sunday breakfast before my newly scheduled flight, he chose to decline.

He chose *for* us.

He chose Rome.

And now my time is up.

I stride through JFK airport at an almost jog, sneakers wrapped around my feet and my carry-on luggage trailing in my wake. I wear headphones in my ears, so my hands remain clear. Making my way toward the luggage carousel, I search every screen, every line of information, every flight number until I find mine.

"You arrived safely?" Unimpressed and uninterested in hiding the scorn in her voice, Alana bounces her baby to sleep on the other end of the line, patting the squeaking infant, and walking laps of her living room.

Or bedroom.

Or maybe even the dock stretching across the lake outside her house.

I'm not sure where she is, but I picture every detail as easily as if I was right there with her.

Jesus, I never thought I'd see the day when I longed for Plainview.

"Your flight was delayed taking off," she grumbles. "But you got there pretty quick."

"Yeah, there was a good tailwind or something." I pause by carousel number 3 and drag my carry-on to a stop by my thigh, my purse nestled on top and my phone tossed haphazardly inside, and because life enjoys smashing me in the face with lemons, I feel the tug of something sticky on the bottom of my shoe. Frowning, I lean on my carry-on and lift my foot, only to find gum stuck to the sole. A little more, tacked against the floor. "Ew." Stubbed toes. Spilled coffee. Gum. *Great!* I dig through my purse in search of a napkin. A wet wipe. Literally *anything* to save me from losing my damn mind.

I've returned to the greatest city in the world. This is supposed to be a happy occasion, dammit.

"I stepped in gum," I grunt, sweeping the contents of my purse from side to side. "Who the hell drops gum inside an airport?"

"Pigs, mostly. Maybe that's a sign you should come back to Plainview."

With a victorious explosion of air, I find a single-wipe sachet in the bottom of my bag, so I yank it out and tear the packet open. Then, I balance on one foot and clean up the mess some other jackoff created. "I stepped in gum in Plainview, too, just so we're on the same page. I'm pretty sure I shattered my little toe on the corner of your dresser. I lost my lucky pen. Oh, and I got my heart broken." I roll my eyes. "I assure you, this is probably not the sign you think it is. How are things back there?"

"Awful. I used to have this best friend—*you might know her*—she committed to visiting me for six weeks. But I guess that was a lie."

"Alana—"

"She said she would run my shop while I recovered from childbirth. Ya know, the life-altering, life-risking situation where a woman brings a whole other human into the world? Yeah, I did that. But then this alleged friend quit. *Without warning*. Pretty unprofessional, if you ask me."

"Alana!"

"Plainview is a little less beautiful today. The sky, a little grayer."

"Good lord, William Shakespeare. Chill out."

"My son cried himself to sleep last night because he was counting on one last week with his Aunty Fox. That week was callously taken from him."

"Alana—"

"There are less stars in the sky now. And my husband?" She scoffs. "Girl, my husband hasn't even had a chance to consummate his marriage."

"What's that got to do with *me*? I wasn't gonna be in the room with you. Jesus! I'm here to support you, Lana, but there are some lines I'd rather not cross." *Especially when your husband looks exactly like the man who crushed my heart.* I peel sticky gum off my shoe, groaning when the mess only seems to grow worse. "You're making an already stressful situation worse. Friends don't do that to friends."

"You didn't even tell him how you feel! People don't do that to people they love."

"He suggested I go to Rome! He didn't *choose* me, Alana. If he wanted me to stay, he could've pulled me aside and said something. He didn't."

"Tommy told me he loves you."

Straightening again, I scrunch the napkin and glance around for a trashcan. "Tommy loves me? That's sweet. A little inappropriate, considering you *just* got married. But sweet all the same."

"No, stupid! Tommy said that Chris loves you. He told me last night, after I held my crying son to sleep because my son is autistic and doesn't handle change very well. He was expecting a week with you, but you cruelly robbed him of that. That makes you inconsiderate and a child abuser."

"For God's sake." I grab my purse and sling it over the crook of my arm, and leaving my carry-on where it is, I stride toward the closest trashcan I can find. "You're laying it on a little thick, don't you think?"

"It's not thick enough until you're back here in my living room. And just so you don't change the subject too easily, I repeat: Tommy said Chris said he loves you."

"That's nice." Be still, my stupid, aching heart. "Chris never told me."

"Tommy said Chris said he was gonna move to New York to be with you."

"He—" I skid to a stop, just eight feet from the trash can. "What?"

"Finally," she growls. "Got your attention. Chris was planning to sell his house and use that money to buy an apartment in New York. He would have given everything up for you, Fox. And he was trying to tell you, but then Booker turned up and ruined everything."

"Chris wouldn't come here. No chance." I start moving again, frowning as I toss the wipe into the trashcan, and then I spin back and head toward the carousel.

Sadly, I arrive… to nothing.

I look to the man on my left, then to the guy on my right—*yep, this is where I was*—then I look down at the small speck of gum still on the floor. "Someone stole my carry-on."

Alana falls silent for a beat. "What?"

"Someone stole my friggin' carry-on! Dammit!" I grab my carousel-neighbor's sleeve and yank him around. "Did you see who took my suitcase?"

He looks to the floor—*no suitcase*—then back into my eyes. Then he drags his arm from my grip and circles to wait elsewhere. So I turn to the dude on my right. "Did you see who took my suitcase?"

"They haven't come out yet." He snags his phone and accepts a call, but he gestures toward the not-yet-moving carousel. "They'll come soon."

"Someone stole your suitcase?" Alana questions. "Seriously?"

"I was gone for ten seconds!" I back up and cast my eyes around the packed airport, searching for the bright monstrosity amongst blacks and blues and grays. "Who took my suitcase!?"

"You're going to get your ass arrested," Alana snickers. "Don't shout in a New York airport, dummy. You know better than that."

"First my pen, and now my suitcase!" I want to scream. I want to sit on the floor and cry. Most of all, I want Chris to emerge amongst the other travelers and tell me he loves me. *Choose me, dammit!* "It's gone, Lana. All my stuff."

"And you didn't check it, right? Are you sure you didn't—"

"Yes, I'm sure! I had it a second ago, but I walked away to put the gum in the trash. Now it's gone."

"Did you have anything important in it? Anything valuable?"

"Well…" I tear my purse open and mentally check off my things. Laptop. Wallet. Cards. Phone. Tampons. "It had my butt plug in it. And cookies from *the bakery*. Raya packed them for me to bring home."

"Cookies and a butt plug?" she snorts. "Honestly, that sounds like a fun suitcase to steal. If I knew the chick beside me at the airport was packing that kinda stuff, I'd do everything I could to become her best friend. She sounds fun."

"Alana!"

"I feel for you," she drawls. "So sad. Devastated. Someone stole from you. Those bastards."

"You don't sound sad at all."

"I am," she snarls. "Just not about the case. I'm mostly focused on the fact you're leaving the freakin' country in three days and moving to Rome! Buy a new butt plug and stop being such a friggin' baby about the things that don't matter."

"He dipped, Alana! He left! He had a chance to say something, *anything*, but he didn't. Then, instead of spending our last day together, he hid away and didn't even say goodbye."

"Because he's hurt! That's who he is, Fox. He feels *deeply*, and now the woman he loves is leaving the country. Maybe we disagree with his coping mechanisms, but we don't get to dictate them. He's in survival mode now, so if he wants to lock himself away to cope, then there isn't a damn thing we can do about it."

"He could've told me he loves me!" I cry out, drawing eyes and cautious steps back from those around me. "He could've been brave, the way you expect me to be brave, and he could've spoken up. But he didn't. And then he didn't even have the decency to hug me goodbye. I haven't seen his face since your fucking wedding. And that just…" I viciously swipe treacherous tears from my cheeks. "It sucks, okay! I've spent my whole life *not* being picked, so excuse me for a minute while I try to pick myself up. *Again*."

"Fox—"

"I thought I was gonna get my Disney moment," I whimper. "I'm the princess whose parents ran out on her, so obviously, *my* prince wouldn't do that. Chris is averse to crowds. He *hates* having eyes on him. So I was kinda hoping for a *Lloyd Dobler* ending."

"Llo—" She pauses. "What?"

"You know in the movie how he's got the boombox over his head? He wanted her to know he loved her, Lana. That's what I want."

"This isn't a movie," she groans. "Not everything comes with a neat little bow."

"But I want the bow! I want him to want me. Loud. Proud. I want him to make it a big deal because that's what *I* need. And he's…" *Stop crying. Stop crying. Stop crying*! "I was so sure he was gonna do it at the wedding." I wipe my stupid, leaking nose. "He said he wanted to talk after. Then he asked me to dance. I thought *that* was my movie moment."

"But then Booker ruined it."

"Then Chris cut and run." I wipe my cheek and look across as the light above the carousel illuminates and the belt begins circling. *Bet my case will be the last one to come out.* "You spent so much time talking about how *he* needed direct communication. How special *he* is and how it's my job to talk straight. But I need that, too. I need '*I choose you, Fox*'. I need '*I'm in it for life. I'll never leave.*' I need someone to choose me because as it stands, I'm an almost-thirty-year-old loser who has retained literally zero relationships because everyone always leaves."

"She sighs, pained and sad. "Fox—"

"Let me wallow for a while. Let me be mad and pathetic. I'm allowed to feel this way, and if you loved me at all, you'd agree."

"Agree that you're pathetic and pitiful?" she scoffs. "Guess we're gonna fight about it then because, dammit, you're supposed to make your own destiny. Stop bitching, and stop expecting someone else's love to dictate how you feel about yourself."

"That's not what I—"

"You want to live in Plainview, but you'll only do it if Chris wants you? No! You want to live in Rome, but only if no one is chasing you around the world? Get the hell out of here with that corny bullshit. You want to live in New York, but you're only happy if a man is there with you? Fuck off with that shit. You're better than this, Fox!"

"Alana—"

"We get it, okay? Your parents suck. You were hurt. You place self-worth in the hands of those around you. But can you make a decision for yourself for once in your fucking life? Be wherever *you* want to be. Do whatever *you* want to do. Do it for *you*. Find *your* happiness. Then, once you're settled and loving yourself like the rest of us love you, *that's* when everything else will click into place."

My jaw trembles with the sob I want so badly to give in to. My eyes burn with the tears filling them. My throat, even, warms with emotion.

"You're being mean to me." I sniffle. "I probably could've done without the tough love today."

"I'm sorry," she murmurs. "It breaks my heart to see you hurt."

"But I need to choose me." I lick my lips and scrub my eyes, clearing my view of the cases finally rolling onto the conveyor belt. "You're saying no one else will be with me as much as I'm with me. So I have to love myself and yada yada yada."

She chokes out a tearful laugh. "Yada, yada, yada. Basically. Maybe Rome *is* the right choice for you. Away from Chris. Away from us, even. It'll just be you, which'll force you to dig deep and find out who you really are. Maybe in five years, you'll come back an Italian-speaking goddess who knows she's a bad bitch, because although I like reminding you every chance I get, I would much rather know *your* brain tells you, too."

Passengers come and go, rushing toward the conveyor belt when they see their luggage and clearing out a single second later when they've got their things. The crowd ebbs and flows, and with them, my emotions.

"I really love him, ya know?" I drag my palms across my face and wipe my tears. "He made me feel like I could conquer the world. Which is kinda new, since I'm usually winging life."

"I know you love him." She exhales a long, gentle sigh that creates a picture in my mind of her rocking her sweet baby. Swaying in the muted light. Existing inside the life she always dreamed of. "I even know how you feel today. I've left a Watkins behind, too. I've walked into a new city, praying he would chase after me, but terrified that he would, too. I know you so well, Fox, because you and I are too damn similar. We were hurt by the people who were supposed to protect us, and then we rebuilt each other with the kind of love only a couple of lost girls could summon."

"It was safe," I whimper. "It was easy."

"And then we had to grow up. I faced my ghosts, Fox. But you keep running from yours."

"I'm not running—"

"Vietnam," she counters. "Canada. Poland. Austria. You've been *everywhere*. You'll go *anywhere*, so long as you don't have to stare at yourself in the mirror."

"Ouch." I press a hand to my aching heart and groan. "That was mean."

"Truthful," she croons. "Sometimes, that shit hurts. So now you're in New York, and Chris *didn't* ask you to stay here. Which, honestly, was the right thing for him to do."

"It would've helped if he had."

"No," she snickers, the sound watery and sad. "Because then you would've stayed. For *him*. We need to find what *you* want."

"I want him to want me." If I was paying attention to how truly fucked my day is, I probably could've predicted what rolls out of the carousel tunnel next. But of course, the universe enjoys taunting me, busting my suitcase open so a pair of my underwear hang off the zipper. My shoes: one in, and one on the conveyor belt. "Damn." I make damn sure my purse is hooked on the crook of my arm before wading through the crowd and getting my hands on the stupid suitcase. I yank its overweight heft across the steel lip and onto the speckled floor. "I'm hanging up now, Lana. I've gotta collect my panties before a creepy basement dweller pockets them."

"You've…" She pauses. "What?"

"Nothing. Just my life. Try to get eyes on Chris for me, okay? Make sure he's alright. It scares me that he's gone underground."

"I'll check on him. I promise. You wanna stay on the line while you get in a cab and head home?"

"No. It's time to be alone, I think." I catch sight of my approaching shoe, so I skip around my suitcase and lunge for it, slamming my ankle against the handle of my bag and hissing as pain radiates up through my leg. Limping, I snag the damn shoe and scowl at the beady-eyed ogling of those around me. "Stop looking at me! I'm from here. I'm not *different*." I crouch in front of my suitcase and work on stuffing everything back inside. "I'll text you when I get back to my apartment, Lana. If by some crazy miracle Chris is there, like this is a giant set-up for his grand *I love yous*, then I probably won't text you. I'll be busy sobbing and having sex."

She snorts. "If he's there when you get there, and you plan your life around whatever he asks, then we'll circle back around and do this all over again in six months. Or a year. Or five years."

"Spoilsport."

"Even if the sex is really, *really* good. It's important you make these choices for you."

"Worst pep talk ever." I roll my eyes and quickly snatch my underwear off the edge of the conveyor belt, stuffing them in the case. "Love you."

She sighs. "Love you, too. Make good choices."

I tap my ear and end our call, so the hubbub of JFK airport on a Sunday evening and the rushed grunts and quick steps of passengers collecting their things replaces the soothing comfort Alana's mere existence brings me.

Who knew I'd eventually miss the tractor-buggy luggage guy from Barlespy Airport?

"Ma'am?" A dark shadow falls over my shoulder, heavy boots popping into my peripherals, and the delicious cologne of a man who buys what smells good hits my lungs. But I don't even hope for the impossible.

He doesn't smell like Chris, anyway.

I peek over my shoulder and up at the dude who towers over me. Six-foot something with broad shoulders and a pleasant smile. He offers a hand, but when I merely stare, narrowed eyes and flat lips, he grabs on and pulls me to my feet, then he places a wad of balled fabric in my palm and leaves me with a pair of my underwear.

"I couldn't think of a more discreet way to hand those back to you," he teases. "Though I won't lie, I considered flinging them off my finger, slingshot style."

"Ha." *Not funny*. I close my fist and meet his eyes. He's handsome, I suppose. In the traditional, normal human being way. But he's not Chris. And he's not this mythological self-loving *me*. So I turn on my heels and continue packing. "Thanks."

"I can't help but notice you're having a tough time." He bends beside me, poking his head back into my space. "And you seem to be traveling alone. If you wanna, I could help you out—"

"No, thank you." I flip the lid of my case closed and sit on top, flopping down with all the weight I possess so I can drag the zipper around. I catch sight of his suitcase, rolled up and sitting safely beside his leg. More importantly, I notice the belt wrapped around it to keep his things together. Rudely, I reach forward with an unladylike harrumph and unsnap the clip, stealing from him without a single lick of remorse. "I'm gonna keep this." I dig the fabric under the bottom of my bag, then around until the buckle meets, and because my case is thicker than his, I adjust the straps until everything comes together, and I'm one step closer to *not* ending up on the news. "If you wanna write your number on a piece of paper or something, I could send it back when I'm done."

"What if..." His eyes flicker across mine. Searching. Flirting. "What if you write your number on a piece of paper or something. Then I'll call you up and take you out to dinner sometime this week?"

"Can't. I'll only be in New York for a few more days, then I'm moving away." I tug my suitcase to its wheels and place my heavy purse on top. Though I make damn sure not to release either handle. "I'm sure you're a nice guy and all that, but I'm already spoken for." By myself. *Gag*. "Thanks for stopping to help me, though." I turn on my heels and jerk my stupid case away, and though I keep my head high and my spine straight, I pray no one notices the *wee-woo-wee-woo* of the broken wheel on the bottom.

This is my life now, even though New York is supposed to be my safe space.

I draw a long breath and fill my lungs with New York air—oddly, the air I considered life-giving five weeks ago tastes kinda gross now after spending so much time beside a beautiful lake. I limp out of the airport and onto the sidewalk, and turning my attention toward the line of cabs that *should* be waiting, I sigh and watch the last one go.

"It's fine." I drag my case to the glass walls at my back and snap the handle down to make room to sit. But I catch my thumb under the metal, hissing as fresh pain stings my digit and adds another ding to my already shitty mood. Snagging my purse and hooking the straps over my arm, I plop onto the top of my case and slouch in on myself, breathing before I lose my shit. Exhaling before I end up on a terrorist watch list for doing something monumentally stupid. "Everything is fine. Everything is going to be just fine."

Chief happiness what?

"Hey!" A man's deep voice draws me around. His wolf whistle echoes in my ears, and a bouquet of flowers clasped to his chest turns my eyes wide.

But they're not for me.

"Hey, babe!" He catches a woman on the fly—*his* woman—and lays a juicy, noisy, over-the-top kiss on her lips.

Her legs wrap around his hips.

His hands cup her ass.

It's loud and lovely and a beautiful declaration of love.

But it's not for me.

My phone trills, music playing through my headphones, so I tap my ear and slump like I'm eighty-five years old and ready to play with my belly button lint. "This is Fox."

"Oh, good!" Booker exclaims. "You've landed."

"Mmhm. Are you back yet?"

"Yeah. I flew into LaGuardia about an hour ago. I tried to call when I landed, but I figured you must've still been in the air."

"Yep." *Chief Unhappiness Orangutan. That's me.* "Glad you made it back safely. I only just walked out of JFK, so I'm gonna get a cab and head back to my apartment."

"Actually, I was gonna ask if you wanted to get that dinner with me and Sherry tonight? Things are moving quickly now that you've accepted the position in Rome. The next few days are going to kick our butts, and I didn't want to miss out on one of our last opportunities to—"

"No, thanks." I left New York in a skirt suit and heels. Perfect hair. *Confidence.* But I've returned feeling like the hunchback who lives at Notre Dame. "It's already dinnertime, Booker. I'm starving and cranky and ridiculously tired. I need a shower and someone to punch me in the face. I'd like to feel literally anything except existential dread."

"Yikes." He laughs. "Bad flight, huh?"

Bad life. Bad... everything. "I can't wait another two hours to eat, and not in a million years am I coming to dinner with plane air on my skin and in my hair. I'm heading home, soaking in the tub, and if I'm lucky, I might slip under the surface and addle my brains a little before someone pulls me out."

"Well..." His laughter falls away. "That doesn't sound good. Anything you wanna talk about?"

"Can't." *You're a guy. And I have to make my choices for me.* "I'm good."

"We're friends, right? You've always been my friend. So if something is wrong, you'd tell me?"

"Nothing's wrong. I'm just really tired." I catch a flash of yellow from the corner of my eye, a cab—my prince charming—driving this way. So I bound from my suitcase and snatch up the handle, and despite the ache in my ankle, the throbbing in my squished thumb, the incessant *wee-woo-wee-woo* of my suitcase, I charge toward the street with one hand in the air. "Taxi!"

"Taxi!" Another guy strides from the airport doors, his shout louder than mine. His eyes swing my way, then back to the cab. Then, like it's a race and he's ready, he drops his shoulder and runs. "Mine!"

"That's my taxi!" *Wee-woo-wee-woo!* "Jerkoff! You know I saw it first!"

"Sorry, lady." He's faster than me by a long shot, swinging the door wide and diving in with an undignified *fwump*. Then they're moving again, and I'm just... I'm me. All alone. With my dumb broken suitcase.

"Er..." Booker clears his throat. "I feel like I probably shouldn't ask. That sounded rough."

"Don't ask! Don't tell. Don't speak at all." I lower my hands and ignore the dumb trembling in my jaw. Hundreds, maybe even thousands, of people loiter outside of the airport. But no one sees me. No one gives a single shit about me or my tears. "That was *my* cab."

"It's like you've forgotten how to New York," he teases. "It's not the first to see the cab, Fox. It's the first to have their butt inside."

"Shut up."

"I'll send a car. Michael can be there in about thirty minutes, so why don't you head back inside and get a cup of coffee or something?"

"No." I walk all the way to the curb and park my suitcase on the very edge, then crossing my ankles, I lower to my butt and *harrumph*. "I've got the next cab, no matter what. I'm ready to fight for it."

"And... dinner tonight?"

"Absolutely not! I'm gonna go try the drowning thing. I'll see you at the office at nine o'clock sharp. Until then, forget I exist. Gah!" Overstimulated and frustrated, I whip loose strands of hair off my face and twist the ends together. But I have no hairclip and I'm not sure I have a hair tie stuffed away in my bag. "I'm hanging up. Leave me alone."

"Fine." He grunts. "Sorry I bothered you on personal time."

"Good." I catch a flash of yellow from the corner of my eye, so I bound to my feet and thrust my arm in the air, and when some other jackass rushes to the curb twenty feet to my left, I stare at the side of his head and snarl when his eyes come to mine.

Wisely, he retreats, dropping his hands and taking a long step back. Then two. Three.

Smart.

As soon as the cab stops in front of me and the trunk pops open, I wheel my case around—*wee-woo-wee-woo*—and lift its stupid weight into the back long before the driver has a chance to get out and do it for me. Slinging my purse onto my arm and slamming the lid down, I stalk to the back door and slide in.

Sweat makes my skin sticky. It makes my shirt cling to my shoulders and my hair grip to my neck. Because despite the fact it's dark out already, and although it's not yet summer, the humidity is thick, and my whole fucking life wants to irritate me.

I meet the driver's eyes in the rearview mirror, and rumbling out my address, I sit back with a heavy, noisy exhale.

"So… you're in a cab now?"

"Jesus, Booker!" I startle at the voice in my ear, scaring the driver, so he jumps and wrenches the wheel dangerously to the left. "I thought we were done?"

"You didn't end the call, and I'm kind of afraid that if I do, I might see you on the news in a little while. Something about an enraged ape climbing the Empire State Building."

I slump back in my seat and close my eyes. "Goodbye, Booker." I tap my headphone and kill our call, and though my phone beeps with incoming texts—one from Alana, asking me to text her when I get to the apartment, and one from Raya, asking if I landed safely—I ignore the robotic phone voice. Because neither is from Chris, and his declaration of undying love is the only thing I want to hear right now.

Is this how he feels when I steal his fork? The itchy skin. The tight control on a temper that wants to blow. When he's sleeping in sheets that annoy him, is it like how my shirt sticks to my skin and feels like a straitjacket? Or when he wears socks with imperfect stitching, does he feel the same frustration I feel when my hair sticks to my neck?

And if this is his life, how *doesn't* he rage against anyone who looks at him? How does he live like this without wanting to kill someone?

"Most of the folks I collect from JFK are tourists with big smiles," my driver murmurs. "They're usually pretty bubbly and energetic and excited to be here."

Exhaling a long, chest-emptying sigh, I peel my eyes open and meet the dark stare of a man easily inching toward sixty. Maybe even sixty-five.

"I know I'm a stranger," he explains. "But seeing as how we have twenty minutes, and you probably won't ever see me again... you wanna talk about it?"

Yes. No.

"Do you ever feel like you just don't belong anywhere?" I look at my purse and drag it open with shaking hands. I'm so hungry that even a stick of gum would be an improvement to my current state. "My parents didn't want me. Neither of them. My foster families didn't want me. My college degree hardly wanted me, and even when I got it, I didn't use it."

He nods, listening without interrupting. Processing without intervening.

"My best friend left. And it's not that she doesn't want me, but she wants her husband and family more. Which, of course, is entirely appropriate." No gum. Not even a breath mint. Frustrated, I settle back in my seat and fold my arms. "I've lived in New York my entire life, but I have no *real* friends. I have colleagues. And I have neighbors who are nice. But I should have more, right? I'm almost thirty years old, so I should have more to show for nearly three decades of existing."

"You haven't found your place yet." Calm and entirely too comforting, he drives us out of the airport and onto regular New York roads, where everyone is kind of crazy and drivers are erratic. Yet, he keeps our progress smooth. Our stops and starts, unhurried. "You're still young. It's okay that you're still looking."

"But I've looked all over the world! I've prioritized plane tickets over groceries more times than I can count. Nowhere wants me."

"Could be because you're looking for a place, when maybe you should be looking for a person."

"My best friend would disagree." I lay my head back and close my eyes. "And if she heard your theory about finding a person, she'd smack me with a newspaper. Then she'd probably smack you, too."

He chuckles, his chest and belly bouncing with the sound. "I meant, *you*. You haven't found you, yet."

"Oh! Well." I open my eyes and meet his in the mirror. "Yeah. She agrees with that. She said I have to figure out what it is I want."

"And you're struggling because you've never belonged, and no one wanted you." He merges lanes and slides us between a bus and another cab. "How can you possibly know what you want, if you don't even know who you are? Your family bailed, so you have no foundation to work with. You have nothing to grow from."

"You're good at this." Smiling for the first time since standing on the dance floor at Alana and Tommy's wedding, I exhale a cathartic snicker. "You get a psych degree before taxi school?"

"No. But I meet all sorts of people every single day. I've developed somewhat of a hobby of trying to understand them in our limited time together."

"Can you understand me? And when you do, tell me what I should do." I chew on my lip and stare out at the partial darkness outside. The sun is down, but this is New York, after all. "I'm honestly so, so tired," I breathe, swallowing my shaky breath before it betrays me. "It's like the universe wants me to solve a ridiculous riddle. But I can't read the words. I can't even *see* the words."

"Why don't you tell me what you think you want to do? Or what you think should happen?"

"But what I want, and what I think should happen, are two different things." I bring my hand up and trap my pinky nail between my teeth. "I *want* to turn around and run back to the crappy little town I just escaped because I left something kind of important behind."

His eyes swing to mine in the mirror. "Luggage?"

"My soul. My family. The ones I choose. I left my best friend behind, though technically, she was the one who left me first. I left this little boy behind, who is basically my nephew, but not really. But I love him like I would love my own son if I had one. I left my niece behind. She's only a month old and was named after me. And I left these two guys behind."

"Two?" His cheeks warm, his blush stretching from his face to his neck. "Seems we've found the root of your confusion."

"They're twin brothers," I snicker. "Identical. One of them married my best friend, and the other..." *Owns me.* "As naïve as it sounds, there's a part of me hoping he snuck across the country while I wasn't watching and is waiting for me at my apartment. Like, that's his grand gesture of love, ya know?"

"You don't think he'll deliver this grand gesture you want so badly?"

"No. Because I was the one who left. I told him we were *just friends*, and then I accepted a new job in Rome."

He hisses, shaking his head gently to the side. "I see. That's a little messy."

"Right. Because *I'm* messy. So, while I'm over here foolishly hoping to be proven wrong, I'm not counting on it. Because even without the friend stuff, and even without Rome hanging over our heads, that's just not who he is."

"So, you know who *he* is? But you don't know who *you* are?"

"He's... quiet," I sigh. "Humble. He's caring and brave. He would choose a night in, instead of a nightclub, any day. A meaningful conversation and dinner on his porch, over pretense and restaurants and sharing a dining room with two hundred other people. He *hates* crowds, but his brother has a job that kinda flies in the face of that, so he tolerates them when he must. He hates sharing his family—he especially hated the idea of sharing them with me—but when it mattered, he welcomed me in and made my existence in that town *better*."

"So, he has *preferences*, but he's willing to step outside them for the people he loves." He flashes a charming smile and meets my eyes. "It's entirely possible he's waiting for you at your apartment."

I breathe out a soft laugh and try not to let that tiny sliver of hope get too large. *The higher I fly, the harder I'll fall...* "Maybe. Maybe not."

"Because your family left you." He nods. "They didn't love you the way you deserved, which probably means, in your mind, you're not worthy of more. You think this guy isn't willing to step away from his preferences to make you happy. Worse, you think his refusal to do so means he never loved you at all."

"Breaking my own heart every time I think it." I hate that my hand shakes. That my stomach turns. I hate that I bounce my knee to work through excess energy, though God knows, I have none to spare. "So that's what I'm doing; spiraling between *I want him to be there for me* and acknowledging that he probably won't be. And honestly, I have no one to blame but myself."

"Because of the *just friends* thing," he guesses. "And Rome."

Mmhmm.

"Self-sabotage. You've got yourself in a loop, and you don't know how to get out."

"That's me." I drop my head back again and close my eyes, because my hunger is making me nauseous, and driving in New York traffic, even with Mr. Smooth at the wheel, is pushing me closer to puking. "I've been sabotaging myself since inception, I think. Pissing people off and forcing them to leave, all so I can say *see! That's what they do.* I've been working a job that literally no one else in the world would hire me for, so if I resign or get fired, I become entirely un-hirable, with a college degree that cost a bunch and *no* experience to show for it."

"You hurt yourself in the quest for…" He pauses for a long beat. "Sheesh. I don't even know. Hurt yourself now, so later, the hurt doesn't catch you by surprise?"

"I'm a mental case," I groan. "I stub my toe in any town or city, and I declare it a *bad fit.* I described myself as a bad organ transplant, and that town I just escaped, was the body. They don't want me, and God knows I hate feeling unwelcome, so I run away and hide."

"But by your own admission, you've traveled extensively."

"Yes."

"Which means you've looked behind *all* the curtains, you've met *all* the people. You've explored the world. But stubbing your toe *sometimes* means you've thrown your hands up and declared that you belong nowhere."

I'm ridiculous, I know. "Correct."

"Can I tell you a story?" He turns at the next corner, and when I feel the warmth of his gaze, I open my eyes and find him waiting for me in the mirror. "If you don't mind?"

"Sure." I flick my wrist in his direction. *Go ahead.* "I'd rather hear about your life than obsess over my own. You'd be doing me a favor."

"I was hoping you would say so." He slows and turns another corner, before speeding up again. "I met the love of my life when we were just fourteen years old. It was a different time," he murmurs. "A very long time ago, when such things were not improper. I was born not so long after soldiers returned from the war when men were… Well… They were not always coping. My parents' marriage withstood the war, and when my father came back, he and my mother made their children and did okay in the shifting economy. Maggie—the woman who would eventually become my wife— and I were born in the same hospital within days of each other, and we lived on the same block our entire childhoods. Her mother and mine met, and as women do, they brought their children together. From that day forward, I was—"

"In love?"

He laughs, loud and jolly, like Santa himself. "Goodness, no. I was annoyed. That girl did *everything* she could to irritate me."

"Oh..." I snort and enjoy the feel of it in my throat. "Not quite where I expected you to take this story. You said she was the love of your life."

"And she was. But she made sure I would never enjoy a moment of peace. If I said I preferred *not* to eat spaghetti for dinner, that woman made it more often. If I said I wanted petunias in the garden, she planted daisies."

"Doesn't sound like she liked you very much."

He chuckles. "Oh, she did. But her father had gone to war, too. She used to tell me her home felt like a museum. It was cold and quiet. It held no love. Just… things. And people." He brings us toward my apartment, rounding a corner and slowing for a set of lights. "She never saw her parents fight. Hell, she couldn't even be sure she'd heard them *speak* to one another. So, by the time we met, she intended to irritate me to death. It never occurred to me, not until now as you tell me your story, that maybe she intended to break us before we started. Send me away early, which she might've considered preferable to losing me later."

She was scared.

It's easier to ruin things when they're new. When the stakes are lower and the pain, less crippling.

"This is why I enjoy meeting new people," he murmurs. "Because understanding them helps me understand myself, too."

"Welp…" I rest my chin on my chest. "You're welcome."

He chortles. "Of course, we eventually reached a point where it no longer felt like she was pushing me away. In fact, she threatened bodily harm to anyone who dared stare at me too long."

"Possessive," I smirk. "That's when you know you've roped her in. She was sticking, and you were, too—whether you liked it or not."

"Right. But still, she planted the flowers I never asked for and cooked meals I told her I didn't much fancy."

"If you were smarter, you would've told her you didn't like the things you did. Trick her."

"If you were less focused on your heartache, you'd realize I loved spaghetti all along," he counters smugly. I bring my eyes up and catch his, dancing in the mirror. "I made it my business to know her better than I knew myself. Though, naturally, I wasn't infallible. Twelve years ago, as we were approaching our fiftieth anniversary, my sweet Maggie decided we should buy a new bedroom suite. I had no clue why, since the one we had was fine. You can't buy quality furniture like we could before, and I had no desire to trade solid oak for whatever cheap crap was at the shops. But that woman usually got whatever she wanted, and a few weeks after our initial conversation—where I said no, we did *not* need a new bed—I arrived home from work and walked into our bedroom to find a whole new look. Instead of dark brown, our new furniture was white. Instead of the mattress my body was used to, I was forced into this monstrosity I hated. Ohhh," he growls under his breath. "When I tell you I was cranky…"

My cheeks ache from my smile, which is a thousand times better than the ache I feel in my heart. "I think she and I would've gotten along."

He rolls his eyes. "No doubt. The point of my story is that I stubbed my toe on that damn bed the very next morning. And then I stubbed my toe again the next day. And the day after that. Until eventually—"

"You learned where the new bed was and stopped running into it?"

He snorts. "No. My toe broke, and now I have a calcified lump that bothers me every single day. But Maggie…" He exhales a sad sigh. "Well, she died. Almost a year to the day after that bed was delivered, she was diagnosed with the kind of cancer that kills. And just seven weeks later, she was gone."

"Jesus!" I shove up straight. "This isn't a happy story! You're breaking my heart."

He pulls onto my street and slows, counting numbers on the side of each building. Finding mine, he brings the cab to a stop and slides the gear into park, until finally, he twists in his seat and meets my eyes for the first time without a mirror between us. "For eleven years, I've lived without the love of my life. But I kept the bed. Because even though I stub my toe, and even though that calcified lump continues to grow and ache—"

"You kept it because you love Maggie."

His eyes glisten, but he draws his lips into a close-mouth smile. "If I got rid of the bed, just because I kept stubbing my toe, I wouldn't wake up to the little love note she scratched into our brand-new wood on that first day."

Surprised, I massage my aching heart. "She scratched it?"

"She knew I'd be cranky, and she figured I might even insist we return it all and get our money back. She knew me, just as I knew her. So she scratched our names into the wood and made damn sure I'd never see that refund. Maybe you stub your toe sometimes in these places where you think you don't belong, but if the cruel passage of time has taught me anything, it's to not focus on the mild inconveniences. Search for the love note, missy. Someday, you might find yours." He hooks a thumb over his shoulder. "Can I walk you to your door? I'm dying to know if he's waiting for you."

"God." I wipe fresh tears from my eyes. Digging a hand into my purse, I take out enough money for the ride and a little extra for the story. "I *dread* getting out of this cab because if he's not there, I might crawl into the corner of my bathroom and sob a little bit."

"Maybe he's here. Or maybe he's sitting in the corner of *his* bathroom right now, waiting for you. It's entirely possible you may be two hearts breaking as one because you're both in the wrong place at the wrong time."

"I wish Maggie was my cab driver tonight." I show him my smile, if only to soften the blow of my words, then I push my door open and step onto the sidewalk. "I bet she'd have better, more direct, problem-solving advice."

He follows me out and opens the trunk, and though I slide my purse along my arm and reach forward to get my suitcase, he playfully slaps my hand away and does the work for me. "If you want her advice, I bet I could predict what she'd say. *Easily*."

"You *did* have a habit of knowing her as well as you knew yourself." I accept my case when he sets it on the road, tugging the handle up while he closes the trunk. Finally, I place my purse on the case and straighten my back.

It's time to be brave.

"I don't know your name."

"Eugene, ma'am." He offers his hand and wraps mine in his over-large palms. "I'm Eugene. And you are?"

"Fox. I know," I add when his brow shoots high. "Strange name. Tell me please, Eugene. What would Maggie advise me to do?"

His eyes dance with taunting humor. "She'd tell you to stop fussing over a dumb guy and do whatever makes *you* happy. Then, once you're doing that, you inform that sorry son of a bitch that he's to fall in line, *or else*."

"Ironic." I snicker and shake my head. "That's basically what Alana said. I have to figure out what I want and go for it. Then if the rest is meant to be, it'll be."

"Sounds like she knows what she's talking about." Sobering, he tilts his head toward my building. "I won't follow you up, since that would not be proper. But maybe, when you get to your door, you could let me know if he's there?"

"Let you know?"

"Yeah. Like, if he's there, flash your living room lights a little bit. If he's not—"

"No flashing." *God, it hurts already.*

I said we were just friends! And then I declared I was moving to Rome. *Of course, he won't be here.*

"I'll do the light thing." I bring my gaze up and meet Eugene's eyes one last time. "Thanks for the ride. You're the first person I've talked to today who didn't annoy me."

He takes my hand between his and squeezes. "And you're the first person I've met in eleven years who kind of reminded me of Maggie. That was a gift."

God! Tear my heart out!

"Wherever you go, Fox, and whatever you choose to do with your life, I hope you waste none of it doubting how truly special you are. Take up space and know you matter. Our lives are too short to worry about what other people think of us."

"Ominous and inspiring at the same time." I take a step forward, nervous and jittery. "C-Can we hug? I feel like this is a hugging moment."

"It would be my pleasure." He drags me in and crushes me close, his beard tickling my neck and his heart thudding heavily against my chest.

He lingers, even when I try to pull back, reaffirming his grip and chuckling because he already knows me so well.

When he's done, he steps back and holds my arms in his broad hands. "My wife and I never had children. It's not that we didn't want to. It just wasn't meant for us. But if we had..." His lips curl higher. "I think our daughter might've been a little like you."

"You have no kids." I reach up and swipe my eyes. "And I have no parents."

"The universe usually knows what she's doing." He presses a kiss to his fingers, then he places his fingers on the center of my forehead. "I'm thankful you chose my car tonight, Fox."

And to think, I would have gotten into the other.

"Now go." He releases me and takes a step back, shooing me along with a flick of his hand.

I don't want to leave, and yet, I want nothing more than to lock myself inside my apartment so I can cry in peace. But to get there, I have to go through the part where I discover if Christian is here, waiting for me.

Or not.

I draw a deep breath, expanding my chest until it aches. Then I wrap my palm around the handle of my bag and *wee-woo-wee-woo* along the sidewalk. Through the building door. Onto the stairs.

I haul forty pounds of clothes and shoes and a few snacks, too—since I'm a weirdo—up three flights, and when I arrive at the next, I round the landing and consider holding my breath to stave off the panic building in my chest.

But I don't do that either, since passing out on the stairs would only send me back to the bottom again.

"If you're up there, maybe you could stomp twice." *Great, I'm talking to myself.* "I know I suck at communication, and I *know* I said we were friends. That was shitty of me. But if you're here, then maybe that means you love me, too. And if that's true, then I would *really* appreciate it if you stomped to save me from the stress of wondering."

I stop and wait. I look up and tilt my head to the side. But all I get is silence... and the sounds of a game show coming from one of my neighbor's apartments.

"No?" Dropping my head, I continue up the stairs and onto my floor, and lugging my suitcase behind me, I steel myself and pray I survive the pain. Then I look at the area in front of my door and find it exactly how I expected I would.

Empty.

"Well..." I *wee-woo-wee-woo* all the way to the door, slipping a key into the lock and opening it to reveal five-week-old air that tastes nothing like the rich, fresh breeze coming off the lake in a little town in Hillbilly Nowhere.

I wasted five weeks hating that place, when all along, it was me I hated the most.

I drag my case over the threshold and toss my keys into the bowl by the door. Then, switching my lights on, I allow my hand to linger a little longer.

There will be no flash coming from my apartment tonight.

You can leave now, Eugene. Show's over.

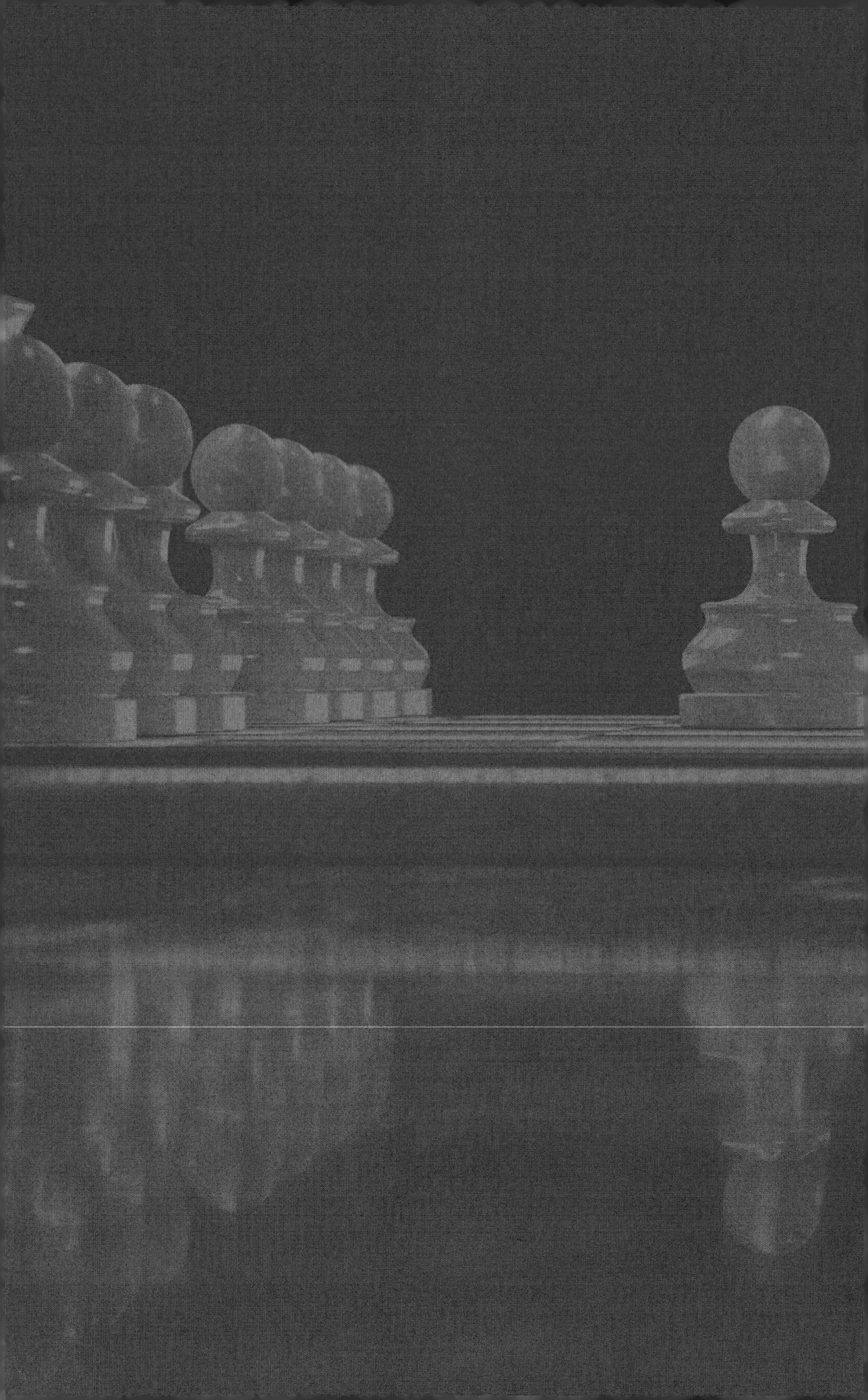

FINAL ROUND
FOX

New day. New week. New me.

Kumbaya and all that shit.

And because I'm all about riding waves of enthusiasm, I spent my entire commute to the office calling moving companies and emailing my landlord to let him know I would no longer need my apartment after this week.

I've come to a decision. For me.

Thanks to Taylor Swift, Chinese food delivery, and a clawfoot tub.

Now, I slide out of my cab—not Eugene's—and stand tall on the sidewalk outside Gable, Gains, and Hemingway. Shaking my hair back, I smooth my jacket and fix my purse on the crook of my arm. Finally, I draw a deep breath until smoggy city air fills my lungs, then release it again and start toward the front doors.

New week. New me. It's time to be intentional.

"Fox! Hey." Brenna bounds from her chair behind the tall receptionist's desk, waving her arms until her entire body sways with the movement. "Welcome back! And congratulations on your promotion."

"Thanks." *Hell yeah.* I forgot how it feels to be a badass bitch inside a workplace where everyone adores me. Like Superman donning his cape, I need only to wear heels and a skirt suit to feel confident again. I stride to the elevator and tap the call button, but while I have a moment, I spin back and meet Brenna's eyes. "Is Booker already in?"

She touches her ear and accepts a call, but she shows me two thumbs up —*affirmative*—so I turn on my heels and head into the elevator.

My phone chirps with a text, and other GGH employees file in, so I back up until my shoulders touch the steel wall, and taking out my phone, I spy Alana's name on my screen.

Though, my spidey senses tell me she's not who sent the text.

> I have to go to school in a minute, but Mom said I could play a game of chess with you. She said you'd feel guilty about leaving Plainview early, so you would for sure play.

My phone vibrates again, but with a picture of a freshly set chessboard. Already, the first white pawn has been moved.

Snorting, I tap at the screen, knowing I have time before we reach the fifty-first floor.

> Emotional manipulation is cold, classless, and an entirely unkind war tactic that violates the Geneva Convention. But since you were upfront about it, I figure I'll allow it.

> Clear communication is, after all, the cornerstone of healthy relationships. Move my pawn to E4. I'm walking into work now, so we'll continue our game this afternoon.

The elevator door opens and closes a half dozen times, allowing new people in and others off. A myriad of perfumes mingle in the air, though thankfully, the nausea I felt last night is gone, replaced with a steely determination for what I know is coming next.

While I wait, I hit reply again, but my message is intended for Alana.

> Your son is a meanie. However, I've gotten especially good at chess in the last month, so prepare him for his inevitable loss. When I'm done, I intend to point and laugh, lording my power over a defenseless ten-year-old.

> I'm heading into my boss' office in a sec to set some shit on fire. Wish me luck. And Franklin, if you're reading this, don't tell your mom I said shit. But do prepare for your humiliation. You're toast.

Swiping out of that chat, I slide over to Chris's next. Though, unlike Alana's, the conversation I've had with him is... sparse. Even when things were good and six weeks felt like an eternity. If I invited him to the bookstore apartment, all I ever received were one-or-two-word responses.

Yes.

No.

When I would send: *I'm thinking of you. And I'm just about to step into the shower.*

I'd receive: *On my way.*

When my emotions got heavy, and Alana was unavailable to talk, I'd say: *I'm in my feelings today because I just remembered Alana named Hazel for me. It's kind of a big deal to me, and I'm annoying myself by obsessing over it.*

He'd send back: *It's a big deal.*

He always acknowledged that I spoke but never provided reassurance that my words were welcome. That's where he and I differed. It was between those cracks that my doubts crept in, and my lacking self-esteem became a smothering blanket I never quite escaped.

But now, cloaked in New York confidence and nerves that've been bolstered, I type the things I forced myself not to send last night.

Last night was for me and Taylor Swift and a bottle of beer.

> I have a million things I never told you and a million more insecurities I never shared. Because, duh, they're embarrassing. They're my reasons for the way I am. They're why I said that thing about friends on Saturday.

> They're not excuses. But they are context. And it's that context that will help you understand why we're probably not a good fit.

I hit send and glance at the elevator control panel. We're still in the teens, so I look down again and keep typing.

> I'm crazy, and you're calm. I'm spontaneous, and you're... not. Ironically, we're both children of trauma. Though unironically, that trauma manifests differently in each of us. I haven't even told you about my parents yet.

> All of the things you crave, I can't be, and all the things I am, make your skin itch. I'm the shirt that doesn't fit quite right, and the sheets that are a bit scratchy.

> And sure, you could still wear the shirt and sleep within the sheets, and life would go on, and everything would be okay. But... I don't want to be the reason you're never quite at peace.

I hit send again, and gulp when I receive instant read receipts. Jesus Christ on a cracker. He's reading my words *now*.

> I fooled myself into hoping you would follow me back to New York last night. Maybe you would've been waiting for me at the luggage carousel, or where the taxis line up, or... and this was my last-ditch hope... maybe you were sitting in the hall outside my apartment when I got home.

> I would've run into your arms and made it into a whole big thing—which you would've hated. Man, oh man, my little Disney heart wanted it so bad. But alas... this isn't the first time I've made an idiot of myself.

> Little girls often wish for declarations of love. Like at my daddy-daughter dance at school, when I was sooooo sure my father would arrive with a bouquet of flowers and all my peers would ooh and ahhhh over how lucky I am.

I hit send each time my texts become too long. Then I keep typing.

> I got my first boyfriend when I was thirteen, and I made damn sure he was entirely inappropriate. He was older and a smoker and an all-around bad boy.

> I did it hoping it would bring my dad back, because him shouting at me about choosing wrong is still a declaration of love. I wanted that declaration so freakin' bad.

I hit send and push on.

> I convinced Alana it was okay for her to leave New York and move back to Plainview. I even called her while she was driving, egging her on.

> But all along, I was kinda hoping she would turn around and siege my office in Manhattan and shout: COME WITH US, FOX! Come to Bumfuckville Hillbillytown.

> Butttttt… kind of like how I said you and I were only friends, I never shut up about how small towns suck, and the chicken poo was a deal breaker for me.

> How could she possibly ask me to come when she was so sure I would hate it? She's too pure for that. Too kind. So the fact I hoped she would ask is, frankly, dumb.

> You and I were never just friends, Chris. In fact, I don't think we were ever friends at all. We're yet to have a conversation that doesn't include fighting with each other. But you wanna know when I fell in love with you?

> It was just after Alana had the baby, and she asked for family time. She didn't mean it the way it sounded, but hoh boy! I took it the way it sounded. I wanted to walk back to the apartment by myself because I wanted to cry. Sooooo much!

> I wanted to rage and scream and accept that, yep, I'm a nobody, and I belonged nowhere. But no. You followed me. You insisted on driving me. And then you read my mind. Somehow, you knew what I was feeling.

> You didn't even like me, but you made damn sure to point out that what she said was not what she meant. And I don't know if you know, but to the little girl waiting on her declaration of love: the fact you followed me and drove me home…

> Well, that was the same kind of magic I'd been waiting for my whole life.

> Which is dumb.

> I was reaching. I was convincing myself that it was something it wasn't.

> Thennnnn, we banged.

> And then you laid in bed with me and showed me this guy who wasn't the same guy I thought I knew.

> Which was the exact moment the younger, impulsive, desperate-for-love me piped up and said, 'Hey, let's not tell anyone about us.'

> Because, duh, it was time to sabotage any spark of happiness I might ever experience.

> I figured I was doing the right thing. And you agreed so easily. I didn't want Alana to find out about us because half of me was scared she'd be mad when I inevitably screwed everything up.

> And the other, louder, meaner half of me was terrified she would be pissed. She spent ten years crying for you, Chris.

> A whole decade, mourning the loss of the love of her life. But also, mourning the brother she no longer had.

> Godddd, the pedestal was HIGH! I had no chance of being good enough for you, and I desperately didn't want her to tell me so.

> My heart couldn't handle it. So I did what I always do, and I sabotaged us before we even got a chance to try something else.

Glancing up when the doors open on the fifty-first floor, I stride forward and type while I walk. Paying attention to no one as I make my way toward Booker's office.

> These texts are starting to drag on, filling the whole screen. Which means your eyes have probably already started glazing over. But I guess I just wanted to say: I love you.

> I loved you.
>
> And since we're on the subject, I want to say a little girl fell in love with the guy who insisted on driving her home that day.
>
> That was the spark that lit this fuse.
>
> But it wasn't the kind of love that lasts. She was incapable. She was just a child, desperate to be chosen just once in her damn life. And good for her. She held on to that love all the way until midnight last night.
>
> I couldn't say these things to you while I was in Plainview, because I was working on immaturity and insecurity.
>
> I wanted you to take the leap and speak your feelings first because I was scared to walk out on that ledge alone.
>
> It's ironic, really, that I would lecture you on comfort, when I was the biggest coward of all. That makes me a hypocrite.

I hit send on that message, too, but when I start typing some more, the speech bubbles on the other side pull me up short.

He's typing, and holy hell, that nausea I thought I'd escaped comes spilling back as violently as a tidal wave.

> Just to clarify: You love(d) me? But you fell out of love with me around midnight last night?

I stop just six feet from Booker's office and slam my back to the wall, tipping my head up and filling my cheeks with air that escapes on a whistle.

But then my phone vibrates with another message.

> What the hell did I do at midnight last night that hurt your feelings? I was in bed, not sleeping, but definitely minding my own business.
>
> How can you blame me for something I had no part in?

I choke out a pathetic laugh and swipe fresh tears from my lashes.

> Firstly, and just because I can't let this moment go without saying so, your texts today contain more words than ALL of your previous texts combined.

> That's interesting!

> Second, you did nothing at midnight last night. But I stopped being mad and sad and weird about the declaration I didn't get at the airport-taxi stand-and/or my apartment door.

> Because that was immature and silly, and it's not what true love is built upon.

> Those declarations were for a little girl who desperately wanted to be chosen. Now...

I pull my bottom lip between my teeth and suckle, tapping send while I contemplate how to finish my sentence.

> Now, what? You met some hunk on the plane and forgot about me?

> Now, I'm a woman who was chosen. Finally. It took me nearly three decades to realize waiting for someone else to love me is ridiculous, when I needed to love me all along.

> I had that power, but I kept tossing it to everyone else, hoping they'd do something magical with it.

> But here's the kicker: I never told these people what I needed. In fact, I told them the opposite.

> Like expecting Alana to beg me to move to Plainview: duh, of course, she wouldn't! I never shut up about hating the place.

> And telling you I wanted us to be a secret: how could I expect you to tell me any different, when I'd already made clear I only wanted casual?

> I kept saying I wanted one thing, but hoped silently for another. And then I kept getting mad when I received the things I asked for and not the things I wished for.

"Fox?"

I startle and spin, locking eyes with a curious Booker waiting in his office door. His gaze flickers down to my phone, then up to my face. And though I know he sees the tears in my eyes, he swallows and pretends, *for my sake,* they don't exist. "We're ready when you are. Take a minute, then join us."

Take a minute and wipe your face, you unhinged whackadoodle.

Nodding, I clean my cheek and clear my throat. "One minute and I'll be ready to start. Thank you."

He drops his chin and backs up, closing the door and giving me my moment of privacy, so when I check my screen again, I'm greeted by a barrage that make my heart skip.

> I'm sorry I have an aversion to itchy sheets and ill-fitting shirts. If I could touch either without wanting to tear my skin off, I would.

> But since we're taking a leap and streaking buck-ass naked out of comfortable and into exposed as fuck: I love you.

> Stupidly, I told Tommy. And I told Alana. Oh, and Cliff knows.

> And Eliza, too.

> And Raya.

> In fact, she told me. And even when I tried to deny it, she called me a liar. A hunky, hunky liar —her words.

> So basically, everyone knows. Except you.

> Yet, you were the only one I needed to tell. I fucked that up, Fox. I swear, I wanted to. I tried to.

> But the idea that you wouldn't feel the same scared the piss out of me, so I shut my trap and wasted our five weeks, and now you're in New York.

> Would you believe me if I told you I was planning to move there, too? I was gonna follow you.

I cough on the emotion trying its best to choke me. Then I type a fast reply.

> Yeah, Alana told me last night.

> But then Rome happened, and Rome is much, much farther away. Now you're telling me, as of midnight last night, you're no longer in love with me anyway?

I snicker.

> It's a different kind of love. Rooted in self-love first. Which, I'm led to believe, is a far superior option anyway.

"Fox?" Less patient now, Booker pulls his door open. "We have to start."

"Yeah, sorry." I wipe my nose and quickly type, despite Chris' moving speech bubbles.

> I have to go into a meeting right now. But I'll call you later. Maybe. If you wanna talk.

> I know we screwed up the first round. But a traditional fight has, like, three rounds, right?

> Five, actually. If we screw up the next one, we're still good for a few more.

> Not sure how long-distance will work, seeing as how I hardly talk, and I really like touching you.

> But I'm open to crappy hotel sheets if you're willing to slum it with a dude who gets weird about forks.

> I'm willing to learn Italian for you. I mean, I'll complain about it, and I'll focus mostly on the cuss words.

> But this is how adults have relationships, right? It's how they move from really great secret sex, into something a little more important.

> I'm sorry I wasn't at the airport to do the big declaration thing you wanted. And now, I can't even do the declaration thing without you assuming I did it because you told me to. Which kinda sucks.
>
> Anyway. You already said you were going into a meeting, so maybe I'm talking to myself. I do that more than you think.
>
> Catch you when I catch you. Kinda wanna tell you I love you. But it feels weird.
>
> So, ya know... I'm thinking it, even if typing it makes my hands shake.

"Fox?!"

"Yep!" I lock my screen and shove my phone into my bag, and tugging out a small white envelope from the depths of my purse, I push off the wall and follow Booker into his office.

Amedeo, our Italian GGH director, waits in one of two of Booker's visitor chairs, a sharp Italian suit draped around a fit body, and dark brown eyes sparkling with amusement as he watches me stumble into the room.

I make a beeline for the only remaining chair, setting my purse on the floor by the leg, then I turn to Amedeo and offer my hand. "Mr. Conti. Welcome to New York. I was thrilled when I found out you'd be here."

"Ciao." He flashes a megawatt grin and stands, wrapping my hands in his much the same way Eugene did last night. "It's good to be back, even if my visit will be short."

"The contracts have been drawn up by legal." Booker sets a stack of paperwork on his desk and unbuttons his suit jacket, before sitting down and gesturing for Amedeo and me to do the same. "You'll want to read them over, Fox, but for expediency's sake, I'll tell you: your job remains the same as it is here in New York. However, the office over there is smaller, and the staff members are fewer. This makes for a perfect opportunity to continue and expand, what you're already doing here and still have time to learn from Amedeo. We've discussed in detail your desire to explore the things we do, and Amedeo has been hinting at bringing you across to Rome for the last little while. So when we came to the conclusion you could do both jobs, an idea was born, and a position was created."

"I feel you will be pleased with the accommodations we have in place for you." Amedeo crosses one leg over the other, resting his elbow on the arm of the chair and his chin in his upturned hand. And because he's not entirely old or ugly, he smiles that way men like him do. "I'd be happy to have you in my city."

"Your contract stipulates five years," Booker continues, "broken down into one-year intervals. At the end of each year, you're welcome to renegotiate terms with Amedeo first, and then us, second. If at any point you decide you're dissatisfied with the change, you would put that in writing and let us know. We would hate to lose you because you think you can't return, so—"

"I'm sorry. Could I stop you for a moment?" I pick up my contract, only to set my small envelope down in its place. I pass it to neither men, nor do I explain its contents. I merely settle back and leaf through the contract, searching for the words I hope desperately to locate. Words I *know* exist. I just have to find them. "I loathe to be *that* person, gentleman. Causing a fuss when no fuss is necessary."

"Please." Amedeo gestures my way. "Fuss, Ms. Tatum. What's on your mind?"

"Well…" I cough out a nervous laugh. "Probably not what you're expecting."

In my peripherals, Booker's eyes narrow to dangerous slits.

"Here." I set the contract on my lap and point at the words that set me free. *Sort of.* They provide me a lifeline. *Ish.* "It's stipulated here I have the option to work remotely three days a week, provided I attend the staff meeting on the first Monday of every month."

Curious, Amedeo rolls his bottom lip between his thumb and finger. "This is correct. Technology removes the limitation on one's workspace. I, myself, am working remotely today. You accept these terms?"

"Not in their entirety." I draw a heavy breath and fill my lungs with the bravery I so desperately need, then exhaling again, I meet Booker's eyes. Since, really, he's my boss. Amedeo needn't even be here. "I wish for five days a week remote work, but I accept monthly meetings, here or in Rome. Or London, even. Wherever you need me to be."

"Five days a—" Booker shakes his head. "How would that be possible? You can't do half of your job remotely."

"Right." I lean forward and slide my envelope closer to him. "Sadly, that leads me to this."

"*This?*"

"My resignation, effective immediately."

"What?" He snatches up the envelope and rips the seal open. Tearing my single sheet of paper out, he speed-reads as fast as his eyes can move. "*Effective as of the date of this letter… resignation from Gable, Gains, and*

Hemingway... appreciate your guidance and..." He swings his eyes back to mine and growls. "I don't accept your resignation." He slaps the paper back to his desk. "I don't know what the hell has come over you, Fox, but *this*," he points at me, "this is not you. We have way too much history for me to let you quit when I damn well know, six weeks ago, you were content exactly the way things were."

"Which leads me to my next confession: I was hoping you wouldn't accept." I close my contract and place my hands over top, then I offer Booker a kind smile and another for Amedeo. "I would love to learn from you both. I mean that with full sincerity. I don't *want* to leave Gable, Gains, and Hemingway. My loyalty remains with the company that took me from my professional infancy, making it possible for me to flourish and learn. However," I bring my focus back to Booker, "I grew way too comfortable in this job. It was easy. It was fun. It was rewarding and fancy, and honestly, it simply made me feel good."

"So, what's the problem?"

"I'm still paying student loans for a degree I don't use. I've allowed myself to become complacent, letting the education I worked really freakin' hard for dissolve in the back of my brain while I fill it with other, less relevant things."

"We're giving you a chance to do exactly as you're asking for," Amedeo counters. "Forgive me. I'm confused by your hesitation."

"Rome is my hesitation." I swallow and drag my eyes back to Booker. "And New York. And London. And literally every other town or city or place that exists where my family *doesn't*."

"Your family?"

"I would've begged you for a lobotomy six weeks ago if I said these words, and I promise you, my hands sweat even now. But..." I lift my shoulders in a nervous shrug. "I'm moving to Plainview."

He barks out a loud, mocking laugh, throwing his head back and slapping the desk.

While he does that, I look at Amedeo and grit my teeth. "Just give him a second. He'll stop."

"Plainview?! Fox, you called it the Hillbilly capital of Bumfuck Alabama!"

I wrinkle my nose. "It's not actually in Alabama."

"I know it's not in Alabama!" His laughter cuts away, and his rage takes over. "Did you go on a cocaine bender while you were out there? Have a mental breakdown? I swear, the Fox who left and the Fox who came back are *not* the same person!"

"They're not." I settle back in my chair and slow my breathing, lest I cry like a tool and ruin every shred of credibility I have with these men. "I'm not that person anymore. And even if that's freaking you out a little bit, I actually think it's a good thing."

"Fox—"

"I healed while I was gone. I hurt. I grew, and I might've thrown a tantrum or two. I was treated badly by some of the locals. And I was treated well by others. I learned what it's like to have a family, and worse, what it's like to sit outside and stare in while they lived their lives. I've spent nearly three decades throwing up walls, preparing my comebacks, and stacking my barbs for whoever broached my defenses. I was determined to expose them before they exposed me."

Heavy black brows pinch above Amedeo's eyes. "What is it you think you are, Ms. Tatum?"

"A coward, mostly. An island of misfits, but I'm the only one who lives there. I'm a child of trauma who wants so badly to be doted on, but when I am, I tell myself I don't deserve it. That's why I like my job so much." I cast my eyes back to Booker. "It's easy and it's fun. But more importantly, it comes with praise. So much freakin' praise. And I figure, I deserved *that* praise. Because we have the data on staff morale that says what I do matters."

"What you do *does* matter! That's why we're offering you oodles of money, dummy."

"Getting paid to be told I'm amazing." I fold my arms and bring my pinky fingernail up to my lips. "It's the easiest, most fulfilling cash I ever made. And I assure you, the idea of letting that go is *terrifying*."

"So don't! If the thought of moving to Rome elicits *this* kind of reaction, then don't go. It's okay to think you wanted something, then change your mind. You don't *have* to accept the job."

"For me to agree with you on that point, I must also acknowledge that it's okay to think I *didn't* want something. But now I do."

Like a true New Yorkian, he turns his nose up in disgust. "You want Plainview?"

"I want Plainview. I want roosters on the fence and cows in the yard. I want the gossip vines, though I look forward to a certain few old ladies kicking over in the next ten or so years."

Like a tennis match and a ball flying from one side of the court to the other, Amedeo's eyes swing to Booker. "Kicking over?"

"You cannot base your happiness—and a whole cross-country move—on the *hope* that some old biddy will up and die, Fox! That's not how grown-ups make decisions. But it sure as hell is one way to tempt karma to come down and whoop your ass."

"It's not like I'll poison the old folks or anything." I roll my eyes and ignore the buzz-buzz-buzz of my phone in my bag. "I just mean, the fact they're pretty old already makes me feel better."

"Fox!"

"Offer me a full-time remote position." I look from one man to the other. "Either of you. I'm begging you. I don't want to leave Gable, Gains, and Hemingway, and lord knows, I don't want to work at Alana's bookstore for the rest of my life. So I'm asking you to please, please consider finding me a position that satisfies us all."

"You're asking me to let you go," Booker groans. "You'll leave New York."

"You were happy to send me to Rome!" I gesture toward Amedeo with both hands. "How is this different?"

"It's different, because this is what you wanted. Rome was your dream, Fox, and I give a shit about you outside of this office. I want you to have everything you want."

"I want Plainview. And I want my family. I want Chris and that stinky gym that smells like balls and all of those people who hardly even like me. I want the stubbed toes. And I want to continue to work with you."

Poor Amedeo. The man speaks fluent English, but not everything makes sense. "You *want* to stub your toes?"

"I'll fly out once a month, every single month, for the rest of my working life, to any office you want me in. I'll even fly economy, if you insist."

Booker scoffs.

"If you want me to be happy, then *this* is it." And because he already wrote it into the contracts, I open them again and jump to the last page. "If at any point I change my mind, you'll bring me back to New York. See? You already provided me an out if the hillbillies get to be too much."

"You're still calling them hillbillies!" he growls. "But now you wanna be one of them?"

"I just want a chance to figure out who I am. I know you don't *have* to. At no point are you required to tolerate me and this ridiculous conversation, so if you wish to end it, end it."

"Then I'm ending it," he quips. "Right now."

"Fair," I sigh, closing the contract again and placing my hands over top. "However, I'm moving this week. With or without your blessing."

"Fox!"

"I would really, really like your blessing." I reach across his desk and grab his hands. "Please, Booker. Don't make me work at the bookstore. Don't let me leave without a steady income and a reason to fly back to civilization once a month. If you send me away today and I become one of *them*, you'll have no one but yourself to blame."

He firms his lips. "Emotional manipulation? You're usually much better at it."

"I know. But I was up until midnight hosting a Taylor Swift concert for the rats living in my walls. I'm tired."

"You know Taylor Swift?" Amedeo questions. "Americans know all other Americans?"

"Please, Booker." I set my elbows on his desk and press my palms together in prayer. "I'll work really hard. I'll learn fast and become your highest-grossing lackey yet. I'll secure accounts you couldn't even dream of, and I'll make damn sure the yearly data shows I deserve my praise."

"Fox—"

"And I won't ask for my salary increase."

He scoffs. "I should hope not."

"I won't need you to pay for accommodations either. Just agree to keep me on. Give me a year to show you I can do this."

"What if I give you the year and you fail? Will you come back to New York?"

"No. But I'll try the emotional manipulation thing again and buy myself another year." I wiggle my hands. "Let me go home, Booker. Rome isn't where I'll be happy. Plainv—" My body rejects the words. My tongue stumbles on each syllable. *Oh, God.* "Plainview is where I need to be. At least for now."

His desk phone trills, startling me where I sit and buying us both a moment to sit back. And though he stares into my eyes, ignoring the phone until it rings out, it starts again and draws his ire. He points at me, then points down—*don't move!*—then snatching up the headset, he slams it to his ear and grits out, "Yes?"

"If he doesn't offer you the job you want," Amedeo leans closer, chuckling under his breath, "I will."

"Really?"

"Sure. You want a job in marketing, Ms. Tatum, and you've convinced me to pay you *not* to work for me. You've a natural talent."

"Stop talking to each other!" Booker snaps, then back to his call. "Push my nine-thirty out, and tell Chauncy I'll call him when I'm done in here. I can't step out right now." He stops and listens, then nods. "Yes. I'm aware.

CRAZY IN LOVE

I'm willing to risk it. Thanks." He drops the phone back into the cradle and glares straight between my eyes.

So I flash a bright smile and pray it simmers his fiery mood. "Willing to risk what?"

"None of your damn business! If you no longer work for Gable, Gains, and Hemingway, then such information will no longer be shared with you."

"But... I *do* still work for Gable, Gains, and Hemingway." I bring my hands up again. "Please?"

"I've offered her a position in Rome," Amedeo counters smugly. "Remotely, of course. Full time. Full salary. Starting immediately."

"This is not a bidding war! She's *my* staff member, and I'll make my decision without a trojan horse from my *now* competitor. That's not what we're doing today." He swings angry eyes back to me. "One week remote, one week in the office. But you don't start remote until six months from now, when I can be assured you've got a handle on your new position."

"One week a month in the office, the rest remote, starting one week from now."

His eyes sizzle and burn. "This is not a negotiation."

"No. But it kinda feels like a game of chess, and this move is what I call the Queen-whoop-de-do. The fact I'm willing to walk away without a job at all means I can be as ridiculous as I want. It's up to you to decide where you'll draw your battle lines." I snag my purse and stand, and setting my contract back on his desk, I tilt closer. "You know my terms, and I welcome your written counteroffer. Also, fun fact: the trojans were not Italian. I read about that war from the side of a condom packet."

"I intend to make a written offer too, Ms. Tatum." Amedeo turns in his chair, grinning. "May the better country win."

"I look forward to hearing from you." I cast one last look to Booker, my friend, my safe place to land for the last ten years, and know I'll accept damn near *any* offer he makes. So long as it includes keeping my job *and* Plainview.

Finally, I slide my purse onto the crook of my arm and circle my chair. "Thank you for your time, gentlemen. You each have my contact details." Turning on my heels and digging my hand into my bag, I scoop my phone out, desperate to see what else Chris has texted. Hungry for whatever words he's sent.

> Cazzo means fuck. I'm already rolling that one into my vocabulary. And vaffanculo means to fuck off.

> I expect to say that one to Tommy pretty often.
>
> Ti amo means I love you. I don't know if you know that. But I looked it up online and that's what it says.

Snickering, I tap at the screen and start my reply, and with my free hand, I tug the office door open and stride through.

"Ti amo. It's kinda smooth, huh?"

Startled, I swing my head around and risk my life when my neck clicks and my stomach somersaults. Then I lock eyes with Christian *freakin'* Watkins, standing right where I stood before I came into the office. His back pressed to the wall, and his phone in his hands.

"Chris?" I spin back to face Booker, still at his desk, then around again to make sure Chris is still where I left him. *I think.* "What are you... what..." I toss my phone into my bag and let my hands dangle by my sides. "You're in New York?"

"I'm wherever you are." He moves off the wall, dragging a carry-on suitcase and stopping it beside his thigh. "Lucky for me, there's still this tiny window where I can make a cheesy declaration of love and you'll know it was because I wanted to, and not because you told me to."

Fat tears well up in my eyes, blinding me to the beautiful, handsome, mildly panicked man in front of me.

"You *know* I hate speaking in front of a crowd. And dammit, Fox, you know my hands are shaking, even if I do a decent job of hiding it."

"Do... do you want to come to my office? So you can speak in privacy?"

"NO!" He shouts at the top of his lungs, drawing eyes from every person on this floor... and possibly security, too. "No, I don't want privacy, Fox Tatum. I want to declare that I LOVE YOU."

"Shh! Jesus." I stumble forward and press my hand to his mouth. "You're making a scene."

"I KNOW I'M MAKING A SCENE!" He pushes my hand off, then throws his in the air, and with exaggerated movements, he stomps in a circle. "MY NAME IS CHRISTIAN WATKINS, AND I'M IN LOVE WITH FOX TATUM."

"Chris!"

"I'M MOVING TO NEW YORK. BECAUSE MY GIRLFRIEND LIVES IN NEW YORK. AND IF SHE MOVES TO ROME, THEN I'LL GO THERE, TOO. I'LL JUST NEED A MINUTE TO WORK ON VISAS."

"Stop shouting!"

"I will not stop shouting! I'm ti amo with my girlfriend!"

"He doesn't speak it properly," Amedeo groans, stopping in the doorway. "Americans always say it wrong. And that accent is..."

"Hillbilly," I murmur. "It's hillbilly."

"I brought you sheets." Chris drops to his knees and feverishly unzips his suitcase, flopping the heavy shell case open and presenting, a'la Simba on pride rock, a package of silky black. "I'll trade my sheets if it means I get to keep you."

"Chris." I lower into a crouch and meet his eyes. "You can stop."

"And my forks, too." He whips open the other side of the case and reveals his entire cutlery set. Not just the forks. "I'll use whatever silverware you ask me to use, if it means we can try for round two."

"You don't have to give anything up. You can keep your sheets and—"

"And my shirts." He stands again, grabbing my hand and yanking me up, then he fists the back of his shirt. "I'll give up the clothes on my back and wear a burlap sack if you need me to." His eyes burn with desperation. "Please don't need me to. That shit is insanely itchy."

"Chris—"

"And your pen." He reaches around and snags my pen from his back pocket, presenting it the way others might a diamond ring. "It fell out of your purse in my truck that first day after I picked you up from the airport. You spent the whole fucking drive arguing with me over who had more claim over Franky, then you jumped out to hug Alana and kicked your bag over. I found the pen the next day, and when you asked me about it, I didn't wanna give it back."

"You had my pen this whole time?"

"I'll sell my house and use the money to buy something here. Or in Rome. Or London. I'll buy you property wherever you need it, and if that means I'm broke and can't afford the sheets I like, then I don't mind."

"Chris, stop—"

"My skin has *never* itched as much as it has in the last forty-eight hours. I don't sleep unless I'm with you. I don't eat unless we're okay. I don't want to be Hazel's godfather if her godmother is on the other side of the world. And I can't invite anyone into my home office to play chess now anyway. Not after we—"

"That's enough of that." I clap my hand over his mouth and burn. I know my cheeks fire red. "Jesus. From no crowds at all, to offering to take your shirt off and telling them that we... That we—"

"Have sex?"

Booker tips his head back and groans.

I draw a fortifying breath and close my eyes, *knowing*, once I open them again, this will all be just a dream. A hallucination brought on by stress. "Maybe I drowned in the bathtub last night, huh? Maybe none of this is real."

"I flew to New York to be with you." Chris takes my hands, pulling me in until our chests touch and his warm breath hits my chin. "I was expecting you to say no, because you have a shitty habit of sabotaging anything good you could have. You're toxic as hell, Fox Tatum, and irritating to boot."

"Well... thanks?"

"But I met this cab driver last night. He brought me to my hotel and told me a story about his wife."

"Wait. What—"

"She's gone now. She died. After fifty years of marriage. And to us, when we're not yet thirty, fifty years of marriage sounds like a really long time. But I swear to you, from where he was sitting, it wasn't nearly enough. He told me about this bed she'd made him buy and how he kicks the wooden leg every damn day. He said he gets sad now on the rare days he *doesn't* kick it."

Eugene. My beloved Eugene.

"I want you to irritate me, Fox. I want you to hide my forks, and destroy my sheets, and disrespect the rules of chess. I want you to do all of these things and tell me, at least once a day, that you *ti amo* me."

"That's wrong!" Amedeo growls. "You're saying it wrong!"

"If you're in Rome, then that's where I'll be. If you're in London, then I'm heading to London."

"And if she's heading to Plainview?" Exhaling a tired sigh, Booker leans against the doorframe and scrubs a hand over his face. "What if she's negotiated a job in that hillbilly backward-ass nowhere? What do you say to that?"

His eyes swing back to mine, wide and questioning and only half panicked. "Plainview?"

"You didn't already sell the house, did you?"

"My house?" he gulps. "You... my house?"

"I could live at the bookstore for a little while, I guess. Make sure we're still in *ti amo*."

"Not. Right!"

"But eventually, I'm gonna get tired of driving across town in the middle of the night, then sneaking out again in the morning before Alana wakes up. That kind of nonsense is for twenty-something-year-olds. I'm turning thirty soon."

"You want to live at my house?" Finally, his lips curl into a smile. "You promise?"

"Can we go bed shopping?"

"Yes!"

"But we have to buy the bed you hate the absolute most. It has to be white and heavy, and if you think it's ugly, that's better."

"Okay." He draws my hands higher, breathing warm air between his palms. "And we'll fly to Rome how often?"

"Once a month," Amedeo declares.

"Never!" Booker snarls. "Our negotiations are not yet complete. For now, she'll fly to New York one week a month." And then he sighs. "Starting next month, once she's settled in at her new place."

"Which will be *your* place." My cheeks stretch higher, and my lips tremble. But my smile is back. And damn, it feels good. "This was a really nice declaration of love, by the way."

"You think so?" He pulls back to study the mess he's made. "It was insanely hard getting that silverware past TSA. I almost got an internal exam."

"Everyone would have been looking at you."

"I hated every single second of it." He slides his hand around to the back of my neck and tugs me to the tips of my toes. "I *amo* you, Fox Tatum."

"Gah!" Amedeo huffs. "You're doing it badly on purpose."

"This is how you feel when you take my forks, huh? You do it on purpose because it's kinda fun."

"Yeah." I study his lips and wait. Wait. Wait. It's not a declaration of love until we kiss. "You love me? Out loud? Are you willing to go to a town meeting and tell all those old bitches to stop looking at me mean?"

"So willing. I'll shout at them if you want me to." He presses his forehead to mine. "You love me, too, right? Not just friends?"

I choke out a silly, trembling laugh. But then I shake my head and set my hands on his shoulders. "Not just friends. Not *even* friends." I lick my lips and wait for the payoff. It's coming. "We're going to annoy the hell out of each other."

"I hope so." He drags me closer and seals his promise with a kiss, swiping my bottom lip with his tongue and squeezing the back of my neck with his fingers until it hurts. But it hurts so good. "My house. On the lake. We'll share Franky and Hazel equally. I'll cook nice food, so you get to smell something other than deep-fried crap all the time. Oh, and I wanna stop at the Galápagos before we go home."

"Okay." I kiss him, too. I'm allowed. He's mine now. "I still have a week left of my vacation time, anyway."

"But what about the olives?"

Stunned, I inch back and search his eyes. "What?"

"The olives." He stares, stares, stares until I feel the heat of his intensity. "Do you, or do you not, like olives?"

"I hate olives." God, it feels good to say so. "I hate them so much, Chris."

"I knew it!" He fists my hair and brings me to the very tips of my toes. "I'm gonna make a point of knowing you better than I know myself. No more olives, I promise."

He's my Lloyd Dobler, and this is my moment.

All along, I thought the moment was about everyone on the outside, watching on and thinking, '*Oh man, she's so lucky*!'

Turns out, I've forgotten about them.

"I *amo* you, Chris. Forever."

Continue the Love & War series with Hard To Love

*Looking for a **free** fake-dating laugh-out-loud romcom where our heroine is forced to attend her cheating ex's wedding—not only attend, but be in the freakin' wedding party!—so she hires a date for the week? Grab your copy of If The Suit Fits today.*

What happens when a vigilante killer and a homicide cop fall in love? Grab Sinful Justice and find out.

ALSO BY EMILIA FINN

(in reading order)

The Rollin On Series

Finding Home

Finding Victory

Finding Forever

Finding Peace

Finding Redemption

Finding Hope

The Survivor Series

Because of You

Surviving You

Without You

Rewriting You

Always You

Take A Chance On Me

The Checkmate Series

Pawns In The Bishop's Game

Till The Sun Dies

Castling The Rook

Playing For Keeps

Rise Of The King

Sacrifice The Knight

Winner Takes All

Checkmate

Stacked Deck - Rollin On Next Gen

Wildcard

Reshuffle

Game of Hearts

Full House

No Limits

Bluff

Seven Card Stud

Crazy Eights

Eleusis

Dynamite

Busted

Gilded Knights (Rosa Brothers)

Redeeming The Rose

Chasing Fire

Animal Instincts

Pure Chemistry

Battle Scars

Safe Haven

Inamorata

The Fiera Princess

The Fiera Ruins

The Fiera Reign

Mayet Justice

Sinful Justice

Sinful Deed

Sinful Truth

Sinful Desire

Sinful Deceit

Sinful Chaos

Sinful Promise

Sinful Surrender

Sinful Fantasy

Sinful Memory

Sinful Obsession

Sinful Summer

Sinful Sorrow

Sinful Corruption

Turkey Trouble

Sinful Deception

Sinful Reality

Hell In A Hand Basket

Sinful Seduction

Lost Boys

MISTAKE

REGRET

Crash & Burn

JUMP

JINXED

Underbelly Enchanted

The Tallest Tower

Diamond In The Rough

Lost Kingdom

Luc and Kari

Tulips and Lost Time

Nick and Mel

If The Suit Fits

Love & War

Tell Me You Love Me

Crazy In Love

Hard To Love

Rollin On Novellas

(Do not read before the Rollin On Series)

Begin Again – A Short Story

Written in the Stars – A Short Story

Full Circle – A Short Story

One More — A Short Story

Worth Fighting For – A Bobby & Kit Novella

ACKNOWLEDGMENTS

It's the end of another story. Another chunk of my soul, floating into the ether to exist long after I'm gone.

Thank you so much for following me, trusting me, and reading my stories.

As always, I want to thank my team for consistently having my back. For caring about me, as a person, before the books, even though the books are what brought us together.

My editor, Britt... I love you so much. Thank you for existing.

My proofreader, Lindsi; thank you for making my books as perfect as they can be.

My cover designer, Amy; thank you for covering my babies and making them so, so beautiful. I adore your work.

My model photographer, Katie Cadwallader; thank you for your art. I appreciate what you do so much.

To my kids; thank you for choosing me to be your mum. Thank you for existing. Thank you for being exactly who you are.

To my readers; thank you for supporting my work, reading my stories, and allowing me to write what I love. I'm living my dreams, and that's because of you.

Thank you for being here.

I appreciate every single book picked up. Every single page read. Every single message sent, comment posted, and review written.

From the bottom of my heart.
Thank you,
Emilia

Printed in Dunstable, United Kingdom